Sarah's Story

Sarah's Story is a controversial novel set in the Eastern Cape, South Africa during three decades, 1961-1986. It chronicles the history of two families who live on a small holding just outside the fictional town, Fort Bedford. Sarah Khumalo is a farm worker, who works all her life for the Crewe family, who own the small holding. Her family story is the story of the Poqo uprisings, forced removals, small town consumer boycotts, change and murder. Her life is a thread which joins the lives in this community. The novel is an unflinching look at the bitter apartheid years.

The novel won the 1996 Bertram's Literature of Africa Award, under the title *Close Up*.

Ann Oosthuizen was born in South Africa. She lectured at Rhodes University, Grahamstown, where she wrote and toured with two plays written in protest at apartheid. In 1972, she moved to New York and then to London.

She has published poetry and short stories in collections and in journals. She was a founder member of Sheba Feminist Publishers, who issued her first novel, *Loneliness and Other Lovers*. She worked as a translator (from Dutch) and as an editor. Her collection of stories by South African women writers, *Sometimes When it Rains*, has been translated into German. She taught creative writing in London and in Carmarthen, Wales.

In 1990, she returned to South Africa for ten years, where she worked as an editor and also wrote radio plays as teaching aids for teachers of English. She now lives in Wales. Her most recent publication is *Mirror, Mirror*, in the eponymous collection of short stories published by Honno Modern Fiction.

Sarah's Story

Ann Oosthuizen

Estuary

This edition first published in 2010 by
Estuary Publishing, 34 Rosamund Road, Oxford OX2 8NU

ISBN: 978-0-9567761-0-5

Designed by Jan at Estuary Publishing
Cover picture from an original painting by Mary Davidson

For David, my brother

Part One

1962 - 1963

Jo

ONE

Jo wandered down the track, which led to the river. She was a skinny eleven year old with a face, still trying to find an harmonious shape, angled towards an over large nose and dreamy eyes. Her straight brown hair was already beginning to work loose from the rubber bands which earlier this morning had fastened her two severe plaits. She was wearing a washed out blue cotton dress, with an inch of darker colour than the rest where the hem had been let out, a while back, to lengthen it. She slithered under the barbed wire fence to avoid snagging the material.

Although Glen Bervie stretched right up to the centre of the river, only the fields were fenced. By constantly changing its course, the river had created a hundred yard wide wilderness between its banks. If the gate were open, a donkey cart with a load of fine, white sand might have been parked there. It was a place where Jo could meet a woman walking with the light, dancer's step needed to balance on her head a huge bundle of thorn branches for firewood. Where James, Sarah's son, would herd the cows to drink from the thick, brown water.

Glancing up at the dark bulk of the krantz, which loomed above the river on its opposite bank, Jo walked towards it with care, avoiding patches of long, dried grasses and clumps of prickly, yellow poppies, which might shelter the sudden rush of snakes.

She haunched down at the water's edge, reaching forward to a flat rock on which dried silt had been curled by the sun into thin, pale wafers. With her fingernail, she peeled one off and held it delicately in her hand. Light, yet golden brown, it seemed to her to be like the manna from heaven, which had fed the homeless Israelites on their journey through the desert. Venturing a small bite, she felt its gritty texture jar against her teeth, and when she wiped her mouth vigorously on her skirt, the thirsty feeling on her tongue contrasted with the tears she discovered travelling down her cheeks in an abandonment of sorrow that she had not expected and did not understand. She held her knees, and rocked backwards and forwards, sobbing.

It had always been accepted that Uncle William and Aunt Vera would take over Glen Bervie, when Ouma died. William was Ouma's first born and only son. The farm was his inheritance. It didn't matter, it seemed, that Millie, his sister, and Jo, her daughter, lived there already. Now, only a year after Ouma had been so small in that high, narrow hospital bed, with her grey hair brushed straight off her face, William, a doctor, had moved his practice from Johannesburg to Fort Bedford, the market town close to the farm.

It bothered Jo that she hadn't said goodbye to Ouma properly. Ouma had roused herself only once in those last days, muttering something as if it were important.

'What is it Mother?' Millie had asked in the loud voice she used with Ouma, because, being ninety, she didn't hear so well.

'Call Sarah,' Ouma had murmured, and subsided back into that deep sleep from which she had not woken again.

'She doesn't mean it really,' Millie had explained because Jo had been so agitated, pressing Millie to drive to the farm to fetch Sarah. 'She's dreaming she's at home.'

Using the blue flowered china jug and bowl, Sarah had washed Ouma every day, gently drying and powdering her brittle, painful body. Ouma's small, white hand had clung like a bird's claw to Sarah's strong, plump arm as Sarah had supported her on the long, slow walk up the passage to the chair set in the dining room window where Ouma stayed all morning. Millie would bring her tight rosebuds in her favourite shades of gold and red, the post she had fetched from town, or a book from the library. 'Another little bioscope,' she would joke as she handed it over. Jo would set out the

10

cards on the green baize table, fitting a red jack on a black queen and turning over the next one so that Ouma could see if the game would come out this time. Towards noon Sarah would pass the window on her way to pick mint in the garden for the roast lamb in the oven that smelled so deliciously through the house.

Although neither Millie nor Sarah had told her, it was clear to Jo that William was going to change everything. Marge, his daughter, would go to Jo's school in town - they'd be in the same class. Today Aunt Vera was flying back from London, where she had been visiting her own family for the past three months. Her plane would be landing in Port Elizabeth at noon.

Earlier that morning, Jo had hid behind the open sitting room door, listening to her mother and Uncle William. She wanted her unseen presence to protect her mother from the harsh, exasperated tone William used towards his sister.

'You'll have to clear up your mess in here.'

'It's only my gramophone and a few records.'

'It's not your room any more, Millie. After Vera comes, you're not to make so free with it.'

William's conversation with his sister was from long habit never more than a series of commands. As he came into Jo's line of vision, she saw him turn to survey with satisfaction, the newly painted dove grey walls and glossed white bookshelves. There was a different carpet in the room, under the lounge suite William had brought down from Johannesburg.

William was calling for Marge to hurry or they'd be late for the plane. It was over a hundred-mile drive and they wouldn't be back before afternoon tea. Jo slipped outside and hung on one of the wooden posts, which held up the veranda roof so that she could watch them leave. William had his 'grown up business' face and pretended not to notice her, but Marge pushed Jo's chest with the flat of her hand.

'See you later, alligator.'

'In a while, crocodile.'

They gave each other their secret thumbs up sign, and Marge waved through the side window until the car disappeared behind the trees.

Inside the living room, Jo's mother was putting a Beethoven sonata back into its sleeve.

'Sarah, Sarah where are you?' she called.

'I'm coming, Miss Millie,' accompanied the sound of Sarah's bare feet slapping against the linoleum as she ran along the passage.

'Please put this under my bed.'

Sarah's strong arms encircled the gramophone, a box affair with a built in speaker.

'Wait - I have to unplug it first.' Millie coiled the flex and laid it on top. 'Be careful with it.'

'It's all right, Miss Millie.'

'Won't we be allowed in the sitting room any more?' whined Jo, defiantly provocative.

'Don't say things like that. Of course we will. But you've lots of other places to play - it's not a children's room.'

'What about - '

But her mother, her grey curls fizzing round her head, was already hurrying to see whether Sarah had scrubbed the cork floor, that marked so easily, in the dining room, whether Leah had started the brawn for supper. She began to beat egg whites into a peaked fluffy mountain to fold into a chocolate cake for tea. Cut off by this high tide of activity, Jo trailed after her, then banged moodily through the screen door which separated the kitchen from the back yard, to join Sarah and Leah, who were eating breakfast, sitting on a sparse patch of grass in the shade of a single pine tree.

Jo plumped down too close to Sarah. 'Hai Miss Jo, Give me some room to eat.'

'Sorry.' Jo moved reluctantly, and watched as Sarah spooned up the creamy white mealie meal porridge, mixing in the sugar, and blowing on it to cool it down.

'I hate Aunt Vera,' Jo blurted out. 'I wish she would stay in England.'

Sarah seemed not to have heard. She said something in Xhosa to Leah, which Jo couldn't understand, and they both laughed.

'What's wrong? What are you saying?' Jo suspected they were

12

making fun of her, and she pulled her skirt tight over her hunched knees.

'No, nothing's wrong,' teased Leah. 'Miss Jo is getting very cross these days.'

'I'm not.' They were turning against her. She worried they would side with the newcomers. She knew everything would be much worse if Sarah did that.

Leah and Sarah were sisters, although they didn't look a bit alike. Leah's skin was a pale caramel, compared to Sarah's reddish brown. Leah, who had not married, had worked in the post office in Port Elizabeth before she had returned home to look after their old mother. She was slim, where Sarah was plump, and she wore a red and black knitted cap on her head, not a white doek, like Sarah.

Jo wanted to confide her fears to someone. William and Vera now owned Glen Bervie. This awesome idea gave her the creeps. Already she'd seen her mother pushed out of the sitting room and Vera hadn't even arrived!

Jo watched Sarah drink her coffee in hot, hurried gulps. 'Where's Nozuko?' she asked. Nozuko was Sarah's eldest daughter, just a little older than Jo.

'She's gone to the clinic with Nontobeko and baby Nontu.' It wasn't worth going over to Sarah's house, then. It was boring having no one to play with; she was better off away from the whole lot of them.

'If my mother asks, tell her I've gone to the river.'

When Jo turned her back on the house, she was, as always, comforted by the scale of the landscape. A clear sky sizzled over fields and paths, which glared back into the sun. It was hot enough to need to linger for a moment in the deep shade of the oak trees that Ouma had planted along the gravel drive. She sniffed the wet, red earth in the furrow, which was used to flood a field of sea green lucerne, already a foot high. Now she could see the krantz rising grey above the tops of a line of poplar trees. Further away still, miles away, blue mountains shimmered in the heat.

TWO

Before she had begun school, Jo spent hours on the river bank with Sarah and Nozuko. Sarah usually carried Nontobeko cradled and asleep in a light blanket tied onto her back. Under Jo's guidance, for Nozuko was a gentle, quiet girl, older than Jo, but awed by Jo's different status on the farm, Jo and Nozuko had built streets of miniature mud huts, and collected pebbles to make walls and paths for elaborate gardens which they decorated with bright yellow fairy powder puffs from the mimosa thorn trees.

Sarah had woven stories about the tokoloshi into the river landscape. 'Don't go that way, Miss Jo. Mamsamsaba lives there. That's her place.'

Jo had gazed with awe towards a wilder area upstream, where a small tributary joined the main watercourse.

'Who is she?'

'A tokoloshi - a spirit - a bad spirit.'

'A witch?'

Sarah shivered. 'Don't talk about her any more.'

Since that time, Jo had kept obediently to Sarah's invisible boundaries. She explored what she took to be her own territory, peopling it with imaginary characters from the books she read. She named the grassy island in the middle of the river after Robinson Crusoe, called the shallow cleft, with its easy climb onto the top of the krantz, the Garden of Eden because in its shade, unlike the rest of the dry, slate surface, plants grew in abundance; freesias in early spring, and later, red hot pokers, dark blue agapanthus, and bright

14

velvet African violets.

This was her very special place. Now Uncle William's shadow fell over it and claimed it. Used to being obeyed, he could order her out, in that voice, which said, Don't contradict me.

If she refused to listen to him, screaming her rebellion, her mother would be shamed and tell her to behave. She hugged her knees, and blew her nose on her skirt. It'll always be mine, she vowed, rocking backwards and forwards, I'll remember every inch of it, every tiny bit. One day I'll come back here, even if I'm very old, and I'll build myself a house - right here. She scooped her hands into the river bank, tunnelling downwards until she reached water level, where the sand, heavy with seepage, collapsed in on itself.

Sitting back on her heels, she was distracted by the flight of a yellow weaver bird darting towards its nest, which dangled with a dozen others over the water. Tied to the very tip of a thorn branch, so that its weight curved the branch downwards like the arc of a fishing rod, it was a grass fortress, a hanging basket with a small, round entrance. She could hear the chicks scream. Wriggling under the trees, she lay on her stomach and leaned as far out as she could in an effort to see what was going on in that living darkness, but the nest was still further over the water, and its opening was turned away from her.

As she edged back, she spotted a pale blue egg, freckled in navy, lying abandoned in the grass. It must have fallen from a nest higher up and rolled, without cracking, to its present position. She felt tender towards it, cradling it, hoping that the life inside was still undamaged. Perfectly balanced, it lay like a feather in the palm of her hand.

Oh, she thought, can I save it? She wanted to find a warm nest to hatch it in. She was too energetic to hold it under her armpit. What about inside her mouth? But no sooner had she popped the egg into the pouch of her cheek, than its fragile shell broke, and her mouth was full of rottenness.

Horrible! She retched yellow slime and fragments of blue shell onto the grass, and cupped her hands to carry river water in all haste to rinse the taste away, taking care not to swallow because the water was impure, probably infected with the bilharzia worm. She couldn't stop shuddering, nor could she get rid of the memory of that sulphur death. Her face and dress were wet, and there was a yellow stain on her front, which she splashed and rubbed.

Escaping, she crossed to the other side of the river, jumping awkwardly from rock to rock. Once, she slipped, soaking her sock and shoe in the brown water, but she kept going, scrambling in a panic up the krantz, grabbing wildly at tufts of grass and juts of rock to steady herself. She was still shaking when she stood on the top and turned to face the view, breathing lungful's of air in great sobs to slow herself down and push the experience deep inside her.

Now she could see the farm. Oupa and Ouma had named it Glen Bervie after the place in Scotland where Oupa had lived before he came to South Africa. A hundred acres: a gentleman's small holding, Oupa joked, because in the Karoo a profitable sheep farm ran to thousands of acres. Glen Bervie supported twenty jersey cows. Every morning the cream was taken in a donkey cart to the train siding, and the money they received from the cheese factory in Cookhouse paid the wages for the people who worked on the farm.

From this height, the plain in front of her looked like the relief map on the table at school, with its green sponge trees and painted match box houses. Only this map was one she knew from living inside it and walking all over it. There was the red farmhouse roof, partly obscured by the leafy greens of all the different kinds of trees, which surrounded it. There was the gum forest at the back, planted as a windbreak, an orange grove, lawns and an ash tree, as well as the three tall pines at the front of the house. Round the tennis court were more trees, hedges and flowerbeds. Then came the gravel drive with its avenue of oaks and the two white gate posts facing onto the brown earth road which linked up with the sleek tarred road going to Fort Bedford, three miles away.

The land on which she now stood belonged to their neighbour, Big Jan Botha, a farm so big that it stretched across an entire mountain. She leaned against one of his fence posts, her gaze taking in not only Glen Bervie, but the whole view. She picked out the other small holdings lying along the curve of the river; a twist of windmill over at the Seaman's place; the Fourie's green tin roof. A red lorry was travelling along the main road. It passed the Fourie's place, and then, before crossing on the bridge over the river, the turn off to a large number of poorer houses that together made up what everyone called the plots.

Jo knew that Leah lived on the plots with her mother because once, with Millie, she had visited her house when Leah was ill. Leah was lying on an iron bedstead in a small, dimly lit kitchen. A very old woman sat on a straight backed chair next to a paraffin stove. There was a big, dark sideboard, and a table with two more straight backed chairs. The uneven floor was covered with cracked linoleum; faded pink roses over green and white squares. Jo stood close to the bed and rubbed its knitted quilt between her thumb and forefinger.

'Now you just stay in bed until you get better. Sarah and I are managing very well.' Millie spoke cheerfully, ignoring an invitation to sit down.

Walking back, Jo had kept close to Millie because the houses were so different from her own. They were squat and crowded together, and the walls and rusted tin roofs were a uniform mud colour, the colour of their swept, dry yards.

She squinted sideways to catch a glimpse of a group of men playing cards in the shade of a grape vine which spread across a doorway; then a tidy vegetable garden with neat rows of mealies, and a roof weighted down with fat, orange pumpkins. A child, her dress the same faded mud colour as the wall of her house, stared as they passed. The whole settlement, as if it had a unified life, hummed with many sounds - a dog barking, voices raised inside a house, a car engine turning over. The total area of the plots was less than one lucerne field, yet they had crossed several uneven narrow roads before they were safely back over the main road and walking between their own wide lands.

Now, from the elevation of the krantz she could see that beyond the plots was another large farm; while holding the whole vision together: the big farms, the small holdings, the plots, the bend of the river, the main road and the innumerable dirt roads and tracks, was the great mountain range which surrounded them all in a high ridge of blue.

Sarah's apron appeared through the trees like a white flag flapping against her long, navy cotton dress. Jo knew exactly what this meant - her mother was calling her for lunch. It had been arranged that they would eat sandwiches on the lawn in order not to spoil the glory of the dining room, where everything had been scrubbed and polished, and where Millie had placed a bowl of orange Barberton daisies, which she had picked first thing this morning before the sun had had a chance to make the stems go limp.

Jo slithered down from her high point, jumped the stones and was at the gate in time to meet Sarah.

'I saw you - you needn't have come all the way.'

Sarah's face was moist with the heat. She held up a strand of barbed wire so that Jo could climb more easily through the fence.

'Miss Jo, how did you get so dirty? What have you been doing?"

'Nothing.'

Jo wiped her hands on her skirt, then inspected her dress, which she now noticed was stained in green and yellow and brown. She pulled up her socks. The right foot was still wet; both the sock and the shoe were muddy.

'I fell into the river - my mother won't mind.'

'What about when Miss Vera comes?'

Prompted, Jo imagined Vera stepping out of the car, not a hair out of place. She could hear her English drawl, 'Good heavens, Jo - have you been living on the mountain with the monkeys?' And then she would snigger at Jo's discomfort. Vera was fanatical about dirt. When she wanted to be particularly damning, she'd wrinkle her nose and call someone 'smelly'.

'I'm not against the natives,' she'd say. 'I just don't think they're very interested in personal hygiene.'

Jo began to feel sick. She crossed her arms over her chest as if trying to become very small.

'I've put rain water on the stove to heat so we can wash your hair,' Sarah comforted her. 'And Leah has ironed a clean dress for you. Don't worry, you will look nice when she comes.'

18

THREE

'I've got my work cut out - this place is in a complete shambles!' William leaned against the bedroom door, enjoying Vera's meticulous toilette. His fingertips pricked as he stared at the blue satin bib she had tied around her neck to protect her shoulders from a dusting of face powder. Always, in the mornings, he watched her dressing. He told himself that the confidences they shared at this time were important in establishing a common front against Millie's insidious anarchy.

'What have you planned to do today?' He asked the question idly, needing intimacy.

'Big Jan has offered to take me riding. I'm to have his grey mare - she's a gorgeous mount.' Vera ran a bright red lipstick over her partly opened upper lip, then imprinted it firmly on the lower one, smoothing the colour with a thin brush.

For an uncontrolled moment, William saw the farmer's hand on Vera's thigh. He almost heard a jovial laugh, and the smack as Big Jan patted the round of Vera's bottom, before she gathered up the reins and the horse skittered away. He deliberately forced the pictures out of his mind.

'I'm going to build on more rooms,' he announced, making it up to her. He'd been planning this, even before Vera's return. 'A music room for you, and a study for me.'

'Well, now, as if the house wasn't big enough already.' They were in accord - he appreciated the sarcasm.

'It's too bad,' he sighed.

'Can you fit a tiny modern kitchenette into your plans? I simply hate that filthy wood stove. Millie has an electric oven in the pantry, but the surfaces there are sluttered - I mean cluttered - ' she giggled, 'with jars and tins.' Vera wrinkled up her nose. 'I'd like to boil an egg without bumping into one of them.'

'Talking about Millie - I've just seen her strolling around outside - of course she's wasn't even dressed. The hem of her gown is stained dark brown with dragging around in the mud!' William's mouth, so often drawn into a straight line, as if the world needed all his determination to keep it on course, relaxed as he sneered at his sister.

'Was she still wearing that hair net?'

'Of course.' William silently thanked his lucky stars for providing him with a wife of whom he need never feel ashamed. As Vera lifted a hand mirror to survey the back of her head, he promised himself yet again that he'd make it up to her for having to live in what was, to her, a god forsaken place in the middle of nowhere.

They'd met in London towards the end of the war. He was nearly forty, she a good ten years younger. She was his ideal: cool, sophisticated, controlled. In spite of her Englishness, or perhaps because of it, she'd been quite a star on the Johannesburg social scene. Then there'd been a scandal; absolutely without foundation, through jealousy probably, she'd been cited in a divorce case.

They'd never discussed it - he was too proud to ask her about it - but he was almost sure she'd been relieved to escape the gossip. He himself had always yearned to make Glen Bervie his home, and now, it seemed, circumstances conspired to make this the right moment to move. Marge would be much healthier in the country, and there would be people to look after her when Vera made her frequent trips home. He'd made that bargain when he proposed. 'I know I'm just a colonial,' he'd joked, 'but I promise you'll always be able to keep in touch with the music and theatre in London. I'll guarantee you that.'

On the morning breeze came the faintest echo of axe on wood.

'Listen!' He stepped quickly to the open window.

'What?' She put down her hand mirror.

'There it is again ... Can't you hear it? They're chopping the trees in the river - I expressly forbad them - I've even wired up the gate.'

20

He was bending to secure his shoe lace, his face red under his tan, the war scar, which ran from the corner of his mouth to his chin blazing white as his jaw tightened.

'Eat your breakfast first ...'

'Later ...'

He caught up with them as the last one stooped to climb through the fence, carefully passing over the wood she had collected before lifting her skirt, as if in a curtsey, to show a delicate ankle and bare feet.

'Hey!' There were three women. Two had already replaced the bundles of wood on their heads, the third was through the fence before he reached them.

'I've told you people you can't come here for wood any more. If you keep cutting down the trees, the river bank will be full of dongas.' His voice rose. 'Understand?'

'Ja, Baas,' the eldest spoke for them all, emotionless. She stood quite still, a caryatid, her right arm raised to steady the load.

'There's no more wood next to the bridge, Baas.' That young one is cheeky, he thought. If the riverbank next to the plots was such a wasteland, they'd only themselves to blame.

'You must buy wood - or cook with paraffin.' Why was he getting into a debate? 'This is my land - it's not your land. I've told you already, you've no right to come. I'll call the police the next time. Tell the others. You'll be arrested for stealing. Understand?'

'Ja, Baas.' All three spoke at once, a chorus.

'Go now. Don't come back again.'

'Ja, Baas.'

He should have taken their axe, but he couldn't bring himself to do that. That was something for the police to handle. He watched them walk up the road, the young one trailing behind as she adjusted the cloth padding on her head. She was running to catch up with the others, yelling something in Xhosa - he caught a few swear words. Made him feel accused.

They'd made him late for work. His hands were shaking and the palms were sweaty, as if he'd just come from a battle. Well, he'd enough war medals to prove he could fight! He'd gladly bet on the

21

winner!

The joke cleared his head. Looking up the gentle slope towards the farmhouse, he could see the smoke from the kitchen fire spiralling above the trees. Higher still, a white egret sailed across the sky, then floated downwards against the backdrop of the mountains. Who would have thought that loving a place you owned would be such hard work? The responsibility was overwhelming.

When his mother had died, he had thought he had inherited a life of ease and plenty; he'd told his new partners that he was too old to do night calls. Why not? Patients made appointments with him during the day because they knew he was good, particularly at diagnosis. He felt so secure in his own judgement, that he was prepared to return the consultation fee if he made a mistake. Yet now, he was being made a fool of, forced to play policeman, get into arguments about what was by right his property.

It wasn't just free firewood. He counted the ones who actually lived on his land: Freddie and Emily and six children; Sarah and Ernest (retired now) and four children. That totalled fourteen. Then Leah and Alfred, who lived on the plots. He didn't mind the men; there was the lucerne and the cows, heavy work, but it was the women who got under his skin - and you could add Millie and Jo to the list if it came to that.

Sometimes he would get into such a rage, he thought he would go mad. Like the evening he came across that piccanin with her billy-can standing at the kitchen door.

'Who's this?' he'd shouted at Sarah.

'She's Sina's granddaughter. She's come for the separated milk that the old Missis and Miss Millie always gives to us.'

'Who's Sina?'

'Sina used to do the washing. She's too old to work now.'

'She must have a pension - I don't suppose like the rest of you she'd even think of paying something for the milk.' He felt that was fair comment, but Sarah and the child just looked at him in that insolent way that natives have when they dig their heels in.

There was too much loud talking in the kitchen. And there were always a couple of big pots steaming away on the stove - Sarah or

Leah were probably cooking for their entire families right there in his house. In his opinion it was degenerate to bring children into the world that you couldn't feed or clothe properly, and then expect someone else to take care of them for you. He himself had decided that one child was quite enough responsibility, and Vera had concurred. After Marge, he had had a vasectomy. He rather thought Vera had something done too, but as he wasn't her doctor, he had no business to ask.

Was it any wonder that he had begun to think there was something inferior in their nature? Sex was for animals - it wasn't what kept him and Vera together. He loved Vera and she loved him - the act itself - so undignified - seemed to him unworthy of expressing that love.

Thinking about personal dignity fed his grudge against Millie. How could his own sister turn out to be the very opposite of everything he most admired? She was untidy, loud. In spite of her size, she refused to wear a decent bra because she said it gave her a migraine, so she slopped around in home-made jumpers with gravy stains down the front and her breasts hanging down like an old bitch. To crown it all, she still behaved as if she owned the place, asking her pals from town to bridge parties in the afternoons, or arranging tennis, without even mentioning the idea first to him, or, for that matter, to Vera.

The trouble was she had come to him together with Glen Bervie, as part of the property. She'd refused to leave home until she was almost an old maid, then she'd finally married that no hope farmer who'd got himself killed because he couldn't drive a tractor properly and the damn thing overturned and fell on top of him. Of course she'd come straight back home again, this time with a child as well.

He hadn't said anything at the time - as a matter of fact it had suited him, what with Father needing special care, and, later, Mother being on her own, but he was paying for it now, with a vengeance.

He looked at his watch: eight o'clock. He'd have to change his shirt - this one smelled of his rage. Sarah would have to clean his shoes again. Lucky he had no ward rounds at the hospital this morning.

23

As he passed through a gap in the pomegranate hedge, the house was visible for the first time. On the steps leading to the veranda sat an old black woman with her arms around a younger one, who appeared to be sobbing, although he could hear nothing from this distance. They were partly obscured by a man in a rusty black suit jacket and wide khaki trousers, who stood in front of them. To William the group looked like a dirty brown stain against the clean white walls of his house.

William left the drive, circled round the rockery, walked swiftly across the lawn and jumped onto the veranda to avoid passing close to them.

'Baas - ' He wasn't stopping, but the man lifted his head, and William couldn't help seeing his face. He glimpsed deep lines around the eyes, a thin mouth and a few yellow teeth.

'Sarah!' he shouted, blinded by the gloom of the house after the bright morning sunlight. As usual, she came running. 'Why didn't you tell those people to wait at the back door?'

'Baas William, they wouldn't listen to me. The woman is very sick. Her husband says they must sit where the Baas will see them, so that they don't miss Baas William. He is afraid she will die.'

'Do you know who they are?'

'No, Baas William. They come from the other side of the river. Baas Botha's place. She got sick in the night.'

'Look, if they walked here, they can walk to town.' He drew a deep breath to calm himself. He was desperately afraid of his own compassion. 'This isn't a clinic. Tell them that. Tell them they must go to the hospital - the doctor there will treat her.'

He washed his hands. Vera was waiting for him in the dining room.

'Have you got rid of them?' she asked.

'I told Sarah to do it.' He helped himself to scrambled eggs from a dish on the sideboard, leaving the bacon.

Vera rang the bell sharply. 'Toast for Baas William,' she ordered, when Leah appeared. 'And hot coffee.'

The group passed in front of the dining room window. Sarah and the older woman were half carrying the other one, who seemed to be unable to walk. Probably acute appendicitis. No, he told himself, don't even think about it. If you get involved it will be just the beginning; they'll come from far and wide and you'd end up being a kaffir doctor with no respectable status and no white patients. How will you support your family? Imagine what it would look if everyone in the district turned up here to be treated! The Hippocratic oath never insisted that one had to be a saint. Besides, they've got a perfectly good doctor at the hospital, and it only costs twenty cents a visit. He ate voraciously, buttering more toast than usual.

Sarah was trying to calm the man down. His loud voice was uneven and breathless, while the woman's sobbing rose almost to a scream. It was an outrage that they should dare to make such a racket on his property.

Now Marge and Jo had turned up - Marge with big sympathetic eyes, and Jo tugging at Sarah, asking her something. They were both dressed in gymslips and white shirts, carrying satchels.

He looked at his watch. 'Millie's late, as usual.'

'I've given up trying to understand Millie.' Vera opened the window and spoke to Marge as if no one else existed. 'Marge - come and wait inside.'

'But, Mother - '

'You heard me.'

'My Mom's bringing the car round now, Aunt Vera.' Jo turned her head momentarily, raising her voice above the hubbub.

'Jo, don't interfere.' Vera closed the window, shutting out some of the noise, and returned to her place at the head of the table. 'We've got to separate Marge and Jo. That girl has been allowed to grow up without any manners at all.'

Marge stood in the doorway. 'Mother, I'm just waiting for Auntie Millie. We're going to be late ...'

'You should have left ten minutes ago. Now stay here until - '

But at that moment the 1948 beige Chevrolet appeared in the drive. Millie had been mistress of her father's car for the past eight years. She sat straight up in the driver's seat, her neck straining to see over the bonnet, as if she were driving a tank. She braked sharply, then leaped out to consult with Sarah.

William noticed she was now wearing her town clothes; a blue cotton dress and navy and white court shoes without stockings. Her hairnet had been removed, but there was still a faint pink line across the middle of her forehead from the tight elastic band, which had held it in place. Millie opened the back door of the car and Sarah bundled the petitioners inside. Jo was standing at the window mouthing, 'Marge - we're going to be late ...' and wringing her hands and jumping up and down in pantomime panic.

Vera put out her cheek for Marge's kiss.

'You and Jo must come to the surgery after school,' reminded William.

'We will, Dad. Goodbye.' Marge fled.

William knew it was going to be a dreadful day. How was he expected to concentrate on his work when he would be plagued by the memory of how he had barely saved himself from these never ending appeals to his charity; and his anger would be further fuelled by the vision of his daughter's sleek blonde head wedged between Millie's grey curls and Jo's mousey plaits, with behind them the muffled shadows of the blanketed women and the black man's shapeless brown hat.

FOUR

During lunch one Saturday, Millie recounted the news she had picked up at her morning's bridge party. 'Bunny Loots says the newspapers call Nelson Mandela "The Black Pimpernel." He's travelling all over the country telling people to strike. He could be in Fort Bedford this minute - or hiding on the plots. The police can't catch him even though he's been on the loose for months. They've hundreds of men out looking for him.' Millie felt inspired by what seemed to her a real live adventurer.

'What do you mean "The Black Pimpernel"?' William was instantly at his most stern.

'Oh! "They sought him here, they sought him there" ... You know.'

'What I'm asking is, why you're presuming he's some kind of hero?'

'I ... Oh ...' Millie's voice trailed away, but she wasn't beaten. She'd come back full of news. At least it was something to talk about. Meal times had become so silent lately. 'Rita Albertyn said her sister, who lives in Port Elizabeth - Connie - I think that's her name - Connie van der Byl - the one who married that farmer from Cradock who lost his farm and went into selling stock feed.'

Vera sighed, and cast her eyes to the ceiling. Millie rushed onwards. 'Connie asked their girl, Agnes, "Agnes, I hear that you've been told to kill us white people, but Agnes would you really kill me and the Master?" Agnes has been with them for years apparently. Anyway, Agnes said, "Oh, Madam, I could never kill you and the Master, but maybe I could kill the people next door, and then Esther from next door could come here."

Millie, who did not believe this story, enjoyed its gruesome theatricality, but her laughter died when she realised the effect her words were having on the two girls who were staring at her wide eyed. Too late she remembered her mother's adage: Little pitchers have big ears. Damn. She should have held her tongue, at least until the grown-ups were alone. 'It's not true, Jo,' she looked at them both, 'It's only a silly story. It couldn't happen.'

'Really Millie - you and your women friends gossip about strike and murder as if it's nothing. That kind of talk could get you into serious trouble.'

'William! The children!' Vera was warning him not to lose his temper in front of the girls, but he was too carried away to stop himself.

'Who's Nelson Mandela?' asked Jo.

'Don't interrupt.' William drew a breath, then turned on Millie once more. 'You don't know the first thing about what you're saying. Mandela's a communist - do you care about that? If he got into power, he'd want to give this farm to Freddie or Ernest, and then what would happen to you?'

To please him, although she thought he was being far-fetched, Millie gestured horror, 'I was only ...'

But there was no stopping him. 'You think it's exciting the police can't catch him? It's against the law to strike - don't you believe in the rule of law?' William didn't want an answer; his mind's eye was now fixed on the argument, so that he didn't really notice her. 'If the natives did what he said, what would they eat if they didn't work? Mind you, it wouldn't make much difference to this farm. Most of them have never done a proper day's work in their lives. They don't know the meaning of real work.' This was one of William's favourite grudges. Millie could see him pause for a moment, hating them.

'He's asking for a minimum wage of two rand a day - we couldn't pay that.' She wanted to show William that she didn't need convincing. To Millie, who had very little money of her own, such a demand was fantasy. It would put up the wage bill astronomically - for a whole month's work, they paid Sarah only four times the daily rate that the strikers would ask for.

'That just shows you. I'd have to sack most of the people here if I had to pay that sort of money. That wouldn't be a bad thing - I sometimes think the place exists just for their benefit. Sarah certainly acts as if it belongs to her.'

Although it was still dangerous to disagree with him, Millie launched herself into a defensive position. 'William, you know Mother said she couldn't have done without Sarah ... and she nursed Father too. She slept in the kitchen at the end - even when she was pregnant with Nontu - so that Mother could ring for her if she needed something in the night. Mother - and Father too - promised we'll always look after her, even when she gets too old to work, because of what she's done for us over the years.'

'I'm not saying she must go, but she must realise that things are different now. She's got to smarten up for one thing.' Millie was glad that William sounded calmer. Luckily he'd started eating again. It was her fault, she shouldn't have upset him.

'I'll see to that,' Vera spoke decisively. 'I've already spoken to her about it. By the way, Millie, to change the subject, Andrew Wilson and his wife are coming to stay next weekend. You know, the pianist from England who's doing the concert in the town hall. I'm asking William's partners and their wives to a small supper party here afterwards. I think it would be better, Millie,' her voice slowed down for emphasis, 'if you and the children ate in the kitchen during their stay. Like all artistes, he's bound to be very highly strung, and I think the less people he has to meet during the day, the better - and afterwards, well, I don't think you'd fit in do you? I also forbid the two of you,' she looked sternly at Marge and Jo, 'to rush around the house while he's here.'

The girls sensibly kept their heads down - staying out of the crossfire, thought Millie grimly, who had herself been mortally wounded. A mouthful of potato stuck in her throat. She poured herself a glass of water. At the bottom of the jug, a tiny mosquito lava jerked itself against the glass wall, like a comma on the loose. They hatched in the rainwater tank. She concentrated on it in a terrified way, wondering blankly whether Vera had spotted it as well and was making a note to complain about the water on some future occasion.

She had known about the concert of course, and had bragged about it that very morning at bridge. Bunny had exclaimed, 'You'll introduce us to the maestro, won't you?' and then Elsie Mills had come out with, 'I bet she'll be much too stuck up to notice the likes of us.' She had said, 'Of course not,' and she'd promised all manner of things. Oh, she had been foolish. Now she'd have to sit by herself and watch Vera shepherd in her party of guests. How would she explain that she hadn't even met him? It would be easier to stay home with the girls and pretend she had a migraine.

Chin up, she told herself, pivoting her face in what was becoming a characteristic gesture, and saw Sarah coming in to clear away the main course. 'The beans were delicious, Sarah,' Millie praised. 'Did you know, William, we were eating Sarah's crop.' Generously, she meant to smooth things over again, but from William's face she could see she had made yet another gaffe.

'What?'

'Sarah grew these beans in the field behind her house - didn't you Sarah?'

'Yes, Miss Millie.' Sarah didn't look up. She was trying to pack the tray as quickly as she could.

His face purple, William threw down his serviette. 'I'm obviously much too stupid to understand.' He stood up so suddenly that his chair crashed to the floor behind him. The girls jumped. 'Someone explain to me -' he was looking at Millie, but turned his head to glare also at Sarah, who had put down her tray and ran to pick up his chair.' I've got one hundred acres of good land. I pay three boys to work on them. I'm trying my damnedest to be self-sufficient, but I end up buying vegetables from one of my own servants, who's doing more for herself on my land than I can myself. What sort of fool does this make me? Why aren't we eating our own beans?'

'You know ours aren't ready yet, William. The carrots and potatoes are, but the beans were put in later ... you wanted to wait ... I thought you'd be pleased that Sarah was so enterprising ...' Millie stood up as well. William shouldn't behave like this. Meals were

30

sacred times celebrating family unity. Now that Mother was dead, there was no one to insist on that.

Her mind flashed back to her childhood, remembering how William had always been the one to give the orders. He was ten years old, in khaki shorts, refusing to play with her. No, you're a girl, girls are sissies. All right, then, but only if you do as I say. You be the nurse. I'm going to bring the wounded back from battle. You get the hospital ready.

Where are we? She would be hurriedly assembling blankets, pillows, glasses of water.

He was making a tremendous noise. At the front, silly. It's the battle of Delville Wood. In order to keep him with her, she allowed him to operate on her dolls. He'd only pretended; they weren't in any real danger. Lately they seemed to be on different sides and he wasn't playing any more. Don't fight him, she told herself.

'I'll get the fruit salad,' she murmured, bringing out her trump card.

'I'm not hungry,' announced William, in a voice which said, Look what you've done now. Millie knew this was meant as a rejection and felt it keenly. She couldn't stop him, although she put out a hand in feeble protest. It wasn't right to leave before the meal was over.

He ignored Millie. 'Vera, please send my coffee to the veranda.'

'I'll join you there, soon,' responded Vera. They worked together seamlessly. Millie knew Vera rejoiced that she had made William angry. She'd have to ride it out - there was no way she could make amends now. It was difficult for Vera, she told herself, trying not to feel too hurt, Vera wasn't used to living at Glen Bervie yet - she had to make so many adjustments.

The fruit salad was a work of art - the oranges and pineapples sliced as thinly as pieces of stained glass. A blue jug contained thick, yellow cream. In spite of everything, Millie was proud of it; she knew she had created a triumph. She ate noisily, deliberately allowing herself to enjoy the flavour, tipping her bowl so that she could gather the last drop of juice onto her spoon, which grated against the china.

'You must still be hungry,' said Vera pointedly. 'Would you like another helping?'

'I shouldn't ... oh, well ... perhaps, just a sensation.' Millie held out her plate.

'Oh, Mom, you always say "just a sensation". Can I have just a sensation too please, Aunt Vera.' Jo and Marge giggled. Marge was whispering to Jo to buck up.

'Can I go, please?' asked Jo, finishing quickly.

'Please may I be excused?' Millie reminded her, using the old fashioned language that was part of the tradition of the house. She felt a stab of sadness, remembering.

'Please may I be excused?'

'You may.'

Marge looked mutely at her mother. 'You may go too, Marge.'

The two women sat for a moment, then Vera stood up. 'I'll have my coffee with William,' she announced, setting her chair back neatly against the table.

Following Vera, but at a distance, Millie hesitated just inside the house. William and Vera sat side by side in comfortable wicker chairs, their backs turned to her, as if they had no idea that she hovered in the doorway. Millie wanted to apologise to William, but it wasn't the right moment. First she must get rid of the suspicion that they didn't really want to live with her at all. It was such a pity that William was so overworked because it made him lose his temper at the slightest thing and that was no good for the atmosphere of the house. Although, after Mother's death she had quite enjoyed running Glen Bervie on her own, she had been delighted when he had decided to come home. Summoning all her strength of character, she vowed to herself to keep on adoring him.

Easily, from long practice, she paged through the photographs in her mind, conjuring up each scene. There was William, a bright faced four year old standing with his arm round Mother's shoulder, while she, still a toddler, sat happily on Father's knee. There were more family photographs: tennis-parties, picnics. She kept them all in a shoe box on the top shelf of the cupboard in her bedroom. There were others, which she had cut out from the newspaper: William, captain of the under fourteen cricket team; William in the mountaineering club; William, head boy. Those were group photographs, with William always somehow in the centre. Then, William in his university cap and gown: Dr William Crewe; William in uniform: Lieutenant Colonel Crewe with a DSO and bar. A sepia tinted war wedding in an old English church: William with his beautiful English bride.

In her estimation, no other man had ever come close to him. Conrad, Jo's father, was different, a comfortable man, not a hero. She hadn't needed another hero. William was a heart throb. Millie believed he looked just like Clark Gable, who was her favourite actor. She wasn't the only one who thought so. Bunny Loots joked that even though she was a middle aged frump, she felt like a schoolgirl when she was with him and she always wore her prettiest dress and put on her reddest lipstick when she visited his surgery.

Mother had adored him. After Father's death, she had relied even more on him, and longed for letters or visits from him. Sometimes he would sit with her for hours, without saying anything, or they'd make decisions about the farm and suddenly there'd be a new dam or a borehole that William had paid for. You could lean on William, Millie knew she herself wanted to do that, so it wasn't surprising that she sometimes confused him with the heroes in the novels she liked to read. He was really such a loving person. She couldn't blame him for being bad tempered sometimes; being a doctor was a terrific strain and he was trying so hard at the same time to make a go of farming.

There wasn't any point in hanging around. It only made her feel bad that they didn't want her with them, so she took her coffee cup to her bedroom and pulled the curtains across the window to soften the sunlight. Unbuttoning her dress, she climbed onto the bed, a high one with a dark mahogany headboard, to lie in her petticoat on the satin bedspread she had inherited from Mother's sister, Aunt Helen, who had never married, but had worked as a teacher in the college in Riebeek East. She stretched out to the bedside table for her glasses and her book, an old one she had read many times. She opened it where she had left off the night before.

Millie read: I worship him, thought Emily dreamily, holding his letter to her breast and looking up at the myriad stars glittering in the black velvet sky. Whatever he does, I'll always love him - no one, no one at all will ever, ever take his place in my heart.

Millie's eyes closed. Soon small, light snores mingled with her soft breathing. Her mouth fell slightly open, her glasses slipped down her nose, and her book tipped quietly from her slack hands.

FIVE

Marge and Jo burst out of the house like corks from a bottle. They blinked at the glare, but the earth was moving towards winter, and the sun, although still warm, had lost the fierce burn of summer heat. Sarah was giving a plate of boiled mealies and gravy to Nozuko, who was waiting for it under the pine tree, with Nontu playing beside her in the soft sand.

'Will you go on strike, Sarah?' Jo was pushy, direct. Her nose was red and shiny from the lunch time eating. Her head reached to Sarah's armpit.

'Hai!' Sarah tried to sound stern. The child was really a nuisance. She was like a dog sniffing out a bone buried in the ground. It must have been news about the strike that had made Baas William so angry at lunch time. Leah was right, when she said that he was waiting to sack them, and if they ever stayed away from work, he'd have his chance. Thixo! What would she do then, with Ernest so ill and tired and that pension of his not even enough to let him have his little bit of tobacco.

Jo craned her neck around Sarah's body to check whether Marge was still in tow. Quicksilver Marge, who never, thank goodness, wanted to talk the way Jo did, had already ducked into one of the outside storerooms to fetch a racquet and a bald tennis ball. She began to hit it against the wall in long, even strokes, moving backwards to give herself more room to swing her arm.

'Has Nelson Mandela come to Fort Bedford yet?' Jo tugged at Sarah's skirt.

'Who?' The men had met secretly at Isaac Gxoyiya's house. She had stopped James from attending, but Ernest had gone - it won't make any difference, she had told herself, don't worry, he has no job any more.

'Nelson Mandela. He wants you to strike for higher wages - stay away from work so you'll get more pay.'

What right had she to ask? It was more than politeness required to give the child an answer. 'Miss Jo, I must look after my children. Ernest is sick now. I can't stay away from work - Baas William won't pay me for not working.'

'Oh, but - ' Angrily, Sarah left her in mid sentence. Jo wanted her to fight Baas William just to suit her own grievances. What does she care about our life, Sarah thought bitterly. She's just a child, but already with more schooling than I've ever had. Didn't Jo ever notice how James and Nozuko had missed out? She was always complaining that something 'wasn't fair' or that she hated someone or other. Why didn't she feel bad that she herself hardly talked to Nozuko any more now that Marge had come to stay, or when she dressed for school, why didn't she worry that the other children on the farm weren't getting the same chance as she had?

Sarah promised herself that her two youngest would be as well educated as any white child. Nontobeko was clever - the teacher said so. Miss Millie had given her two hundred Rand when her old Missis had died, which she had put away in the old cocoa tin she kept at the back of the wardrobe. She would need it to pay for the books and the uniforms. It wouldn't be enough, but she would find more somehow even if it meant growing beans and walking the long road to town to sell them to the Chinaman in the general store, and she would do it, whatever Baas William said to her.

Leah brought the final tray of dirty dishes from the dining room. It was Sarah's turn to wash up. She stacked the plates and slid them into the soapy water.

Do you know what Jo said to me?' she asked. 'She said were we going on strike with Nelson Mandela!'

'Yehova! We are in trouble!' Leah's face looked so stricken that Sarah had to laugh.

36

'It's all right. They were talking about it at lunchtime, but they don't know anything. That's why Baas William was shouting.'

'Serious? They don't know?'

'Serious - it's all right. I told Jo we couldn't strike, because how would we live?'

'Those men from Jo'burg know nothing about what it's like here in Fort Bedford. The police in Port Elizabeth are putting people on trains and sending them back to the rural areas - to no jobs and no food. Every day another hungry someone is asking me if they are wanting a girl to work here on the farm. Cha!'

'Don't talk about the meeting any more. The less we know about it the better.'

Leah was piling the leftovers into the white enamel basins they carried away with them each day. Sarah busied herself with the washing up, but she couldn't help worrying that Ernest would get into trouble. She told herself it wasn't dangerous for him because he was too weak to do anything active. Isaac Gxoyiya had probably only asked him out of respect.

Still, if Baas William got to know about it, would she keep her job? In spite of the old Missis's promise to her that this family would always employ her, she could never be sure of William.

SIX

Big Jan Botha cleared away a pair of angular dried thorns, like two sharp horns, before spreading out his jacket on the ground. 'You can sit here,' he told Vera, smoothing out the torn bit of lining under the right arm pit, where sweat had darkened and weakened the material.

They were hidden from the main river by a curved sand bank and a thick hedge of mimosa scrub. Vera glanced backwards as if poised for flight. Her forehead was damp and her cheeks flushed by the quick walk from the house. Although she had had an excuse ready, she had not wanted to bump into anybody who mattered. She dabbed at her face with a white lawn handkerchief scented with eau de cologne. She was in Mamsamsaba territory, although she didn't know it.

'You're sure no one will see?'

'Positive. You're safe with me.' He grinned at her. 'You look like one of those china dolls they sell at Johnston's. Pink and white. A beautiful English doll.'

She sat down gingerly. Her thighs were wet. A week ago, she'd stayed for tea after their ride because Olive Botha had insisted. The tea table was laden with Afrikaner delicacies: melktert - custard pastry, scones topped with finely grated biltong, chocolate cake, green figs preserved in syrup. Although she had made everything herself, Olive ate nothing. She was immensely fat. William had told her Olive's size was due to something hormonal. Her forearms, pushing out of the puffed sleeves of her home made cotton dress had a blue, veined look, like lardy joints of mutton.

'Next time you come, you must bring the girls with you,' wheezed Olive. 'And Millie, I always like to see Millie.' She wrapped slices of the chocolate cake in grease proof paper for her to take back with her to the children.

Big Jan winked at Vera and said that he had to go out to check on the boys, who were dipping the sheep and he wanted to make sure they were doing it right. He stopped her car at the cattle grid, and stuck his head through the window.

'You look good enough to eat, Vera, and I'm still hungry. How about giving me a nibble?' His lips smacked, and swerved towards her ear, but she moved her head quickly, and giggled.

'You'll have to do better than that.'

'I have.' He tossed a white gardenia into her lap, freshly picked from a bush growing at the base of the gate post with its large sign: Sunnyside: Pedigree Friesland Herd. Bulls for Sale. 'How about it?'

'About ... what?' she held the flower to her eyes like a fan, inhaling its sweet perfume.

'Meet me at the river tomorrow.'

'Well, Jan,' she drawled, pretending to be shocked, but not avoiding his stare. She was weak from the ride, and the sweet food. 'You're a fast worker.'

'Did I say anything? Just want us to have a chat in private. Nothing wrong in that, is there?'

'Next Wednesday - after lunch.' She said it so quietly that he seemed at first not to have noticed. Then he whistled through his teeth as he withdrew his head from the window, and gave the car a triumphant pat.

'Well, well, Mrs Doctor Crewe! I'll be waiting for you!'

She'd known what she was letting herself in for. She'd thought about it constantly during the intervening days, imagining with a kind of fascination what they might do together. Living in that house which was full of William's mother's furniture, and his dreadful sister and that awful child, she'd smiled to herself, thinking they'd never guess what was going on in her mind. Adultery. The word was forbidden in their Calvinist vocabulary - and vulgar was another one. You could never enjoy a giggle or a slap and a tickle. The talk was always sport and missionaries. And the relatives! Cousin this and Great Aunt that. She'd only been back a couple of months and already it was getting her down.

If she was going to survive here, she'd simply have to keep some secret life of her own. Besides, although William thought he and his wife were too good for sex, he was not above getting a kick from flirting with the women who came to his consulting rooms. She'd seen how they looked at him with their calf's eyes when he paid them particular attention. And what on earth did he suppose she should do with herself in this damn place when he was fine and dandy and too busy to notice her? Deep down, she felt, he colluded in what she was up to and was content to let it happen as long as she made sure she wasn't found out. This way they'd be able to keep what she didn't doubt was the most important thing in both their lives - their marriage.

Mrs Doctor Crewe - even Big Jan knew that this was what she was and always would be. A neighbour, their lands adjoining, he was a very suitable choice and she was sure she could trust him not to blab. The affair would cheer her up and give her the push she needed to take control of Glen Bervie. If she must live here, she would make it her own place, and no sister in law or family servant was going to tell her how to run it.

Big Jan squashed down next to her. His face was red, like a butcher's, his hair vigorous and blonde. He was pulling at the straps of her sun-dress.

'Wait - you'll tear the material.'

'I can't wait. You're my strawberry milk-shake.'

As she unfastened the buttons on her bodice, his hands were crawling up her legs. They were large and fleshy, smoother than she had expected for a man who worked so much out of doors. She began to tremble.

'Naughty girl ... you're not wearing bloomers.'

'Bloomers?' she laughed, but her teeth were chattering. 'They stopped making them years ago! Does Olive still ...?' She must remember to think about Olive's bloomers, when she had more time.

'Panties, then?' His fingers had found her.

40

'No ... I never ... wear them.'

'Ever?'

But there wasn't time to answer. He was inside her. They strained together. His face shone like the sun. His tongue was in her mouth. He smelled like a horse. He covered her: heavy, heavy.

Unsatisfied, she moved her hips, trying to find her own climax, but it was hopeless. He was going, she could feel him slip.

'I must get my handkerchief.' After desire, the mess. Unfulfilled, she knew she would be coming back for more even as she pushed him off and sat up, pulling on her dress. Five minutes!

He was still flat out. His trousers were around his knees. She wanted to kick his buttocks, they revolted her so.

'Sexy!' he murmured, his eyes closed.

SEVEN

Vera, bathed and wearing a cool, green afternoon frock, acted hostess for Millie's tennis guests. William had been persuaded to play, but he felt ungracious about it. He wasn't keen on Millie's friends. He despised Father O'Reilly for being, what he described as physically stunted, with short, muscular legs. The Irish, he felt, had been degraded as a race by generations of poverty, by inbreeding and by the iron hand of the church. The Father's own congregation lived mostly in the location and when Father O'Reilly had once, in William's consulting rooms, confessed that he found the young women almost irresistibly beautiful, William judged him. Sex over the colour line was, of course, illegal. William found it unthinkable. The priest's admission had compounded William's dislike of him. More than anything, it confirmed his opinion of the man's weak character.

'You've missed some terrific rallies, Vera. William has a tremendous backhand,' Bunny Loots praised extravagantly and gazed at William with large, innocent eyes. Her curly hair framed her pleasant, round face in damp ringlets. Bob Loots, the third guest, was the manager of Barclays Bank. William felt he was wasting his time in the company of two men who were locked into the received wisdom of God and Mammon.

William found it hard not to grab Bunny's arm and take her away from the table to where they could talk more easily. He preferred dialogue to general conversation and today he felt more than a little irritated. His consulting rooms - where he battled to understand the functions of the body, struggling on the side of Life itself - were far

42

more stimulating than this bunch.

'I'm looking forward to watching the sets after tea,' drawled Vera, who wouldn't be seen dead on the tennis court. William admired her for not playing if she couldn't excel at the game. That's my Vera, he thought approvingly.

The men clustered at the end of the table. They wore white shorts and knee-high white socks, and their tennis shoes were freshly cleaned. Bob, tall with round spectacles, sat between William and the grey-haired priest. William's face had an inward look. His bad temper had put him in a metaphysical mood. He felt a certain need for revenge; it would give him satisfaction to catch these dull people in a net of his own making; to show them up, in fact.

'Father,' he began, 'you're the theologian amongst us.'

'Oh, William, don't mock me,' laughed the priest, embarrassed. 'A poor parish priest, that's all I am.'

'No, no - you're much too modest. I have a moral problem, which keeps me awake nights. I need your advice - yours too, Bob. It's financial as well. Morals and money are often linked, don't you agree? Will you allow me to tell you all a story?' He smiled at Bunny and Vera, including them, and waited for permission from his audience.

'Fire ahead.' Bob was on his second cup of tea. His tall body, which he had allowed to slump gently against his chair, looked pleasantly tired. 'Can't do any harm.'

Harm? How dare this man, who spent his time counting money, patronise him? I'll show him, thought William, and went into battle. 'Right. I want you to imagine an island. Two families live on this island, and they've divided the place exactly in half. Half each, you understand. That's fair, isn't it?'

Father O'Reilly gave a guarded nod as if he at least recognised that his soul was in danger. It's like fishing, William thought, beginning to regain his good humour. I'm tempting him with a juicy worm.

'Let's call the one family, the Brown family and the other, the Green family. The Browns and the Greens, okay? Now, the Brown family are very conscientious and hard-working. They get up early every morning and dig like mad in their gardens. At night, they study.

They are careful to limit the number of children they have so that they can afford to feed them and to educate them to be teachers and doctors, farmers and even artists. By their industry, they build an ideal society which provides them with everything they need.'

William could see that Millie was beginning to twitch. She was pulling her mouth round in all directions, and her one shoulder had dropped forward over the table. Knowing her dislike of arguments, William thought it likely she'd start a diversion. He'd better buck up before she interrupted.

'The Green family are the exact opposite to the Brown family. They hate work. They drink and fight and sleep late. When they drink, they fornicate.' William pronounced each syllable, emphasising the final consonant, as if he was spitting. Although in his own mind he was trying to be objective, he couldn't help imagining such license as a personal affront to himself.

'They don't care a damn about the future. They have a baby every year - at least. Sometimes more. They don't keep their children clean, let alone save up to give them a good education. Quite often,' the worst sin of all, 'Quite often, a child won't even know who his father is.'

There was an embarrassed silence, into which Millie rushed. 'What about some more chocolate cake, anyone? Father, do have some - just a little slice? Bunny? Bob?' They had all had quite enough thank you. It had been delicious, but so filling. William assessed Millie's intervention as an attempt to protect Father O'Reilly from having to defend the Catholic Church's policy on contraception. She was about to announce the recipe for the chocolate cake, but he glared her into silence, and raised his voice as if he had not been interrupted.

'So, you see, we now have two distinctly different kinds of societies sharing the same island. On the one side live the Browns, a cultured people, with music, wealth and scholarship. On the other, the Greens are suffering from the effects of overpopulation, ignorance and idleness.'

Millie wouldn't dare interrupt again, so William felt able to allow the pause to become uncomfortable. Bob Loots drained his cup and

44

stared earnestly at the tea-leaves as if they might reveal the answer to the problem that William was about to articulate. Finally he looked up into William's brilliant blue gaze. 'So?'

William took this as permission to continue, although he knew that it was given with some reluctance. 'After a few years, the Greens are in a terrible shape. They've got all the diseases you can imagine - tuberculosis, smallpox, kwashiorkor, gastro-enteritis. Their babies are dying. The people who reach old age walk about begging for food. They've got no hospitals, no decent schools, no industries or proper housing. And to top it all, they've had such a population explosion that they simply can't produce enough food to feed everybody, even if, at this late stage, they reform their habits entirely.

'Well, naturally, they look over to the Browns' side of the island and can't help seeing that things are going pretty well there. The dairy herds are giving tremendous yields of milk, the gardens are full of vegetables, the children are healthy and clever. There's enough room for everyone. They begin to feel envious of the Browns. They even start to blame the Browns for what has happened to them.

'Now, Father, you must please tell me: is it the Browns' fault that the Greens are starving?'

Father O'Reilly looked unhappily at William. 'In your story, no, it's not their fault.'

'You're quite sure?'

'Yes.'

'Go on, please William,' urged Bunny. 'What happens next?'

'Well, the next part is when things get really difficult,' William laughed. 'The Greens send a delegation over to the Browns' side. They say to them, "Listen, we're more than you. We need more than half the island. Our children and our old people are starving. Our cattle have nowhere to graze. Please give us food. You must let us graze our cattle on your land?"'

'Do they let them?' Bunny leaned forward eagerly. She was plump and healthy, with some of her bloom still on her. She reminded William of the girls he'd taken out at university. He felt inclined to flirt with her.

'I don't know the answer - that's why I'm asking you. Should they?' He smiled encouragingly.

'Can they afford to?' In the afternoon light, the sun's low rays made Bob's eyes look like two golden coins.

'It sounds as if they can.' Bunny's words came tumbling out. 'They could at least give them some food, and then, afterwards, maybe try to get them to work harder. Teach them how. They could send over doctors and missionaries. The trouble is,' she made the jump into what had been William's unacknowledged model from the beginning, 'they're not civilised yet - that's why they behave like they do. They're not like us, you know; it'll take thousands of years before they can catch up.' Like everyone she knew, she saw the 'natives' as separate from her, a different species, characterised by 'they' rather than 'us', a vast number of people, seen in dark shadow, the details washed over with layers of cliché. William was too astute to make such a mistake.

William didn't want the argument to end without a principle being established. Like all women, she was sentimental. No one wanted to face the really difficult thing. 'Charity - that's a good Christian virtue, eh Father?' Why didn't the priest say something. The man was a coward. He lived among them.

'It depends,' answered Bob, 'how much they want.'

'You've got it. Just suppose the Greens start to say things like, "Look how big your houses are. We don't have houses like you - you don't need so many rooms. Look at the size of your farms - you don't need all that land. You ought to give us more land because there's more of us."'

'Oh, no! They can't do that.' Bunny glanced miserably at her husband as if she wished he could save her. 'The Browns worked for what they have. They deserve - '

Bob interrupted her. 'Why don't you admit that you're both talking about the natives. South Africans spend all their time discussing the native problem.' He laughed heartily. 'Ha! Ha! It's a national sport!'

'Why should you think we're talking about the natives?' William was obstinate. This was ethics, not politics. One had to have something to hang on to - some rule of thumb, so you knew what

46

was right and what was wrong.

'I can't see the point of the problem otherwise.' Bob pushed his cup and plate away from him, dismissing it.

'But the Browns have to decide,' Bunny was still passionately involved. 'Is it wrong if they say no? If they say yes, they could lose everything. Like in Communism.'

'There could be a war.' Millie spoke involuntarily, as if she was surprising even herself. She caught her head in her hands. 'I'm sorry ... I had this picture of a lot of poor people surrounding Glen Bervie ... and of them being shot.' She looked helplessly at William. 'I'm ... I'm sorry.'

'Millie, are you all right?' asked Bunny.

Millie's blue eyes - the same shade as William's - were reddening with tears. 'I saw flames ...'

'Imagination,' said Vera. 'William, you've upset Millie again.' Using a slightly sing-song tone, she gave the impression that Millie was abnormally sensitive.

William was furious. 'So they should lose it all out of fear?' He wasn't going to let Millie get away with spoiling everything.

'Out of love,' murmured the priest. He bent down to tie his shoe-lace so that William almost didn't catch the words. He won't even say it to my face, William sneered, glad at least that his opinion of the man was being substantiated.

Bob unrolled his height out of the chair. 'Well, William - you've certainly set us a knotty problem.' He sounded as though he was dismissing someone from his office.

'You'll miss the last two sets if you don't get going,' urged Vera, trying to get them out of the house. She was warning him that these metaphysical conversations always ended in anger, especially his own.

'Although really, it isn't at all like that.' Millie still sounded a little dazed.

'What isn't?' William's voice was sharp. He felt like a cornered terrier and wished he could bite her. He wanted to draw blood.

'I mean, some of them work very hard. Ours do.'

'When we're watching them.'

'Oh, but that's their way,' Bunny sounded as if she was climbing back onto familiar ground. 'It's a different culture and they're generations behind us. They're like our children - we have to teach them.'

'They must accept responsibility for themselves. Take a look at the plots on your way home. It's amazing the number of people living there and it's right on my doorstep.' William's vision of the island was specific to his own landscape. His problem, although he had not yet admitted this to himself, came from the urgency of his own dilemma. Although he was already thinking of ways to clear the people off the settlement, he was unconsciously still struggling with his better nature.

'It's quite true,' shuddered Vera. 'I hold my breath when I drive past. The place is a sewer.'

'They've built a school.' Millie seemed to have regained her old interfering manner. 'The government made them pay for it themselves. Mother donated some furniture. The headmaster was very grateful. Mr Matama - that's his name. He's a very intelligent and educated man, Mother said.'

Everyone was on their feet. They were picking up racquets and moving towards the door. William realised he had lost them. It wasn't such a bad thing. People without a scientific background had no experience in patiently testing hypotheses until you found one that stood firm.

'Father, you play this set,' said Millie. 'I must be there when they start the milking and I know you always have to leave early for mass.'

'It's an interesting idea, William,' Bob joined William on the way to the tennis court. Because of his gangling stoop, he looked shorter than William, who held himself straight, like a soldier.

'I'm a thorn in everyone's flesh,' William tried to laugh. 'I just have to ask these questions that no one wants to answer.'

It was like diagnosing an illness, he thought. You've got to get to the centre of things. No good letting the symptoms cloud your judgement. Try out different solutions until you get the right one. Ask questions until you find the clarity to make a judgement. His mother used to be a better antagonist. He missed her more than ever. He wasn't afraid to face up to what the natives were really like, but he

48

wanted to be sure. A good doctor would never operate just on a hunch - but then again, a patient could be lost if you hesitated. He gripped his racquet and swung it in a practise shot. He swore he wouldn't be afraid to act if he could just be sure of the right course.

EIGHT

Sarah was certain it must be past midnight. Beside her, Ernest slept the exhausted sleep of a man who is fighting a losing battle against a serious illness. Her leg felt stiff, and she moved it slightly, careful lest she wake him. Where was James? This was the third night this week that he'd gone out without a word to her.

She heard the front door creak, and she raised herself cautiously to look towards the kitchen, where a thin sliver of moonlight, like the blade of a knife, fell across the room. She could feel a cold draught. On these starry winter nights, the frost had a sharp bite. When she needed water in the morning, she had to break icicles off the tap outside.

Thank goodness James had closed the door at last. Now he had taken off his shoes. He wasn't usually so considerate. It must be even later than she thought. If she got up to ask questions, Ernest would wake too, and she didn't want him worrying. She listened to the sounds: the furtive scrape of the table legs across the floor as he pushed it out of the way; the padded slide of the mattress when he rolled it open; the way his body shifted, looking for a soft crease to rest his hip bone.

She worried about her son - he was so thin! Her heart ached when he came in from the fields with his sleeves rolled up. She had tried only yesterday to place her hands round his upper arm to measure its size, but he had pulled away, not willing to let her fuss over him. It didn't matter how much she fed him, saving bits of meat from the house to give him extra treats, his body stayed as thin as a piece of string.

She had been so proud that her first-born was a son! She had named him Mkhuseli, the protector, thinking that he might grow up to look after her and Ernest one day. Proudly, she'd taken him to the big house.

'He's a beautiful baby! May I hold him?' the old Missis had praised.

'Yes, Missis.' Sarah had smiled at the baby's bright brown eyes and his perfect face. She'd handed him over so that Mrs Crewe could cradle him in her arms and coo over him, and the little spirit had opened his mouth in a big chuckle.

'Oh, he's so wonderful, he must have a proper Scots name. You must call him James, after the Master. Yes, that's the best thing. I'll tell Mr Crewe - he'll be most honoured.'

Thinking about the years that followed, it seemed as if Mrs Crewe had put a collar round her son's neck that day. Now, only nineteen, he too worked on the farm. She knew it wasn't what he wanted to do - and it wasn't what she had hoped for him either.

She could remember the first day he went to school. It was like yesterday. He was already seven, and tall for his age. She had thought her heart would burst when she watched him so solemn-faced among the other, older children, pretending to be accustomed to their talk about sums and spelling. There wasn't a school on the plots yet - they'd walked into town. If she closed her eyes, she could still see him, holding his new slate as if it was the most precious thing in the whole world.

He had done well at school, and then, just before James was due to go to the senior school, just when he'd passed his Standard Six, Ernest had begun the pains in his stomach which made him double up, helpless, in the middle of milking. Baas William had said that the operation would help, but Ernest had come home weak, and never got strong again.

When the old Missis had said, why not send James to work in Ernest's place, she had wanted to cry No straight away, but she had kept silent. What could she say?

'Well Sarah?'

'I'll ask Ernest, Missis.'

'James must be close to fifteen now, he's a strong boy and old enough to work - Freddie can train him. It's a good chance for him, Sarah, and you know we can't afford to keep on paying Ernest's wages when he's not doing anything.'

She had wanted to say, I wished for James to have a different life from us on the farm. Then she had thought of Ernest, the way he needed his rest, the way he looked - all used up. Finished.

That was five years ago. James was a good son, he'd not complained. He'd listened carefully to everything Freddie had taught him, but he wasn't really willing - you could tell by the way he walked round the farm, as if there was nothing in his work that gave him pleasure. Lately he'd started to read in his lunch-break, and when he got home he'd sit at the table with a newspaper or a book. She knew that it was Mr Matama who was lending him the books. At first Sarah had been pleased because he seemed to be studying again, but when she'd wanted to read over his shoulder, he'd covered the page with his hands. She'd felt excluded and began to be worried when Leah told her that Mr Matama was talking politics with a group of young men, and that James was with them. Politics were not safe, Sarah knew, especially if people started to notice.

Ernest lay on his back so that his breathing deepened. Even though the sickness had made him old, he looked handsome in the early morning light, with his high forehead, the thin line of his cheek-bone and his strong chin with its tidy grey beard. She couldn't bear to think that his life might be almost over. She worried that there was nothing but sorrow and trouble ahead for all of them - no wonder she had lain awake most of the night.

She was first up, dressing quickly without disturbing the others, but she gave Nozuko a shake when she was ready to leave, to tell her it was time to make breakfast. The air was clean and sharp, and Sarah's breath came out in a warm cloud in front of her when she hurried towards the big house. As she got closer, she could hear the buckets clinking like bells against each other as Alfred carried them out of the dairy before taking them down to the cow-shed.

Millie was already standing on the kitchen steps, holding her blue dressing gown tight under her chin. Sarah missed her old Missis, and

52

she could see Millie did too, the way she tried to keep everything the way it had been.

'Sarah, I've boiled the milk for the coffee on the primus. Alfred's ready to start.'

'It's all right, Miss Millie.' Glancing back, she could see how her footsteps had melted their shapes onto the stiffly frosted grass. She stamped her bare feet on the wooden kitchen floor, trying to bring the feeling back into them.

Alfred was in the doorway. She handed him a mug of coffee, and he held it in both hands, warming his face against the steam. 'It's cold, Ma!' he laughed, his face round and innocent. She liked him; such a pleasant, polite boy.

She began to set the fire in the stove, tearing strips of newspaper, breaking thin sticks, and pushing them in delicately to build the flame, which started hesitant and small. She piled on a few fatter sticks, then some sharp splinters off the logs. The fire was yellow now, growing fast. She levered off the top back plate, and, suddenly catching, it roared through. She manoeuvred two bigger logs on top. It was time to fill the pots with water.

From then on the morning was just a rush. Jo was cross because there wasn't enough hot milk.

'Wait,' Sarah soothed, 'it's coming - soon, soon.' She danced round Jo, trying to make her laugh so that she would be more pleasant. 'Come on, don't look like that.'

'But I have to leave for school.'

'No, no. There's still time.'

Leah was putting bacon into the frying pan. Sarah took Vera her coffee, then laid the table for breakfast. While they ate, she dusted the sitting room. Afterwards there was clearing up the dining room, the bedrooms, morning tea, lunch. There was no moment when she could speak with James, although she thought about him. The house was bright now with winter sun. Vera was expecting visitors - she wanted the spare room floor polished, and the beds made up with clean, starched sheets.

It wasn't until the afternoon, when she took the men their samp and meat, that she saw James again.

'Son, we must talk.'

'Not now, Ma.'

'You know why it is so?'

'Yes, Ma.' It was grudgingly said, and then, 'Please.'

He was sitting next to Alfred on a fallen tree stump, both of them leaning against the corrugated iron shed, where Emily hung the washing when it rained. Alfred was the happy-go-lucky one. Musical, he'd got hold of an old accordion, and he played in a band sometimes when there was a wedding or a celebration. He wore his cap rakishly on the back of his head and had, while waiting for his lunch, tapped a rhythm on his knee with the back of his spoon. James glanced swiftly at him as if to check whether he was listening, but Alfred was too busy mixing the gravy with the white mealies to bother with what they were saying.

'The food is great, Ma!' Alfred smacked his lips in appreciation. Was that relief on James's face? She wasn't a fool. She straightened her back in a gesture James must have remembered instinctively from childhood, because he lost that defiant, shut-off look, just for the moment.

'Tonight, Son?'

'All right, Ma.'

James didn't go out that evening. He sat silently in the chair next to the stove, his hands empty on his lap, but Sarah could feel his restlessness under her skin. She waited too, not daring to order the family to go to bed in case Ernest suspected something. At last the girls said goodnight. Nozuko had wanted to finish sewing a skirt, but Sarah told her the light was too bad.

Sarah busied herself with the ironing. Luckily there were a few sheets and a shirt waiting, but she was clumsy. When she put the iron on the stove to heat, she left it too long, and the room smelled of scorched cotton. In desperation she started cleaning the side-board, taking each ornament, and the cups as well, to the table where she could see them properly, wiping them down with a damp cloth. The paraffin lamp left dark smudges in the corners of the room and on the ceiling, and her own shadow was very big along the wall.

'You make my eyes tired, Wife,' complained Ernest. 'What's getting you to jump around?'

'It's nothing. I'm just sick of the dust here. Why don't you lie down and rest?'

It was after ten o'clock when he finally settled. 'I want to check the chickens, James,' she said. 'I heard them carrying on last night, the way they do when they're frightened. Maybe a dog or a jackal's got his eye on them. Will you come with me?'

The moon made a deep purple shadow along the side of the house. They kept to the path, walking close together within its narrow limits, although she was taking two steps to his one stride. In the distance she could see a rock face glitter on the mountain, where snow had fallen. She shivered.

'It feels strange to have such a tall son.' It surprised her that her laugh was unsteady, almost as if she were crying.

'What is it you want to know, Ma?' He sounded puzzled. Was he pretending?

The chickens were huddled together at the back of the hok, where there was straw and a wooden shelter. It was very quiet, except for lonely sounds far away - a car engine, a dog barking. She stood leaning forward, her fingers caught in the wire mesh of the enclosure.

'I'm sorry if you've been worried. I know it's not easy, with Father ...' He tested the gate and tightened the rope which kept it closed, talking softly, almost to himself.

'Wouldn't you like to get married, James?'

He gave an involuntary snort, like a bitter laugh, as if he were spitting out air. 'Ma, with these wages?'

'With your schooling, you could try for something better in town.'

'If I leave, will he let you keep the house?'

'Thixo!' She hadn't imagined anything like that. 'My old Missis promised me I would be all right. Where must we go if he turns us off? Ernest is too sick to move.'

They stared ahead at the comfortable feathered darkness inside the rickety wooden shelter.

'My old Missis,' Sarah spoke slowly, describing someone she could still see clearly in her mind's eye, 'she was so frail, I had to wash her and dress her as gently as if she were a baby. She used to say I was the only one who could put on her clothes without it hurting. "Call Sarah," she'd tell Miss Millie, "I'd like to get up." Then we'd walk along the passage - slowly, slowly - and she'd hold my arm, pulling strongly as if all her strength was flowing into that hand so that she could keep me with her. After a few steps, she'd say, "Can we rest a minute, please, Sarah?" We'd take five, maybe even ten minutes, just to get to the dining room. Poor Gogo.'

'You loved her,' his voice was full of a kind of pain. She couldn't see his face; it was turned away from her.

'Yes, I did. I would have helped her out of respect too, but she

56

always used to say, "I won't ever forget your great kindness, Sarah. You have my solemn promise. And Baas William too will not forget."'

'Do you still believe that?'

'I don't know.' She sighed, resting her forehead on her hands. 'After the funeral,' she was remembering again, 'Baas William came to me without a smile, his face closed - you know how he looks - and he said, "I want you to have this from me, Sarah, for what you did for my mother." Five - pounds it was then! A tip!'

She couldn't stand still any more - she walked a few steps away from him, and then returned. 'No, you are wrong - Miss Millie will stop him if he tells us to go. Besides, however he may seem, he is still the son of his mother. He must have his own honour.' Her voice was firm again.

'Turn around,' he asked urgently, and she looked back along the path they had walked together. She saw their home, its walls washed a pale blue by the moon, then the winter stubble shining silver in the fields, the farm road. The big house was hidden by a copse of gum trees and the outbuildings round the yard.

'Look!' He pointed to the Fourie place on the other side of the fence. Their cement dam was built close by. A slight breeze turned the head of the windmill so that it gave out a rusty whine, and a spurt of water splashed from the pipe. Mrs Fourie ran a shop for the people who lived on the plots. She sold everything dearer than the Chinaman in town, but in quantities they could afford, weighing out three cents sugar, or handing over one cigarette. With only two cents to spend, it wasn't worth the walk into town.

'Look!' and there was the main road, tarred now. She remembered when it was just gravel, when the cars trailed clouds of dust. She'd paid for that new surface, was still paying, with the yearly road-tax. Leah always got into a bad mood when the tax demand came. 'I don't need that road. Besides, what do we do to that road, hey? My feet aren't so hard that I can wear it down!' she'd exclaim.

'This was all ours once, Ma,' James was saying. 'Izwe Lethu. Our Land. They buy and sell it to each other as if they have the right. They chase us off. But they are like dogs guarding a piece of stolen meat. Mr Matama is writing down how we once had our own farms here, which were well kept with tall mealies and fat pumpkins. How the men were rich with herds of red cows. How our people were healthy, not like now, when we are poor and the children die.'

'But Son, it's gone. It only hurts to talk about it.'

'You want me to forget? We are tired of forgetting. Come, let's walk a little.'

He led her through the gate next to the main road. Right there, where the traffic juddered past, was the graveyard for those who died on the plots, and on the nearby small-holdings; a narrow, triangular piece of land bumped up into graves and enclosed by a barbed wire fence.

'We live without respect, Ma, and when we die it's the same. How can we honour our ancestors, when we ourselves are without honour.'

Was it possible that he was saying these things to her, his own mother? She tried not to be hurt, but to understand him. In the moonlight a few wooden crosses cast crooked shadows. Several had fallen over, or stood at a precipitous slant. On one mound was a jug with a broken handle half buried in the loose earth, on another a golden-syrup tin held a few dead chrysanthemums. A cracked glass dome no longer protected a spray of faded artificial lilies.

'Do you think you are the first to feel like this?' Sarah caught his eyes, willing him to hear what she was saying. 'Ernest was in the ANC. I remember I went to a meeting where they told us that one day the whites would again share with us those things they had taken from us. But for now, we were like children to them. They had the education, and we had many things to learn from them. Our leader, John Dube promised: "Where once was a pool, water will collect again."'

'Do you still believe that?'

'I don't know. Nelson Mandela came in the night like a thief. Your father went to the meeting, although he forbad me to tell you so. We are not the same as the factory workers in the Bay. There are no other jobs for us than the ones we have.' Sarah looked bleakly across the tarred road towards the first few houses on the plots, no lights now, all asleep.

'It will get worse, Ma. How can you believe in a white person's honour, even that of Baas William or Miss Millie, when they have already taken so much. Perhaps not those two themselves, but why do they not know what has happened to our people? Just living here with them, we must remind them of that history they would like to pretend never happened, or maybe it's just that they can't stand for us to have even this little bit for ourselves. It itches at them, like a sore place, or a bite of an insect so that they will want to take away the small piece that we have left.' He scuffed the soil at his feet. She heard the despair in his voice, but there was something else there too - a hint of the preacher, the politician.

'And you think you will be able to stop them?' The words made strange shapes in her mouth.

'We are many more than they are.' There was a change in his voice, which was infused with a kind of excitement. 'It's not just what Mr Matama says. It's not just us, here. There are meetings happening, groups coming together all over the country: in the Bay, in Queenstown, Cookhouse, Cradock - even far away, in Cape Town, and places I haven't even heard of - Paarl, Wellingon, Worcester.

'This is serious?'

'Serious.'

The knowledge was too heavy for her. How she wished she hadn't spoken to him! She tried to save what should be within her power to look after - surely he would listen to her. 'James, can't you wait just a little while? We're not so badly off. We've got a nice house. I'm making some extra money on the vegetables. The two girls are still to do their schooling. Nozuko isn't old enough to be married, and Father is very ill.'

'You think that what is to be will wait until you are able to live better? It will never happen that you will be safe from the future. The only way you can be safe is to join hands with it and greet it.'

'James - you have always been a good son to me. If I were to ask you to stop?'

She read his silence.

She wanted to take hold of his shoulders and shake him. She wanted to say, 'You think we can force them to make our lives better?' How could he risk so much? She knew the posture of the white man. The policemen in town were six feet tall with hard flesh under their khaki trousers. They wore leather belts and leather shoes; they carried leather sticks and guns in leather holsters. They used the sjambok! They swore at all Black people, and when they arrested anyone, even for no crime at all, they beat them when they got them inside the cells. The farmers were the same. She'd seen the scars that Baas Botha had left on the two men who worked for him and had stolen his milk while he was on holiday. They'd never get a job again. They sat in the shade of the vines, and gambled, leading others astray. She didn't want James to become like them. Please God, it wouldn't go that far.

'Promise me you will do nothing illegal.'

He gave a hopeless laugh. 'Even when we say the things that are on our hearts, it is illegal. The government makes laws to close out mouths. It is against the law to say they must change.'

'And you think they won't find out, when everyone is suspicious and Ethel Mhlusi lives next door to the school, with a son who works secretly for the police?'

'That is so. I will tell the others to be more careful.' It was the only concession he was going to make.

'You could -' In an attempt to convince him that the group could jeopardise their own fragile community, she made a large gesture with her arms that took in the graves at their feet, the cemetery and the plots across the road, but even as she made it, she was conscious of the desolation around her and she dropped her arms with the 'Tsk!' of anger. And what will happen to you? She was crying silently now, hating her own weakness. He too remained silent.

'Come - it's getting late. Father will wonder what has kept us.' She turned her head away and dried her eyes on her sleeve. They walked back to the house in silence. I can't ask again, she resolved. He knows how I feel.

TEN

Although Fort Bedford Girls' School, Senior and Junior, was bilingual in English and Afrikaans, the number of English-speaking girls was so small that Miss Belmont taught Standards Three to Six in one classroom. In desperation she sent the four girls in Standard Six into the playground and charged them to revise for their History test.

'I don't feel like learning History,' yawned Jo. 'It's boring.'

'If you really thought it was boring, you wouldn't remember it,' rebuked Marge. 'You just pretend that because you're clever.'

'I'm not.'

'Yes, you are.'

'I'm not.'

'Yes, you are.'

The girls had settled on a bench against a north-facing wall so that they could catch the winter sun. Rita Snyman, who was repeating Standard Six for the third time, was the first to sit down. She jerked her gym down at the back to cushion her legs from the wooden slats of the bench. She had decided she wasn't going to bother with school because she was old enough to leave at the end of the year, and she bragged to the others that she had a job waiting for her as a receptionist at her father's garage. Placing her unopened history book under the bench, she unbuttoned her shirt in order to tan her cleavage. Then, producing an emery board from the top pocket of her blazer, she began to file her nails, taking care to keep the white edges as long as she could without breaking them.

'Shut up you two. If Jelly Belly hears the way you're carrying on, she'll make us go back inside.'

The four girls strung out along the bench. Alice Morgan closed pale sparse lashes over her meek, uncurious eyes. A blue vein on her forehead beat under porcelain white skin. Because she was often absent from school, she was out of her depth in all subjects, and hardly ever ventured to speak in lessons. Once she had murmured to Jo that her father was a bully, but when Jo, who always wanted to know everything, had asked 'why did she say that?', Alice had become silent again, and then stayed away from school for almost a fortnight.

Jo didn't want to admit it, but it was easy to be clever in this class. She knew she was smarter than Marge. Uncle William hated it that Jo's marks were usually higher. It was almost worth not working, or making deliberate mistakes, so that Marge wouldn't get into trouble after the test.

'You'd learn better if you weren't so worried about doing well,' Jo wanted to help.

'It's easy for you. Auntie Millie doesn't fuss over you - she says school made her sick.'

Millie's migraine attacks had kept her out of school. Although Marge was clearly much impressed with Millie's remark, Jo remembered the way Vera had sniffed and said perhaps it would have been better for Millie if she had made an effort, then she'd have been able to get a job.

Jo's eyes smarted. Her mother didn't seem to mind the way Vera spoke to her.

'Oh, I've quite enough to do,' she'd replied airily, and pretended not to hear Vera's tight-lipped retort.

'Yes, sponging off other people all your life.'

Her mother would never let Jo discuss Uncle William and Aunt Vera. To herself, Jo had nicknamed them The Interlopers. The word made her think of a thick dark company of locusts which had once swarmed catastrophically over the lands, crawling and hopping on every bit of green they could find and destroying a whole crop of lucerne. She magnified two of them a thousand fold and imagined their grotesque angular legs and large eyes, their blue, red, yellow and green scales, their hungry jaws consuming every living thing in Glen Bervie. Sometimes the impression that it had all gone was so strong that she'd get up early to make sure the trees and lawns and flowerbeds were still in place.

Suspicious of what they might be up to next, she had begun to spy on Aunt Vera and had spotted her sneaking down to the river to meet Big Jan Botha. Later, she had watched her return, and noticed that her hair and dress, usually so immaculately permed and pressed, were covered in bits of grass, as if she had been rolling in it. She suspected that they had been kissing. She couldn't tell anyone; it was too embarrassing. Marge would be horrified.

It was easier to get on with schoolwork than worry about what was happening at home. Marge was already whispering to herself the list of the names of the Presidents of the Republics of The Orange Free State and The Transvaal. Jo turned to the next chapter, which covered the discovery of diamonds. A child had picked up a pretty stone without realising what it was worth. Who was she? They should have mentioned her name! thought Jo. All the grown-ups in the history book had names. Imagine if it had been herself who had found it first - the injustice of not being credited!

In her mind she pretended she was five years old, playing on the riverbank. Sarah was looking after her and Nozuko. Nozuko was collecting smooth pebbles, which Jo was placing in patterns on the pale river sand. Jo hummed,

'You are my sunshine
My only sunshine
You make me happy
When skies are grey ...'

She ran over to a thorn tree to pull off a bunch of mimosa flowers to plant in the sand. The yellow pollen dusted her hands.

'Look, Miss Jo.' Nozuko gave her a sparkling stone. She balanced it on her open palm, and it sucked in the sunlight, turning it blue and purple and deep gold.

'Oh, it's so pretty! Can have it?' Always, in their games, Nozuko did what she told her, and this time would be no exception. Finder's keepers, thought Jo, so why do I think I have a right to it? She brushed this niggling doubt aside and went on making up the story.

At the house, her mother was giving a tennis party. Jo sat with her legs dangling over the edge of the veranda. She threw the stone up and caught it again, so that it scattered brightness between her hands. She wanted the grown-ups to notice what she had, and to make a fuss of her.

'That's very pretty, Jo. Bob - take a look at what Jo's found,' Mrs Loots exclaimed. Mr Loots' back curved like a question mark over Jo. There were beads of sweat on the tips of his ears, which were bright pink from running around on the court. He wiped his glasses with his handkerchief.

'May I hold it, Jo? Aah! It's very fine - I've not seen anything like it before. Must be some kind of rock crystal, I would say - I'd love to have it for my collection.'

'Millie, did you know Bob collects stones. He's quite an amateur geologist. Look how he's drooling over this one.'

'Jo'll let him have it, won't you Jo? She was only playing with it. She won't mind.'

She did. She had a secret garden in amongst the gum trees where she had planned to give it a special place. 'But Mo-om -' When she started to object, Millie frowned, pulling a face at her from behind the two Lootses, who were holding the stone up against the sun and squinting at it as if it already belonged to them. You can't argue with grown-ups.

'I'll give Jo something for it. Look, here's fifty cents, Jo. Is that all right now?' He knew she didn't want to give it up.

'But that's much too generous,' Millie protested, although her mother always told her never to be mean and always to give more than what was asked for.

'No, no - it's a proper exchange. Jo found the stone, and now I've bought it from her.'

Jo could almost feel the coin's hard round surface pressing against her palm. Half a crown was a lot of money. What would she have done next, she wondered?

I'd hide the money in the drawer in my bedroom, she thought. I'd save it up to go to bioscope. You could sit on a kitchen chair in the first three rows for just ten cents. She imagined that, and then saw herself drifting out to the back yard where Nozuko was minding Nontobeko while Sarah washed up the cups and the cake plates after the tennis party. She sat down next to Nozuko, and she knew Nozuko would never find out about the transaction that had just taken place on the veranda. Besides, Nozuko wasn't allowed to go to bioscope anyway, which was for whites only.

Jo had a vision of Nozuko's plump face with the kindly eyes that always tried to please her. She had hardly seen her lately. Just last week, she and Marge had passed Nozuko on their way to the tennis court. Jo had stopped to say hello, but she hadn't known what to say after that and Nozuko had seemed terribly shy, so she'd just smiled and said 'I'm sorry, I've got to go,' and she'd run after Marge. If someone - a friend - had done that to her, it would have hurt, it would have been terrible.

'What's wrong with Jo?' Rita's voice had a sort of echo to it, and came from very far away. 'She's gone all greeny.'

There were black and white spots dancing and swimming on her eyeballs. Only a small area in the middle was clear, but she couldn't concentrate on it. She put her head in her hands, and it lay there as if it had fallen off her neck. Marge made her stand up and dragged her towards a tap set in the hedge, even though her legs had no bones in them.

'Give us a hand, Rita,' she heard Marge as if she was speaking through an eiderdown.

'No chance. I don't want yukky vomit on my gym.'

Rita was right to be wary, Jo's body was shuddering and she couldn't keep the sour, burning taste out of her mouth. Marge made her bend over and a stream of lumpy brown stuff shot out of her mouth onto the grass. Marge turned on the tap and splashed Jo's face, and Jo, shaking, discovered that the spots had cleared. Placing her mouth under the jet of brackish water, she drank greedily and gratefully.

'Got a hanky?' asked Marge. 'Use mine.'

'Sun stroke,' pronounced Rita.

ELEVEN

Jo and Marge dawdled after school. They had over an hour before it would be time to meet William. 'Let's play "Spot the Hermit"', giggled Marge. To both of them it was one of those terrifying games, like chewing silver paper, which held an element of danger. They had never seen the man, but his secret presence in a world, where he managed to evade all social obligations, gave Jo the idea that he was not quite human. Did he have a mother, Jo wondered, or a father? Had he been an orphan and brought himself up without the help of grown-ups? What if - the idea was awesome - he had never been a child at all, but had turned up in Fort Bedford out of nowhere, fully grown?

Jo's satchel bumped against her back as she ran towards the hermit's house, which was behind the school and higher up against the mountain. On their way, they repeated the stories they already knew about him.

'He won't let anyone inside,' declared Marge.

'He hasn't been out for ten years - except maybe at night when no one's awake,' Jo whispered, fearful lest he overhear them, imagining his lonely figure sliding along in the dark. Perhaps he was very tall, or very tiny. He couldn't eat much if he never went shopping. When asked what he looked like, Millie was evasive, 'I don't remember ever having seen him,' she'd replied to Jo's urgent questions, but Jo knew Millie was capable of lying - a white lie, she'd say - if she didn't want to give an answer.

'They had to break the front door down when he was ill and they took him to hospital,' Marge continued.

'They knew something was wrong because his milk was going sour outside on the stoep.' Jo gave a dry retch as she conjured up the smell of rancid milk. She hoped she wasn't going to be sick again.

'Aunt Kitty asked him to Christmas dinner, but he wouldn't go.' No one, Marge implied, nodding her head and pursing her lips, no one had ever before refused an invitation from Aunt Kitty.

The house stood by itself in a small cul de sac. It was single-storied with a brick front bay. A creeper with heavy, dark green leaves climbed over the roof, across the window and completely covered the veranda, which was closed in with wire mesh. The shadow of the mountain lay like a cold shroud over the overgrown garden.

Jo was affronted that the man managed to hide away from everyone in Fort Bedford. She wanted to flush him out.

The day had a bitter flavour. Her mind was still jumping with images. One moment she could see Vera's spiteful face, the next her mother was becoming dimmer and dimmer, fading into nothingness. Then she conjured up two locusts, sitting in deck chairs on the lawn, with Sarah carrying a tray of scones and tea to them. It wasn't a nightmare because she was awake, but she couldn't stop it either.

If I had lots of money, I'd give some to Nozuko, wouldn't I? And then she could go to school, too, somewhere. Jo was unclear where Nozuko would go, as she wouldn't be allowed to attend the whites-only Fort Bedford Junior Girls'. Maybe I'd need every penny to buy Glen Bervie from Uncle William and there'd be nothing left, she excused herself. She'd make it up to Nozuko somehow.

She felt like breaking something. 'I'm going to throw a stone at his window,' she told Marge. Why should the hermit be allowed to get off scot free from being with other people?

'You wouldn't dare,' Marge giggled.

'Yes I would.' Jo picked up a stone from the road, but her throw was clumsy, and the stone sank into the hedge, which divided the garden from the street. Marge had her face in a gap in the greenery.

'Ooooh!' Marge snatched up her satchel, which she had dropped onto the ground, and took off.

'What's it? What's it?' But Marge had streaked away on her long legs and was already waiting at the corner for Jo to join her. They scooted downhill towards Main Street. Three more corners and it was clear no one was following them.

'It moved.' Marge's teeth were chattering. Her straight blonde hair was cut in a bob, which stuck out round her head like a dandelion.

'What? Where?'

'Inside the house. I saw a white face.'

'Him?'

'Must have been.'

'Looking at us?'

The horror of his gaze made them scream with hysterical laughter, and they linked arms and skipped into Main Street. In spite of Jo's misgivings about William and Vera, she decided she wanted Marge to live with them always. She lengthened her step to keep up.

The Dutch Reformed Church was next door to William's surgery. 'Are we going in?' asked Jo. It was a ritual they followed every afternoon while they waited for William's lift back to the farm.

The church was locked during the week, but not the garden. The tall, iron gate screamed as Jo pushed it open. The walls of the building were painted the same granite grey as the straight gravel paths laid out in dry squares in the garden. The windows were of clear glass, without pictures or colours and they stared at Jo as if they were eyes that could see right through her.

Although Ouma's father, Jo's great-grandfather, had built this church, it wasn't their family church. Ouma had married a Scottish immigrant, and the family had joined the Presbyterian Church, which was smaller, and built in the newer part of the town. Millie took Jo and Marge to the Sunday morning service there, where Millie sang loud and slightly off-key, enjoying the hymns, and Jo, embarrassed by the noise her mother was making, mouthed the words without making a sound, while Marge joined in with a sweet, clear voice.

The most important thing to Jo about the Dutch Reformed Church, was the statue of their great-grandfather, which stood on a plinth just inside the gate. Jo gazed, as she did every day, at this man, all made out of white marble, even his hat, beard, morning coat and high, winged collar. His right hand rested on the bible, his left was

68

extended slightly away from his body towards her. The Italian artist, working from a photograph, had produced, Ouma had said, a passable likeness.

She was the only girl in her school, besides Marge, of course, who had a statue of her great-grandfather. Although she didn't own the statue, it seemed proof that their family was special. It was the reason why, when she trailed behind her mother to the shops, everyone stopped to enquire after their health; why, however disregarded she felt at Glen Bervie, the farm was still the only place to live. It was not only more beautiful than anywhere else, it was the source for Millie's generosity - the cream cakes she baked for the school fete, or the buckets of roses, like wet sweet-smelling rainbows, which Millie gave to less fortunate friends in town whose gardens were too dry and small for such abundance. Everyone, even Uncle William, always sighed with pleasure when, on returning to Glen Bervie, they drove the car through the gates and up the drive.

Marge, who never stood in one place for more than a few seconds, was balancing on the brick borders of the barren flower-beds. 'Any um-berellas, any um-berellas, to sell today?' she carolled. She had already forgotten about the hermit. Jo thought that Marge had every reason to feel comfortable. She was not treated to the daily insults that she and Millie suffered. The trouble Jo was having was that every time she pictured the white face Marge had seen staring out of the dark, enclosed house, she could only imagine it as Millie's.

Jo concentrated hard. She wanted the statue to know what was happening. What was the good of a great-grandfather like this one if he didn't help when things got bad? Vera had stopped her mother's bridge parties, using the excuse that she needed quiet in the mornings, and couldn't stand all that coming and going, and besides, Elsie Mills's laugh sounded like a horse neighing.

Jo had noticed how her mother's chin had begun to firm up, as if she were having to tell herself all the time to be brave. She had seen Millie pause and draw herself together before entering the sitting room, as if unsure of her right to be there. She would often say she wanted an early night. Jo was positive that this was because she wanted to avoid an evening alone with William and Vera.

There wasn't anything Jo could do. Vera hated her even more than she hated her mother. Last Saturday morning, Vera had taken Marge to tea with Olive Botha. Marge had worn a new dress, and they had sailed down the drive without even a backward glance. Jo had told Marge to say she wanted Jo to go with them, but Marge just shook her head and replied that it wouldn't make any difference. Her clear blue eyes looked puzzled as if she couldn't understand why Jo was making such a fuss, which made it worse. Jo had turned away and hid behind the rockery when they left. It was an awful, lonely morning, and she'd ended up feeling so disregarded that she'd refused to talk to anyone at lunch.

'I'm not having you sulk like this, Jo. You could at least try to be pleasant when you're at table.' William terrified her with the ferocity of his glare.

'She's probably copying the baboon ancestors she left behind on the mountain,' Vera sniped, making her feel even more that she wasn't really part of the family.

Millie had taken her for a walk down to the cow-shed after lunch. They stood for a while and gazed at the three golden-brown calves in the fenced-off enclosure. The calves rushed optimistically to them. Pitying them because they had been separated from their mothers, Jo put out her hand for one to suck. Its tongue was like wet sandpaper pulling at her fingers.

'You let me down when you're rude to William and Vera,' her mother began.

The accusation was unjust, when all she had done was try to defend Millie. 'I wasn't,' she blurted out.

'Don't contradict me, Jo. That's just the way children are not supposed to speak to grown-ups.'

'And grown-ups - how are they supposed to behave? They're beastly to us.'

'I won't let you say that, Jo.'

'Why not, when you know it's true?'

'Jo, you're a child. You must let me decide.'

'But -'

'No. That's enough. I could make a handbag out of your bottom

70

lip.' Although she was joking, Jo could tell that this was the final warning.

Millie made up for the scolding with chocolate ice-cream at the Palladium cafe, and an afternoon at the bioscope for her and Marge. They'd even been allowed to stay for the serial, but it hadn't changed her sense of outrage at the way all the grown-ups ganged up against her.

The church clock struck four-thirty. 'Time,' announced Marge, jumping over the flower-beds and running ahead of her to the gate.

Jo was for a moment frightened of her own intentions, then, gathering all the spit she had in her mouth, she aimed at the statue. A frothy blob hit his left hand, and glistened on the palm before beginning to slide off. Jo glanced up at the all-seeing, all-condemning eyes of the church windows, then ran hell for leather after Marge.

TWELVE

Millie dreamed she was back in the past, when the farmhouse was being built. Although she had been only two years' old at the time, in her dream she was eleven, the same age as Jo was now. She and William were helping their father, who was a wiry man with a red beard. Like all immigrants from Europe, he burned badly. His face was blotchy from the exertion of hacking down prickly pear trees to clear the site for the house.

William was chopping at the leaves, separating them from each other, while Millie had been given a rusty agricultural mincing machine with which to mash them into food for the hens. She had to fork the leaves into the mouth of the machine, then press them down with a wooden spade before turning the handle. The fork and spade were much too big for her, so that all her movements were clumsy. She dared not give the leaves a shove with her hands, fearing their delicate, sandy-coloured thorns, like a fuzz of hair. If they attached themselves to her skin, they would hurt at the slightest touch, and her mother would need a magnifying glass to find each one before pulling it out.

'The work's too much for one man and a boy.' Her father mopped his forehead with a large blue handkerchief. William retorted angrily that he wasn't a boy. William's white shirt was immaculately clean, with neatly rolled up sleeves, and his wide trousers had a knife-edge crease in them. His cool, untroubled face was without his war scar - the way he had looked in the photographs taken just before he went to university.

William shouldn't talk back to Father, Millie worried. She concentrated on producing piles and piles of minced cactus leaves, as if this would somehow encourage William to behave himself. When she pushed the heavy, giant handle, which took an age to go round, a green slime oozed out of the holes in the mincer and plopped onto the rusty trough beneath it.

'Look!' she cried to them both, 'I'm nearly finished. You'll have to chop down more trees!' All round her dense shapes shut out the light. Her voice sounded thin and high, without resonance, as if it were sucked away into the fat, fleshy leaves.

'Tell Ernest to help us,' ordered her father. In her dream she knew that both he and Ernest were dead, but it didn't make any difference. Her father had taken off his jacket, and his silver watch chain was looped across the front of his waistcoat.

'I don't want him!' shouted William. The blade of his axe sparked as he struck out at a cactus twice his size. It turned slowly on its base like a large peaceful animal, then fell, displacing the dusty earth with a puff.

She could hear her mother ringing the little silver bell to announce lunch. She pulled at William's sleeve, but he jerked his arm up and raised the axe towards her. His white face and his blue eyes with their cold glare terrified her.

Her mother was already sitting at the dining room table. It was laid with the best china: white with patterns of small rosebuds round the edges. The silver butter dish and the salt and pepper reflected circles of light onto the ceiling. She was ladling out soup from the blue Minton tureen, which they had inherited from her grandmother's dinner service. She handed Millie a plate of soup, and indicated that she should carry it to her father's place.

'Millie, I count on you to stop William from disobeying his father.' Her mother's voice had an accusing edge. Her mouth was set in a thin line.

Against her will, Millie began to sob. The tears ran down her cheeks and fell into the soup. Putting down the plate as quickly as she could, she wiped her face with her knuckles. Her hands were stained with the sap from the leaves, and she knew with a terrible dread, that her nose was clogged with the same green slime. She glanced fearfully at her mother to see whether she had noticed, but Mrs Crewe was absorbed in watching the approach of her husband. Her face had lost that irritated, judging look, and was transformed with love.

Millie's sense of desolation was total. She stood, unclean, watching her father and her brother sit down to eat at the table, afraid to move in case they noticed the state she was in.

She held this dread even in the moment of waking. Choking with the tears she had shed in her sleep, she reached for the handkerchief under her pillow, and sat up to give her nose a good blow. Trembling, she looked slowly round the room, placing in the early morning light the solid shapes of the wash-stand and wardrobe, the floral curtains, her clothes piled onto a chair. She allowed relief to flow through her and lay back floppy with gladness that she was not still in the dream.

Turning to her bedside alarm, she saw that it was not yet five o'clock. Although it was earlier than she usually got up, she did not wish to dream again. Sliding out of bed, she put on her dressing gown and, because the garden would be muddy from the night's dew, her heavy shoes and socks. Anticipating the joy of being the only person awake and watching over the house, she tip-toed quickly down the passage, picked up a basket and secateurs, and dived into the clean, pale morning.

She had at least an hour before anyone else would wake. She began to hum, keeping her voice down while she was still close to the house, but she knew the song was growing in her, and she longed to let it out. The sky was lilac coloured, with a few wisps of pink clouds just above the trees. A spider had spun a web in the night from the rain-water tank across to the grape pergola and sat, speckled yellow with crabby grey legs, at its centre. The web would be broken later by the traffic from the back door to the tank, but for the moment she gazed at it, its intricacies silvered with dew, and ducked, as if in homage, beneath it.

Now she was out in the open, drifting light as a seed towards the front of the house, the drive and the rose-garden. She had in mind to pick some early buds she had noticed the day before - a few white

74

Virgo, a tawny Sutter's Gold, a fairy pink spray of Cécile Brunner. She would place them in a blue jug in the sitting room. She paused to look back at the house; white and safe on a green sea of lawns. The view filled her heart.

She had lived in this house for nearly half a century. Only two years ago, her mother, who had created it all, had rested all morning in a grass chair under the ash tree so that she could enjoy the garden. Her father, in his last illness, had gazed out from his seat on the veranda at Jan Botha's farm. He watched the speckled black and white Friesland cows graze along a field, or the busy tractors push red earth into a wall for a new dam. His straw hat had shaded his eyes, and his beard, which had grown white, had scratched her cheek as she leaned her head on his shoulder. That was ten years ago, when Jo lay asleep in a pram on the lawn, with a white bridal net thrown over the top to keep off insects. Later, Millie would see her toddle down to the river with Sarah and Nozuko, talking so much that Sarah called her Little Bird, after the weaver birds that never stop chattering as they dart in and out of their basket nests.

The conviction that all the generations were still present and active in the landscape, swelled her song. She sang her favourite hymn, and as she passed out of earshot of the house, she let it out from her full lungs.

'Shall we gather at the river
The beautiful, the beautiful river ...'

She snipped as far down the rose stems as possible, pulling them out and away from the bush, careful not to let the thorns snag on her gown. When they were children, she and William had been allowed to select hymns for a sing-song at home on Sunday evenings. She had liked it best when it was winter, and there was a fire in the dining room. The wood crackled and spat and the flames dazzled. She waited until it was her turn, so she could ask for the one that sounded like a picnic.

'Shall we gather at the river
That flows by the throne of God.'

She could see her mother and father and Aunt Helen, all smiling at her and sitting on golden thrones set on the river bank. Ernest was on one too now, looking like in his younger days, his beard dark, not flecked with grey. Her mother turned to say something to him and he put his hand on her arm and laughed as if responding to a joke.

There was such a crowd of people, such a generous and happy hum of laughter and talking. Everyone she knew was there in beautiful new clothes: William and Vera, arm in arm, with Marge at their side; Jo, next to Marge, without that sulky, dull look her face had taken on lately, but radiant and energetic, was holding Nozuko by the hand and talking earnestly to her. Father O'Reilly walked among them as if giving them all his blessing. Sarah and Leah were there with their old mother, and James and Nontobeko and Nontu, as well as Bunny Loots and Bob, and Jan and Olive Botha. Freddie and Emily were there with their children, and Isaac Gxoyiya, the builder, as well as Mr_Matama and all his pupils from the school. She imagined the whole crowd floating over the ground, the women's dresses billowing and shining in the balmy air.

'Shall we gather at the river ...'

The sun was rising like a huge golden balloon, touching the trees with a yellow light, making a halo around the house.

'That flows by the throne of God.'

She didn't want to go inside yet. She kept to the lawn, circling the house, past the front door towards the orange grove on the other side. She had been keeping an eye on a few navels. The large orange globes were puckered to contain a second, baby orange packed neatly inside. She'd been waiting for them to lose their faint green tinge. They had disappeared. Perhaps William had picked them? Her eye caught a flicker of movement between the glossy roundness of the trees.

'Stop!'

They turned towards her; two small children, with large, innocent eyes. The pockets in their short pants bulged. They kept their hands behind their backs.

'Come here.'

Obedient, but silent, they approached. A pocket ripped, and an orange rolled onto the ground.

'Pick it up.' She gestured the command in case they didn't

76

understand her.

One child bent sideways. Now she could see he was in difficulty because he already held an orange in each hand. Oh! The little sinners! She kept back a smile as he juggled the three oranges, which were too large for him to keep comfortably together.

'Put them in here.'

She held out the basket. Half a dozen oranges tumbled in among the roses. Then another two. She put on her sternest voice.

'That's very naughty.'

They gazed at her, uncomprehending.

'Oh, I don't know what to do with you. Go to the kitchen, the kitchen door. Wait for me. Wag by die kombuis.'

They scampered off, their heels kicking up. One wore a dun-coloured vest, torn under the arm, the other a shirt several sizes too big, which flapped over his knees. The little devils!

There was a squawking in the gum trees. A colony of egrets were nesting in the topmost branches, like white washing spread out to dry over the leaves. A tree swayed as one bird stretched its wings to the morning. Vera complained about the noise and William said the droppings were killing the gums. This was undoubtedly true. Mother had prophesied it would happen when they first came to nest there. Mother had paid the farm children to beat pots and pans in a loud clatter, hoping to scare them off, but the birds usually wheeled up, and then settled immediately the banging stopped. They were a protected species, but William had told Millie just the other day that he was going to write to the magistrate for permission to shoot them.

She passed through the sitting room. The roses will look lovely on the bookcase, she thought. As she entered the passage, she bumped into William, who was already dressed.

'Lovely morning,' she beamed.

'Yes.' Conscious that she hadn't washed yet, she headed for the kitchen, but he called her back. At high speed, she reviewed all the things he might be angry about, but when he spoke, she was taken by surprise.

'Can you please not enter the house through the sitting room door? Imagine if I had been a visitor. I don't want my guests to meet you in the sort of state you are in.' His voice was flat, like a man on the wireless. His face and form were shadowy in the dark passage.

'All right,' she kept her tone gay and light.

'I'm talking about you and Jo - at all times, mind. Could you both use the kitchen door from now on?' he persisted.

'Fine.' Wanting urgently to escape from him, she gestured with her basket towards the kitchen. 'I just want ... put ... these ...'

'As long as you understand.' He turned away and she was released. Her stomach pulled. What was it she had been doing? Oh yes, the roses. Putting the basket down in the scullery, she went to fill the blue vase at the tank. Was he really saying she should never use the front door? Surely not. He was just in a bad mood. Chin up, she told herself.

The two small boys were huddled under the pine tree. She had forgotten all about them.

'Sarah - I caught them stealing oranges. Whose children are they?'

'They're from the Fourie place.' A shack across the road from the cow-shed. A family with at least a dozen children. Their very existence was an affront to William.

'Scold them, Sarah. Say that if I catch them stealing again they'll have to talk to the Baas.'

While Sarah was putting all this into Xhosa, Millie studied their wily, innocent faces.

'Oh, I don't know. Make them wait, I'll give them some bread and jam.'

Spreading home-made apricot jam on thick slices of bread, Millie deliberately plunged her mind back into her early morning happiness. Going over each different event, she remembered the egrets. Maybe, she thought, that old trick with the pots and pans will work after all.

The children politely held out both hands for their bread and jam, and waited to be given permission to leave. Millie called Sarah outside once more.

'Ask them to come back tonight, with all their brothers and sisters. They must be here at six, just when the sky is turning colour. We'll make them bang the pots and pans under the trees, like we

78

used to - to stop the birds from roosting. Say I'll pay them three cents each. You can bring Nozuko and Nontobeko as well, and Freddie's children.

It would be like a children's orchestra. Her imagination was leaping again. She couldn't see William objecting if she could give a good reason for the noise. Besides, she'd pay for it herself. One big bang instead of having to shoot those beautiful birds. And if it failed - well, it would still be a gorgeous event. And the children would have a fine time and even earn a little money.

'Miss Millie -'

Millie glanced at Sarah. It was too bad, she thought momentarily, that this morning everyone seemed determined to interrupt the fragile dreams she used to keep herself going, but when she studied Sarah's face properly, she began to understand that something terrible had happened. Sarah hadn't yet recovered from Ernest's death, but this morning she staggered slightly, as if she had been in a storm. Her eyes seemed to have sunk right into her face.

Millie put a hand on Sarah's shoulder, and guided her back into the kitchen, pulling out a chair for her to sit down.

'What is it, Sarah?'

THIRTEEN

Suddenly there was the scream of fast cars braking, there were headlights at the window, men shouting. Then the front door was kicked open, and there were white policemen and black policemen with torches in every room. They were shining the light into Sarah's eyes so that she couldn't see for the dazzle; they were pulling her roughly out of bed.

'Meid, waar's jou man?'

'He's passed away, Baas.' Sarah pulled the blanket tighter around her shoulders as she followed the men into the kitchen. The little girls clung to her; they weren't even crying, they were so frightened.

'Vat die boy - get him!' James stood naked in the torchlight, trying to cover himself with his hands. The sergeant, a heavy, white man, twice his size, with hard, pink skin, tipped the sideboard over with his boot and the cups and saucers shattered on the floor. Sarah had a sudden glimpse of the pretty china lady with the green dress, which Millie had given her, lying without hands, her painted face broken in two. The next moment two more policemen hurriedly opened the drawers and threw everything out onto the floor as well. A black policeman whom she'd never seen before, slashed open the mattresses, like slaughtered animals. She watched them like someone who has broken a bone. She could see the damage, but was too bewildered to feel the pain.

'Take the books!' ordered the sergeant. He was a man who had come to make war.

Then another policeman brought him something. 'Well, well, what

80

have we here?' You could tell he was pleased by the oily way his voice changed into bullying triumph. 'What's this, Khumalo?' He held up a knitted balaclava cap, which covered the head and ears, leaving holes for the eyes and mouth. The Chinaman stocked them for the winter; it wasn't anything special. James sometimes wore it when he went out at night.

'That's it. He's one.' Quite without warning, the sergeant hit James across the mouth with the butt of his gun, so that James staggered forward, losing his balance. 'Jou donder! You rotten bastard. You'll pay for this. 'Then, slowing down, he sneered, playing his torch over the James's man's smooth body.' Get yourself decent.'

James struggled into his trousers. Sarah wanted to speak to him, but he avoided her gaze, and anyway he was surrounded by at least four white men. They were handcuffing him and kicking him towards the police van. At last he turned his head and she saw his fear.

'No -' she rushed towards him, but they pushed her back.

'Shut up, bitch. Your son's had it. He's lucky we don't shoot him right now. You won't see him again.' They shoved James so hard into the back of the van, that he fell forward on his face and when he scrambled to his feet, his face was full of blood.

'James!' she screamed above their harsh commands, above the sound of the engines revving up. 'James!'

Then in the grey early morning light, she and the girls were left alone in the wrecked house. How would she manage now? How she wished Ernest were still alive. What was going to happen to James?

Nozuko crouched down amongst the bits of china. She was trying to fit three pieces of a broken saucer together.

'We'll clean up later,' Sarah took the shards from her stiff fingers. 'Make a fire now, so we can eat something hot.'

Nontobeko and Nontu were clinging to each other, shivering. Their lips were blue. Sarah tucked a blanket round them and tried to make her voice sound reassuring.

'I'll find someone to mend the door. It's still early - it's not yet time to go to work.' She was deliberately not speaking about James because she didn't want to show the children how bad she felt. When she was dressed and the children were having something to eat, she hurried over to her mother's house to tell Leah.

Although it was earlier than usual, the people on the plots were already awake. From a flicker of a curtain at a window, or a door opening a few inches, she could see she was being observed from almost every house. Ethel Mhlusi was standing at her gate.

'Molo Mama.'

'Molo Sisi.'

'Did they take James, Mama?'

She didn't want to speak. She nodded her head.

'They've got the schoolteacher too, and five others. Sammy Skweyiya is one.'

Sarah didn't stop. If she talked to Ethel, the whole place would find out her business.

Leah told her the rest. 'Everyone seems to know a little, but it's not safe to speak about it. Mr Matama has formed a group of the men around James's age here on the plots. There were many other groups in other places. There's been trouble in the Transkei and a farmer was murdered. Now the police are arresting people on the trains coming from Cape Town because they say it was started by men working away from home.

Sarah drew in her breath. They were whispering together even though the front door was closed.

'Poqo!' She could see Leah was almost too scared to say the word. 'That's what they are called. They say Africa is for Africans. Didn't James tell you anything, Sisi?'

Sarah shook her head. The less she knew, the better! She kept on seeing the way James had tried to stop the blood pouring from his nose. What were they doing to her baby now?

'No one was murdered here!' Sarah cried out at last. 'How can they be taken for what happens in the Transkei, or in Cape Town?'

'Leah,' her mother called. She was hard of hearing and had slept through the noise which had woken everyone else.

'I'm coming, Ma. Sarah's here too.' Leah turned to Sarah. 'She'll be asking questions about you now. I'll say you came for some sugar. Go to the big house and tell Miss Millie what has happened. Maybe she can get them to release James.'

82

Sarah fastened her hopes on Millie. Millie had friends in Fort Bedford who could speak to the police. Surely, she thought, they wouldn't need to keep a child in prison. He hadn't done anything.

But Millie looked worried when Sarah told her. 'There's been a lot in the papers and on the news. Everyone is scared of Poqo. Is James really a member?'

'No, Miss Millie!' Sarah cried out. Denial was best.

Yet Sarah remembered that when she told Leah about the knitted balaclava, Leah had exclaimed that this was bad because that thing was their uniform - and a sort of disguise, when they went to kill someone, or set fire to a church or a bank. Had they worn them too, elsewhere? Sarah had asked, but Leah couldn't say.

'How do you know these things?' Sarah had exclaimed. 'Why didn't you tell me before now?'

'It's all over the streets today. Everyone is talking about it, even though we didn't know anything yesterday. It's like a wind that came up after the police left. Poor Mrs Matama is crying in her house. He pretended to her he was giving the young men extra schooling.'

The thoughts in Sarah's mind made her feel stupid. She couldn't move, couldn't speak. Millie's voice seemed to come from far away.

'It's best I tell William myself. Vera needn't know yet. I'll phone Father O'Reilly - no, I've got to go to town. I'll see him there.'

Sarah put her head on the kitchen table.

'You'll have to work today, Sarah, I'm afraid, otherwise Vera will be furious, especially as she's got visitors coming. Can you manage that?'

Sarah pushed herself to her feet, and Millie helped her to stand. 'I promise I'll get Father O'Reilly to sort something out. Courage, Sarah.' Millie patted her shoulders awkwardly. 'I'm sure they'll see how young he is.'

Oh God, thought Sarah. Oh please God. For the first time that morning, she cried, the tears rushing down her cheeks. She put her apron over her head to hide her face from Millie, so that she wouldn't be shamed.

At that moment, Leah came in through the outside door.

'Try to comfort her, Leah,' said Millie. She was already taking off her hairnet, and shaking out her curls. 'I've got to talk to Baas William first, but I'll wait until the children have gone to school. If he asks where James is, just tell him you don't know.'

FOURTEEN

William accosted Sarah later that morning. His eyes were blue stones. 'Millie says you knew nothing about this sabotage James was plotting.'

'No, Baas William.'

'Look, I'm not sure whether you are lying, but I've thought it over, and you can stay on here until we know everything.'

Yehova! thought Sarah.

'But I'm telling you now, if that son of yours ever gets out of prison, and personally I hope they hang him, he's never to set foot anywhere near here again, because if he does I'll shoot him for trespassing.'

She was trembling. She told herself it was his rage talking. It couldn't be true that they would sentence James to death. Not for doing nothing.

After he turned away, the day seemed to pile on her without stopping. Then, when Vera called her to tell her to lay two extra places for lunch, Sarah made herself run. She couldn't afford to give them more chances to be angry with her.

'Clean yourself up, will you Sarah, before you wait at table,' snapped Vera.

Leah ironed a freshly starched apron for Sarah. 'Do what you can,' she soothed. 'I'll be there to help.'

Father O'Reilly drove out in the evening to visit Sarah in her house. He touched the broken door with his small, white priest's hands that were used to blessings and rituals.

'Did the police do this?'

Sarah nodded, and led him inside. The room was tidy now. Nozuko had covered up the mattresses with blankets and swept up the broken china. She was very subdued - too quiet, Sarah knew.

Father O'Reilly didn't sit down. 'It's bad news, I'm afraid.' His face was in the shadow of the lamp, but his voice was kind. 'They've all been taken to Port Elizabeth. They're being held under the ninety-day law, which means no visitors, not even a lawyer. You can give me clean clothes for James and I'll make sure they're handed in at the police station. It's all we can do.'

She couldn't stop expecting James to walk in at the door. She knew it was ridiculous, but she kept food ready for him each day. After work, when she was alone with Leah, she cried. No one else talked to her about her son. It was as if they were afraid of being arrested if they did. Although, sometimes, she noticed a few extra flowers on Ernest's grave that she hadn't put there - a jam jar with white daisies, and, once, a single pink rose.

She didn't make contact with the other families whose relatives were in prison with James. Her reticence was partly out of respect for Mrs Matama, who held her head high and refused to speak about her husband to anyone. Besides, Sarah only knew the other relatives by sight. Nosisa Skweyiya, Sammy's mother, nodded to her in church and would have come over, but Sarah avoided her because Leah had told her that she'd heard Sammy was going to be released soon as he had agreed to give evidence against the others. Nosisa had already travelled by train to Port Elizabeth, where she had been allowed to visit Sammy, but although Sarah longed for news, she did not ask her to find out how James was

Two months after the arrest, Father O'Reilly brought Sarah a bundle of clothes. They were James's clothes, but what had the police been doing to him? There was blood on his shirt, and on the trousers, which were soiled and smelled terrible with the ammonia smell of urine as well as a scorched, burnt smell. She soaked them in disinfectant, and rinsed them, and then washed them with soap - and with her tears.

Four months after that, there was the trial. Millie said it was lucky William and Vera were away in Pretoria, because now James could have visitors and Father O'Reilly would drive Sarah down to Port Elizabeth to attend the closing days of the trial. Sarah and Mrs Matama stayed in the women's hostel in New Brighton, and caught a bus into the centre of town, where the accused were being held. Inside the police station, window panes painted over with what was once white paint, now yellowy grey with city dirt, let in feeble daylight. The dingy entrance was like a dark cave, where the faces of the white policemen glimmered like angry ghosts staring at her and Mrs Matama.

Millie had given Sarah a sober grey dress which had been her church dress, and Sarah had made herself a new long dark blue skirt to go with the white blouse which she had been given after the old Missis had died. 'Wear the grey dress,' Mrs Matama, who was wearing black, advised. 'It makes you look the decent motherly woman you are. Maybe they will pity us and give us longer time with our men.' Mrs Matama wore glasses, which seemed to turn her into a different class of person to Sarah. Like her husband, she too had a matric, and when they were on the bus she read a book just like a white somebody.

James was an insubstantial shadow behind a wire mesh screen. It wasn't that Sarah couldn't touch him, although she longed to, nor that she couldn't see him properly, although that was terrible also, but what hurt the most was that he sounded so tired. As if somewhere in that cold, cold building he'd lost the James she knew, and accepted whatever this place chose to make him.

'They will let you free,' Sarah's voice pleaded with him to agree with her.

'Try to understand, Ma. Sammy Skweyiya has turned state witness. We've all signed confessions.' He spoke in a heavy, dull voice.

She found herself telling him instead about Nontobeko's school report. They had a new teacher at the school to take Mr Matama's place. 'Nontobeko says she wants to be a nurse when she grows up, so she can help sick people get better.'

James smiled for the first time.

In the morning, the two women stood together with a small crowd in the damp shadow of the court house, and waited for the van load of prisoners due to be tried inside the huge stone building with its five different courts. As the van, with wire mesh screens instead of windows, swung through the narrow gates, she heard the prisoners singing.

Thina sizwe
We, the people
Thina sizwe esintsundu
We, the Black people
We are crying
We are crying for our land
Which was taken away by the white people.
They must leave our country alone
They must leave our country alone
Let them leave our country alone
Let them leave our country alone.'

Men's voices, singing without the usual interwoven melody of women's voices joined in with them. Their voices had been in that cold, bruising place where all commands echoed harshly against cement floors and iron doors. She knew about it; she had been there too and seen it for herself. How sorrowful they sounded, yet how the singing moulded them together! Miriam - Mrs Matama had asked her to be more familiar with her - was weeping openly now. They both lifted their heads and sang with their men.

Thina sizwe
Thina sizwe esintsundu'

Inside the courtroom, the 'non-European' benches were crowded with attentive people. In the larger, whites-only gallery opposite them, there were rows of empty seats. James and six others were being led up the stairs from below the court. As they shuffled in, Sarah realised with a shock that the men were handcuffed together in an awkward line. They had chains on their legs too. She knew all the accused by sight, if not by name. Mr Matama had lost a lot of weight - they all had. James - James was thinner than he'd ever been and looked years older.

All the officers of the court spoke to each other in a gabble of

English, which was hard to understand. Sarah strained forward in her seat because she was afraid she might miss something important.

'The court will rise,' shouted a small cross man with his hair combed like a cap across a shiny, bald head.

Without recognising the command, Sarah rose with the others, but it was only after she had sat down that she realised that those on trial would have to remain standing, because the usual place for the accused persons was too small for their number.

The judge came in from a side door. He swept his long black cloak together like a blanket, before taking his seat. He spoke with the men near him in the court in that same complicated and unfamiliar English. James was leaning forward like all the others. On each face was an anxious attempt to follow the proceedings, because that understanding would give them knowledge of what would happen to them.

'What is the prosecutor saying?' Sarah whispered to Miriam.

'I'll tell you afterwards.' Miriam was frowning, her eyes fixed on her husband, who stood very straight, his face without expression. Only once did he turn to look at her and Sarah could see a light flash between them. He may have lied to her, but now was not the time to talk about that, it was a time to show the love she felt for him, and she did so.

In the recess they went outside into the street. They had no money for food or drink, so they stood against the grey building, where a strong wind blew sweet papers and dirt over their shoes in little dusty whirlwinds, and the air was stale and full of sadness. Miriam's voice was a whisper, although cars passed them on the tarred road without slowing down and no one seemed near enough to hear what she said.

'The prosecutor said they were planning to put dynamite in the Dutch Reformed Church.'

'What?' Sarah couldn't believe it.

'And in the magistrate's court, and in the location office.' Miriam spoke tonelessly, like one in shock, or as if she were trying desperately not to give the words their full meaning. 'He said they were going to bomb the police station.' Her husband, the schoolteacher, had been the leader of a group, which talked about such things. James had been there and then come home to Sarah's house and rolled out his mattress and slept. Now Sarah knew why he had not wanted to discuss the group with her.

'How?' Sarah's eyes were wide with the fear of it.

'I don't know. Perhaps they had only begun to talk about what they could do. He said they planned to kill policemen. I'm sorry -' Miriam gave a dry sob. Sarah knew how much Mrs Matama had valued the status of being the headmaster's wife. Other people had blamed her for being too proud. Now she apologised to the mother of one of the young men her husband had led into prison.

In the afternoon there was a court interpreter, who spoke in Xhosa and Sammy Skweyiya pointed to the school-teacher. 'He told us, "The whites deserve to die! Not one of them is innocent."' Miriam put her hands over her face.

Sarah and Miriam waited again the next morning to join with the men in their singing. They sang their desperate and hopeless longing to be united with them.

Nkosi sikelel' iAfrika
God bless Africa
Yiza moya oyingewele
Come Holy Spirit
Usisikelele
And bless
Thina lusapho lwayo
Us, her children.'

This is happening to my son, thought Sarah. They are going to take him away from me, she told herself. She knew from James's face that there was no hope. What good would it do to confide in Miriam what she feared? The two women suffered, but not together.

Sammy Sweyiya was given his freedom in exchange for the things he had told the court about the others. James and four more were sentenced to ten years' hard labour. Then there was silence and the judge put a black cloth over his head and spoke to Ezekiel Matama.

'You are a wicked man accused of a serious crime, which has been proved against you. You misused your position as a teacher to

90

mislead the young men over whom you had influence. You planned the overthrow of the state. The punishment for treason is death, and in your case there are no extenuating circumstances. I therefore sentence you to be taken to a place of execution, where you will hang by your neck until you are dead.'

Part Two

1973 - 1974

Millie

FIFTEEN

'What are you up to, Millie?'

Millie raised her head and her gaze rested calmly on William's trousered legs. She had learned when quite small to keep her attention fixed only on the present moment. She had been busy contemplating the sky in an empty, benign way. Once she had thrown herself down on the ground - and that decision had been made in a flash, like the way she jumped out of bed in the morning - she hadn't had any second thoughts. Lying on her back, she had immediately lost herself in the unusual view of the sky, which arched above her. The colour, as it entered her mind, was not a uniform blue, but grew from the palest duck egg at the edges, to this deep cerulean - she tasted the word, it sounded heavenly - right in its centre.

'What?' she asked vaguely.

'I want to know what you think you're doing?'

She wasn't going to care if William was furious with her. The twin trunks of trousers were too tall to allow her to see his face, whose expression in any case she could imagine. Careful lest she might get a migraine from the angle of her neck, Millie returned to her stubborn stare at the sky.

'You're lying in the dirt like an old, broken doll.'

'I'm saving the tennis court.'

Millie reviewed the events, which had caused her to end up where she was. She'd heard the tractor - that was the first thing. The noise was closer to the house than usual. William allowed only Freddie to drive the tractor. He said the other boys hadn't the brains to understand machinery. She'd looked out for Freddie's intent body hunched over the heavy, clumsy vehicle. Instead of appearing in the drive, the thump, thump had remained constant, and it had niggled at her. William never consulted her about his plans for the farm. She was always nervous about what he might think up next.

Deciding to take a look, she'd strolled towards the sound. As she'd rounded the plumbago hedge - flowering now with sticky bunches of smoky-blue flowers - she had caught her breath. The tractor was on the tennis court! The two posts that had held up the net were laid side by side on the grass outside the wire enclosure, like teeth that had been extracted. One row along the length of the court had already been ploughed up. Freddie was making the turn for the next row.

'No!' she had cried out. 'No! No! No!'

Freddie couldn't hear her above the racket of the engine. She'd run, stumbling across the overturned earth, caught up with the rattling machine and flailed her arms against its huge, turning wheels.

'Stop! Stop!' she had screamed again, but helplessly, pitifully unequal to the noise and movement of the tractor. Then, just as she threw herself into its path, she had somehow flapped herself into Freddie's line of vision. She could have been killed, if he hadn't braked in time. I could be dead now, she thought. The idea, with its sense of release, was almost comforting. She couldn't see how she could win against William, especially as he had the advantage of making her feel continually in the wrong.

She'd had a vague impression of Freddie's shocked face bending over her. He couldn't help her up because that would be too intimate a gesture. Poor Freddie! She'd given him a terrible fright. She couldn't blame him for calling William.

'Millie, please stop humiliating yourself like this.' William's tone was conciliatory, which was unusual for him. She maintained her silence. No, he'd have to do much more than that to move her.

'Please stand up, Millie. We can't talk when you're like this.'

She lifted her head again; was it a disguise, or did he seem less frightening?

'I promise. I won't do anything without your agreement.'

96

Well, she was positive she wouldn't give that. Her head swam as she sat up. He put an arm around her shoulders and helped her gently to her feet. He kept the arm there as they walked together to a bench placed outside the court. It was ages since he had touched her, or even talked kindly to her. It made her feel differently towards him, not so cut off.

They sat down so close together that she could feel his warmth. 'It's a wonderful surface,' Millie sobbed into his shoulder. Once she started to talk, she could feel her longing to confide in him surge up. 'You said so yourself - that it was the best court you'd ever played on. Mother told the boys to put on layer after layer of anthill sand, the purest, free of all stones, and then they wet it and rolled it, wet it and rolled it until it was hard and smooth ...' She fumbled for her handkerchief which was tucked into the sleeve of her cardigan, and blew her nose loudly. The tennis court had been something to boast about. 'It's taken years and years to get like this ...'

'But Millie, we don't use it anymore.'

'We could. We could ask people out to tennis again - '

'I prefer golf now, and you haven't played in weeks.'

It was true. Bunny Loots had developed a bad knee. She and Millie had been dropped from the Fort Bedford tennis team. After all, she was over sixty. Elsie Mills had chosen years ago to stick to bridge, saying she was much too old to run around like a young thing.

'Father O'Reilly ...'

'But he hasn't been out for months!'

'He's on holiday in Ireland. When he gets back - '

'I can't be expected to keep up a tennis court just for the benefit of a priest who comes once a fortnight for a few sets. Millie, be reasonable!'

'The girls ...' This was her last card. In the holidays, the tennis court was what pulled everyone together. The spectators sat under flowery cotton sunshades, or in the shade of the Camdebo stinkwood - a tree, Mother had said, which was as elegant as an English beech. Millie always made hop beer for the summer parties; the ice-cold bottles dripped from the condensation in the fridge. Oh the pop of the corks! The sweet fizz!

Marge was a first-class player, she was always worth watching, and if she said so herself, Millie still played a good game in spite of her bad knee, which only troubled her occasionally. All Millie's finest memories were around this court. Here, and at the big family meals, with several extra guests: cousins, uncles and aunts, as well as friends - everyone together. Lately William and Vera preferred to eat in their own dining room, and sent her her meals on a tray. When they had visitors, it was usually people from the city or overseas, whom she didn't know, like those ballet dancers who had been staying last week. Vera had explained that it would upset the numbers if she joined them. She had never thought the farm could become so lonely, and now its very heart was to be cut out.

'Marge only gets a fortnight's holiday.' William continued. Marge was nursing in a large Port Elizabeth hospital. 'She gets more than enough tennis in P.E. because she plays for the nurses' team, and, when she comes home, she's much too tired to be sociable. She doesn't want you to organise tennis parties with old school friends she hasn't seen in years.'

Millie couldn't help hurting when he talked like that about what Marge thought. Now he was starting on Jo.

'As for Jo, you know as well as I do that she doesn't even want to come here for her holidays. She'd rather be plotting sabotage with her left-wing cronies than visiting her mother.'

It was true that Jo didn't like coming home to Glen Bervie anymore. She had told Millie that she hated her aunt and uncle and, if she had the choice, wouldn't even cross the street to speak to them. It made Millie feel bad when Jo said she couldn't bear to eat their food - 'to be beholden' she had called it. She complained that they patronised her and made her feel like a pauper, which wasn't a very kind thing to say, Millie thought.

Millie couldn't make Jo come home for the holidays - she was an independent woman now, with a loan from the Provincial Education Department. Of course Millie visited her, but she never stayed for long. The other young people with whom Jo shared a house were very nice and polite, but Millie felt awkward there. They were all so clever and busy.

Besides, Jo had never really enjoyed tennis the way Marge had. She could see it was unreasonable to expect William to keep up the court just for the children.

William must have noticed her hesitation, but it seemed to make him even kinder towards her. He drew her closer into the circle of his arm. 'Millie, you know how I love Glen Bervie. How could you believe I'd want to harm it?'

'Oh - ' Millie wailed. His shoulder was drenched with her tears.

'I know you feel the same as me. That's why we're both stuck here. Vera doesn't understand, but you do. Whenever I've gone anywhere else, it's always been away from here. I used to cry with happiness whenever I came home.'

'You'd wear dark glasses so we couldn't see your eyes,' Millie blubbered, laughing gently.

'Sit up now, please,' he begged her, and helped her straighten up, but she steadfastly refused to look into his face. She wasn't going to let him talk her round. It was important, even if she couldn't say why.

'Poor Vera - she's a city person really, and she's had to put up with this obsession of mine. She's been a saint over the years. It's tough being married to an old plaas japie, a country cousin, like me!' It was a rare moment for him to confide in her. She was sure he was sincere, and she felt for him.

He gave Millie's shoulder a pat, and she acknowledged the joke with a weak cough of a laugh, and blew her nose again in a hopeless way. My eyes must be dreadfully swollen from all this crying, she thought, conscious, for the first time of her appearance. He probably hates having the wet on his shirt.

But it didn't seem as if he did. 'Remember when we were little? Remember the time we spotted that cobra curled up next to the old cement dam - the one that used to be for the windmill, before the electric pump and the new borehole? It was lying in the grass. We almost didn't see it because it was the same greeny-yellow colour. We put a bucket over it before it could wake up and spit at us. Remember? You were brave and sat on the bucket to keep it from sliding out, while I ran to call Father.'

'I only did it because you told me to ...' She was laughing properly now, and gazed at him, her blue eyes the same shade as his, but gentler. 'We both got a good hiding for that!'

'Do you remember how you crowned me King of Glen Bervie? You made the crown out of ivy and stuck in pomegranate flowers for jewels.'

'And you carved a sceptre for yourself from a willow branch.'

'Funny how things like that stick in one's memory ... King of Glen Bervie! What do you think of that, hey?' His voice was soft now, and it was as if he belonged to her. She remembered how he had pronounced: You are my subject now. Kneel! How he had ordered: When you pass my plate at dinner, don't curl your thumb over. I'm the king, you'll contaminate my food if you touch it. Holding his plate from underneath had made it slip, and Mother had exclaimed in exasperation, 'Millie, hold the plate properly, or you'll drop it, for goodness sake!' And William, when she had glanced quickly at him, had nodded, imperceptibly, like a man bidding at an auction.

William was speaking softly to her, confiding in her. 'It's not just the owning of it - the title deeds and so on. When I came back here to live - well, I was fifty-five. I wanted to grow old here. I'd come back to my beginning.'

She didn't dare interrupt; he was in full flow. Besides, his face was suffused with warmth towards her.

'Ten years! My God, Millie, it's been more worry and trouble than I've had in all the rest of my life.' He was opening himself to her, and she had his full attention. 'Even the war was easy compared to this - this feeling that if I shut an eye, they'll take everything, everything! Tools from the garage, that don't mean anything to them - that they don't know how to use. They steal the fruit from the trees even before it's ripe. I wouldn't mind so much if they waited - but they leave green apples with just one bite out of them lying all over the lawn. The waste!'

'It's the children ...'

'I'm not so sure!' William was beginning to work himself into one of his rages against the natives. The arm around her shoulder became taut. As usual, Millie tried to deflect his anger.

100

'But, Wil - '

'I swear their parents send them out to steal out of spite. You'd think I had more than enough land and the water to be self-sufficient, but I'm stopped every time I plant anything, from getting the benefit. The whole thing is driving me mad. I can't sleep at night thinking about it. You say it's the children - whose children? You don't know, do you? Freddie and Sarah pretend they don't know either. Imagine what it would look like if I stayed out all night, waiting to see who it was? And if I caught one? Can I send a child to prison for stealing green apples? I'd like to shoot them, you know, like vermin. Millie - I'm close to committing murder!'

Suddenly he switched off his frustrated anger, as if it were something he could tap into at will in order to show her the depth of his feelings. Instead, he focused all his attention onto her, turning to face her and settling comfortably back into their rare intimacy.

'Just look at us two,' he caught a laugh in his throat, giving the sound a tender seduction, 'the only ones who remember this place right from the beginning. Two old people quarrelling over a tennis court. It's not worth it, Millie. We've got so much to bind us together. It'll spoil everything if we fall out over this.'

She turned to him, a spark of hope in her eyes. 'You won't...'

'Please, Millie, can't you see my point of view? I don't like doing it either, but they force me - don't you see? And look on the bright side - it wouldn't be destroying something, it would be an improvement. Imagine how well everything would grow here in this light soil, and how pretty it would look. I'd plant asparagus, strawberries ... It would be something to boast about.'

'But there's so much other land, why here?' She was beginning to see the pictures in his mind. It tired her and made her uncertain. She told herself to be steadfast. She tried to remember the deep blue centre of the sky, but she was beginning to feel her resolve melt.

On his part, there was irritation, as if he hated having to go over it all again. 'Because the court's got this high fence, and I can padlock the gate. It's perfect - and close to the house too. They won't get in so easily.'

'The fence will keep them out?'

101

'Yes.'

She surveyed it. High enough. When Sarah's James was just a little boy, she had paid him a penny an afternoon to fetch the balls, which were hit out of the court. She remembered how he'd sat, with his legs dangling into the irrigation furrow, passing the time by throwing up small stones and catching them on the back of his hand. Now he was in prison on Robben Island. William had been about to tell Sarah to pack up and go, but in the end it had been Vera who'd stopped him. 'I'm not training another housemaid,' Vera had said, and it was true that most girls never stayed long with Vera. 'Besides,' she had continued, 'you can see from the state Sarah's in, that she can't have known anything about it.'

William had still been suspicious of Sarah - he'd talked about the Trojan horse and the enemy within the gates - and this had increased his sense of being under siege. Ploughing up the tennis court must be hurting him as much as it did her, and he would be blaming the natives for making him do it. Millie hated the way she could so easily be affected by other people's emotions. This morning, when she had seen what the tractor was doing, it had all been quite clear in her mind, but now she was losing her grip. His anger was tearing her apart. She laid her hands on her stomach in what was becoming an instinctive gesture.

But William's mood changed as he gazed into the future. 'Millie, imagine it! Like a child's drawing, with everything in rows: beetroot, carrots, cabbages, runner-beans on bamboo stakes. A proper vegetable garden.' His voice became enthusiastic. 'It could look like those walled gardens in English country houses! Man, it would be something, some sight to see! We could grow plants they've never even heard of in Fort Bedford: English artichokes, green peppers, aubergines, herbs. That would make your bridge pals sit up, hey?' His face had a gentler, peaceful look, with all the hate washed away.

Millie lost her footing. 'If it would mean ...'

He had been waiting for this, and turned immediately. 'Yes?' He gave her his full attention, holding her again in his arm.

'If ... perhaps ... if it could stop you from feeling ... if it kept everything safe ...'

102

She couldn't say it now, but there was this longing in her for harmony: the way it used to be. The tennis court could still, as he was describing it, be the centre.

'Please, Millie.'

'If it would give you peace of mind.'

'That's my girl. Now you're beginning to see it my way.'

If it gave him safety in his ownership of Glen Bervie. If the lock on the gate kept out the thieves. She began to picture him striding into the house, carrying huge bunches of beetroot, feathery carrots. She could breathe the fresh smell of newly dug earth, see him with his arms full of lettuces. He'd be relaxed, generous. Some of the old atmosphere might return. She could take vegetables to Father O'Reilly and he would give them to his parishioners. Vera might ask her to make lettuce salad again. There'd be work laying in the beans for winter, bottling the tomatoes. She could make chutney. It was wrong to cling to something you no longer used, foolish to insist that things stayed the same, when they no longer meant anything to anyone else.

'I'd better go and wash my face,' she said tremulously.

He helped her to her feet, then turned away from her. 'I must find Freddie. You'll be all right now, will you?'

'Yes.'

Victory gave his old irritation a chance to surface. He had been on his way to golf when Freddie had called him. 'Probably missed the first hole,' he muttered. He noticed the mess on his shirt. 'I'll have to change too.'

'Oh dear. I'm sorry, William.'

'Well,' he sighed. He was blaming her again.

She was on her own once more, walking stiffly towards the house. She felt done in. She must have damaged her knee when she'd thrown herself down because it hurt when she put her weight on it.

SIXTEEN

'They told us to dig holes for planting trees ... they made us build walls of sand to keep out the sea. We worked without spades or picks and they beat us if we stopped to rest.' James rubbed his eyes as if trying to erase the memory of broken, septic fingernails, crippled hands. His mother exclaimed in horror and his sisters wanted to know more, but he couldn't go on, and stared out of the window at the windy, untidy street outside rather than at his hands, which looked healthy now and without pain. Most of all he wanted to forget the icy island gales, which killed the sapling trees. He wanted never again to see those pitiless grey waves eating the wet, gritty sand-banks that he and the other prisoners had so laboriously piled up against the sea.

Nozuko had prepared a lamb stew for all the family to celebrate his homecoming. Because of William's threats it was important that James should avoid meeting him. Although there was nothing that Sarah wanted more than to have him with her, it was clear that James could not return to live with his mother. Instead Raymond and Nozuko had made room for him in their two-roomed council house in Fort Bedford.

Nozuko has married a good man, thought James. Raymond Goniwe held his two sons comfortably in his lap. Two years and four years old, they stared wordlessly at the uncle who had just come back from prison. What do they know about those things, thought James bitterly. What do they know about police and Special Branch, about detention without trial, about why I went to prison. Are these things

even talked about outside prison? Nozuko gave him extra meat, and Sarah looked as if she was restraining herself from catching him in her arms in a huge hug as if he were still a baby. Occasionally she leaned forward to touch James on the shoulder or to stroke his arm or his leg, as if she were testing whether he wasn't just a beautiful dream. Her face was so radiant that Nontobeko would nudge Nozuko every now and then with a nod towards their mother and chuckle in sympathy.

'The first thing you must do is get a driving licence,' Raymond was saying. 'Happy Ntwasa will teach you. He's good, and he doesn't mind if you start paying after you have a job. I know Oxford Furnitures is always looking for drivers and I will take you myself to see Mr Albertyn. The pay is not too bad.'

Raymond worked as a salesman for the same firm, selling furniture on hire purchase to people in the township, who bought living room and bedroom suites to cram into their tiny rented houses. Although his job encouraged customers to make debts they couldn't afford, Sarah had told James that Raymond believed that, even if the shop reclaimed the suites after six months or a year, at least the people had had a chance to live comfortably for a little while.

James was grateful to Raymond for planning his future, but just being with this number of people was confusing him. He felt the pressure. First the boat, bumping over the choppy cold early-morning sea; then the noisy, crowded train; then trees, houses, shops, markets, people shouting, all of it spinning before his eyes. He hadn't slept for the two nights on the journey, and that wasn't even counting the fitful, feverish sleep he'd had on his last night in prison. He had been told of his release the day before they let him go.

'Khumalo, get moving. You're going home tomorrow. The Governor wants to see you.' Greasy, the chief warder on the block earned his nickname because of his thick, unwashed hair.

'Here's some soap so you can make sure you don't stink him out like the dirty kaffir you are.'

'Ja Baas. Thank you, Baas.' James was clumsy with excitement and fear. He dropped the soap, and Greasy swore at him for being such a dom kaffir.

There was another man present at the interview with the prison Governor. Because he was dressed in a brown suit with a lime green shirt and darker green tie, James identified him easily by his vulgarly fashionable clothes as Special Branch. The man lounged in an easy chair in a corner of the office, staring at James without moving his head, the way a lizard stalks its prey. James felt the eyes as he stood to attention in front of the Governor's desk.

'Now you don't want to come back here again, do you Khumalo?' said the Governor, a thin, old white man with a mouth like the lock on a cell door.

'No Sir.'

'You will be returning to Fort Bedford?'

'Yes Sir.'

'We haven't placed any restrictions on you when you are released, except that you must report to the police once a week. Don't forget to do that. The report from the warders tells me that they believe you are a reformed man. Are you, Khumalo?' The Governor's mouth changed shape a little, as if attempting a rusty smile.

'Yes Sir.' He had been so eager to agree. Would they really let him go free?

'It will please us if you co-operate with the police.'

'Yes Sir.' What else could he have said?

The Governor was looking through his prison report. 'The government needs reliable people like you in the locations to warn them who the trouble makers are - the agitators and communists. You don't want to get involved with people like that again - do you Khumalo?'

'No Sir.'

'Good boy. This is Warrant Officer Gouws from Port Elizabeth. He'll be getting in touch with you. He'll make it worth your while. You don't have a job to go back to?'

'No Sir.'

'Good, good.'

The man in the lime-green shirt said nothing. During James's interrogation before his trial, there had been a team of sweaty policemen who had screamed at him, beat him, placed electrodes on

106

tender parts of his body, made him stand for days on end until his legs had filled up with fluid. He couldn't remember their faces, but this man had the same degenerate, yet infinitely powerful look about him.

The Governor was repeating a question. 'I said, "Where will you be staying?"'

'In the location, Sir. Zone B, 29 First Avenue. It's my brother-in-law's house, Sir.'

James didn't like it that the Governor had written down his address, and so had Gouws. He couldn't think of a way to get out of this liaison, yet now he daren't ask advice from his family. In the past, if someone had confided in him that the police were giving him a hard time to make him inform on others, no matter who that man was, he would have assumed the speaker was trying to cover up. He didn't want people to suspect him of being an informer.

At least he hadn't taken the money the Governor had offered, so there was no way they could say he was on their payroll. He'd pretended he didn't understand, protesting that he'd enough for the journey, and that his family would help him when he got home. He'd pretended he hadn't realised he was being paid for future services. Perhaps, he hoped fervently, they would think him too dom to use. These worries were like a curtain between him and his mother and sisters. He tried to concentrate on what his mother was saying.

'I'm sure Miss Millie will give me the money.' Sarah was enthusiastic. 'Then, Son, you'll have a something of your own.'

'What?'

'I've told you - we'll put up a room for you.' Sarah had been talking for some time and wasn't going to repeat herself. She merely waved an arm towards the outside wall. The house was attached on one side to the neighbours, but the other side was free, and there was a bit of garden. 'I'll ask Miss Millie for the money for the zinc plates, and you can build your room yourself to save money. Then you'll have your own place here.'

SEVENTEEN

Sarah spoke to Millie the following morning. 'Miss Millie, James is back.'

'On the farm?' Millie was startled. They were in the old kitchen, not Vera's shiny new modern one. Millie was baking trays of fairy cakes for the church bazaar. She beat the yellow mixture vigorously.

'No, Miss Millie, he's staying in town.'

Millie felt relieved. 'Is he all right? How does he look?'

Sarah's face was radiant, her skin glowed. Millie caught her joy. She put down the wooden spoon carefully, and clasped her hands together, 'Oh - I'm glad. I'd love to see him. Where is he living?'

'He's with Nozuko and her husband.' Millie knew how cramped the council house would be with two children and three adults. There was a terribly long waiting list for empty houses in the location, and James didn't have a chance without children of his own. William, of course, blamed them for having too many children; he said it was their own fault if there was overcrowding, but it stood to reason that even a man on his own would want more than two rooms. William said they were lucky they got houses built for them with no worries about mortgages or upkeep and that he himself would be happy not to have bills to pay, but she wasn't so sure whether she believed him. She'd found herself thinking lately how nice it would be if she had a cottage to herself on the bottom lucerne field, close to the river ...

'We have to build on a room for him,' persisted Sarah.

'Oh, yes?' Apprehensively, Millie realised this was going to be a request for funds.

'We must have money for the zincs.' Sarah was determined. She was talking about corrugated iron sheeting for a lean-to addition.

'Oh Sarah! How much will it be?'

'I don't know for sure. The Chinaman is selling the zincs cheap - second hand. Maybe seventy rand.'

'I'll see what I can do.' It was an enormous sum for Millie, who drew a small widow's pension from the state and relied on William for free board. Her bank account hardly ever showed a credit of more than twenty rand, but she understood that this was an emergency.

'That boy!' William had raged only months ago. 'When I think what I've done - what this family has done for his blood-sucking mother and for all his damn sisters. He'd better never come out of prison because if I lay my hands on him I'll thrash him to an inch of his life. The things he planned to do! And the rhetoric - their rights to the land - the same land they don't care a jot about unless I'm standing over them all the time to see they work properly. If the natives farmed this place it would go to pot in five weeks!'

'But he didn't really do anything,' protested Millie.

'Don't be more of an idiot than you already are. They planned to murder us, to rape our women and to blow up buildings and then you say they didn't do anything.'

'All they wanted was to have a just society,' Jo had joined in. She was home for a brief four days. 'They have a right to ask to be treated equally as human beings.'

'Ag, don't talk rubbish. You lefties are all the same - you always want something for nothing. Human being? He is a human being. I am a human being. What's so special about that?'

'But he wants to be treated the same as you - to own his own home - to earn a proper wage - to have a decent education.'

'Look, I've worked for what I've got. I'm still working dammit, even at my age when a lot of other people have retired already, and I work a damn sight harder than any native for miles around. You people are all the same, whining and complaining about what you haven't got, and always wanting something for nothing.'

'But the law -'

'Don't argue against the law. That's what we all live under - that's a given. If you want to change it - then stand for parliament and see how many votes you get.'

They were outside on the veranda. William's rage had made him jump up to stand directly in front of Jo, blocking out her view. His face was in shadow, while her's was lit by the bright sun. Watching them, Millie thought how young she looked, and how pretty. That's my girl, she thought. It's good that she cares about other people. And then, with a sudden shaft of pain, He's going to say something that will make her never come back.

William was wagging his forefinger so close to Jo's face, that she twisted to one side to get away. 'You people can't accept that it takes hard,' he paused for emphasis, 'work to succeed at anything. Oh no! That would be too much trouble. You and your friends talk about bombs, and plan sabotage. You're neurotic, that's what you are - a bunch of neurotic misfits: you can't live with yourselves, so you want to blow up the rest of society.'

'Uncle William - Uncle William -' Jo kept on interjecting, turning her head back to look him in the eyes.

'Let me finish. You've got to learn that there's no such thing as rights - no such abstract thing. Where do you expect them to come from? God? I thought your lot had given Him up long ago. You demand to run the country just the way YOU want. Why should you be allowed? The only person who can do that is a man living on his own on a desert island - and even then he can't do exactly as he wants. He hasn't got the right to fly up into the sky; he hasn't got the right to walk way down to the bottom of the sea, he's got to find his way on the rocks. No one can do just what they want.'

'But, Uncle William, the laws are different for Africans. That's wrong isn't it? We want to change that.'

'The natives don't want to change. They want to keep on blaming us for what they are. Degenerates! They've brought it on themselves. They can't ask us to give away the country to them. It's not their right.'

'If you were black, you'd think differently.'

She shouldn't have said that, thought Millie. William will see it as

110

an attack on his integrity. Watching them, Millie wanted to run forward to drag Jo away. William seemed to sway, as if about to fall on her, but he regained his balance and made himself taller, the bones in his legs locking together, his rib-cage expanding. Jo hadn't noticed. Her face was flushed and she rubbed her knuckles into her eyes.

'I've fought in the war - in Egypt and in Italy. I know what it's like under fire. I've got the medals to prove it - no one can take that from me. You'd never see me begging in the streets - begging ... for rights.'

If such rage had been directed at Millie, it would have terrified her. She's game, thought Millie, as Jo opened her mouth to reply. She's a fighter.

'But you might be different. You might have lost all that feeling of power, or never had it - ' Jo was still appealing to his sense of fair play.

'It's not a feeling. That's what I've been trying to tell you, but you're such an ignorant, twisted little girl, you don't know what you're talking about. It's not worth discussing anything with you. I know there is nothing anyone on this earth could do to me, which would take away the dignity I have - the human dignity - which is so lacking, which I can plainly see the natives haven't got. Man, they've no guts, no backbone. Look at them! You could starve me, torture me, keep me in solitary confinement - even that! - but you'd never ever be able to take away my human dignity. I don't have to ask anyone for that. Ugh! It's no good wasting my time on you,' he was already turning away. 'You snivelling liberals, you make me want to puke. You're in it up to your necks in the filthy, communist slime. You haven't the faintest idea ...'

He was gone. Millie knelt by Jo's side and held her, using her own body to absorb the shuddering sobs, which had taken hold of Jo. 'It's all right ... it's all right ...' she murmured, stroking Jo's hair. 'He was just angry ... you got him on a raw spot ... he's not really like that inside ... he's kind really ... it's all right my girl ... it's all right ...' She was saying the first things that came into her head. Probably Jo wasn't paying any attention anyway, but her sobbing was slowing down and her shaking was becoming less violent.

Lifting her head, Millie caught sight of Vera's face at the sitting-room window. She must have been watching all the time. There was a look - Millie couldn't believe it - was it pleasure? As if she were rejoicing that William was driving Jo away from Glen Bervie. It could have been a trick of the light, but for a moment she had been like the Cheshire Cat. Smiling.

'Come,' Millie urged, taking Jo's arm. 'Let's go for a walk.' And of course they had gone down to the river. They'd climbed the krantz and gazed out over the riverbed. It was July, and millions of aloes had sent up red spikes, like flaming swords, all over the mountainside.

'I remember Ouma telling me that when the English soldiers came, they thought the aloes were the Boers, and shot at them by mistake.' Jo's voice was still unsteady. It was clear she was looking for safer ground. 'But, she said, the Boers weren't such fools as to dress up in bright colours, and were in their old khaki clothes, taking pot shots at the English from behind the rocks. They couldn't believe these soldiers, dressed in their full military uniforms, were really fighting. They thought they were on parade!

But the English won anyway. Funny how the Afrikaners hold on so tightly, when they know more than anyone what it's like to be dispossessed.' Jo sighed. 'They want to make sure they keep it this time.'

While Jo looked bleakly down on the river landscape below them, Millie struggled with what felt like a migraine coming on. The colour of the aloes vibrated like heartbeats against her head. She could feel the blood drip through.

'Whose side were we on during the Boer War?' Jo asked.

'Our family?' Millie strained to reply normally, so that Jo wouldn't worry about her health. 'Hard to say.' She took a breath, 'Oupa and Ouma weren't married. Oupa was an immigrant from Scotland, so he was in the home guard for Fort Bedford, but Ouma had cousins who fought with General Smuts, and two of her sisters were farmer's wives and were sent to concentration camps. One of them died there, with her two children.'

'At school in the English class there was only Marge and me and Rita Snyman - oh yes, and Alice. Once a girl in the Afrikaans class told me she hated the English because of the women and children who'd died in the camps. Do you remember the fête at the senior school, with bands and gymnastics, when South Africa became a republic?'

'It was like they'd finally won the Boer War,' acknowledged Millie.

'A victory celebration. Now they're consolidating the country for the Afrikaners. They're moving black people off places they've lived in for generations, land that they own, and dumping them in what they call resettlement camps. Terrible places. I visited one. Just a lot of tiny shacks as far as you can see. Nothing grows there ... they're not allowed to keep animals ... there's no work. It's genocide.'

Jo's body seemed poised at the very edge of the krantz. Her hair was cut short, her face was without make-up, like a boy's. Millie could hear Vera sneer, 'You can't tell them apart these days - unisex,' as if it were a perversion for the young to dress like that. Jo was wearing a turtle-necked black jumper and black corduroy trousers tucked into high black boots - she looked like a soldier in uniform.

'Stand back,' Millie called. 'You'll fall.' She pulled at Jo's arm.

'I'm not afraid. I've always stood here - it's my spot,' Jo laughed, but she stepped back and sat down on a rock, her elbows on her knees, her chin on her hands, her white face glimmering against the black of her clothes and the grey gravel krantz.

'You should play more tennis,' scolded Millie, thinking that with all her studying, Jo didn't get out of doors enough and that she'd make herself ill.

'Oh Mother, don't fuss. I was never any good - you are the tennis player.' Jo sighed, remembering Millie's loss, and she embraced her impulsively. 'I'm so sorry!'

Millie didn't trust herself to speak - she didn't want them both to weep. The tennis court was a wound still and nothing had come of her sacrifice.

'I used to think I'd come back here one day,' Jo continued after a moment, 'and build a hut under the wild fig tree.' She pointed straight downwards to a strip of meadow, bleached golden by the frosty nights, which nestled against the rock face. 'I thought I'd be no trouble to anyone. I'd collect firewood like everybody else, and claim

113

just this small part of the river as my own. I'd have Mamsamsaba to tea - '

'Who?'

'Oh - just a story from when I was small. I used to think that if you loved a place very much, and would look after it, that it should be yours. Should be. Crazy idea. Now I feel as if everywhere around here is so bloody - an old battlefield, but one that's still dangerous with unexploded mines everywhere, and they go off at intervals, even random intervals with no apparent cause, just when you think you're safe. It's not possible to have a dream of a pastoral idyll, the idea of a hut by a riverside - "Nine bean rows will I plant there ..." That kind of thing is just not on. Not here in Africa, anyway.'

And Jo put her head on her knees and cried until Millie feared they would be stuck up there until sunset, even all night, or that they'd have to swim back to Glen Bervie across Jo's tears, the stepping stones and the meadow all flooded away.

Almost as if Jo had known it would happen, she had, on her return to Cape Town, been served with a banning order confining her to the magisterial district of Rondebosch. Student politics, William had said. Communists, William had said. It was no good saying Jo wasn't a communist, and that Millie knew that for certain. There's no smoke without a fire, William had said. She asked for it the way she was behaving, you saw that for yourself. You should be grateful they haven't locked her up.

Serves her right, Vera had said.

114

EIGHTEEN

What would Mother say? worried Millie. Darn it, she wouldn't have fussed over a silver teapot - not when James needed somewhere to live. Millie knew very well what William would think - shout rather! But she wasn't going to let him find out if she could help it. Luckily, because Vera had her own silver, Mother's heirlooms were kept out of sight in the cupboard below the bookcase in the sitting room.

If he asks, I'll tell him they're mine - that Mother gave them to me, she muttered to herself, preparing the lie, as she watched William and Vera disappearing down the drive on their way to a drinks party with Bennie van Zyl, William's partner. This time, at least, she wasn't sorry to be left behind. When the cat's away, the mice will play, she told herself.

Her mind looped around all the old sayings. Who's she? The cat's mother. Was she cat or mouse? When she thought about it, she was amazed that she was a mother. The way William treated her, she remained five years old to his ten. It gave him permission to override anything she wanted. Even if she asked him, he would never allow her to have the silver teapot, or even to leave it to Jo. That amounted to being disinherited, didn't it? It was a harsh thing to say about him, but sometimes that was just what she felt like.

She imagined Jo's surprise that it should worry her. 'A teapot? No thanks - I'd have to clean it all the time.' On the other hand, Jo might treasure it because it came from Glen Bervie, a place Millie knew she loved deeply.

No, she'd made up her mind. Stubbornly, and feeling a little in the wrong, Millie entered the sitting room. Although she knew they'd be gone for several hours, she was still jumpy. Her hand shook as she turned the key in the cupboard door. She told herself sternly to slow down. She had all the time in the world.

Funny thing about smells - the aromatic, wooden, dusty air inside the cupboard pushed her straight back into childhood. She could see herself kneeling on this very spot, on one of those rare rainy days when the sky turned to water and it was too muddy to go outside. There used to be a tea set made of small gilded bones. Ah - there it was! She took it out on its red and gold papier-mâché tray and re-arranged the tiny cups and saucers. She used to imagine a lady mouse's tea-party when she played with it!

She must stop dreaming and get back to business. The silver teapot was there, as well as a silver sugar, milk and hot water jug. Might as well be hung for a sheep as a lamb - or was it a goat? They were a little tarnished, but not too badly. She wrapped each piece in newspaper and placed them all together at the very bottom of her shopping basket. The next day she took the lot to town, as bold as brass.

Harry Cohen, the jeweller, turned the teapot upside down.

'It's got a hallmark,' Millie ventured.

'Yes, I can see that.' His steel-rimmed glasses were perched on the tip of his nose, and he held the teapot up to the light. 'Very nice,' he said. 'A very fine piece.'

'How much do you think it's worth? I don't want to you to sell it in Fort Bedford. Can you send it to Port Elizabeth?'

'Possibly.' Harry Cohen was lost in contemplation.

'There's more.' Millie dived into her basket, scattering sheets of The Fort Bedford Chronicle all over the floor. 'A set.' She placed the rest on the shop counter.

'A hundred rand?' suggested Harry Cohen hopefully.

'Done.'

116

NINETEEN

Sarah was looking for the right girl for James to marry. She had been thinking about it all the time he was in prison. She pictured someone young, but not too young, because James was twenty-nine already. Sarah also knew she wanted a someone special, not just any girl. A someone, who would have a good job, but would also know the duties of a wife. A someone, who would give him children, and anchor him; who would stop him from worrying about things that got him into trouble.

In the first few months, James had spent most of his time asleep, or pretending to sleep as he lay under a blanket, his back curved towards the room, on the iron cot in Nozuko's kitchen. Slowly, slowly - and she had had the sensitivity to wait for it - he had come alive. He was building the lean-to now. Millie had come through with the seventy rand, and had added another ten rand for furniture.

'I've had a windfall,' she'd whispered, pressing the notes confidentially into Sarah's apron pocket one afternoon after lunch, when William and Vera had been entertaining in their special dining room. At the same time, Millie had indicated to Sarah, with a slight pulling of the left side of her face towards Nomzamo, the new 'girl', that she should not say anything to her. Nomzamo hadn't seen what was happening. She was up to her elbows in soapy water. Nomzamo was the replacement for Leah, who had taken on a cleaning job with the Fort Bedford Town Council. The hours were better for Leah, especially necessary now that their mother was becoming very old. Sarah envied her. She didn't have to be at work so early, and her weekends were free.

Sarah had her eye on Nomzamo for James. She was charming: slim and smart with a sharp tongue that really made Sarah laugh. Her schooling had been good, and although Nomzamo hadn't told Vera, who would not then have given her the job, she was working only for the few months until it was time to go on her nursing course. It made Sarah smile to know that Vera had no idea that Nomzamo's father was Mr Matama, the schoolteacher. Vera hadn't bothered to ask who Nomzamo's father was, or even her surname.

Sarah admired Miriam Matama. Although she had lost her husband as well as her home, her silent endurance had been an example to all the wives and mothers of the men who had been sentenced. During those long ten years of waiting for James to come home, Sarah had stopped blaming Mr Matama for what had happened to James. Ever since their time together at the trial, she had sympathised with Miriam, who had not broken down, who had never spoken a word against her husband, even though she had known nothing until that morning when the police had come to take him away.

Perhaps he had been afraid to tell her - she was a religious woman, who ran the Mothers' Union every Thursday afternoon. They wore impressively bright red blouses with wide starched white collars. Leah, who also belonged, had said that Mrs Matama was a proud woman, who would never show her troubles to others. It must have been hard for her to accept the little bit of food and money that her neighbours had brought round.

'We want to help the teacher's family,' people would say. 'Here's a something for you and his daughter,' and Miriam Matama had made her back even straighter, and nodded unsmiling thanks for the gift.

Nomzamo had done well in her schoolwork. Her mother, who was, because of her husband's political stand, now banned from employment as a teacher with the Bantu Education Board, had insisted she keep on with her studies, even though money was tight. Miriam Matama had walked into town every day to a job at Paula's Styles, where she did alterations to the new dresses that were not the right fit for the white customers. She suffered the indignity of being

118

Paula's alteration 'girl', and had crawled on the floor in front of women who had less education than herself, but it had been worth it, because Nomzamo had worked hard, she'd passed with a first class! Now she and Nontobeko would be going to Mount Frere Training Hospital in six months' time to start their nursing courses.

TWENTY

One afternoon, James was nailing the corrugated iron sheets onto the wooden frame he had erected, when Nontobeko brought Nomzamo round to see the building work. He'd known Nomzamo as a young girl, when he'd visited her father's house, but she was a woman now, and he was suddenly foolish in her presence. He could think of nothing to say, just stood there, yet he couldn't help smiling in an awkward, unfocused way at her so that she must consider him to be quite without brains.

'Are you having an outside door?' she asked.

'Oh yes,' and he laughed again, calling out to Nozuko, who was busy in the kitchen. 'Then, when the hammering stops, you won't even know I'm living here, Sister!'

'Because you'll be fast asleep again,' Nozuko responded in the same teasing manner, appearing broad and smiling in the doorway, like he remembered his mother used to look. Was that before he went to prison? Or before his father had died? Or before William had taken over Glen Bervie?

The past was squashed into one picture with the word 'before' written below it. Yet, thinking about his time in prison, as he had done so much over the last weeks, he couldn't deny that the experience had changed him - set him apart from his relatives and friends. Inside, they'd often referred to prison as a 'university'. Whatever it was that he had learned there, and this was what he had been puzzling and puzzling about, it wasn't nothing. Nor was it something he wished to forget either.

120

'Tell them about Vera,' Nontobeko nudged Nomzamo.

'Hai! No!' Nomzamo giggled, gracefully twirling round, looking for somewhere to sit which wouldn't soil her dress.

'Sit here, please,' James jumped forward to dust the chair he'd been standing on. 'No, wait - I'll get a better one from the kitchen.'

'He must like you, Nomzamo, he's not normally so hospitable,' teased Nozuko, but gently, as if she were pleased that he was making such a fuss of her.

'Nomzamo was fed up with Miss Vera,' prompted Nontobeko.

'Thixo! That scorpion!'

'Yes, but tell them what happened!'

'She didn't want me to wear shoes inside the house - like it's some holy place. Your mother never does, and I suppose no one else has dared. She says they are too noisy.' Nomzamo sucked in her cheeks. 'Ai cawn't hear myself think with all your clip clop ping.' Nomzamo enunciated the words in an exaggerated English accent, and then squinted hideously.

Her audience laughed appreciatively. There was a sudden hiss from the kitchen and Nozuko jumped up to attend to a pot boiling over.

'Don't say anything more until I get back, please.'

James couldn't take his eyes off Nomzamo, noticing how graceful her arms were, and how her narrow fingers danced - now curled around each other, now adjusting the hem of her dress so it didn't trail on the floor, which was not yet smooth and clean. He wished he could think of something to say, but it felt as if his tongue had grown to fill his whole mouth, and he was scared that if he tried to speak, he would only manage a croak, because his throat was so dry.

Then Nozuko was back. 'And - ?'

Nomzamo shook her head, and looked at each person in the group as if unsure whether they really wanted to hear.

'Go on - ' prompted Nontobeko.

'Well, I was mad. I'm supposed to walk around with no shoes? Do we have a new law: black people must never wear shoes in white people's houses? We must clean for them, but they don't want to hear us or see us. Soon they'll tell us not to breathe.'

121

'Did you say that?' asked Nozuko, awed. James remained silent, fascinated. She belonged to a generation who had reached adulthood while he was in prison. Her irreverence made her seem so much less bound by the laws, both written and unwritten, under which they all lived.

'No, I didn't tell her what I was thinking, but I made sure she knew I was angry. I banged the pots around, making as much noise as an earthquake! And of course I kept my shoes on.'

'What did she do?'

'What could she do? I don't care because I'm leaving soon, and anyway she can't sack me straight away because then who will do the work? Besides, she had visitors - imagine having an argument with a cheeky servant in front of some visitors! Then she came into the kitchen after lunch for something, and we all - even your mother, even old Emily, who usually never says boo to a goose - turned our backs on her, so that we couldn't notice she had come into the room. But we had eyes at the backs of our heads. We knew she just stood there, and then she had to leave!' Nomzamo giggled. 'No one said anything. We just got on with our work, and then, in only a minute, she was back again.'

Nomzamo sucked in her cheeks for her English accent. 'Look here, I can't come into my own kitchen and be greeted by all these black looks.'

Nomzamo paused, enjoying the moment. 'I couldn't help myself - it just came out - "Those are our natural faces, Madam," I said.'

'What! Really?' Nozuko was screaming with laughter, James too. Nontobeko was doubled up, even though she had heard it before.

'Well, I'm not ashamed of being black. You've all heard it by now. Black is beautiful.'

She is beautiful, thought James. He would have gone on his knees, if only he had something to offer her.

He thought about her all the time. Those are our natural faces. It made him laugh. It gave him the courage to dream.

He stood looking at the 1956 Buick for sale in Snyman's Garage.

The young white woman with the frizzy yellow hair, who sat in the glass cubicle suspended above the pumps, glared at him as if she expected him to leave dirty finger marks on its shining surface, but he made himself take no notice. Three hundred rand! With this car he could set himself up in a taxi business. He could drive passengers to Cookhouse to catch the train, or convey people to weddings or funerals. It would carry at least seven - five in the back seat, another two in the front, and the boot was enormous. They made the old cars nice and wide, and the seat covers were still not too bad - just that one place where there was a tear.

If he had a proper business, with prospects, he could ask Nomzamo to marry him. If she consented, she could still do her training as a nurse - he wouldn't stop her from going away to study. He'd be proud of her if she did that. If they had children, it needn't interrupt her training. Nozuko would help, or even his mother. He didn't want his wife to work as a servant for white people anyhow.

He looked admiringly at the huge winged mudguards, walked slowly round to the front to gaze at the broad chrome radiator, which seemed to give him a conspiratorial silver grin. The bumper and headlight casings were dazzling. It was definitely a bargain. Wondering about its mileage, he sauntered round to the driver's window and peered through the glass.

'Hey, Boy, what you up to?' She had opened the window of the booth and was yelling at him. Her neck and face had gone an ugly pink. 'Take your hands off that car, you hear? If you don't listen to me, I'll call the baas.'

The baas was probably her father. Who else would employ her to do nothing but sit watching the place? He wished he could just walk up to her and count out the money right there. He would pay her in one rand notes and throw them in her face. She'd have to shut up and smile and smirk at him too, like she probably did to all the white customers, especially the white men. She'd summed him up as a thief - a black thief because that's what they always thought of black people.

Those are our natural faces. Oh Nomzamo! He straightened his back, and sauntered towards the street corner. He wouldn't give that white bitch the benefit of seeing him hurry. Waiting to cross, he checked to the right, and spotted Millie driving the dusty Chevrolet on her way into town from Glen Bervie.

TWENTY-ONE

Millie was telling herself jokes. The one about the woman who was in the toilet when the train stopped at Port Elizabeth.

The conductor banged on the door. 'P.E.?' he yelled at her.

'No,' the woman replied. 'I'm just brushing my teeth.'

Millie sniggered. 'P.E.?' she said out loud, frothing with giggles. Her body felt the pleasure. When she told herself jokes, especially risqué jokes like this one, it was as if she had a special second laugh in the soft folds between her legs.

'P.E.?' she repeated, and felt the same sweet laugh again.

She noticed James standing on the corner and caught his eye. He's terribly thin, she thought. He's even gone a little grey. She stopped the car and leaned over to the passenger side to roll down the window.

'Hello James! Welcome back! How are you?'

'I'm well, Miss Millie, thank you.' James smiled at her with such a friendly smile. Prison has changed him, thought Millie. I know he's older, but he's different in another way. He's always been quiet, but now he's got something extra. He's grown into an impressive person. He's a fine son. No wonder Sarah is looking so happy.

'How's the building? Are you living in your room yet?'

'It's almost ready. Thank you for helping with the zincs, Miss Millie.'

He was obviously not working. 'What have you been doing otherwise?'

'Oh ... I've been learning to drive.'

He had bent down to the window on her side of the car, and over his shoulder she spotted the buick. The figures R300 in orange letters were pasted onto the windscreen. A car hooted behind her, but she did not hear it.

'Will you get a job as a driver?'

'I'm hoping. My brother-in-law, Nozuko's husband, says they need someone at Oxford Furnitures.'

Millie had heard about his plans from Sarah. If Mother had been alive, or Father, they would surely have taken him back on the farm, but maybe he was better off in town. Farm wages! Nowadays there was never enough money. In the old days there seemed to be more. Well, things had cost less in the first place. She remembered how Father had paid each year for Sarah and Ernest and the children to go to the seaside on holiday. They'd pack themselves onto the train with baskets of food and an old cardboard suitcase tied up with rope. Mother always gave them a roast chicken for the journey. Now all she ever heard was how hard up William was and how the servants cost him more than they were worth.

On Sundays, which was the only meal they still ate together, Vera sat and watched each mouthful she put into her mouth, as if it were made of gold. It was impossible to ask for a second helping without Vera raising an eyebrow. Not that she had much of an appetite any more. As a matter of fact, she could barely swallow the food. Somehow she'd lost all pleasure in the taste of things. When she was on her own, she even read a book to take her mind off her meal, or so that she could have something to think about.

No point in getting morbid. She started to fantasise to cheer up James, whose face had taken on a bleak look now that he wasn't smiling.

'That car over there would make a marvellous taxi, you know.'

'Oh yes!' His brown eyes shone.

'One could make a good living out of it.'

He nodded.

'Not work for anyone else - that's the only way.'

They gazed at it. Silvery grey, it seemed a phantom of hope. She could imagine it flying along, packed full of well-dressed people, laughing and talking because they were on their way to a wedding. The car behind Millie hooted again, insisting she take notice, and then swerved out, drawing parallel to her.

'Mrs Rorig, you can't stop here. Don't you know you're blocking he road?' It was Lenny Dawson, of Dawson's Bakery. He sounded exasperated.

'Oh, I'm so sorry.' In a fluster, Millie pushed the gear handle into first and the car jerked forward. Then she remembered James. 'You get your driving licence,' she said firmly, pulling up the hand-brake again. 'First things first. You never know what will happen.' She gave him a brief, awkward wave.

'I will, Miss Millie.' He raised his arm in farewell, but with her neck stretched out like a turtle in order to see over the bonnet, she was already negotiating the turn into Main Street.

Millie was thinking that talking to James had made her forget that she wasn't well. Not that it was urgent, just a feeling, like travel sickness. Bilious, without throwing up and sometimes a nasty, dry cough. She didn't get migraines any more. It was probably the same thing, but in a different place.

She decided she'd ask William about it when he and Vera came back from the wedding. Big Jan Botha, who had been a widower for four years since Olive died, was marrying again. She was glad for him. No one had seen the bride yet and there was much speculation about her. Apparently she was thirty years younger than him. She was an old girlfriend of Little Jan Botha's, and Big Jan had met her when Little Jan had brought her to the farm on holiday. It had been a whirlwind romance. Little Jan didn't mind - he knew plenty of other girls he could choose from.

The wedding was to be on a farm in the Cradock district; only a hundred miles away ... but too far to drive on her own in case she got a puncture. The reception would be huge. She conjured up the bride and bridesmaids, wearing long dresses in peach or sky blue satin stretched tightly across ample busts and buttocks, with sweat stains spreading under their armpits. It would have been a nice little holiday away. Cousin George would have been delighted to put her up, and it was ages since she'd seen that branch of the family.

Millie told herself crossly that she was getting a Cinderella complex, imagining that Vera was some kind of ugly sister, or more likely a wicked step-mother. That was because William was becoming more like a father than the older brother she used to play with long ago. Still, she had felt awful when they'd made their plans to attend the wedding without asking whether she'd like to go with them. Something about staying over in Cradock on their way to Pretoria and then obviously they wouldn't be able to give her a lift home again and she'd be stranded. Then she'd somehow stopped thinking about going. She could, she scolded herself, have arranged a lift with someone else, but it would have been embarrassing to let on to friends in town how her brother was treating her these days.

'Here comes the bride,' she hummed firmly to herself, blotting out sadness.

Fair, fat and wide
See how she wobbles
From side to side.'

There was a parking space in front of Dawson's Bakery large enough to get into without reversing, which wasn't her forte. She'd buy the bread for the servants - apologise to Lenny, if he was at the counter, for holding him up just now - then rush through the groceries so that she could flop down at Bunny Loots for a cup of tea. Damn. They were also away at the wedding. Never mind. The library. Get out some little romance to read through the afternoon.

TWENTY-TWO

'Good morning, Doctor.' William's hand rested lightly, like a dry, brown leaf in the magistrate's fleshy palm. He needs a check-up, thought William. Afrikaners ate meat three times a day. He was always warning his patients that if they didn't exercise, they could be in danger of a stroke.

'Please take a seat. Would you like a cigarette?' Mr van Jaarsveld opened a silver box and held it out to William.

'No, thank you. I'm going to live a long time,' laughed William. He was determined to occupy the high moral ground during this interview and was using the refusal as censure. The chair was leather-covered and comfortable. The dingy passages in the Magistrate's Court had been crowded with what Vera called the smelly poor, but inside this room, William was relieved to see, there was some hope of rational discourse. His spirits rose. He looked approvingly round at the panelled walls and the bookcase filled with large leather-bound textbooks on Roman Dutch law. The man was nobody's fool.

'I'm sorry, Doctor, that I had to ask you to come to see me.' van Jaarsveld settled back in his chair with a soft sigh.

'It's about my letter, isn't it?' William's blue eyes ordered the magistrate to come to the point.

'That's right. I ...' van Jaarsveld was searching for words.

I'll have to help him along, thought William. 'Don't worry man. I'm busy, but if it's necessary for me to come to you, why then, I'm only too pleased to take the time. Just so we get this matter settled.' William crossed his legs. The windows needed cleaning, he noticed.

There was some kind of argument going on outside - a black policeman was yelling at two men in prison clothes: khaki singlets with wide khaki shorts. The men ran round to the back of the building.

Van Jaarsveld spoke English with a heavy Afrikaans accent. William thought momentarily of switching to Afrikaans to help him out, but decided he had the advantage if he kept to his own language. Besides, he told himself, English was still one of the official languages in spite of the Nationalist Government and it was van Jaarsveld's duty to speak it properly.

Van Jaarsveld held up William's letter as if he wanted to return it to him. 'I would normally - in the normal course of events that is, send your letter straight to the relevant government department - in this case the Department of Population and Planning. This matter, as you know, falls under the Group Areas Act.'

'Yes?' William calculated the odds. Surely the man wasn't trying to block him?

'Believe me, it's not that I'm trying to hold things up - nothing like that. I just thought ... just considering how drastic ... Forgive me, Doctor, but I thought we should talk things over first.'

William held the silence, but kept his gaze steady.

'My problem is ...' van Jaarsveld looked down at his hands which lay clasped together, resting on his desk top. They were the white hands of a man who spends even his off-hours indoors but the right fore-finger was stained with nicotine. He's a worrier, thought William, and he knew suddenly, with some pleasure, that it would be all right.

'My problem is, I can't help feeling sympathetic. Ag, I come into contact with them every day. You could say it's once in a blue moon that a white person is in the dock in this court. Every day it's the Bantu: drunks, thieving, pass-laws, fighting - that sort of crime. Not really wickedness ... I feel - well, they're not yet educated to our standard ... they're still ... our children really.'

William let van Jaarsveld's words fall about him like crumbs. The magistrate lit a cigarette, drawing in the smoke with an inverted sigh, and holding his breath. William turned to stare out of the window. A

130

dark green van passed by. Through the wire mesh windows, William could make out shadowy silhouettes of bodies slumped forward.

'Ja nee,' sighed van Jaarsveld. The words were Afrikaans for a social stalemate.

He's not going to preach to me, thought William grimly. I know the law.

Van Jaarsveld seemed to pull himself together. 'You see - what we have on the plots is a settled community. There's no criminal elements to speak of. They've built their own school. Doctor, the government doesn't spoil them. There was some political trouble a few years ago, but that's all over now. By right of ownership they've got hold of a bit of land - something to pass on to their children. Now you've laid a complaint.'

William was taken aback at the position van Jaarsveld was taking. 'It's all in my letter. I'm not saying they're a bad lot, but there's overcrowding, and so many people living on my doorstep is a nuisance.' William had not expected to have to debate with an humanitarian, but in a way he was glad of the test. He laughed gently to prove his disinterestedness. The most important thing was not to feel sorry for them. What about himself and his own family?

'It's a problem for me too, man. You say there's no criminal elements among them, but they steal everything I grow. I've had to lock up my vegetable garden - literally! Now it's my milk. However hard I try, I can never get to my cows before they do. If I milk at six, they come at five. If I milk at five, they come at four ...' He stopped, fearing the choking feeling his anger gave him would invalidate his rational stance. He made a small gesture with his right hand, briefly removing it from his pocket and extending it, palm upwards, towards Mr van Jaarsveld. He didn't enjoy being a petitioner.

'The police can't catch the culprits?'

'No.'

Mr van Jaarsveld sighed again. They were approaching the substance of William's letter. What had gone before was merely a preliminary. 'Well, you are correct in what you say here, Doctor. What's there is clearly a black spot: an area of land where the Bantu people have resided with freehold rights for a number of years, situated in a designated white area.'

The man was moving so slowly, William was finding it difficult not to interrupt. 'Look, they may own the land, but I can assure you, they don't care about their places like we do. They're not the same as us. It's so overcrowded - an eyesore - there's no drainage, no sewage disposal, they simply throw the stuff out wherever they feel like it! They used to drink the water from the river, but as a doctor I felt it was a definite health hazard to all of us - and I've got a wife and child to think of, so I put up a tap from my own borehole. I did it myself! I tried to get them to pay for it, but of course - ' He shrugged. 'Now there's this swamp all round the tap. We farmers and small-holders, we're all trying to improve our land, while these people, they simply do nothing except spoil it for us.

'Besides,' he added, calming down, 'it's against government policy for them to be here, isn't it?' That was the point, dammit. The man had already said as much.

'Doctor, it's terrible. Everyone is telling me the same thing.' van Jaarsveld looked earnestly into William's eyes, leaning forward across his desk. 'It's happening on all the farms round here. Sometimes a farmer has a hundred people living on his land. Maybe he's got ten boys working for him and they're all with wives; what happens when the children grow up? Don't think you are the only one coming to me with his hands in the air; say a boy hasn't been working properly, or his children are stealing, or just because there are too many of them, then it's something on the farmer's conscience if he gets rid of them. They can't go to the city, they can't live in town, or on another farm, unless they can get a job there, which is unlikely because it's the same everywhere -'

William was beginning to lose his temper. He didn't want to be burdened with the whole country's problems. Why did the man keep avoiding the main issue in this emotional fashion? He tried his best to make the conversation sound like one reasonable person discussing government policy with another. 'But I was told the government is doing something about all this - building towns where people can go, where they can have a house even, and get work. It doesn't just endorse people out with no proper planning beforehand.

132

That's why I sent my letter. I know they have to live somewhere, but I myself can't put up with them living near me any more.'

van Jaarsveld's hands fumbled with the pencils on his desk. He pressed them into a neat bundle, and aligned them parallel to the ink-well. His cigarette burned sideways in a blue squiggle. Then he stubbed it out with a decisive gesture, and William wrinkled his nose at the stale smell.

'Doctor, I must now speak personally to you. You know in my job I'm not allowed to criticise the government, but ...' To William it looked as if he was bracing himself. 'My wife's relatives farm just outside Queenstown. The place has been in the family for donkey's years. We visit twice a year, Christmas or Easter and one other weekend.' He put his hands together in his lap and rocked his chair backwards, looking up at the ceiling. 'Last Christmas, I thought, why not make a detour Cathcart way to take a look at the mountains. It's really shorter, but the road isn't tarred, so we'd never been before. Then we came across ... I'm sorry, you must think I am talking nonsense. You see, our Bantu, the Bantu from this part, the ones who come in front of me every day, they get sent to this place called Sada - it's a newly built town in the Ciskei. It's been put up 'specially for surplus Bantu from the Karoo. They get taken there in lorries. The Government even transports their furniture free for them. They get some rations, and later on the men can get work on the Cape Town docks, or the mines. The big firms, like construction firms, which make roads and so on, they go there every year to recruit labour.

'Anyway, we were driving along this road - dirt, but not too bad, actually - and it went over the hill.' He shut his eyes, and his voice became thin, as if he were in a bad dream. 'You won't believe it unless you see it. You know what the veld is like there even at the best of times - grey or brown as far as you can see. In summer nothing grows because of the heat, in winter the wind off the mountains cuts sharp.'

He paused. William let the man's voice soak into the books and the leather chair. He refused to give the words purchase in his mind.

The magistrate continued. 'Imagine thousands of little houses set down in rows on the veld, each one the size of your bathroom - smaller. Forty thousand people. That's the government figure, and they say the one near East London, Mdantsane, is even bigger. Doctor, I'm sorry to say this, and I'm a good Nationalist. It's a hell-hole.'

He'll lose his job if I report him, thought William. But that wasn't the way to win. If he couldn't convince van Jaarsveld, he wouldn't feel comfortable with himself. He deliberately relaxed his body so that his tone became more intimate.

'Mr van Jaarsveld, let me congratulate you! You are a man after my own heart. As you rightly say, this is a moral problem, and I'm very glad that you have put this point. All my life I've worried about things to do with morality. You have described a pathetic sight, but we must remember, those places are at the beginning of their development. I'm told the government is making it very attractive for industry to set up in the homelands. What they are doing is centralising the surplus labour. I approve of that. In Europe it's done all the time. They call places like these New Towns.

'The plots, on the other hand, are a slum, don't you agree?' The magistrate nodded. 'I'm a humanitarian, like you, but overpopulation is a health hazard. I'm talking about epidemics that could sweep through the country killing thousands. Sometimes individual people have to suffer for the greater good and often the people themselves don't realise they would be much better off somewhere else.'

The magistrate sighed. 'I can see you look at this from a medical point of view, Doctor. You're right. Things can't go on as they are.'

William worried about a certain lack of conviction in the magistrate's voice, as if the man were holding out on him. It was important that he leave the courthouse not only having got his way, but also feeling that he had done the right thing. van Jaarsveld was proving quite an opponent. He changed tack.

'Look Mr van Jaarsveld, I myself haven't got a lot of money. It hasn't been an easy life for me either. My parents did without to send me to university and I started my practice owing quite a few thousands - pounds it was in those days. I had my mother to look after, and now I've the responsibility of my sister and her child as

134

well as my own family. In addition a doctor is expected to put on a certain show ... I expect it's much the same for you?'

'Well, yes, Doctor.'

'William - please call me William ... er ...'

'Hannes, my name is Hannes, William.' William's expectant silence sucked further confidences from him. 'I'm a farmer at heart, William. You wouldn't think so to look at me, but sometimes, in this office, I don't know why I'm here - I feel out of my depth.'

My God, thought William. Spit it out, man. He laughed, politely disbelieving. 'You look like someone who's studied hard.' He nodded towards the bookshelves, waiting.

'It wasn't my first choice. I was my parents' only surviving son, a laat lammetjie - born when my mother was in her forties. She had another baby, a brother to me, who died in the camp in Mossel Bay. My father was a rebel against the English, you see. When my parents got back to the farm there wasn't a stick standing. The house was burned, and all the cattle slaughtered. They had to start all over again, with nothing, except the bare earth.'

Well, talking about himself has put some stuffing back in him, thought William. van Jaarsveld was meeting William's eyes with a clear gaze.

'We're a very close family. When the depression came, we'd have lost everything if I hadn't gone into the civil service and over the years I've been able to help them. My parents still farm, even at their age now! My father gets up at four in the morning! He says he's too old to learn to do anything else.' He laughed proudly.

'So you don't have any other brothers and sisters?'

'No. It is a sadness, but my mother says the Lord was merciful to let her conceive so late, like Sarah, the barren wife of Abraham.'

'I can't tell you how much I admire you people,' said William heartily. 'I expect you think I'm just another blerrie Engelsman, but I'm not really. My mother was a true Afrikaner, a boerenooi. She had sisters in the camps too, one of them died there.'

'You don't have to tell me that, William. In Fort Bedford we've learned to live together - the English and the Afrikaners. I can't hate the English for the war any more. That's nearly seventy years ago. We were neither of us born then.'

'Besides,' William took over smoothly, 'your lot have won now, surely, and as far as I'm concerned that's the best thing that could have happened. I look on life from the side-lines. I'm a bit of a philosopher, you know, and I've got a tremendous admiration for you Nationalists. I'm glad the country is in such safe hands. During the Boer War, our families were on opposite sides, but now you're the magistrate, and I'm sitting here asking you to help me.' He laughed, and van Jaarsveld joined in. 'That's the way it should be, Hannes.'

It had worked. van Jaarsveld no longer held the letter as if he wished to return it to William. He became business-like, shuffling the papers on his desk. 'Well, then, William, I won't keep you any longer. I'll send your complaint straight to Pretoria with a recommendation that the area should be declared a Black spot and zoned for removal.'

'One more thing, Hannes. Could I ask you a small favour?'

'Of course, William.'

'Well, just like you said, it's not a pleasant matter. I don't actually want to be personally involved. It's not that I've got anything against these people as such, it's just the situation, and, of course, the principle of the thing. I'd be grateful if my name wasn't mentioned in connection with it.'

Now the magistrate could be generous. 'Don't you worry, William. There's no need for anyone to know there was an original complaint. What will happen is that they will first send an inspector. He will interview the farmers, and the small-holders in the area, and then go round to the Bantu. They usually ask the police to come with them at that stage. The inspector will find out who has title deeds and so on. They probably won't have much - they didn't register land in those days like we do now. Then, these places usually attract a lot of skollies. Those we can deal with in the courts straight away. Their passes will tell us where they are from.'

William waited. Surely he wasn't going to change his mind? Was he going to leave the home-owners where they were?

'Those who work in town will be put on the waiting list for a house in the location. I reckon that will leave us with about two hundred people, and most of them will probably be only too pleased

136

to be sent where there is a house already waiting for them, and a chance of a job too.'

Whew! William breathed a sigh of relief. He imagined Vera's smooth face wreathed in smiles. 'How long will all this take?'

'Probably less than nine months altogether. When they get going, our administration is pretty efficient.'

van Jaarsveld was on his feet, and holding open the door. Glancing through the window, William glimpsed a column of convicts laden with picks and shovels. The magistrate followed his gaze.

'They're working on the little park behind the post office - the one on the corner of van Riebeek street, that used to be a vacant site.'

'Oh yes - I know the place. Jolly good idea. I'm very grateful to you, Hannes.'

'Ag no, man, William, it's my pleasure.'

TWENTY-THREE

Waking from her drugged sleep, Millie pushed, like a child, with fisted hands at the tube fitted into her nostrils.

'Mrs Rorig, you must keep still.' The nurse was a starched armadillo. A watch ticked where her heart should be.

'What time is it?'

'It's four in the morning.'

'What - ?'

'I'm just fixing your pillows. You've had an operation. I'll give you another injection to make you sleep.'

Millie closed her eyes. She had never felt so uncomfortable. She forced herself to imagine morning mist lift from meadow grass, the early sun glint silver on wet spider-webs. She tried to remember the rank smell of over-ripe grapes, the plumpness of figs after she peeled away the soft skin.

She plummeted into a nightmare in which the plots were on fire. She was on the other side of the tarred road. She could see sparks exploding high in the air, singeing the feathery tops of the gum trees before they caught and went whoosh! like torches, crackling and straining until they crashed onto the homes beneath them. She could hear screaming, and saw people silhouetted against hot gold and red, rushing out of the burning houses with babies, suitcases, bundles of blankets, chairs and mattresses.

'Over here!' she shouted. The roar of the fire was too loud. The heat was a great, shimmering wall between her and the people she wanted to save. The road was a river of boiling tar.

'Over here!' she sobbed, and woke to find Marge holding down

138

her arms.

'Auntie Millie! Auntie Millie!' Tears were streaming down Marge's cheeks. 'Oh, thank goodness you're awake!'

'I - '

'Don't try to talk. I'll wash your face. Just lie still.'

Marge soothed her and combed her hair. 'Jo is coming this afternoon. She's been given permission to break her banning order for a week.'

The doctor visited the same morning. He wasn't Bennie van Zyl, her own doctor in Fort Bedford, but the sleek young surgeon who had performed the operation. Of course, Millie reminded herself, muddled, she was in the Port Elizabeth General. The operation had been yesterday. Marge was a ward sister. That was why Marge was with her.

'Well, Mrs ... ' The Doctor read her name off her chart. '... Rorig, you'll be up and about in no time, I'm sure. He stood on his left foot, his right already on its way to the next patient. He consulted his notes. 'We managed to cut out the tumour, and I'm hoping we got it all out.'

'When will ...?' Millie had trouble pronouncing the words. Her false teeth were in a glass of water on her bedside cabinet. The tube dragged against the tender flesh in her nose.

The doctor gave a tight, polite smile. 'The nurse will explain. You'll be with us for a little over a week, probably.'

He whisked himself away with a clatter of brass rings as the curtain round her bed gave way to his exit. Millie allowed herself the luxury of a few self-pitying tears.

'Oh, Marge, please give me my teeth. I've had the most terrible things done to me.' She gestured feebly towards the tube. 'It's the worst time of my whole life.'

'I'll stay all day, Auntie Millie.' Marge settled into the chair next to her bed and held her hand. Millie's mouth felt more comfortable with her teeth in. Marge spoke while she gently wiped away Millie's tears. 'I've brought you a clean nightie, and I've found one of your books in your locker. Shall I read it to you?'

'Yes, please,' Millie nodded, closing her eyes.

TWENTY-FOUR

When the grandfathers Isaac Gxoyiya and Matthew Ntuli came to the kitchen door, Sarah was overcome with the burden of their presence. They should not have to walk so far! Grandfather Isaac Gxoyiya was well over ninety. His hair was white against his dark, polished skull. He walked slowly, pausing to rest on a stick which was carved in intricate loops snaking up its length towards a round knob worn smooth over the years by the palm of his hand. Grandfather Matthew Ntuli was not much younger. His face was wrinkled all over like a map of his life, and he was so frail you would think a breeze might blow him over.

This wasn't the first time Sarah had wished that Millie were home, and today she was still shaky herself from the events of the previous night. No one had come to her house, but she had been woken at four in the morning by barking Alsatian dogs, men shouting in Afrikaans, and the unforgiving sound of breaking glass and splintering wood - the customary noise of a police raid. Across the road on the plots there must have been at least a hundred policemen, and a whole fleet of vans. She was told they had made over forty arrests, but the worst thing was the notices they had left behind, and about which, surely, these old men had come to speak with William.

She had lain in her bed, stiff with listening, until she heard the vans leave, then she had dressed quickly. It was still the half-dark of early morning as she rushed over to find out whether Leah and their mother had been disturbed. She found Leah rubbing her mother's chest.

140

'How are you?' Sarah asked gently, lightly stroking her mother's forehead.

The old woman's skin had lost lustre, but her smile creased the corners of her eyes. She did not have breath to speak, but she nodded weakly.

'They broke the door - take a look Sisi! Mother was fast asleep, but the noise!'

'We'll take her to my house. She can't stay here.' Alfred had helped them lift their mother and carry her along the road. He and Leah made a chair for her with their hands, and Sarah supported her back and kept the blanket around her shoulders. There was a fractured silence in the houses they passed. People who had relatives arrested, were dressing hurriedly, preparing for the walk to town and the long day at the police station. Others were standing together in small groups, sad and silent, as if unable to comment on the events of the previous night.

'She won't remember what happened - or know the difference between your house and mine,' whispered Leah as they settled the old woman into Sarah's bed. 'She'll sleep now. I'll try to fix our place up.' A rather unwilling Nontu was forbidden to go to school and left in charge of her grandmother.

'Baas William,' it was so unlike William to put down his newspaper at once when Sarah spoke to him, that she almost lost her words. 'Baas William, the old builder Isaac Gxoyiya, is here. He wants to speak to Baas William, please.'

He didn't question why. 'Make our guests some coffee, Sarah,' he ordered, which was again unusual. She had never seen him being hospitable to black people. Curious to see how he treated the old men, Sarah leaned round the shadow of the water tank listening, while Nomzamo made the coffee.

'Well, if it isn't old Isaac - am I right?' William asked heartily, shaking hands.

The frail, old man laughed, showing pink gums where front teeth were missing. 'Yes, Doctor.'

'And who is this with you?'

'He is Matthew Ntuli, Doctor.' Again William extended his hand.

Grandfather Ntuli's fingers were all bones. Sarah thought she could hear them rattle together.

'Well, well, well. What can I do for you this morning?' William's tone acknowledged that the men were the elders of the community come on important business. She had misjudged him, Sarah told herself, he did have respect.

'Doctor, I have been living here in his area for a lo...o...ng time.' Grandfather Gxoyiya made the word reflect not only the span of his life, but also the length of his service to the community. 'I built this house - ' He gestured towards the cream farmhouse with its red roof.

'I know that. I was old enough to remember when you built on those extra rooms at the end of the passage. I was nine then - ten maybe. You showed me how to lay bricks. I learned the bricklaying trade from you.'

Grandfather Gxoyiya's pink gums showed again as he laughed with William. Grandfather Ntuli laughed too, politely. Everyone knew William was a difficult man, and that they had to walk carefully because of his terrible temper. 'Doctor, you can see I am an old man and Matthew Ntuli is an old man, but the people have sent us to you because today is a bad day for us.'

William said nothing, but spread his legs wider, as if wanting to grow roots in the ground. His face became serious.

'Doctor, you know our people were given our land even before the war between the English and the Boers. Queen Victoria, who was our Queen then, said we could stay here, next to the river, and our children forever, because our people, the Fingoes, helped her soldiers in the wars with the Xhosa tribes. Before my father's father, we were living here. Our ancestors are buried here.'

Grandfather Ntuli nodded in agreement. 'Ewe!' he murmured.

'Now they are telling us our land is not our land any more. The police came with pieces of paper.' He took out his passbook from his jacket pocket. Between the limp, brown covers of the small, worn book were several folded sheets of paper. He selected one, and offered it to William. Sarah strained forward as William, holding the notice a little away from his body, read aloud.

'You are hereby given notice that from ...' he had difficulty reading

142

the date ... '31st March, 1974 ... all houses in the Cleveland area, shown on the map attached, in the magisterial district of Fort Bedford ...' William gabbled through the official-sounding language. Sarah heard the words 'Group Areas' and 'Proclamation'. Then he slowed down again. 'Any persons displaced under this proclamation are hereby ordered to give their names to the Fort Bedford police station, where transport of furniture and effects as well as persons will be arranged to alternative accommodation in a designated resettlement area.'

'Have you all been given one of these?' asked William.

'Each house. The police brought them.' He didn't mention how it was.

'Well, Isaac - what do you expect me to do?' William's back was like an iron pole. The two men looked anywhere but in his face. What would they see there, Sarah wondered. She knew from experience how closed it would be.

'The Doctor's family has always been good to our people. You, yourself, Doctor, gave us the borehole so that we could drink clean water. Now we have had a meeting. The magistrate will not listen to us black people. We ask you to speak on our behalf.'

In the pause, Sarah saw William's hands clasp and unclasp behind his back. He would surely speak to the magistrate! Yet when the answer came, Sarah shivered at a sudden vision of William, looking like the judge at James's trial and placing a black cloth on his head. 'Isaac, Matthew, I would like to help you, but what can I say to the magistrate? The government has decided that no Bantu is allowed to own land in a white area. There is now a law that says your people must move over to the other side of the Great Fish River. You are not to think of South Africa as your home any more. Your homelands are the Transkei and the Ciskei. That is where your ancestors came from, not here among the whites.'

'The Doctor knows we do not come from those places. We were born here, our fathers and grandfathers were born here. How can the government talk of homelands? How can it be called a homeland when we have never seen it?' Grandfather Gxoyiya's arm swung in an arc as he said never, as if it indicated a whole world full of nothing,

143

which was foreign to him and to the people on whose behalf he was speaking.

'Look here, Isaac,' William was becoming less polite, more bullying. Soon, Sarah knew, he would lose his temper. 'I didn't make these laws. It's no good talking to me, they're nothing to do with me. They are made by parliament and we just have to do what they say.'

'Doctor, we want to stay on our own land. We want to die in our own house and in our father's house.'

There was something different about William, he wasn't getting angry, it was as if he truly wanted the respect of the elders. He touched Grandfather Gxoyiya's shoulder, but Sarah could see the Grandfather did not even notice, he was past caring about such a gesture. 'Isaac, the government isn't heartless. It may seem so to you, but that isn't so. It will not leave you without somewhere to live. It's just that things have got bad here. Soon the new place will be your home, and your children's home. You will see that I am right. Isaac. For instance how many people are living in your house at the moment?'

The old man counted on his fingers, speaking the names silently. Sarah counted too: his wife, Ethel; his brother-in- law and his sister and their two daughters whose husbands worked in Cape Town; his own son, and his wife, and the six grandchildren, who worked in his garden in the afternoons.

Sarah could see him sitting on the wooden chair outside his front door, directing his troops. He had a big mealie patch and was proud of his pumpkins. 'What next, Tatamkhulu?' the little ones would ask. 'Fetch more water' he'd order, or 'Sweep up those leaves.'

'Fourteen people, Master.'

'It's too many for one house.'

'It's too many, Master, but it would be better if I could buy more land - '

'You see, even you agree with me. The white people don't live like that because we know that sickness comes when there are too many people living all together. The government is thinking what is best for you. They also know you can't buy more land here. The farmers don't want to lose their land, and, besides, it's against the law to sell

144

to you. When there is overcrowding like you have, there is danger of sickness.'

Now William was lecturing them. His voice rose and became more confident. 'I have seen the conditions getting worse since I came to live here more than ten years ago. There are too many children. I see them growing up wild - I'm sure I'm not talking about your children, I'm sure you keep a very strict eye on them.' He laughed, pulling in his anger, trying to placate the old men, but this time they did not smile.

'Isaac, you must agree there are bad ones amongst you - tsotsies, who won't work and who think they can just steal from the white farmers. Who steal from me! These plots were never meant to have so many people living on them. The government is only doing the sensible thing.

'It doesn't happen in South Africa only. It happens overseas too, even in England, where the Queen lives, even there people are moved out of their homes to new houses. Some of them don't like it either and they complain too, just like you are doing now - even white people are moved. It's called slum clearance - the same as here. Believe me, the government is doing it for your own good.'

There was a long pause, then Grandfather Ntuli spoke to Grandfather Gxoyiya in Xhosa, which he knew William would not be able to understand. Sarah froze as she listened, thinking, he will guess what is being said about him. 'Let us go,' said Grandfather Ntuli. 'We are wasting our time with this umlungu, this white man who knows only to keep for himself. We are digging a well where there is no water.'

Grandfather Gxoyiya was weeping silently. The tears got lost among the deep furrows on his dark, old face. 'Doctor,' he said, 'you will not defend us because in your heart you want us to be destroyed.'

Sarah drew in her breath with a sharp hiss. William's back stiffened, but then, again to her surprise, he seemed to soften. It was almost as if he was begging Grandfather Gxoyiya to believe him.

'No, Isaac, you are wrong to say things like that about me, because they aren't true. I am a doctor, my job is to save lives. I take my job very seriously and I have sworn an oath to do that. In fact I could take you to court for what you have just said, but I know you are distressed now. What will happen will be for the best in the long run. You will see that I am right.'

There seemed no answer to this - only silence. The two old men stared at the ground, while William clasped and unclasped the hands he held behind his back. Sarah began to worry that William might spot her watching them, and was about to step back towards the kitchen, when he turned. 'Where is that coffee? Sarah!' he called. 'Sarah!'

In spite of her resolve to stay hidden, Sarah rushed forward. 'Yes, Baas William?' Luckily he was too preoccupied to notice where she had been.

'I thought I told you to make coffee for these two gentlemen.'

'It's coming, Master. It's nearly ready.'

'Right, then.' He turned back to the old men. 'I have to hurry off now, I'm afraid - I'm already late for an appointment in town.' He made it sound as if they had kept him from important business, but he was still hearty with them. 'It's been good to see you again, Isaac, and you too Matthew. Reminds me of old times.' He extended his hand again, and they took it in turn, politely. 'Goodbye. Goodbye. Please wait for the coffee, which I am sure will soon be brought to you.'

Through the kitchen window, Sarah and Nomzamo watched William and Vera drive their white Cortina smoothly away from Glen Bervie. Then Sarah took out a plate of bread and jam together with the mugs of coffee which William had ordered, and she and Nomzamo stood at a respectful distance from their visitors. Grandfather Gxoyiya had sunk onto his haunches, his hands resting above his head on the worn comfort of his upright stick.

'I am not hungry,' he said. 'Thank you all the same, Mother. How is the old Grandmother today?'

'My mother is sleeping at my house, but she is badly shocked. Their front door was smashed open last night.'

The two old men shook their heads and clicked their tongues in sympathy. Grandfather Gxoyiya's voice seemed to come from the

146

very depths of his stomach, it was so low and quiet. 'My father died when I was still a young man. He is buried here. How can I take care of his grave if we are moved away from where he is lying?'

'I have heard of these places where they will send us.' Grandfather Ntuli was drinking his coffee, talking between quick, hot gulps. 'They say, when the people arrive, they see there are many small graves already dug, because it is known there will be deaths, especially of the children. The Doctor tells us there will be work, but there is no work in that place, and everyone is a stranger to the people in the next house. It is a place where each one is alone and you sit all day with your little bit of nothing, and watch it, like a white man.'

Sarah wished Grandfather Gxoyiya would eat something because he would need his strength to walk back to the plots, but the old man spoke in a voice which seemed to float past her and Nomzamo and end up as a whispering in the leaves of the trees. 'They are taking us away from the place of our ancestors. They will destroy everything, not only what we own, but the spirits themselves will be crying and lost. We will be a people with nothing at all.'

Grandfather Ntuli shook his head. 'Hai! The white Baas is full of tricks!' It didn't seem as if he was excluding William from this judgement, and although Sarah could not believe enough in William's wickedness to think that he had caused this terrible judgement on the community, yet he had acted so strangely, so unlike the person she knew, who never cared what black people thought of him. Today he had tried so hard to make the visitors believe he was right and to feel friendly towards him. She had never before seen him act like this and it germinated a tiny seed of mistrust in her.

Grandfather Gxoyiya stood up slowly. His hand on the stick shook with the effort, and then he steadied himself. 'We eat their bread; we have been delivered into their hands. Come,' he turned to his companion, 'we must go. Stay well, Mother. Stay well, Daughter.'

Sarah and Nomzamo watched the two old men in their stiff, slow walk along the path towards the back gate. It is my own bare feet that made that path, thought Sarah - a whole lifetime of coming and going. Running to be on time because there were lots of visitors; because it was Christmas, or New Year; because someone was sick. I

147

nursed the old Master and the old Missis up to their deaths, she remembered. She had washed the old man and laid out his body. She'd carried Nontobeko and then Nontu in her belly or on her back. She'd had to serve in the big house whatever her troubles, like the time she'd left her dear Ernest sitting by himself at home, day after day; Nontobeko when she was so bad with the measles; the two babies that had died.

'Did they really think William would help?' mused Nomzamo, helping herself to a slice of bread the old men hadn't touched. She reached for a mug of coffee.

'The old Master would have.'

'But even the old Master, whoever he was and however good you say he was, must have taken from our people. It's obvious, isn't it, when you see what they have and what we have?'

'It was better then, there was more for everyone, or perhaps neither our people nor theirs wanted so much. My parents walked easily from town to town without shoes. They worked as far away as the mealie fields in the Transvaal. In the beginning, the old Master didn't have a car and he too travelled long distances with a horse and cart. We didn't live badly - meat was cheap - our people still had plenty of cattle and good gardens.'

'But where have they gone then, the cattle and the good gardens?'

'Hai! It's all gone.' Reluctantly, Sarah was finding a bitterness, which had come together with her newly aroused suspicion of William. It was a tiny tick, sucking at her blood and growing. She didn't want to speak about it to Nomzamo. It wasn't something yet that had words.

She gathered up the plates and mugs. 'Come, let's finish the work. I am going to run home to check on Mother before they get back from town and notice I've been away from the house.

TWENTY-FIVE

Mr Freeman, the location superintendent, had, so to speak, grown up on the job. He was young Mr Freeman, whose father, old Mr Freeman, had been location superintendent before him. As a child, he had played in his father's office, and learned to speak Xhosa there, but an imperious Xhosa, which was full of commands and the harsh jokes of the conquerors. He parked his battered, grey station wagon (he told his wife it wasn't worth getting anything better for these roads) in a spatter of stones, closing the door with a bang.

He gave a sidelong glance at the two women camped with their babies and bundles on the coarse grass on the side of the road, and then spoke to the group of black policemen lounging in the sun outside the location office.

'Not again?' His eyes looked heavenwards in a facial grimace.

'Baas, she says you must give her a house of her own - ' one of the policemen replied after the general laughter, but shaking his head at such a ridiculous notion.

Mr Freeman slewed round to speak to the younger of the two women. 'I told you not to bother me anymore. Go home and sleep with your husband. Hamba! Clear off! I can't help you.'

'Baas, my husband is hitting me - ' The woman held onto a three-year-old boy, who was about to toddle into the road. Under his nose were two scabs of dried snot.

'Go home and clean the house for your husband. Wash that child also - look at his face!'

The men laughed again, but the woman was crying. Her friend

spoke up for her. 'She wants a house for herself now. Her husband has thrown her out. He's got someone else.'

'Ag, don't make me mad. You know a woman can't rent a house for herself. You're just making trouble for her - tell her she's got to say sorry to him.' Mr Freeman walked quickly up to the location office and then turned on the row of policemen. 'Don't just stand there. I've work to do and I want some tea.'

Unlike the location policemen, who wore khaki trousers with knife-edge creases, shirts with brass buttons, and shiny brown boots and belts, Mr Freeman was in civilian clothes, which were on the shabby side. His shoes were unpolished and dusty, his collar frayed, his grey trousers baggy and crumpled. He had resigned himself to the knowledge that his job brought him no status in the other part of town. His imperious position in the location didn't accustom him to speak to whites, whom he hardly saw, and who had, even from childhood, treated him as if some of the unpleasantness of being black had rubbed off on him. He was embarrassed when he saw Father O'Reilly sitting in the charge office, and hoped the priest hadn't passed a judgement on his tone with the woman petitioner.

'Father, these people, you know what they're like. You can tell them something a hundred times, but they never listen, hey? How are you Father?'

Father O'Reilly had jumped up when Mr Freeman had entered the sparsely-furnished room. The two men shook hands.

'Come and sit inside my office, Father. I've been on the building sites and I need my cup of tea.' As if bullying the policeman, who was busy with the kettle, would make the Father feel welcome, he yelled, 'Two cups, you hear? One for the Father. Make it now.'

Shepherding Father O'Reilly through to his private office, Mr Freeman's commands were an attempt to disguise what had in fact been his morning's business. He considered the takings from the municipal beer-hall to be one of the perks of his job. The council used the profits from the sale of alcohol in the location to finance all kinds of projects, such as the new enlarged swimming-pool, that benefited the white town, so they themselves weren't likely to look too closely at his accounting. Luckily the priest couldn't have any idea

150

of the significance of the bulge in his jacket pocket, made by the various cheque-books and banking books he used.

Nevertheless, he liked the muscular, little Irishman. He was clever, that one, never getting involved in politics and that meant he was acceptable everywhere. He'd be at a posh wedding in town in the morning - it might even be in the Dutch Reformed Church - and then that same evening he'd be holding Mass in the location. Never made any trouble though, and the natives thought the world of him. No doubt about it, the priest had a secret way with him. It wasn't a bad thing to stay in his good books.

So Mr Freeman wasn't obstructive with Father O'Reilly and before long the two men were in accord. If people from the plots had jobs in town, Mr Freeman would stamp their passes, and those of members of their family, with permission to reside in Fort Bedford. This meant that they could squash into any accommodation they could find. There was a waiting list for houses which, even if no more names were added, would take several years to clear - or never, with this clamp-down on new houses for Bantu in white areas - but Mr Freeman promised to siphon people onto the list, if he could do so in a way which wasn't too obvious. Luckily there was a new location nearing completion further up the side of the mountain, which had been planned and started years before the latest legislation.

As for the old people, if they had relatives who would look after them, both men agreed that it was charitable that they weren't moved far away. Mr Freeman joked that they wouldn't be around for long, anyway, and Father O'Reilly sighed and said something about how he was sure the good Lord would be pleased to receive them. Mr Freeman thought that was quite a clever joke too, and said he liked a man with a sense of humour.

By these arrangements, the majority of the population on the plots squeezed into the Fort Bedford township, leaving a little over one hundred souls, together with a family who had been kicked off the Fourie's small-holding, and a dozen more from farms in the district, to await the government lorries, which would take them and their possessions away to the 'resettlement camp'.

TWENTY-SIX

James had stopped himself from thinking about women for so long that he was unaccustomed even to dream of a closeness of that nature and he was certainly not planning on getting married. For the moment he was just so relieved to be out of prison, and would have been content enough with his life if it weren't for Warrant Officer Gouws, who was sitting in his car, waiting for James on the road back into the township, almost as if he had spies out reporting on his whereabouts.

'Okay, friend?'

James stiffened at the casual familiarity of the greeting, but he was afraid to object.

'You remembered to report in this week?'

'Yes.' James's terse reply was thickened by clenched teeth.

'Jus' reminding you, hey?'

Should he dodge and run? But then it would look as if he had something to hide. 'Can I go now, please, Sir? My sister's waiting for me.'

'Your sister's a nice girl, hey? You should bring her with to the police station one day, hey? Hey, Khumalo?'

'What do you mean?'

'Sir - "What do you mean, Sir" - No, man, I was jus' joking. P'raps she needs a job. She could do my washing, hey? Or sewing.' He laughed casually, his dark glasses winking in the sun, as he scratched himself delicately in the groin.

Very funny. James knew as well as anyone that sewing was a dirty word in Afrikaans.

Gouws let the pause grow. Then, 'I want you at the usual place - tomorrow at three. You better be there, or maybe someone will find herself in trouble. Got it?'

It was as if he had a noose round his neck and they had just jerked it. All the next night he worried about what he would say at the meeting. Would he be able to stall them again? They wanted information, had said they'd put him on their payroll, but up till now he'd managed to get out of it by protesting that he was still unfamiliar with township life. How could he help them when he had been away for so long, he had told them.

The following morning, when he was still undecided, Nomzamo had stepped through the kitchen door as if her appearance in his room was the most ordinary thing in the world.

'You need a break,' she announced, looking around her critically and wrinkling her nose as if she could smell the anxiety he felt. 'You've been working too hard and it's hurting your soul. All work and no play, you know what comes of that.'

He'd not kept his appointment with Gouws that day, but went with her instead, and that was how he and Nomzamo began going out for walks together. Then, after he started working at Oxford Furnitures, they changed the time to Sunday afternoons. It was odd, because, although they never discussed the new arrangement, it was just somehow assumed between them. They always walked in the same direction: down to the river where it looped itself past the town, under the bridge, and then along the river-bank next to the white people's farmlands. They had no right of way, no right there at all, so they never went far, but stopped where the krantz made a shady overhang, and the brown river curled over a grey, pebbled beach.

James told Nomzamo about his childhood and what it was like walking to school in the early morning light, and back again in the hot afternoon, his mind jumping with all the new things he had learned. After a few weeks, she asked him about her father.

'He was marvellous. A brave man ...'

'Were you with him, when ...'

He knew she must be wanting to know about the hanging. 'No, I was already on the island.' He tried not to dwell on her father's death. It was too hard for her if she remembered only that.

'He was a brilliant teacher, you know. He taught me how to read - I mean, really take in what I read. He wouldn't accept anything I said if it was just a quotation from someone else. He'd ask: "And you James? What do you, yourself think? Justify that opinion." And I was so awkward, so ... green. Amazing to think he was only the same age as I am now.'

'My mother won't talk about him. Sometimes she gets the dumps, and I know she misses him. I can't ... ' She shook her head to get rid of the tears. 'I have so little memory of him, I hardly remember his face.' With a quick movement, she jumped to her feet. 'We must go - look, the sun is almost gone.'

It was the time of day when the sun grows bigger and gentler, and they gazed without speech at the orange orb as it slid slowly behind the mountain, leaving a glowing apricot sky to light them home.

James's family made no comments about his walks with Nomzamo, although he knew they were watching closely, and with a joy that was the same as his own. Slowly there grew a kind of song in his heart. He said nothing to Nomzamo about how he was feeling, nor did she speak about love to him, but sometimes, when he helped her through a fence, or gave her his hand to steady her as she jumped across a patch of water, their two hands lingered just an extra second together. For the moment it was all he asked. His happiness needed no future, only the enchantment he felt around them when they were together.

He was glad that Sarah had worked with Nomzamo and clearly liked her, while everyone knew that Nomzamo was Nontobeko's best friend. About Mrs Matama, Sarah commented one day, 'Well, of course we are both widows', and James liked the remark, and was delighted when the two older women sat companionably together on the rare occasion when Nozuko asked Mrs Matama, Nomzamo and Sarah to share a meal.

Nozuko didn't need any prompting to offer Mrs Matama and

154

Nomzamo temporary accommodation, when they lost their home. She hung a curtain on a washing line which she put across a corner of the kitchen to give them some privacy. Nomzamo, who was on the brink of leaving for her nursing course, helped her mother carry their clothing and blankets into town. They balanced the heavy bundles on their heads and, when they brought them into the house, they stored most of what they contained under the bed behind the curtain.

James made a quick detour to the plots just after four-thirty on a Friday afternoon to fetch the furniture, the sewing machine and the kitchen stuff. Oxford Furnitures didn't like him to keep the van in the location overnight, partly because they felt it wouldn't be safe, but mostly because the manager, Tommy Albertyn, deeply suspicious of all black people, imagined James junketing off in it to all-night revels in nearby towns like Cookhouse or Cradock. Maybe I will one day, thought James. Maybe I'll make off with it and they won't see me for dust. His rebellion was short-lived. I'd never get away with it. There's my pass-book, with my employer's name on it. The police always stop black drivers and anyway I have to report to them once a week. They've got me in a net - if I move it just gets tighter.

So he enjoyed the feeling of cheating Mr Albertyn by fetching the furniture, even though it had to be done in a nervous rush. 'Hurry, hurry, you must run with the things - ' he urged the small boys from the neighbourhood whom Mrs Matama had roped in to help them. 'The Baas will catch you if you take too long!' Nomzamo and Mrs Matama carried the chairs out and stacked them on the ground beside the van. James was working at such a tempo that his shirt under his overalls was wringing wet. The bedroom furniture, especially the wardrobe, was very heavy, but the youngsters were wiry and willing. When it was all packed up, Mrs Matama distributed one cent pieces, while James waited for her to get into the front seat beside Nomzamo. Ma Matama had changed over the years. Hardship had made her stouter, as if layering her against hurt, and she was now built like a ship, so that he needed to give her a substantial push to help her in.

'Where will it all go!' wailed Nomzamo. 'There's such a lot!' Mrs

Matama, panting from the exertion, dabbed her forehead with her handkerchief.

James stretched his arms, bracing himself away from the steering wheel. 'I can stack it against the wall of my room. You'd be surprised how tidy it will look - I do it every day in the shop.'

Ma Matama gazed gratefully at him. 'It can't be for very long. I'll find a place for myself soon.'

They were approaching the town. 'When we are across the bridge, you must hide under the dashboard,' warned James. 'I'm not allowed to take on passengers.'

As they slipped off the seat, and bent themselves double, Nomzamo's giggles infected her mother. 'Oh! Help! I'm getting myself into a knot!' Ma Matama shrieked. Her headscarf slipped over one eye, like a bandit, James thought. He was sure she'd never lost her dignity like this before. Nomzamo had told him that when they travelled to Pretoria to say goodbye to her father before the hanging, she had shown no emotion. When she had had to mourn for him at a funeral when his body was not yet cold, even then her face had given nothing away. Nomzamo had told him that she sometimes imagined her mother had jammed a poker down her throat to enable her to keep going during that time.

James smiled, but in a kindly way. Although he was sorry she was uncomfortable, he was glad to see her laughing like this. It must have been terrible to endure without crying out. From his own experience he knew that that kind of reserve was the last resort of those who have no other defence left to them.

'Here comes Mrs Fourie!' warned James and the two women ducked even further down as the green Volkswagen approached.

Ma Matama was shrieking, 'I can't! Help! My leg!' and Nomzamo was crying that her dress was caught in the gear lever.

Mrs Fourie, who had known James since he was a boy and chose to think, so she had informed him, that he had learned his lesson, passed him with a stately wave. Her hair had the perfect corrugations of a recent set, her black-rimmed glasses with the little diamante studs twinkled at him. He waved respectfully back. He loved it.

'I think I've done something to my neck,' cried Ma Matama.

'Ma, you'll be all right.' As Nomzamo kissed her mother, their tears of laughter mingled.

'I'll take the short cut past the white cemetery,' said James. 'It's dirt, so hold tight for the pot-holes.'

Protesting noisily as they bumped to a stop in front of the house, the two women erupted onto the road like fizz from a bottle.

While they were waiting for James to open the back of the van, Mrs Matama pulled her dress straight, and stood still so that Nomzamo could re-tie her head-scarf for her. James called to the children from next door, who had run up out of curiosity, to fetch their big brother.

'You can both rest,' he assured the women. 'Lighty will help - we'll fix everything.'

Nomzamo linked arms with her mother as they went inside. 'Now you know what fun it is to do something wrong!' she joked.

'Wrong?' Ma Matama replied quickly. 'It's not allowed by the white people, but I don't believe what we did was wrong!'

'Ma, you're learning fast!' Nomzamo laughed admiringly and winked at James, who was waiting for her dear face to turn towards his, before getting to work.

TWENTY-SEVEN

Leaving the house through the front door, William noticed Father O'Reilly and Millie seated together on the veranda. It was late afternoon; their two figures were dark against the white walls of the house, while on the grass their elongated shadows swallowed up the last yellow patches of sunlight. William paused for a moment, curious that the priest had been spending so much time with his sister. Considering that Millie's obstinate refusal to attend school had meant that in his opinion she was virtually uneducated and had achieved nothing with her life, he had come to judge her to be without value. He had to admit that he was ashamed of her. She had been pretty once, he remembered, but as an old woman she was really not interesting. It amazed him that Father O'Reilly seemed to be genuinely fond of her.

Millie had become very frail. For the past few months he had noticed on her what one of his medical colleagues at the hospital, where he had trained, had once dubbed 'the mark of Zorro'. The phrase had stuck with him over the years and had helped him in a funny way not to mind too much when his patients no longer responded to treatment. He estimated that she had weeks, rather than months of life still ahead of her. Pity the operation hadn't been a success. On the contrary, it had clearly weakened her and would probably hasten her death. He had predicted the outcome, but of course he couldn't interfere with Bennie's treatment, as he was her doctor. If she had been his patient - well, no point in going into that now.

Father O'Reilly was telling Millie about a wedding he had attended that morning. 'Oh,' he sighed, William thought swooned would be a better word for the way he was carrying on, not at all like a dignified man of the cloth, 'the girls were so young and pretty! The bride - her veil made her look mysterious - beautiful. You know how on these special occasions women, especially young women, attain a kind of inner glow.' William notched these remarks up against the priest. The way he spoke about coloured women was clearly illegal.

Now the man was praising the bride's parents. 'They couldn't do enough for me - not enough. "Have something more to eat, Father", they kept on at me.' He patted his little round stomach. 'I need exercise. They really spoil me - my congregation must be the most generous in the whole world.'

'More than in Ireland, Father?' Millie's voice was breathless, but she could still tease.

'Oh the Irish! Now you're talking.'

Father O'Reilly took her right hand and held it gently between his small, stubby fingers. Millie had lost an enormous amount of weight - she seemed to have aged ten, even twenty years, especially when compared to his wired-up energy.

'I'm missing my tennis, Millie,' he was saying. 'You were the first person to ring me up when I came to Fort Bedford. Do you remember? "Hello Father," you said. "Do you play tennis?" ... Tennis!' He laughed. 'It was the last thing on my mind. The place was so strange to me: brown and blue instead of the greens and greys I was used to. And there were all these new languages to learn.'

'You managed.' Millie's eyes, gazing at him, were very blue in her wasted face.

'Oh yes. Ek kan die taal praat nou.' William noticed that his accent was foreign, but passable. 'Imagine me, unpacking my suitcase in that empty rectory, and then, out of nowhere - "Do you play tennis?" I jumped at it, even though I had to go out and buy myself a racquet!' Millie laughed gently as the priest continued. 'I was still a young man, but you always managed to beat me hollow! You won every set for twenty years!'

'You must be exaggerating!' she protested.

'No, it's the honest truth.'

'I was younger too.' Millie's voice was light, like a bird. Strange how there seemed to be no regret in it, as if she was standing apart from that other time. After all, it was only a year or two ago.

'It was my great good fortune to find you here.' William supposed Father O'Reilly was referring to the tennis, but found that he was wrong. 'You've always beaten me hollow, Millie - in all things. I should say it another way: I believe it was God's will that you should be a blessing and a guidance to me.'

They were getting maudlin, William thought. He stepped out of the doorway. 'Good afternoon, Father. It's good to see you here again so soon. Kind of you to find the time to call on my sister. I hope she's not being a nuisance to you.'

Father O'Reilly jumped up. 'I was just about to take my leave. I - ' He turned back to Millie, who seemed to have shrunk even further. William thought that even in her illness, Millie had this irritating habit of eluding him.

Yet when the priest bent over her to say goodbye, William caught her gaze and its swift intelligence startled him. It embarrassed him to believe that she might know everything he'd been thinking about her. The light was playing tricks on him, for surely he could have sworn he could read forgiveness in her eyes. He dismissed the idea as an unpleasant fancy, which had caught him in a weak moment. He must be more affected by her dying than he had imagined.

Politely, William accompanied the priest to his car, to find, instead, a new bakkie, a small, pick-up truck.

'That's a handsome vehicle,' complimented William.

'My home parish in Donegal collected for it. It will come in useful when people need to move bits and pieces - and it'll carry a lot of passengers.' Father O'Reilly smacked the shiny, red bodywork proudly. 'Well, William, I must take my leave.'

'You haven't inspected my vegetable garden yet, have you Father? Come and take a look. I'll dig you up some of my beetroot and carrots to take back with you - I've a tremendous crop.' Say it, he thought. Why don't you say it? You think I ploughed up the tennis court out of spite. You think I killed my sister. You think I've been unkind to her and that's why she's dying. You think I want her to die. He dared the man to attack him. He was ready and willing to defend himself.

Father O'Reilly opened the door of his bakkie. 'I'm sorry, William, I'm late already. Next time I'm out, perhaps.'

The priest was too cowardly to accept his challenge, and this allowed William to feel superior, although that wasn't the same as winning, and he found himself even angrier than before. That meek morality! People like him wouldn't fight for what they believed in. Justice! It was one of their cant phrases, and they didn't even have the guts to fight for it.

'I don't expect you'll find me here next time you visit. Vera and I are taking off on a holiday overseas. She's been away from London for a long stretch and she's homesick for England - concerts; art galleries. Nothing to compare with that in this country, is there?'

The priest looked at him in surprise. William answered his unspoken question brusquely, indicating by his tone that this wasn't the man's business.

'No, I'll not be here when Millie dies. It's well-known that doctors don't like death. We're trained to cure, and when we can't, it upsets us and we're worse than useless. I believe in leaving that job to your profession, Father. I avoided my mother's dying. I knew it would be a problem for me and I didn't want to break down. It wouldn't have helped anyone and I prefer to do my mourning in private. Millie'll be all right. Sarah's an excellent nurse, and Jo will be coming next week.'

'She's been given permission to leave Cape Town?'

'Of course. Spot of bother at first, but in the end, when they saw it wasn't a trick, they said okay. The Government isn't heartless, you know, in spite of what you people say.'

'Well - I must be going, William.'

William remained standing a long time after the priest had roared down the drive. Pity his poor passengers - he drove that vehicle as if it were a lethal weapon. It wasn't pleasant to feel rebuked, even though he was sure he was right to act as he did. He loved his mother more - much more than that fool could ever understand. His mind jiggled a little with snapshot memories of her, especially in her later days after his father had died, when, although not yet living there, he'd been virtually in charge of Glen Bervie. They'd had so many conversations in the garden about the farm. He remembered the tea table, the smell of hot grass, bees humming, her overwhelming presence. It was hard to get his thoughts under control. There must be something that needed his attention. Ah yes, talking about Jo's visit reminded him of an earlier conversation with Vera.

He walked round to the kitchen to avoid passing Millie on his way back inside the house. He felt the pressure of her suffering. He averted his eyes when he saw her shuffling on Sarah's arm towards her room. Her faded blue dressing-gown hung over-large and awkward on her thin body. Her hair, damp and lifeless, stuck up without grace where she had lain too long on one side. He wanted the relief of her death both for her and for himself. He knew he was waiting for it just as much as she was and the process paralysed him, making it impossible to get on with anything else. He stopped himself from blaming her for delaying her dying.

William had to admit he needed Vera's cold strength to keep him steady. He admired her enormously, couldn't bear to be out of her company for long, and found himself confiding in her more now than he had ever before - even in the days when they were courting.

Vera, an excellent needlewoman, was preparing her wardrobe for their trip. Darning the toe of a silver-grey stocking, she held it up to the light, establishing its insubstantial form. Her eyes quizzed him as he entered the room. A performance of Bach cello variations gave the air substance. Vera left the farming, even the garden, to him. Inside the house was her domain.

'I haven't written to the magistrate about Jo's visit.' He knew this was a diversion - something to keep him busy. 'He knows that she will be in his district.' Preparing to take a seat close to Vera, he fetched paper from the desk and unscrewed his fountain pen. 'What shall I say?'

'About Jo?' Vera rolled the stocking into a gossamer ball, like the spider nests full of baby tarantulas that hung in the plumbago hedge. He'd come face to face with one once as a five-year-old, when,

162

tunnelling through the hedge the hairy mother spider had seemed enormous, eyeball to eyeball, and had terrified him so much he had scooted backwards out of the tangle of branches. He stopped himself from telling Vera about it. She must get so bored with his endless stories about his childhood, especially now when he should be concentrating on his letter.

'She's nothing to do with us. Tell him simply that we'll be away. If she's here when we get back, I'll throw her out.'

He liked the way she said that - such clarity, no pretence. 'Dear Mr van Jaarsveld ...' he began.

'Didn't you say his name was Hannes? You told me the two of you had got quite chummy when you met him.'

'All right.' William started again. 'Dear Hannes, My niece, Josephine Rorig, will be spending the next few weeks at Glen Bervie. The purpose of her visit is to be with her mother, my sister, Millie Rorig, who has advanced carcinoma of the stomach and liver. Do you think, as a doctor, I ought to say that?'

Vera's hand slid slowly down the leg of the next stocking. She held it away from her body and turned it. It was free of any ladders and she gave a satisfied nod. 'Millie knows what's wrong with her. Everybody in town knows.'

William carried on. 'New paragraph. I am aware that my niece is a banned person, and am writing to give you my assurance that my wife and I have no sympathy with her political opinions. However, it is unlikely that she will have either the time or the opportunity to cause trouble while she is in Fort Bedford. I gather that she has to report to the police station once a week during her time here, which is no doubt a precautionary measure on the part of the police.

My wife and I will be away from Glen Bervie, travelling in Great Britain and Europe for the duration of her visit, but I should like to take this opportunity to assure you of our loyalty to the South African Government at all times.'

'Couldn't be clearer,' pronounced Vera.

William prayed that everything would be cleaned up while they were away, not only Millie's dying, but the removals from the plots as well. He certainly didn't want to go through another interview with

Isaac Gxoyiya. If they sent another deputation of venerable men to beg him to stop the bulldozers from clearing the site, he'd have an awful job refusing to try to help. Luckily Vera, whom he admired more and more these days, didn't have any of his weaknesses. He could rely on her to keep the flag flying, so to speak.

TWENTY-EIGHT

Warrant Officer Gouws walked into Oxford Furnitures, and tapped curtly on the glass window, which divided off Tommy Albertyn's office from the rest of the shop. He then stood sideways to the glass, studying the rolls of carpet stacked up against the wall. His right hand rattled the keys in his pocket.

Tommy glanced at him over the tops of his spectacles. There was no mistaking who he was because of that combination, even though he wore no uniform, of power and threat. Special Branch. Something about the way his hair was cut short above the ears, or the way he stood; feet apart in soft, grey shoes, as if he knew he could have anything he wanted. Tommy pretended to be finishing a line of figures, although he found he was no longer able to count. Was it something he'd done? Surely they couldn't know he hadn't voted Nat? He closed the ledger, and walked round to the shop floor.

'Good morning, Sir. Can I be of assistance?'

'Warrant Officer Gouws. You are Thomas Cecil Albertyn?'

'Yes, I am.' Just like them to know about the Cecil, even though he never told anyone because people tended to make jokes about it. Politely, Tommy extended his hand, but it was ignored.

'Mr Albertyn, you've got a boy working for you called Khumalo. James Khumalo.'

'That's right. He's - '

'Any trouble?'

'No, I don't think so.' What was he expected to say? 'He ... seems honest - you know how it is with them, you only find out if they're

165

bad when they walk off with something and leave you flat.' Tommy gave a weak laugh, but the policeman wasn't amused.

'He's here now?'

'Yes. At the back. They're loading the van - I'll call him.' Tommy couldn't wait to get away. Whew! Those Branch fellows really gave him the creeps.

'Wait.'

Tommy turned in the doorway. He wore a beige dust-coat, with Oxford Furnitures embroidered in green over his right breast. He was a small, balding man, and his face had gone very red. Warrant Officer Gouws moved closer to him.

'This boy, James,' he didn't bother to drop his voice, 'he's been in trouble before. Poqo. You knew about that?'

'Er ...' Tommy was speechless. James hadn't told him, neither had Raymond, who had recommended him.

'He's been in prison - spent ten years on Robben Island. It was serious, man. Sabotage.'

Tommy felt sick. He had a jailbird working for him! A terrorist! What if head office found out about it? Poqo. The boy could have slit his throat!

'I'll get him - ' He bolted outside. He was in a funk.

'James - there's a baas in the shop wants to see you. When he's finished, come to my office. I've a few things to say to you.'

TWENTY-NINE

'So, I got the sack,' James spread his hands helplessly. He and Nomzamo were sitting side by side on his bed. 'I was thinking we might get married - and now ...' He closed his left hand into a fist and brought the right hand down onto it with a slap. 'That bloody Gouws. He's always asking - what's going on, hey Khumalo? Come boy, give me the low down. What are they saying on the plots, what are the school children planning, what are the people, die volkies, talking about now? - and I won't answer. I just look at him and act stupid as if I don't know what he's going on about.'

'Where've you been seeing him?'

'I'm supposed to meet him on Wednesday afternoons, on the mountain road, just past the Coloured cemetery, but I haven't been for weeks. Ag - ' he sat back on the bed with a hopeless thump. 'I was sick of meeting him. When I left him, my skin was itching with his dirt. Coming to see the boss was his revenge. I knew something like this was bound to happen. Oh, Nomzamo!' He turned to her, and she held him.

Still in the embrace, he nuzzled his face into the downy hollow of her neck. 'When I was on the island, the sea wind seemed to get in everywhere ... the blankets they give you are as thin as paper. I used to imagine holding someone soft and warm, a woman - I used to make myself fall asleep like that ... but meeting you has been so much more than finding someone to keep warm with.'

Nomzamo broke away. She did not hide her tears, but flicked them angrily with the tips of her fingers. 'It makes me so mad ...

Whatever good things we want, they take them away, even before we get them. Even if it's ours, they take it from us. We dance for them, and now our music belongs to them. It's a joke for them to steal from us.'

He couldn't bear to let go of her, and caught her again in his arms. 'Oh, I love you!' His arms were so tight around her that she cried out. Then they were kissing, their hungry mouths feasting on each other. When she slipped out of her cotton frock, she was a miracle to him - her small, tight breasts, her smooth belly, her furry bush.

'Oh, James!' Shy, she made him hold her close again. Their bodies trembled.

'Do you love me?' he whispered, looking into her eyes.

'Yes, I do. I love you.'

For neither of them was this the first time. Yet for them both the overwhelming sense of a beginning gave the moment the solemnity of a promise. Afterwards, they wrapped themselves in his blanket, and lay, sticky with the juices of love, planning their future.

'I must go back to nursing college next week.' Nomzamo was tentative, unsure of what he was going to ask of her. 'I've got two more years after this one. Do you want me to finish?'

'Of course. I want to be proud of you. I don't want you to have to clean white people's houses like my mother. Will you get a job in the clinic when you are qualified? You could deliver babies.'

'That takes another year - Midwifery is a separate course. I'd like to, but what will you do when I'm not here?'

He turned onto his back and looked up at the roof. There was no ceiling, just the beams and roof plates. A small hole in the corrugated iron, perhaps from an old nail, let in a sparkle of light. 'I'll look for another job. Anything. Gardening. Don't worry, I've friends among the white people. Although Miss Millie is passed away, she wasn't the only one. Mrs Fourie will look out for me too - she likes me, you know.' He tickled her, and they laughed together. It felt like home already. 'Remember the time we brought Ma Miriam's furniture?'

Nomzamo stretched her arms past his head in a huge gesture of delight. 'You made us sit on the floor of the van! My mother - hoo! hoo! - I thought I'd die laughing!'

He hugged her quickly, filling himself again with her life. 'Until I work again, Nozuko will let me eat with them. You already live here - just keep your things in my room, for now. I'll speak to Ma Miriam. If she's happy about it, we could be betrothed soon.'

Having someone in his future with him was a new feeling. He hadn't realised how much it would mean. 'I don't want to go to the mines, or the factories in the Bay.' He couldn't tell her how much his time in prison still haunted him, how it had taken away his hope. He needed to wait for her here.

'Now I've got you - ' he turned again to her, their eyes inches apart, her soft breath on his face. 'Now I know that we are together - ' He felt immensely energetic. He wanted to go outside, to be in the world again, not to hide in his room. His love for her didn't mean that they must dig a pit together. She was the very person who could lead him out of himself.

He pulled her up with him. 'I heard the bulldozers are coming to the plots today. Let's walk over to there.'

THIRTY

Jo was sorting through a clutter of papers and photographs that Millie had kept in old shoe-boxes on top of her wardrobe. She picked out a curled and yellow picture of Millie, standing dreamily on the front lawn, dressed to kill, holding a frilly parasol. She must have been the same age as I am now, estimated Jo, and found herself shaking with dry, aching sobs. I can't bear this, she told herself, gazing through the window of Millie's bedroom at the vine-covered pergola outside. There was a strong wine smell from grapes rotting on the unpicked bunches. A bee battered its body against the window gauze.

When Jo had arrived at Glen Bervie, she had found her mother so thin that she could see the outline of her skull beneath her skin. Millie was outside on the veranda, waiting for her, and as Jo ran towards her, her blue eyes were bright with the joy of seeing her daughter.

'Oh, Mother!' Jo knelt beside her chair, in an ancient gesture which begged for the blessing which her mother had never denied her. Millie's hand rested lightly on her head, then, without a pause, ruffled her hair.

'Get up with you! Bring a chair and sit next to me.'

When Sarah had come out to greet her, Jo had rushed to her embrace too, wetting her shoulder with the tears she had not dared to show her mother. Jo had sat all the rest of the morning with Millie, but when Millie had gone to her afternoon rest, Sarah had helped Jo carry her suitcases from the car.

'It's lovely not having to bother with William and Vera. Seems like the old days again,' Jo blurted, pressing Sarah, as usual, to sanction her dislike of her uncle and aunt, but Sarah turned an anxious face to her.

'Will Miss Millie get better?' They had put down the cases and stood momentarily together.

'I don't think so.' Jo's voice was high from the strain of saying it, but Sarah did not stay to comfort her. She threw her apron over her face, and was gone.

That had been two months ago. Relentlessly the cancer set its tentacles into every part of Millie's body. When the pain in her stomach became unbearable, Millie had been admitted to the hospital in Fort Bedford for intensive care. She waited until this time to speak about her dying. She was washed and ready when Jo came in with a bunch of roses fresh with dew, which she had picked that morning. Millie spoke as if she were repeating a speech she had composed during the night's darkness. 'Jo, I want you to know that I am glad, very glad, that this will soon be over.'

'Oh, Mother. You can't go yet. Please fight. I know it's hard, but please.'

Millie smiled as Jo held a sweet-smelling bud close to her face, but she was beyond even such pleasures. 'I've so many friends to see ...' She was drowsy with the drugs and fell back into sleep.

Jo drove Sarah to the hospital to say goodbye. Sarah was dressed in a dark green wool dress, draped across the bosom, perhaps, thought Jo, one that Millie had once worn, but she wasn't sure.

They found Father O'Reilly sitting at Millie's bedside. Now Millie was allowing herself to float free down a flowing river. Because of the medication, the pain no longer held her back. Father O'Reilly was telling Millie about an old mystical text that he had been reading. As he repeated it to them, the words sounded like both a prayer and like a promise. 'And all shall be well, and all shall be well, and all manner of things shall be well.'

Millie smiled. 'That's right.' She looked at Sarah. 'I'll tell Ernest...'

Sarah stepped forward, but Millie had slipped away into unconsciousness.

In the time that Jo was staying on the farm, Marge, who was still nursing in Port Elizabeth, had spent every weekend she had free at Glen Bervie. Strangely, now that the two women were no longer living around Millie's bedroom, but spent long hours at the hospital, the farm became more like the place they had known as children. Avoiding Vera's rooms, they sat mostly in the dining-room, which was still furnished as it had been in Ouma's time. Sarah, who cooked for them, made mint sauce for the lamb, and served the vegetables in the old polite manner.

'As if we were grown-ups,' giggled Marge.

They ate cold lamb at subsequent meals, spooning mint sauce over the cold potatoes.

'Like a picnic,' commented Jo.

They clung to the memory of what they had been.

Jo drove Marge to the funeral in the Chevrolet, with Sarah, Freddie, Emily and Alfred crowded into the back seat. Jo helped Sarah out, and walked with her to the church door. A man she half-knew, perhaps a shopkeeper, or the owner of the Palladium Cafe was handing out hymnbooks. He seemed uncertain about giving a book to her passengers, but she glared at him and helped herself to five copies from the pile next to his elbow.

'They'll have to sit at the back,' he whispered. 'It's against the law, you know.'

'No, it's not,' Jo hissed back, but she felt unable to confront society all the time. She'd had enough trouble getting permission to attend the funeral herself, which, as it was a gathering, was against her banning order. It was Millie's funeral anyway, not her show. The farm people were used to such treatment. Their faces showed neither hurt nor surprise. Keeping a hold on their books, they filed quietly into the back pew.

To Jo's surprise, the church was full. Jesu, Joy of Man's Desiring was being played extremely slowly on the organ. She recognised the white face and hair of the manageress of Cuthbert's Shoe Store. Her slow rendering of the hymn tunes had always been a cause for complaint. Jo and Marge had got the giggles - oh, it must be ten years ago now - when, during one of the hymns, Bobbie van Niekerk had nudged Millie and whispered very loudly: 'Needs a dose of Epsom salts!' Smiling at the memory, Jo lost control and began to sob.

At Jo's request, Father O'Reilly shared the pulpit with the Presbyterian minister from Cradock. She had also asked for Millie's favourite hymn.

Shall we gather at the river,
The beautiful, the beautiful river.
Shall we gather at the river,
That flows by the throne of God.

Overcome, Jo nudged Marge. 'Marge!' she whispered.

'I know,' Marge nodded, turning streaming eyes to her. From that moment neither she nor Marge could stop, and they wept buckets, both during the service and at the dry, gravel-grey cemetery.

Millie was buried in the family plot next to the heavy, flat, polished stone which marked the place where her mother and father lay. Her wooden coffin slid easily into the earth. Scuffing aside the green plastic cloth which covered the sides of the grave, Jo picked up a handful of dusty soil. The stones rattled on the coffin in a chorus of goodbyes. Her tears, and the uneven ground made Jo unsteady. She clung to Marge, who seemed more able to keep her balance.

'Where's Sarah?' moaned Jo.

'Don't worry. She's in the car.'

THIRTY-ONE

'Who was the heavy-set man with the double chins, who said my mother was the best-looking girl in the family?' asked Jo the next morning at breakfast.

'The big man was Cousin George from Steynsburg. He's a second cousin really. Used to send Auntie Millie springbuck in the shooting season. Auntie Millie was popular with everyone in the family - except Father and Mother.'

'I remember the springbuck! Once the train service was delayed - a derailment or something - and we had to bury it, the meat was so high!'

But Marge wasn't talking about Cousin George any more. 'For me ... when I think about it ... Aunt Millie was the one who made my childhood ...' Marge's voice was unsteady, '...shine.' She blurted out the final word as if scared of losing control.

Jo was crying again. She seemed to do it all the time.

'My mother was always so perfectly dressed. Everyone said she was beautiful - but she never hugged me or told me she loved me. Before we came here I always had nannies - white nannies, who wore starched, creaky uniforms. I hardly ever saw my mother. Auntie Millie made me feel loved. She used - on my birthday - she used to make a whole tin of fudge, just for me ... You know, those old cake tins, the round ones with the pictures of a kitten, or a spaniel on them? Must have been more than ten pounds of fudge, all for me! I could be as greedy as I liked!'

'Aah! The fudge!' Jo's voice was high, like baby's. She was five years' old again, licking the pot, with a teaspoon. The sweet hot fudge came off the sides of the pot, in ribbons.

'And the pancakes. Nobody could make pancakes like her. Do you remember how she used to make pancakes when it rained?'

'And the roses ...' At the image of her mother in the rose garden, Jo pushed her plate away and laid her head on the table. Marge knelt at her side, comforting her, and crying.

'I have such a dream that one day I'll have pots of money, and I'll buy Glen Bervie from Father, or inherit it, or something, and then I'll restore this place to how it used to be. You know, keep open house, like Ouma and Aunt Millie ... fix up the tennis court ...' During Millie's illness the garden had gone wild. There was grass in the rockery and the roses had begun to look neglected. It was frightening how quickly the place had changed. It wasn't just the tennis court, although that had been the beginning.

'I probably won't ever come back again,' Jo sobbed.

'You'll be here for holidays sometimes, won't you?'

'No, I'm emigrating. If I stay I'm part of the system - there's nothing to keep me now that my mother's gone.'

Marge was shocked. 'You've been too mixed up in politics. South Africa's a great country, you know. You need to be more relaxed about apartheid.'

'I can't.'

Later that same morning, the taxi came to take Marge to the station. She kissed Jo goodbye. 'I'm sure you'll be back - South Africa is still the best country in the world, you know. You'll find out, when you see what the others are like.' She waved out of the back window, as she used to, until the car turned into the trees.

It was time to pack up Millie's treasures. There was no one to share Jo's sadness over the photograph of Millie as a young woman. It overwhelmed her. She couldn't continue. In one quick movement, she ran all the clothes in the wardrobe together, unhooked them, and carried the bundle to Sarah and Emily, who were in the kitchen.

'Do you want these?' Jo asked, laying them on the table.

'Thank you!' Sarah tried to dance in mimic joy, but it was a poor performance.

'Oh, Sarah! Please - ' Jo begged her to stop, holding her until she was quiet. 'If they don't fit, maybe someone on the plots ...'

Sarah pulled away, serious. 'Miss Jo doesn't know?'

'Know what, Sarah?'

Sarah turned towards Emily with a 'Cha!' of disgust.

'Know what, Sarah. Please. What am I supposed to know?'

'The last people staying on the plots were moved today. Everyone had to leave. Didn't you see how empty the place has become?'

'I'm sorry. I've not been paying attention. Why is this happening?'

'Everyone had to go.' Sarah was sullen, as if unwilling to talk about it any more. She emphasised the words, 'They say it is a black spot.'

With hindsight, Jo realised that she had noticed something, a lack. She had met no one down at the river. It was bad that she hadn't wondered where the people were, who used to walk casually in the evening over to Big Jan Botha's place, and why there wasn't anyone needing to chop wood any more, or to water their donkeys. No one had mentioned the removals to her. None of the neighbours, who had visited Millie in her illness, no one in town, no one at the funeral - not even Father O'Reilly had said anything. It hadn't been in the local paper. How could everyone pretend it wasn't happening? If she'd known, she'd have ... But her imagination gave out. What would she have done?

Ashamed, she remembered Sarah's mother and Leah, and asked where they were living.

'My mother passed away three months ago. Leah is back in Port Elizabeth again.'

'I'm so sorry, Sarah. I've been thinking only of my own.' She would have embraced Sarah, but felt her stiffness, her not wanting. 'Is your mother buried here?'

Sarah nodded. She pushed helplessly at the bundle of clothes.

'Please, Sarah, walk with me to your mother's grave. I'd like to pay my respects. There's no one else visiting - we can do the work tomorrow. I'll pick some flowers to take with us.'

They took the path that went past Sarah's house. It's so small and shabby, thought Jo. It seemed almost abandoned.

'Are you living here alone now?'

'Nozuko's children sleep with me sometimes.'

'James?'

'He's in town.'

'Oh yes - William.'

Sarah didn't wait to comment, but entered the shadowy interior, returning with a yellow and green enamel jug, which she filled from the standing tap in the yard. The walls of the house looked dirty and damp, with a muddy six-inch tidal stain at ground level.

When I was little, thought Jo, it didn't look so cramped and neglected, and there were always people here. Doesn't William ever paint the place?

The rusted bottom rail of the cemetery gate fell out. When they lifted it up, the hinges went, and it collapsed completely so that they had to step over it. Sarah's mother lay under a new mound of red earth. Planted in the centre was a jam jar, which had held marigolds, but the flowers were dead.

'They don't last,' muttered Sarah, taking up the jar, and flinging the flowers and the greenish water out against the fence. Jo arranged the roses she had picked, and pushed the jar firmly back into the soil.

'Ernest is here too, isn't he?' asked Jo, and Sarah showed her. Next to his grave were two smaller humps.

'My two babies,' murmured Sarah. 'All my people are sleeping here.' She gestured towards more graves. 'My mother and father ... Ernest's first wife ... I must stay close to them.'

'I'm going away - ' began Jo, but she was interrupted by the appearance of James and a tall, slim young woman in a straight cotton frock and a woollen cardigan. They were walking hand in hand, and as she went over to greet James, she was aware that the two women were talking intently. Sarah was being told something which caused her to exclaim, and which made her face lift, even in its sadness.

James's hair had greyed at the temples. Jo could hear her mother's soft voice telling her, 'James has changed. I wish you could meet him again. He's looking more and more like Ernest in the old days - there's something of the preacher in him. Did you know Ernest used

177

to preach on Sundays? I think it was the Church of Ethiopia. Oupa had to buy him a black suit. He walked miles to all the farms around about. That was when he was younger, of course, and now James is the spitting image of him.'

Jo shook James's hand and felt herself becoming very formal. 'My condolences on the passing away of your grandmother.'

'And mine for Miss Millie. She was a very kind somebody.'

'Thank you.' Jo was speechless. She could feel the dead tug at her ankles. If I don't get out of this country, I'll die soon myself, she was screaming inside. As a diversion, she pointed across the road to where a red dust cloud hung over the plots. There was the ominous sound of breaking glass and a rumble, like thunder. 'Shall we go over there to see what's happening?'

Sarah introduced Nomzamo to Jo before they crossed the road. Wasn't Matama the name of the school-teacher who ... it was all such years ago. Jo felt angry she hadn't paid more attention to everything, even though she'd been only eleven or twelve at the time. You get punished for not paying attention, she told herself. You blame other people for that.

The houses flanking the main road had been pushed over into piles of bricks and twisted corrugated iron. Some distance away, Jo could hear a bulldozer's engine straining. The noise stopped, then started up again.

Close by, a wire fence still defined someone's yard. It had netted rubbish blown against it: a torn coat, a scrap of a navy and white spotted dress, three petrol cans, several plastic bags. A woman hurried past them. She was carrying on her head, a chipped white enamel washing bowl which contained pots and pans, judging from the shape of the greyish cloth in which they were tied up. A heavy black handle, perhaps a frying pan, was sticking out between the knots in the fabric.

'Are there any people still in the houses?' Sarah asked her.

'Ma? No, the police made everyone get on the lorries or leave. I was hiding by the trees,' she pointed to a sparse coppice of gum trees further along the main road. 'I still had some things to fetch from my house.'

178

Jo began to cough. The dust was terrible. A mongrel dog, its ribs skeletal under fur so rubbed and malnourished that the raw skin showed through in patches, was scavenging amongst the bags washed up against the fence. Jo didn't know whether her tears were from the dust, or from the coughing. She'd done so much crying lately.

'The lorries came when everyone was still asleep.' The woman spoke as if excited, hysterically. Jo could see now that although she appeared composed, she was, in fact, shaking uncontrollably. 'The police were in such a hurry, they took everything from inside the houses without waiting for it to be packed. They just threw the furniture onto the lorries. The bulldozers started knocking down the houses while the people were still making ready. Hai!' She was laughing and crying. 'Tatamkhulu Gxoyiya was putting on his trousers when his house came down around his ears!'

'Thixo!' Sarah swore. James's fists were tightly clenched.

'Is the school still standing?' Nomzamo asked softly, and James put an arm around her shoulder.

The woman couldn't tell them. She hurried away, disappearing into the red cloud. They continued towards where the noise was loudest, the air more difficult to breathe. The road was uneven, and Jo tripped over a stone so that she almost fell, then ran to keep up with the others. Sarah was pressing a handkerchief to her mouth and Jo fished out a tissue from her pocket to do the same.

'Hey!' A man in white overalls appeared out of the cloud. He was tall, taller than James, with a stomach that in a woman, would have been about to produce twins. A meat and beer man, thought Jo bitterly, her mind in chaos from the devastation around them, imagining him stuffing himself, surrounded by starving children, their bellies full of wind, their small hands held out to him for food.

'You can't walk here!' he shouted. 'What you think you're doing? This is a demolition area.'

'These people used to live here - it was their home,' Jo answered, speaking as one white to another, mediating. 'Can't they look at what's going on?'

'It's not a side-show, lady. The police have already cleared the site of interested persons. Take your kaffirs away with you, and clear off.

If the police find you, they'll arrest you, I'm telling you now.'

'But why - ' Jo was angry. 'You can't arrest people for just looking.'

'Don't argue with me, lady. This is a prohibited area.' He turned to James. 'Hamba suka!' The hard Xhosa words were ones used to address a dog.

James stepped towards him, but Nomzamo, speaking in rapid Xhosa, pulled him away. The group turned to straggle back towards the main road, and in doing so, seemed to Jo to turn their backs on her as well. She caught up with Sarah.

'I'm leaving the country,' she told Sarah, trying to distance herself from everything about them. 'Nothing I do makes any difference - I'm sorry.' She was howling again. You silly cow, she thought, why cry for yourself? You should be crying for them.

'In Cape Town,' she went on, 'I'm banned. I can't go outside the area I live in. I can't go to the theatre or the bioscope. I've got a job - in an office. I had to give up teaching because of my banning order. Not allowed in an educational institution.'

Sarah kept her distance still. Jo acknowledged silently, angry with herself for feeling special, that they weren't allowed to do any of these things either, not because they were banned, but because they were black.

They were on the main road now, and could see Sarah's house, and the trees around the Glen Bervie farmhouse. Jo's companions merged into a solid group, seemingly to turn against her. She could feel their despair, and sympathised, but she continued desperately trying to make them open up for her.

'I've got a friend, a black friend, a student. He's told me that the time has come for black people to work without whites - that we hold them back because we're never willing not to be the boss, even in liberation politics.' She spoke earnestly, wanting so much to be understood and she looked at each face in turn, but they would not meet her eyes. 'He says I'll never be able to understand what black people suffer. You've been in prison, James, for your politics. You know what I'm talking about.'

'Miss Jo?' Why was he still so formal? Making sure that she knew she would always be a white madam in his eyes?

180

'James lost his job today,' said Sarah. Her face was grim.

They stared at each other, Jo on one side, Sarah and James and Nomzamo bunched together. All of them were grotesquely changed. The gritty particles of sand had stuck to their eyelashes, reddened their hair, and marked their faces with patterns of sweat and tears. The noise of the bulldozer continued to remind them of the annihilation of streets and homes. The sun lit up the dust cloud in shafts, heightening its colour.

'It's like being in a fire,' commented Jo, and suddenly she was reminded of Millie. 'We must all go back to Glen Bervie,' she urged them. 'I've got something important to tell you. James, will you come too, please.' James looked at his mother and sensing the question, Jo continued, 'No, it's all right - William is away. I've been forgetful, I have to give you something.'

At last she could make a contribution - something that might change their lives. No longer worried about being accepted, but buoyed up with her sense of mission, Jo led them to the garage and opened its doors to reveal Millie's 1948 Chevrolet.

'James, my mother left you her car in her will,' she said quietly. 'It's not new, I know, but it hasn't done much mileage.' She opened the driver's door to check. '35,000 -' she laughed a little, weak laugh. 'All she did was drive it the three miles to town and back again.'

James said nothing, but he looked as if he had been struck by lightning.

'You can have it now. I'll get the keys and the papers - they're in her bedroom.'

When Jo returned, James was already in the driver's seat, his hands on the wheel. She gave him the keys and the engine turned over smoothly. He backed it carefully out of the garage.

'Come, Nomzamo,' he called, leaning over to open the door for her, and Nomzamo stepped in, her controlled excitement showing briefly only when she had a little difficulty closing the door.

'I'll take it home with me, if that's all right,' James's eyes had a different light in them - not friendly, but at least they were no longer standing on opposite shores.

'Fine. Of course ... It's yours.' Jo was stumbling over the words.

Her eyes were dripping again - sentimental weeping at your own beneficence, she scolded herself, but it felt good anyway. She wiped her nose with her hand, and stood beside Sarah as they waved goodbye, watching the car turn into the drive, noticing Nomzamo's casual elbow balanced on the open window as it sailed into the trees.

Jo took Sarah's arm as they turned back to the house. 'My mother left you money, Sarah. Only R200, I'm afraid - she didn't have much - and it'll take a little longer before you get it.'

'We were not servants to Miss Millie,' Sarah said proudly.

Turning her gaze for the first time since her mother's death to flowers and trees and to the far blue mountains, Jo fancied she caught a glimpse of Millie's gentle face floating away from her, until it merged softly with the cloudless sky.

Part Three

1985 - 1986

Sarah

Sarah had been sitting in the empty house for hours, waiting. William and Vera were returning from a visit to Port Elizabeth that same afternoon. She had resolved that she would speak to William straight away. If she couldn't ask in the very first moment of greeting, she would be caught up in serving them and lose her chance.

When she'd left her house, Nontu had remarked, 'Ma - going so soon? It's still early - you said yourself they'll not be back until almost dark.'

She'd smiled and shrugged. She didn't want to let Nontu see what was in her heart - not yet, not until it was settled with William. Nomhle, Nontu's two-year-old, had put up her face to be kissed by her gogo, and Sarah had scooped her up in a hug, which made her squeal and giggle. Nozinzile was the quiet one. Two years older than her sister, she was drawing intently in an exercise book that her mother had brought her from the Bay.

Nontu had asked her mother to look after the children while she was teaching in Port Elizabeth. If Nontu had to pay someone in the township to do the job on a daily basis, it would take almost all her wages. Besides it would be better for the little ones to be in the country than to live in the crowded city, where there was too much traffic and too many people.

Sarah had felt so lonely with all her children grown up and gone from home. Looking after her two grandchildren would bring back company into the house. If she got sick, young as they were, they would be there to help her. Nozinzile knew how to make tea and she could cut a loaf of bread like a little housewife! Sarah was seventy, and beginning to know it. It was time to slow down. Often, when she woke up in the morning, she would stumble out of bed with legs that felt like pieces of wood. Or she'd be so dizzy, she'd make her way across the fields to the big house with the pale morning sky whirling above her head.

Staring at her hands, lying in unaccustomed idleness on the milky wood of the scrubbed kitchen table, she repeated in her mind the walk she had taken that day through the empty house when all her work had been done. She'd stood quietly in the dining room, gauging the shine on the polished mahogany table, checking the shower, spread, as if for a new bride, across the supper dishes and silver cutlery to keep off the flies. She'd paused at the sitting room doorway, smelling its bookish smell, muffled by the carpet, and had heard the soft chime of the clock striking the quarter hour. She'd paced the forty-five steps down the passage, past the worn patch of linoleum where the telephone was fixed to the wall, past Millie's room, where her royal blue curtains with their white roses, still hung, past the bathroom, with its gleaming white tiles and white painted wooden dresser, past her old Missis's room, a spare room now, although it would always be a sickroom in Sarah's mind. All these doors had stood open, but when she came to the new wing, which William had built on for Vera, she was pleased at how shut off it was, not caring to be reminded of the sight of Vera's glass-topped dressing table with its assortment of creams and powders, nor the smart kitchenette which only Vera used, nor the antiques and paintings in the big, light study that was where the two of them mostly sat together, even now after Millie's death, when they had the whole house to themselves. All these rooms had been built after they had made Glen Bervie their home. Vera had trained a succession of new 'girls' to clean them for her, leaving the parameters of the old house in Sarah's care, and Sarah had kept it all perfect, just as if Millie was about to walk back in at any moment.

Now she reflected that in her headlong dash through each day, there was never time to look back on her life here. What had it been for? She bent her head and blew softly on her hands, as if asking

186

them. They were strong still, with fingernails that gleamed from all that cleaning. How she'd scrubbed and polished for fifty years! She'd moved away cupboards to clear out spider webs, she'd dusted and made up beds. How she'd knelt and bent in that house!

I'm old, she thought, they must let me rest now. When Vera asks me to sleep in the kitchen because William is away, it's not right any more, for my bones hurt too much in the morning. I can't stay in for her like I did for Millie and the old Missis.

She heard the car engine, and the sound of wheels on the gravel drive. Then she stood and waited. She heard Vera's heels click on the linoleum. There she was.

'Sarah, after you've sliced the salami, and made a potato salad and put out the cheese, and then made the tea, you can go home. Leave the washing up until the morning.' It was not Vera's custom to greet those who worked for her.

Sarah bowed her head. 'Madam - ' She paused. Her voice was tired from waiting and she was afraid, so afraid of asking.

'What is it?'

'Madam, please, I must speak to the Master.'

'Can't you speak to me?'

'No, Madam.'

Sarah flinched inwardly at Vera's sigh. No, she wouldn't be put off. 'Really Sarah, you people are too much. He's been driving for three hours without a break. He's had enough for one day without you bothering him. Can't it wait until tomorrow?'

She'd made up her mind. 'No, Madam.'

'He won't be pleased, you know. Take my advice for your own good. You'd do better to speak to him after he's had a rest.'

'I must speak now.'

She didn't know how long she stood this time. It seemed an age, but it really could only have been a few minutes before William was filling up the doorway. Although she still kept her eyes lowered out of respect, she made herself peep sideways at him. He had grown old like her, and his head, she now realised with the kind of shock you get when the you glimpse a familiar person as if he is a stranger, was without hair, like a freckled, sunburnt egg. He was older than herself, but he stood much straighter than she did.

'Well, Sarah?' He was almost hearty. She could see he was trying to control his impatience and that, at least, was a good omen - she must get him to listen to her.

'Baas William - '

'You're not in any trouble are you, Sarah?'

'No, Baas William, no ... it's not that.' She looked helplessly at the floor. She could not meet his gaze. Then for a moment she did. His blue eyes glittered like buttons.

She took a breath. 'Baas William - when the old Missis was alive, my old Missis ... when I was nursing her all those years, and she knew I had helped her with the old Master before her, when I was sleeping in her room at night to help her when she couldn't manage ...' William shifted a little in the doorway, making it clear that he wasn't interested in the details of what she had done in the past. She would have to get on with it. Nomzamo said that black people were only hands and feet for the whites, but she herself wouldn't believe that. 'The old Missis was saying that one day Baas William would look after me. She was promising that I would be able to live well in my old age.'

William remained silent. She felt terrible that she was reminding him of the pension, but what could she do? Surely he could see that it was time?

'Baas William, I'm getting old now, and I want to stop working. I would like to move to town. I want Baas William to give me the pension that the old Missis promised me.'

'Are you asking me or are you telling me?'

'Hai, no, Baas William.' He was saying she was being cheeky. She didn't see how she could proceed in any other fashion. She was only claiming what had been promised to her.

'I'm asking, Baas William. Please, Baas William.'

'Sarah, you do nothing but ask.' He was angry, scolding. 'I have no idea what my mother said to you. She didn't tell me about it.'

There was, inside Sarah, an enormous surprise. It wasn't anything like she had expected. She had not, until this moment, doubted this family's honour.

188

'For all I know, you're making up a lot of nonsense just to suit yourself.' She could see William's body judder in the doorway - he put a hand against the frame to steady himself. 'My mother never said anything about a pension to me. You come to me with this ... story that I owe you something ...' He stuck his hands suddenly in his pockets, but she could see they were balled into fists. Would he hit her? 'You must get this quite clear, Sarah. I don't owe you anything. I've given you a house, and good wages all these years. You've earned more than any other girl on any of the farms, more even than girls in Fort Bedford, but you people are never satisfied. You pretended to be so fond of my mother, but all you really wanted was her money. You people don't know the meaning of giving. You would never think of doing anything for nothing - or out of gratitude for that matter.'

'I'm not complaining about my wages, Baas - '

'You're the kind who never stops complaining. Now you say I owe you a life of luxury. You want to be paid, but you don't want to work. There's nothing wrong with you - you're fit and strong.'

'Baas William, I was born during the first war. I'm old enough for a pension. I've been working in this place since 1933.' The words came out without breath, as if she had been hit in the stomach.

'Then, why don't you ask the government for a pension if you're so old. You don't need to bother me for one.'

She refused to answer. Ernest had received the government pension. It wasn't much more than would pay for the rent, and perhaps a few pounds of mealie meal. Hardly anything was left for paraffin, or bread, and never any meat. She knew how her old people had to live.

Her silence made him believe he had won the argument and he relaxed slightly. 'Sarah, I'm not asking you to leave. I'm not wanting someone else to take your place. Why don't you keep on here - it's not hard work - then you can stay on in your house and have good money. You're better off that way.'

'But, Baas William - perhaps one day the Baas will sell the farm, and the new Baas will say I'm too old to work for them. Where will I go then?' Sarah didn't see how she could argue against William any more. In her disappointment she began to tremble, and she put her hands on the table to steady herself.

He gave an irritated 'Tsk!' brushing the idea away as if it were a fly troubling him, but she had seen the old people from the plots who had no one to take them in, huddled in their blankets, waiting for the lorries to fetch them to the resettlement camp near Queenstown. They had never returned, not even once, for a visit.

'Look Sarah,' he had his bullying voice back again. 'Now you're making out we're driving you away. You stay in your house - when we think of selling, there'll be plenty of time for you to find somewhere else to live.'

'Baas William doesn't understand; there are no houses in town just for asking. The township is full. I have to start looking for a long time before I find anything.'

'All right, I don't mind if you start looking, but you must never think that I owe you anything. What I owe to someone, I pay straight away. You know that about me, don't you?'

'Ja, Baas.' What else could she say?

'If my mother said something, and I'm not at all sure she did, mind, it's nothing to do with me. Did I promise anything?'

She shook her head, but wouldn't look up at him. He had her like a doll in his hands. What could she do?

'You're still fit - you carry on with your work here. You get good wages. You get your food. You get your house. Consider yourself lucky. I'll speak to Miss Vera. Maybe we can give you some time off - on Sundays, or perhaps in the evenings.'

'What about sleeping the night here?' She gestured to the floor as if pushing it away, seeing in her mind's eye, herself, wrapped in a blanket, a cold draught seeping under the outer door, the wooden boards bruising her hip and shoulder.

'What?' He couldn't believe she had the cheek to continue to ask for something from him.

'Please, I can't sleep here anymore for Miss Vera.'

'Sarah, it's not your place to say what you can and what you can't do. If we want you to sleep here, you'll do it. You've been a great complainer all your life. Don't think I haven't watched you getting the

190

better of Miss Millie and my mother. Well, you're dealing with different people now. You'll do as we say and not as you ask. I won't hear any more about it.'

He turned. It was no good running after him because he had surely closed himself from her. It was no good explaining how she had waited. How she felt she'd earned a peaceful retirement pension. She wanted to stay at home and look after her two granddaughters. They were still too young, and would need her in the house, not away all day working for someone else. It was no good grabbing him by the shoulders to make him pay attention to her life. She was nothing to him. Nothing! Not a person who could become tired. Not a someone who had spent all her time working for this one family, who had seen the end radiated by a promise - that she would be looked after, that she would not die poor and hungry. Her people did not treat any old person in the careless way he had treated her. She should have known. She had seen his mercilessness towards Miss Millie. She should have known.

She stood as if her hands were nailed to that kitchen table and let the harsh words he had spoken burn deep scars in her heart. There was blood pumping in her head and she could hear the pulse beat loudly there. It made her head so heavy that she sat down again and pressed it against the table.

Then, like hammer blows, she heard the confident tap of heels in the passage. The sound stopped. Slowly, like one who is wounded, she lifted her gaze to Vera, who stood, washed and perfumed, in front of her.

'Sarah, can you get on with the supper now, please. I'll stack the dishes for you so that you can wash up in the morning.' Vera offered this concession as if she were doing Sarah a favour.

Sarah's practised hands sliced boiled eggs onto the potato salad, cut up salami, and fetched cheese and butter from the fridge, but in her mind she felt utterly degraded, like a dog that has been struck down and punished; a mangy old bitch, cringing in the yard, kept by her owners for her bark against strangers, not for any beauty or value of its own.

When she brought the tray into the dining room, William and

Vera were sitting in the comfortable chairs that faced the view from the window. The sky outside was rose coloured and the grass had taken on a vivid yellow in the fading light. Putting down the tray, Sarah picked up the white net shower that covered the table, and folded it. Vera looked up from her book.

'Oh ... thank you, Sarah,' she drawled, in that surprised voice of hers, as if she knew nothing about the meal, had not even ordered it. William did not turn his head.

THIRTY-THREE

The way they sat at their ease in the window - such an ordinary thing - crystallised everything in Sarah's mind and propelled her out of the kitchen and across the fields before she had time to work out what she had left behind, or where she was going. Her feet took no notice of the uneven ground, yet she did not stumble. She was tall, as tall as a tree. When she reached her house, she wasn't even out of breath.

'Ma, what's happened?'

'Nontu, come. We are not sleeping here tonight.'

'But - I have already made food.'

'Carry it on your head. We will not eat here again.'

Sarah was putting on her coat. She was flinging clothes into a suitcase, then leaving it open on the bed. James would have to fetch everything for her. They would take only the food, and her few rand savings, which she kept in the bottom of the wardrobe.

Nontu and her two grandchildren were looking at her as if she were a stranger. She stared at herself in the round mirror in the bedroom and was surprised it didn't crack. There was someone else there: an old, dark face, wrinkled and with such a stern gaze. Eyes that had seen a snake at the bottom of a deep pit and knew its ugliness. No. No. No. No. Her heart felt this so deeply it thudded with each word of denial. Her watchers were big-eyed with fright, but she was beyond explaining her resolve.

She picked up little Nomhle and tied her slight body securely onto her back with a blanket.

'Come.'

Nontu wanted to lock the front door, but Sarah gestured impatiently for her not to bother. Sarah had Nozinzile by the hand and was already on her way. Her urgency made no allowance for the child's pace as she pulled her along. They passed the cemetery where Ernest and their two babies lay buried. Her mother and father were there too. Her neck hurt as she turned her face towards her sleeping dead. Then they were rushing along the straight, tarred road. Nomhle put her arms under her grandmother's chin, and Sarah hitched up the blanket that cradled the child, so that her weight was easier to carry. She glanced down at Nozinzile, seeing, for a moment's pity, her solemn four-year-old's face as she struggled to keep up.

After a mile and a half, the road crested a rise and the town came into view. What was happening there? No street lights were on, but flames illuminated a pall of smoke. It seemed as if the whole township was on fire. Because of the conflagration in her mind, it was not surprising to Sarah that everyone else should also be fighting. About a half mile ahead of them, several vans were parked on the road and to the side of it, revealing in their headlights blue-black tarmac, shapes of bushes and rocks and glittering fence wire in funnels of light: it was surely a police road-block. Luckily they themselves carried no torches and could not yet have been spotted.

'We'll take the path to the river, and cross before the bridge,' she whispered to Nontu. 'Then we can catch the road through the top houses. They can't guard every way in.'

So they stumbled across the river bed, which was almost dry, but treacherous with scattered boulders that stubbed her toes, and tree roots that tried to trip them, and thorn trees that caught hold of their clothes. Nozinzile fell, and had to be helped back onto her feet. She began to whimper. Nontu wanted to jettison the basin of food, but Sarah said, no, they would lose it to the ants or to the rats. They had brought it so far it would be foolish to throw it away now.

'You told us we must never walk here, Ma. I'm afraid,' Nontu was crying too.

'The spirits must all help us tonight, otherwise we will surely die.' Sarah couldn't recognise the cracked, harsh tones as her own voice.

Then they were scrambling up the krantz on the other side. Sarah

194

felt the sharp jab of a thorn in her foot. When she pulled it out, her hand was wet with her own warm blood. It roused her to feel pity for the others and made her sympathetic towards their exhaustion and their sobbing fear. It was time that Nontu carried Nozinzile, and for this reason it was necessary that they find a safe place to leave the basin of food.

She quietened them with a 'Hush,' and held them back so that they stood silently, listening to the small movements in the bush all around them. In the end she placed the covered basin in the shallow branches of a thorn tree, hoping that the night creatures would not discover it before she could send someone to retrieve it. Perhaps, she thought grimly, it is a further sign that I will be allowed to take nothing away with me from Glen Bervie.

They saw no patrols as they entered the township. As they drew closer, they discovered that it was the beer-hall that had been burning so brightly, but the flames were no longer leaping. It was just smouldering now. There was no one nearby. Perhaps the army had been pulled back to gather strength for one of their early morning raids. The two women and the two children sped through streets, where the silent houses had been closed for safety since mid-day. They arrived at Nozuko's door with their clothes ripped, their hands and feet bleeding. The two girls were dumb with fright. Sarah paused to pat down her grey hair, which stood up on her head in tufts. Then they burst into Nozuko's kitchen, but once inside, she could not utter a word.

Sarah registered James and Nozuko's shocked gaze. Then she was being embraced, being taken gently to a chair. The light from the paraffin lamp threw golden rings onto the ceiling. The stuffy warmth of the room was like a blanket around her. She eased Nomhle off her back, and cradled the child in her arms. Nozinzile climbed onto her lap as well. Nozuko was kneeling at her feet, washing them tenderly with a soft cloth, which she rinsed in a basin of warm water. Nozuko was crying. She put her face against her mother's torn legs, and wept. 'Oh, Ma!'

Nontu had crossed her arms over her breasts so that she held herself tightly together as she rocked backwards and forwards. 'Don't ask me!' she wailed. It seemed the whole room was sobbing. It tore Sarah's heart out of her body. She couldn't bear it. If it went on any longer, she would die from it.

'James,' she struggled to sit upright. Where was he? Had she gone blind as well?

'Ma?' He was standing in front of her. He was holding her hands. He was covering them with his big ones. It was comforting to have a son, especially one as large as he. He was even taller than Ernest had been.

'You must go at once to my house, and bring everything back here.'

'But Ma - '

'I've made up my mind. I won't stay there any more.'

'Tomorrow, Ma - '

'It can't wait. You must go now now!'

'It's too late - past the curfew. The soldiers are blocking the exit roads.'

'All right. Tomorrow then.'

The sky paled into day. James was out with the first cock crow to ask Mr Mzizi, the shop-keeper, whether he could borrow his bakkie. He explained to Sarah that he would take his car as well, but he wanted there to be only one trip so as to meet as little trouble as possible. Raymond would stay away from work to drive the pick-up.

The flight had exhausted Sarah, and she found that her legs would not to move. 'You stay home, Ma,' Nozuko comforted her. 'You stay with the children.'

'But the packing?'

'Nomzamo and I will do it.'

And they did. Her whole life fitted into that bakkie. Her children had expected a confrontation with William, but when they returned, they told her there had been no sign of him or Vera.

'They won't miss me ...' Sarah thought bitterly, and remembered one of the white children's sayings: Good riddance to bad rubbish. Her mouth felt bitter, as if she tasted the juice of aloes. Stiff in all her joints from the night's flight, she sat like a stone in the chair.

Nozuko brought her coffee, and put an arm around her shoulders,

196

bringing the mug to her mouth because her hands shook too much to hold it.

'Never mind, Ma. Rest. Raymond and I and the boys are moving to the Transkei. I wasn't going to tell you until we were sure, but it is almost definite that they want him to run the branch there. You can take over the house from us when we go. James can sign the rent book. We'll arrange it with Mr Freeman. It'll be okay, don't you worry. That's the way he likes to arrange tenants in the houses. In the meantime, I'll store your boxes until you are ready to unpack. This will be your own place from now.'

THIRTY-FOUR

The Fort Bedford High School cadets marched to *'My Sarie Marais'*
set to a slow two-step. Sitting on the dais with the Mayor and other
members of the Fort Bedford Town Council, William and Vera had
the best view. The school History master, now dressed in his khaki
army uniform, was taking the parade. He tucked his officer's baton
firmly under his right arm and marched jauntily to his position at the
head of his troops.

'Pre-sent arms!'

There was a clatter of rifles. Fifty pairs of eyes were seriously
ready to die for their country. When they brought their brown
polished boots together, a few parents clapped enthusiastically.
William smiled. He delighted in such faux pas.

'At ease!'

A slight breeze riffled the orange and white striped awning above
William's head, making it trill against its metal support. In the chair
next to him, Maggie van Zyl, Bennie's wife, put up a gloved hand to
steady her new, chiffon-draped hat. In the pause before the ceremony
began, William, savouring the irony of his remark, had
complimented her on it, saying she looked like a butterfly; a remark
which had caused her to blush and giggle like a delighted overweight
schoolgirl. Actually, he had thought she looked ridiculous. Vera knew,
he congratulated himself for the umpteenth time on his choice of
wife, just what to wear to make all the other women seem like over-
iced wedding cakes.

Bennie van Zyl, his mayoral chain dangling round a neck

thickened by numerous golf swings, stood up to present William with the freedom of Fort Bedford. Today's events were the climax of a week's festivities celebrating the anniversary of the year the British garrison, stationed in this remote farming community, had laid out the grid of streets that formed the town they called Fort Bedford.

To friends at the golf club, William had played down the honour he was about to receive. 'I'm just the oldest - the most decrepit person they could find,' he had joked, but actually, he was proud as Punch. It was the first time in the town's history that they had thought to make such a gesture to anyone.

On the whole, William felt that it was only right that he had been chosen. It confirmed the special feeling he had always had about himself. Was he not the descendant on his mother's side of the Dutch-Afrikaner theologian, trained in Holland, who could read Greek and Hebrew, and who had built a church for his flock here, as grand as any overseas? While on his other side, his father, an immigrant Scottish educationalist, had taught Mathematics and Philosophy in this very school, moulding the children of simple farming people into doctors, missionaries, university professors and members of parliament. In his veins, he felt, flowed the very best blood from the two white South African races - English and Afrikaans. He liked to believe that his own body reconciled the civil war that had been fought so bitterly between the two groups.

'Every town of consequence,' Bennie was saying, 'has an impressive historical background consisting of the memories and milestones of the past. Let us celebrate this our 150th anniversary in a spirit of respect and gratitude for the foresight and industry of our forefathers.' His pompous language was saved and made homely by his strong Eastern Cape accent. William smiled to himself, Bennie must have sweated blood over those sentences - he'd never heard him speak like that before.

Bennie had been William's partner, and still sent patients to him for a second opinion. When he turned to William, his look of gratitude and respect was one with which William was familiar and to which he responded. William listened solemnly as Bennie catalogued his achievements: an impressive school record, his courage and decorations during the war, his academic successes.

'You all know Dr William Crewe. You've all consulted him on your problems, great and small. Some of them even matters of life and death. Like our forefathers, he's never been afraid to face the truth. He's been honoured outside his home-town, but he didn't forget where he came from. He came back to us because his roots are here. Now it's our turn to pay our respects to him. He's a scientist, but a man with the common touch. He's someone you won't find easily in today's world. One of a kind which few men can equal in these modern times.'

William could feel the tears prick at his eyes, and he held himself a little straighter. That's so, he told himself. I've always done what I thought was right, and I've never been afraid of anyone. They were all clapping him. He stood up and walked forward. A good chap, Bennie. One of the best. Glad his old practice was in such capable hands. Bennie was handing him a scroll with a red seal.

'I was born in this town,' William told the rows of faces, the loudspeaker making his voice ring robustly round the field and echo against the pavilion wall. 'My mother was born here too. You all know what my grandfather built for the town. His statue is there for us all to see. My father's memorial is this school. God bless his memory.' Involuntarily his voice broke from the emotion of remembering his forefathers. Damn. Damn. Piddling people. Don't let yourself down in front of them. It was time to stop speechmaking. 'I'll treasure this honour as long as I live - ' he smiled, 'although it may not be for very much longer.' There was some laughter.

Bennie pumped his hand, reluctant to let go. 'You'll outlast us all ...' Bennie's shock of grey-black hair showed a youthfulness which William could not claim although he was equally bronzed and, when he considered his old partner's life-style, probably healthier.

It was time to stand up for the national anthem. Advocates, doctors, hoteliers, farmers, clerks, teachers, shopkeepers, and all their wives, rose to their feet. The men bared their heads for the hymn. Those children not in the cadets were massed along the sides of the green rugby field. William nodded, approving their young vitality.

Tidily dressed in their school blazers, the girls, innocent and healthy, their faces framed by white panama hats, seemed to him like a flock of pretty birds.

My father wouldn't recognise this place now, thought William proudly. He'd been content with that faded gothic school building, like something out of the Middle Ages. Now they had a new hall, modern classrooms, the best teaching equipment, the Science and Domestic Science blocks, the Crewe Library. That wasn't even counting the new boarding houses for the boys and the girls, as well as the new sports stadium where the audience now sat. Fort Bedford Girls', where Marge had gone, had recently merged with Fort Bedford Boys'; these days the government believed in co-education. Although William wasn't against progress, he was grateful that this change had happened after Marge had finished school. The classrooms and boarding house left vacant by the move had been snapped up by the army for use as their headquarters in the town.

The grave promise in the words of the national anthem made him choke again with emotion. *We will live and we will die, For you, South Africa.* He meant every word of it. He'd proved it -not like some of those singing so lustily, who'd refused, not even so long ago, to fight against Hitler. He supposed that was something that did make him feel superior to the Afrikaners in this town. Still, they were in control now. They'd lost the Boer War, but they were resilient and wily and had made sure over the years that they'd won in the end.

He himself was glad they were running the show. You could trust them not to sell out to those scum who were stirring up the natives. They knew what to do with commies and agitators and would always keep a firm hold on what was theirs. They'd never bothered to please those clever crooks in Europe and America. The Boers always acted independently, even when the Dutch were still in control, long before the English had claimed what they'd never had any right to in the first place.

In the silence before the dedication, the wind carried echoes from the location: a confused mixture of shouting, crying, screaming, and the occasional pop of what must be a teargas canister. Was that rifle fire? A machine gun? The Dominie was praying, 'Dear Lord our

201

God, bless us, your people ...' He raised his voice as if to block out the noise.

William noticed Father O'Reilly look up, as if trying to distinguish individual voices. He'd be willing to bet that the damn priest knew more than he let on. Why would he be looking so worried if he'd nothing to do with it? Although tempted to expose the priest as another one of those agitators masquerading under a clerical disguise, William decided that it would be prudent to keep his suspicions to himself.

Everyone he knew was doing their best to ignore what was happening in the location. He himself had never thought he'd get used to seeing tanks trundle down Main Street, yet now you ran into them every day. If he allowed himself to dwell on the sight of them, he would be reminded of the scarred towns he'd driven through during the Italian campaign. The soldiers today were so young, almost children. Yet their faces had that set, inward look that all soldiers have, even though he recognised most of them as sons of his patients, or of his neighbours.

He straightened his back. He wasn't asking anyone to protect him. Even if he was seventy-six, he could still shoot to kill, and he promised whoever would listen - God Himself if He were interested - that he'd take on any black bastard who came anywhere near Glen Bervie. He would manage without those tanks ploughing up his property, thank you very much. Those savages wouldn't get into his house and rape Vera. He rubbed his hands, which were sweating, against each other, and closed his eyes, the better to concentrate on keeping out those black faces he couldn't recognise, but which he suddenly saw massing round his home. In his mind he was barring doors, pushing heavy cupboards against them, piling up chairs and tables in a frenzy of activity. Where was his gun? He had to find his gun.

'Master ... Baas William ...' That bastard, Freddie, was trying to trick him into opening up so that they could grab Vera and take her away with them, but he wouldn't let them fool him. He was loading his shotgun, but the barrel - he couldn't get the barrel to stay still. Vera was pulling his sleeve. That was why. Couldn't she see he was busy? He turned sharply on her. The bitch! Couldn't she understand that he was all that stood between her and -

'William,' Vera's tugging at his sleeve continued. He opened his eyes and the green rugby field tilted crazily, then slowly righted itself. 'You're holding up the line,' she hissed. Bennie was waiting for them. He made himself very straight, and gave his arm to Vera with his usual courtesy as they joined up with the others.

THIRTY-FIVE

Like everyone else, Vera heard the shots and the screaming. Although she would never allow her face to show her fear, she was conscious of the goose-pimples rising all over her body, especially on her upper thighs. Suppose the riot spread? There was just her and William at Glen Bervie, and the Fourie's place was at least a mile away. She'd never wanted to live on the farm, and now her life was beginning to take on that nightmarish quality which one found in the kind of films she didn't like to watch. Every night they locked the six outside doors, but it was no use locking the windows, which anyone could see would shatter easily with a well-aimed rock. The Fouries kept four large Dobermans and a Rottweiler, but both she and William hated dogs and didn't want them barking and snarling every time they went outside. William's answer was to buy her a gun, but she found its cold weight in her hand repulsive, and besides she refused to stand for hours aiming at an empty beer can set up on a stump in the yard.

Three months ago, William had been called to Grahamstown for a consultation. When he'd phoned to say he wasn't coming back until the following day, she'd been furious. 'Call Sarah and tell her to sleep in the kitchen,' he'd replied when she'd explained that she couldn't be alone in the house at night. She'd actually had to walk over to Sarah's house and ask! In fact Sarah had tried to get out of it by saying she was too old to lie on the floor all night. She'd had to beg, she'd had to promise more money! Well, now she didn't even have her on the farm!

204

'I don't care if your beloved Glen Bervie goes up in flames!' she'd shouted at William when he'd returned. 'I won't be caretaker for you. If you want to stay away again, you've got to take me with you, or otherwise I'll call a taxi, not Sarah, and spend the night in the hotel.'

The situation was getting really too much for her. With Sarah gone, the new girls were completely unreliable. She'd had the carpenter put locks on all the pantry cupboards because the stuff was disappearing before her very eyes. She'd even got him to put a padlock on the fridge! Vera sighed. Millie had always taken care of things like that and took the blame if the stores disappeared. If someone had told her beforehand, that she would miss Millie, she would never have believed him. Now she had to measure out sugar, coffee, tea and bread every morning as if she were a farmer's wife, as if this is what she had come to Africa to do.

William had his eyes shut while the Dominie prayed. They had bought his suit in London on their last visit overseas and it gave him that distinguished look that made him, in her eyes, still the best 'catch' in town. She didn't regret marrying him, in fact her status here was far higher than she could have aspired to had she remained at home. After the 'Amen', she nudged him as a wife might, but his face remained empty, as if he were far away from her and the people around him.

'William!' she hissed, pulling harder at his sleeve. He jumped a little, and swayed slightly, but turned immediately and gave her his arm. He was always courteous towards her, she reflected proudly, remembering how good-looking and attentive he had been when he was still in uniform and she a student at the Royal College of Music. His war scar was a silver line on his tanned face, like one of those decorative duelling scars.

At the reception she managed to avoid Maggie van Zyl, who was looking a fright in lots of frilly blue chiffon. William was being button-holed by Bennie, who was telling him a complicated golfing story, so Vera drifted casually towards Big Jan Botha, who was standing alone in a posture as puzzled and unhappy as one of his old bulls. His second marriage hadn't been a success - she could have predicted that. Everyone said that Eileen would have left him long ago, if she wasn't waiting for him to die so she could inherit Sunnyside. Little Jan, who farmed with his father now, had still not married and had turned into a complete misanthrope. It was common knowledge that he regarded all women with suspicion and had already consulted a hot-shot lawyer in Port Elizabeth in preparation for the time when he would fight Eileen for possession of the farm.

'Hello, Jan,' she drawled.

His eyes lit up. 'Oh Vera, you're a sight for sore eyes! If I wasn't past it - '

'Shhh ... Where's Eileen?' she asked sweetly. She liked him to talk dirty to her, but there were too many people with their ears cocked. 'Cocked' was the right word for it! Smiling, she almost shared the joke - not that she'd go prancing down to the river now! They were both much too old for rolling around in the grass, but she had a fondness for him, which came from those times.

When it was all over and they rattled across the grid onto the Glen Bervie drive, William got that glazed look in his eyes again. The frequency with which he suffered from what she had begun to call his 'attacks' was beginning to scare her, especially as they came on so unexpectedly. One day he'd drive the car into a tree and that would be the end of both of them. It was the damn farm doing it. The place was sucking at his mind.

'You must get some of the boys to tidy up under the trees,' she exclaimed testily, scared of what was happening to him and trying to bring him back.

'Wha-at? Oh yes, tidy up under the trees.' He repeated her words so that she wouldn't notice he wasn't really taking them in. It was a new trick he had adopted to cope with the way he wasn't listening to her any more - and she hated it.

It was almost as if she could hear his mind whirring, like an engine out of control. 'You must be tired after the excitement.' She didn't know if he was listening. She was trying to comfort herself, not him.

The evening sun slanted green-gold through the oaks. When the drive curved and one suddenly came face to face with the house, it was still something to remark on, although there was no doubt it was getting shabby. The paint was stained and uneven and there was a long, deep crack upwards from the corner of the dining room window. William never did anything about things like that now. 'Don't bother me,' he'd say testily if she pointed it out, 'I've got much more urgent work to do.'

In fact, the only part of the farm that was doing well was the vegetable garden, which seemed to thrive and grow in inverse proportion to the way the rest of the place fell daily further into decay. The carrots and beetroot were enormous, the beans rampant, the lettuces too big for any salad bowl. There was so much, she was always throwing stuff away. William spent most of the day and half the night there. She'd even heard him crooning some sort of dirge-like hymn over the plants.

Glen Bervie had shrunk to the size of a tennis court! Alfred looked after the cows in such a lackadaisical fashion that they lived from one crisis to the next, usually caused by a broken fence, which meant the cows had strayed into the river, or worse, into the fresh green lucerne field so that their stomachs were blown up with gas. William kept on saying how this wouldn't have happened if Freddie were still alive. Fancy dying of a heart attack, right on their front lawn!

'I'll change,' she told William pointedly, but he just flopped into an armchair at the window, and continued to stare blankly forward, without hearing a word she said. She put on water to boil while she took off her dress. Soft boiled eggs and bread and butter. A children's tea, that's what she'd give him. If he wanted anything more lavish, in the old style, she'd tell him straight that it wasn't her that had quarrelled with Sarah and driven her away.

THIRTY-SIX

Sarah, James and Nozuko stood closely together in the front doorway, straining to catch sight of the origin of the dark column of smoke, which reached into the heavens. 'It's Mr Freeman's office,' pronounced James. 'They're burning the location office.'

'And the secondary school. The flames are from the school burning. Look how high they are!' Nozuko pointed to the left of the smoke, where there was a deep orange glow.

Two adolescents ran swiftly down the uneven dirt road towards them. 'Please go inside the house, Gogo, Mama, the police are coming this way. Close your windows - they're spraying tear-smoke.' The young man hardly paused while he spoke; his companion, a young woman of not more than fifteen was already further along the street, warning people in the next house.

'Have you seen Sipho? Have you seen Thobeka?' Nozuko shouted after him.

'Hai! No Mama! Sorry!' He called back.

Nozuko would have remained outside, just in case she could catch a glimpse of her sons, but James urged her to heed the advice they had been given. 'If the door is open, the police will shoot us. Come. Come inside.' He put his arm round his mother and sister and steered them into the kitchen, locking the door behind them.

'But how will my children get in?' wailed Nozuko.

'We aren't far away. We'll hear them if they come back.'

They sat at the kitchen table with the curtains drawn across the window. 'Oh Sipho! O Thobeka! What will become of them,' wailed

Nozuko. She dabbed her handkerchief at the corners of her eyes to wipe the tears, which flowed freely.

'You should have kept them at home.' Immediately James was sorry he had spoken sharply, and he patted his sister's hand in an attempt to soften his words. He was desperately worried about his nephews, and about Nomzamo, who, because she was a nurse, was right in the front line. On top of that he was afraid his mother was not used to the kind of militancy that the young people were using, confronting the police, making the beer halls and the schools a site of struggle. To be honest he'd been out of the way of political thinking for so long that it scared him too. The children should have been back hours ago ... If they were involved ... Nozuko should never have let them go to school this morning ... If they were his children, he'd be more strict with them ... Yet he scolded himself for blaming Nozuko, who was desperate enough already.

'Nomzamo says, at the clinic, if the children come in to have their wounds dressed - the police take away anyone with a bullet wound even before they are attended to. She says they ask for the doctors' case notes, and then go to their houses to pick up the ones who've been sent home.' He picked at a splinter of wood off the table, then banged his fist before standing up to stare through a gap in the curtains.

'Aah! Sipho!' Sarah cried out in fear. Sipho was the younger of the two boys, only twelve years old. James could have bit off his tongue. What was he doing speaking about all that? He searched through the window, but couldn't see anything move outside, just the houses across the street, shut up tight, like their own. Remorsefully, he turned and pressed his hands on Nozuko's shoulders.

'Don't worry. They're smart. They're probably hiding somewhere until it's safe to walk in the street. It's good that Raymond has asked for a transfer to the branch in the Transkei. The rural children are quieter, and your boys won't lose any more of their schooling. When was it they were last attending?'

'January - ' she counted on her fingers. 'Six months! I remember how I wanted to go to school so much it hurt me just to think about it, but now they don't care anything for it.' Her eyes were looking inward at that other time. 'After a while Miss Jo got so clever she didn't want to speak to me any more. And James, you ... you just jumped away each morning, leaving me, when I was caring for the small ones, without looking back to say you knew how I felt.' She glanced at Sarah. 'I'm sorry Mama, I don't blame you, but I have to speak about it, when everything is so different now.'

James had forgotten how it had been for Nozuko. He felt bad that he'd been so hard on her today, and, it seemed, even in the past. He could still vividly remember those days when the sky arched blue over his head, when his feet scarcely touched the ground. Three miles to town hadn't seemed far! Enchanted by the memory, he sat down quietly. If he closed his eyes the dark small kitchen disappeared, and he could see himself on the road with the other children.

He held Nozuko's and Sarah's hands across the table and looked earnestly at them. 'That's why I was so willing to let Nomzamo finish her studies even though it meant she went away for the two whole years, and then another one for her midwifery - why I worry about those two now.'

'The children say that prison is a better school.' Nozuko seemed bewildered. Her moon-shaped face, meant for kindness and mothering, had aged. His sister wasn't an old woman!

'They've left us behind, Nozuko. It's the generation gap. What they have experienced makes them stronger than we were. I admire them for it. They won't accept any more what we longed for. Now the government sends the army into the schools to force the students to learn - as if that will make them study! They send white boys, not much older than the students themselves, who think nothing of killing, even a child in a school uniform. What have the whites taught their sons to make them happy to kill us?'

Nozuko's eyes were wet. 'Thobeka is always arguing with Raymond. What kind of respect is that? You've heard him, Brother! How can he say his father is a drunkard? You've never seen him drunk - that's true, isn't it?' She put her hands briefly to her face, pushing tightly against her cheekbones.

'Thula! Thula!' Sarah hushed her, but her eyes were wet too, and

210

frightened.

'Now Thobeka says his father's weakness pays the police wages,' Nozuko went on, 'and Sipho says school is a rubbish building where they teach us black people we are rubbish too.'

'Well, it's gone up in flames today!' James couldn't help smiling, and then he was laughing without being able to stop himself. Nozuko caught on, and then his mother, and they laughed and cried at the same time, at the fearsomeness of it, and, he had to admit, at the beauty of it too.

But their laughter could not live while the children played with their lives. 'His teacher said Thobeka is very clever and might do well if he worked harder,' Nozuko mourned. 'Perhaps if he had some learning he could do more for our people than he is doing now.'

James sighed and leaned his back against the uncomfortable wooden chair. Perhaps his mother should lie down and rest - he should make her, but how could she sleep when she was so anxious? No one in the whole township would sleep tonight. He followed Nozuko's thoughts. 'I used to think education was like yeast - that those who received it would lift up everyone else - the whole people. Mr Matama believed that.' Despair caught him again, as he imagined that small energetic man being led to the place of hanging. What had he always said? Analyse your situation, and then act on it. If enough people believe strongly about something, we can change it. He had never been one to think like a victim.

'The white people are used to having their own way,' he continued. 'They swallow everything that's good - the land, then the jobs. Even the schooling they saved for themselves. Now they kill our children when they refuse to accept second best any longer. We should be proud of our children, not angry because they are critical of us.'

Nozuko pushed her chair back and began to pace the room. Four steps to the stove, four steps back again. She picked up the chair and put it against the wall. It was almost as if she were getting the place ready for the removal van. 'As soon as they come home, I'm going - I don't care what they say, I'm taking them away. I'm not waiting for Raymond to find us a place to stay.'

There were shots, then a sustained burst of machine-gun fire, then a loud explosion, like a car's petrol tank blowing up.

'My God!' James was on his feet. What had he been thinking about that he'd forgotten the car!

'Don't show your face at the window!' screamed Nozuko. She stood rigid, her fingers in her ears.

'It's in the next street.' In his relief James put his arms around Nozuko and held her tightly. Remembering his mother, he moved back to her, explaining that there was no danger as yet. Sarah sat stoically, without a murmur of fear. There's a stubbornness in the old people, thought James. It's a strength that has kept us going all these years.

'I should have moved the car, Ma. I'm not sure where, maybe out of town altogether. If the soldiers come into our street, the comrades would think nothing of using it as a barricade and that will be the end of it. Fire is our weapon, when we don't have guns.'

There was nothing more to say between them. 'Please God,' James prayed silently. 'I'm only a poor man. This car is all I have. My wife is having a baby - she has already lost the first one. Please help us now so that we can still live.'

THIRTY-SEVEN

William met Marge's train at Cookhouse station. He gazed at her - his daughter - as she strode towards him, looking tall and stringy, her straight blonde hair held back from her face with tortoise-shell clips.

'Hello Dad!' Her voice was frank, her face freckled, her mouth wide and thin. He had forgotten how much she resembled him both in her features and in the way she moved. There was nothing of Vera's controlled femininity in her. He took one of her suitcases, and they walked together to the car, which was parked with several others outside the office, which sold tickets to whites only. Whatever was happening to petty apartheid in the rest of the country, where there seemed to be a general scramble to dismantle the 'Europeans Only/Slegs vir Blankes' signs in banks and post offices and on park benches, William admired the South African Railways for keeping to the racial divisions which had been set down when apartheid was still respectable. They at least had the courage to stand firm against outside pressure.

'Good trip?'

'Yes, thanks. Slept like a log, and then I woke at six to watch the mountains.'

While he was unlocking the boot, she marked out a noughts and crosses game with her middle finger in the dust on the car roof. He wanted to say irritably, 'Don't do that!' but held himself back.

'Playing a lot of tennis?' he asked. She had brought her tennis racquet.

'Quite a lot. I'm in the hospital A-team. We have matches on

Saturday afternoons.'

'The Transvalers still won't let you play tennis on Sundays?' She had moved to a teaching hospital in Pretoria.

'That's right!' They laughed. He felt as if his face would crack. God, he couldn't stay on his best behaviour forever!

'Your mother's very pleased you're coming. She's not as strong as she was. I thought the drive to the station would tire her.'

'Fine.' Marge was looking at the veldt as they travelled towards the farm. 'You need rain badly.'

'It's terrible. We've not enough grazing for the cows. I've had to buy in feed.'

'Look!' he exclaimed, stopping the car.

A whole family of grey monkeys - at least a dozen - were crossing the road. They moved in a smooth, uneven bound, their bums in the air, their tails high. One carried a baby, which held tightly onto her from underneath her body. They swung over the barbed wire fence on the side of the road, glancing fearfully towards their watchers. Their eyes, outlined in black, showed up on delicate, alert faces. In the same fluid movement, they disappeared into a clump of wild plum trees, shaking the leaves as they clambered along the branches.

'Oh - marvellous!' breathed Marge. Tears were streaming down her face. She was sniffing and wiping her eyes with the knuckles of her right hand. Just like Millie, thought William, disgusted. He hated the idea of his own daughter taking after his sister.

He felt his old anger at Millie clotting the blood vessels in his neck and, moving his shoulders to loosen them, he launched into a diversionary anecdote. 'The monkeys are a damn nuisance. They come right up to the house to scavenge. With the drought, there isn't a lot for them in the veldt, so I was feeding them oranges, tempting them onto the veranda. I wanted to see how close they would dare to come - one of them even ran right into the bedroom. Your mother said I had to choose between them and her!' He laughed. 'In the end I was forced to shoot one to drive them away.'

'Shoot a monkey?' He wished he hadn't told her. Now he'd revived the memory of his tender victim. He'd had to order the boys to bury its pathetic, limp, body.

214

He started the car. 'We'd best get on.'

Vera appeared on the veranda to greet them. It was unusual for her to make this kind of gesture for visitors, and Marge looked surprised.

'Hello Mother.'

'Hel-lo dear.' Both women presented a cheek to be kissed. The two faces collided briefly. Good heavens, this was going to be more than he'd bargained for.

Marge was already heading for the kitchen. 'Sarah, Sarah, where are you?' she called.

Vera raised an eyebrow to William, who hurried after Marge. Vera had never stopped blaming him for Sarah's departure. Said he must have behaved quite frightfully to make Sarah go off like that. Said she couldn't run the house without her. It was Vera's way of demanding that it was time to move to town. She hated being stuck out on the farm when there was trouble all over the place, but he wasn't going to let go of Glen Bervie so easily. He had his own plan of action. He hurried after Marge, who was talking in the kitchen to the latest new girl Vera was trying out. Marge turned to him, looking surprised.

'She says Sarah has gone to live in town. Is this true?'

'I'll explain.' William urged her back to the front of the house, taking her arm in a friendly coercive gesture. 'Let's all settle down first - okay?'

'Mother used to be so pernickety,' Marge dropped the statement into the silence after Vera had gone to bed. She said it, not as an accusation, but quietly, as if out of a need to understand.

'Everything costs the earth,' William grumbled, watching Marge's face closely as she gazed round the sitting room. He was suddenly acutely aware of the dinginess of the velvet curtains, and the grey film of dust, which seemed to have settled on the china, which was supposed to decorate the mantelpiece. It wasn't his business to see to things like that. He uncrossed his legs to stop them from stiffening.

'I told you Vera hasn't been herself. She's been looking forward to your visit, you know.'

William knew it was an odd thing to say about Vera. Marge had been summoned, there was no way round it. She would want to know why.

'You haven't been home for a long time,' he began.

'Don't blame me. Everything's changed here. It's not the same place.'

'I don't know why you keep saying that.'

'But it's true. Now even Sarah's gone. It started before - before Auntie Millie died ... The tennis court - I mean that was truly a terrible ...'

'Now you're being unfair. That's still the best improvement I've made around here.'

'It's ... it's not just the tennis ... although .... Oh drat, I can't explain, but for me everything's gone sour. People don't get the welcome they used to. Well, anyway, the people I knew who visited here. Aunt Millie never made anyone feel she was doing him a favour.'

William was on his feet. He wanted to get out ... clear off somewhere else. He strode to the door, but knew that it wouldn't do to leave her before he'd put his proposal to her, so he returned to stand in front of the empty fireplace. 'We're your parents. You've no right to criticise us, and keep on comparing us to your Aunt Millie. You'd think she was some kind of saint the way you go on about her, or an angel. She was no angel, just a perfectly ordinary woman. Well, she wasn't even ordinary - a damn idiot most of the time. You were lucky you never had to live with her.'

'I did.'

'Not as an adult. She was really most infuriating - pigheaded, like a child really, irresponsible, doing exactly what she liked. She was - unreliable. Your saintly Aunt Millie. Do you know - no you don't - she was a dirty thief. There you are. I've said it.' He had run out of words. The audacity of accusing his own sister in public - that is to anyone except Vera - almost floored him.

'What do you mean?' Marge was on her guard.

'I wouldn't say it if I couldn't prove it.'

'How?' Her eyes, so like his own, stared blue.

He softened his voice. He couldn't afford to fight with her. 'No, honestly. She lives here rent-free. She eats everything we put on the

216

table - she's greedy, always having second helpings - huge amounts of pudding. She never buys anything except what she fancies. I mean, we don't eat fudge and meringues and the kind of unhealthy treats which she and her friends stuff themselves with. Rorig didn't leave her a penny, so what could we do? Mother supported her, and now she's dumped on me.'

'You sound like she's still alive.'

'Do I?' Startled, he tried to explain. 'People in town gossip about us. Not our friends - hers. I've been keeping a book, a sort of book of reckoning. I write down everything that happened as I remember it. Maybe that's what makes me imagine it's still going on. One day I'll make that midget Father O'Reilly read it and eat his words. I'll fetch it.'

He rushed to his study. When he saw the tall black accounts ledger on his desk, despair caught him. It was useless to show it to her - she'd never bother to read it.

'Here it is.' Returning with the book, he flicked through pages of closely written text. 'This is like the balance sheet of my life: good and bad. I've not left anything out. Read it.'

'No, thank you.'

Her rejection hurt. 'I'm your father. Even if you aren't on my side, you should listen to what I have to say. If you think I treat Millie badly, you have to remember there's two sides to everything. Doesn't matter to you what she costs me. Doesn't matter to you that she never does a stroke of work. Doesn't matter that her personal hygiene is such that I'm ashamed to be seen in public with her.'

'Dad - I won't have you say that.'

'I've written it all down - everything is proved. Even her stealing from me.' As he tapped the book, he heard in his head the echo of a judge's gavel. They were both on trial here and he was fighting every inch of the way.

'Stealing?'

'Nasty word isn't it?' He put all his days and weeks of disgust into his voice.

'But what? What would she steal?'

'The family silver! Sounds like old-fashioned melodrama, doesn't

217

it, but it's true. Mother's silver teapot and hot water jug, and the matching cream and sugar dishes. Worth over a hundred Rand - not that that's the point. One day I look for it - I don't know why I suddenly suspect it's gone, and I'm right. Man, William, I say to myself, it's got to be somewhere. I look all over the place, but it's nowhere to be found. Millie's too ill to ask her - I've got some finer feelings even if you don't think so - so I drive into town to Harry Cohen. You know the jewellery shop next to MacIntosh's Chemist?'

Marge nodded. He had her attention at last, he could see that. '"Harry," I say, "Between you and me. Don't breathe a word." I have to admit it was embarrassing talking about such things outside the family, but he was very understanding. Do you know what he says? Says he'd been worried about it at the time. He'd almost rung me, but then thought it wasn't his place to interfere. Old Harry saw the position I was in all right. He was very apologetic.'

Marge opened her mouth, but this time, he held up his hands to stop her. 'No, I'm not finished yet. You know the blue and white soup tureen that used to stand on the sideboard? I'm not very observant about things like that, so I didn't miss it until Vera pointed it out to me when we were having dinner with the Lootses. Large as life in their china cupboard! Our tureen! Vera says it was Minton. What am I supposed to say? Ask for it back? Goodness knows what else has gone.'

'But you inherited the farm, didn't you? I mean you had more than your share. Surely the silver and china …'

'Look, you have to get this into your head: the farm's nothing more than a liability. I often think I run it as a charity for the servants. I've done nothing but pour money into it ever since I got it. Even before that, when Mother was alive, I was paying her a monthly allowance as well as for all the repairs and so on. I've bought this place twice over. You just come here for holidays - you don't see it like it really is.'

How could he explain to her how he felt about the place? He walked over to the window and opened the curtains a little. The light reflected the image of the room back at him until he put his forehead against the cool glass and stared into the outside darkness.

218

'Millie crowned me king of Glen Bervie once, you know.' He stood for a moment with his head still touching the pane. Its smooth cold surface calmed him and he was able to turn back to Marge with a laugh at childhood folly. 'She made me a crown - I even had a sceptre. Oh - we did everything by the book! Years' later I was actually given a piece of paper to prove it was mine. Nobody could take it away from me, nobody could prospect here, or drill for oil, or anything. No one could live here without my permission.'

He kept silent for a moment feeling the pressure build up inside him. He wanted to put a fist through the glass - anything to distract his rage.

'Then I find it's not quite as simple as that. Little bits are being taken from me all the time. The natives - even if they've worked for me for years - help themselves to everything the minute I turn my back. I padlock my vegetable garden. I get the Government to take the surplus people off the plots. But they're really perverse, you know, and they just have more children to replace the ones we removed. Now when I go into town, the piccaninnies besiege the car, asking for money. It's like a plague - I can't get rid of them.'

'You mean they shouldn't have been born?' Marge seemed to have drawn a shadow round her. He rubbed his eyes, which were playing tricks with him in the electric light. It was the way she was sitting - that stillness - for a moment he could have sworn it was his mother there.

'Don't put words into my mouth.'

'I just meant that they have a right to be here the same as us, surely?'

'You're talking like that damn cousin of yours with her twisted ideas. I thought everyone with those kinds of opinions had packed up and left years ago. Or perhaps,' he was sneering at her now, bullying her into going his way, 'you've been listening to those murderers in the locations, who necklace anyone who doesn't toe the party line. Have you thought about them, hey? This country is in danger from people like that. I've told you many times: no one has rights, except what the government gives us. We don't get asked if we want to be born. Sometimes it's better that we hadn't been.

What's so wrong about saying that?'

He had never heard Marge argue back before. Now her voice was so soft he could hardly catch what she said, so that he had to lean forward towards her from his position in front of the fireplace. He held on tight to his book of accounts.

'When I was little, you always talked like this with the visitors, but I never listened. I can't argue with you. I like to be doing things. Aunt Millie used to coach my tennis. Jo would be reading, but Aunt Millie and I would be on the court for hours. She used to give me these marvellous shots to return. No matter where I hit the ball, she'd manage to send it right back to me each time. The rallies would last for ages. I dream about them still as if they are the most perfect moments of my life. If I had the money, I'd restore the tennis court - whatever you say.'

'You?' William snorted. 'A nurse doesn't make that kind of money.'

'I know.' Marge's voice was like a scratch.

William wanted to say, 'Fat lot you really care about the place - you don't visit much,' but he kept quiet. The clock began to strike eleven. It whirred and groaned. It was a most lugubrious clock, William decided. He didn't know why he hadn't thought so before.

'Dad, doesn't the cricket worry you?' Marge's voice rose. 'It's been driving me crazy all evening.'

'Oh - I'm sorry. I don't hear the notes in the top register any more. Where's the noise coming from?'

They moved the sofa along its casters, finding, at last, a shiny, jet creature under the carpet. William caught it and held it between his forefingers, then opened the front door to throw it outside. They stood for a moment in the doorway. He could not see the moon, but when he looked up to the sky, the stars dazzled his eyes. Outside, on the rockery, a tall aloe silhouetted a huge, shaggy head.

'If you don't come home to be with your mother, I'll have to sell this place.'

'You can't blackmail me like that!'

There was a pause, then William tried again. 'Please, Marge, think it over first.'

'Dad, I've got my own life now. It's really impossible for me to let

220

it go.'

William hadn't expected her to refuse. She wasn't married yet, and this was her home. Surely it was a daughter's duty to look after her mother. 'You could get a job in Fort Bedford Hospital, but you wouldn't even have to work. You wouldn't need money.'

'Like Aunt Millie?'

'Marge, please don't push me. It's not easy to ask.'

'It's not easy to refuse either, but it's really impossible - it wouldn't work at all. What about Sarah? Can't you ask her to come back?'

He avoided looking at her. He wasn't going to let her see how desperate he was. Not even Vera would ever get that close. The light from the open door lit up a green rectangle on the lawn into which their shadows fitted. He talked to them.

'You haven't heard the whole of it. After all these years with Mother, with being with the family, Sarah doesn't care a toss about us. She refuses to work just when we need her most. Oh, she wants the money all right, but she doesn't want to work for it.'

'But why did she move to town?'

'More of her damn cheekiness. One day she didn't turn up for work, and when I went to see if she was ill or something, the whole house had been cleared out - without a word to us!'

'Maybe you should ask her. Maybe she'll come back if you talk to her.'

'Go crawling to her?' He couldn't get over the fact that she and Vera both wanted him to do that. They were forcing him.

'Look, you need her. It's not such a terrible thing to have to tell her that.'

He stiffened. How could she say that he needed a native?

'Mother does, anyway. Do it for her sake. You asked me for her sake.'

'I'd rather sell up.'

'Oh, Dad, please don't ... it's ... Glen Bervie's not something you can sell.'

He wasn't going to listen to her getting sentimental about Glen Bervie, especially when she wouldn't lift a finger to save it. It would be on her head, if he sold it, and anyway, she would never be able to afford to live here after he died.

'We're getting to the stage where we're too old to stay out here alone. I have to sleep with a rifle next to my bed in case we're attacked. If I died tomorrow, your mother would be in the soup.'

She put a hand on his arm. It took all his will-power not to shake it off. 'At least try to get Sarah back. Maybe then it'll feel easier.'

'You don't give me much choice.' He hoped she felt badly about it. 'Mind you, Vera and I aren't sentimental about Sarah, the way you are. All the natives I've ever met are selfish and unreliable and just out to get as much as they can from us.'

'I'm sure there was a reason - '

He'd had enough. He shook off her arm. 'Are you calling me a liar?'

'I just thought ...'

'Well, don't.'

Bats were swooping across the sky into the eaves. Their quick shapes crossed his retina like the flicker of a migraine. He had to be alone. 'I'm going for a walk - '

'Goodnight, then. I'll turn in - you should as well, it's really late, you know.'

He'd finished with her - gave her a wave and was already hurrying down the drive. His feet crunched on the gravel, telling him, in spite of the darkness, that he was still on track. He didn't have to think about the direction he was going because he knew it would be to the river. The night air was blessedly cold against his hot face. He lifted his arms as if he were swimming, taking in deep breaths.

The lucerne field was already heavy with dew that drenched his shoes as he crossed it. He had forgotten to take the key to the gate into the river-bed, so he climbed over it like a thief. Now that people no longer walked over from Big Jan's place to visit on the plots, the path along the bank was overgrown with mimosa scrub. Acacia Karoo. A thorn snagged his trouser leg. Damn, without the moon there wasn't enough light to see properly. Another branch pulled him back. This time the material ripped. If he wasn't careful, he'd get back to the house with his clothes in shreds. Slow down, he commanded himself. Look before crashing through. He wanted the high ground of the krantz. When he reached it, after stumbling against sharp rocks, grazing his hands on shale that crumbled beneath his fingertips, he straightened up and turned to stare back at Glen Bervie. Marge must have turned off the lights because the house was invisible except for a darker mass of trees where he expected it to be. He couldn't discern any of the roads - not even the white gate-posts.

Because of the drought, the river was no longer running through the pool at the foot of the krantz. The stench of the water drifted upwards, making him wrinkle his nose in disgust. A night owl screeched - it was hunting probably. His mind was whirring again. He hated the jumble his thoughts made. Walking helped him to sort through the words and images over which, these days, he seemed to have so little control. As he followed the path down again, across the dry river-bed and over the gate, he found he was talking to himself.

'You promised it would all be mine one day, Mother.' As he came up the drive, she was drinking tea on the lawn next to the house. He waved at her in a friendly, loving way. A sunshade was stuck into the back of her chair.

She seemed to ignore him. 'Don't you care about what's happening to the place?' he muttered, gesturing violently with both hands above his head. He had caught her attention at last, and she smiled graciously, putting down her cup and saucer on the green-painted garden table.

'Please help me.' He was sobbing and she wouldn't like that. Men don't cry. 'You're on a losing wicket,' he told himself sternly. 'Pull yourself together, man.' He stiffened his shoulders and began to hum. The tune was one of the hymns they used to sing on Sunday evenings after supper - wish he could remember the words. He gave it a marching beat and dug his heels into the gravel in a military fashion.

'A title deed is just a scrap of paper, man,' he interrupted the hymn to scold himself. 'What did you expect? Like holding onto ... air!' He laughed at the idea, grabbing at nothing in a burlesque pantomime. He nodded towards his mother, who smiled lovingly at him. 'I'll be a good loser, Mother,' he called to her. 'I promise you won't see me make a song and dance about it.'

He turned away from her and began to plan. 'Buy a house in town - no, a flat,' he muttered. 'No garden; no land at all. Better that way. Serviced.' He loved that touch. 'Get Sarah back, then tell her to bugger off.' The idea gave him more comfort than he had expected. At least he'd be free of them at last.

He was at the tennis court. He kept the key for the padlock on his belt. It opened smoothly, as always. Six hundred perfect square yards. The rows dug and banked with military precision; beans staked; asparagus mulched; lettuces just beginning to head. He turned on the tap that started the sprinklers, sniffing like a dog at the rich smell of dry earth receiving moisture. Paradise! This was as he had planned it.

The words of the hymn came back to him and he sang to the tune, which crashed through his head.

Oh God of Bethel by whose hand
Thy people still are fed;
Who through this earthly pilgrimage
Hast all our fathers led:

Our vows, our prayers, we now present
Before thy throne of grace:
God of our fathers, be the God
Of their succeeding race.

Hearing the other voices join with him, hearing his own young voice, he stood, as if in a trance, his face and hair streaming, his clothes sodden with the water from the turning spray.

THIRTY-EIGHT

'Next!'

The skinny sister on Sarah's left nudged at her knee, and then pointed to the white clerk who had called out. Flustered, Sarah gathered up her pass-book, and moved quickly to the counter. The man flicked through the pages.

'Jou naam is Sarah Khumalo?'

'Ja, Baas.'

'You want to apply for a pension?'

'Ja Baas. Please Baas.'

'Where's your husband. Is he working?'

'He's late, Baas. A long time ago.

'What else have you got to prove your age and status?'

Surely he could see that she was old? He barked out his words in a flat, bored voice. 'Birth Certificate. Baptism Certificate. School Certificate. Marriage Certificate. Your husband's Death Certificate.' He sighed as if it exhausted him to have to explain such elementary things to such a stupid someone.

'I've got papers at home, Baas - the Death Certificate and Marriage Certificate too. We were married in 1930.'

'Bring them with you. Next.' The room was hot and stuffy. The man looked as yellow-pale as the dust that had settled on the files piled up at the end of the counter. He smoothed down his thin, reddish hair.

Applications for pensions were processed only on the first Tuesday of the month. She had to wait four weeks before she could

225

spend another day at the magistrate's court in the long, patient queue. This time she brought all her papers. The same man looked through them. It didn't take him more than a minute. He scribbled on a form and pointed an inky finger at the place where she had to sign.

'When will I get the pension, Baas?'

'We'll let you know.'

'How long will I have to wait, Baas?'

'This application has to go to Pretoria,' he gabbled at her. 'They look at it there first. If they pass it, maybe three to six months. Sometimes a year. I can't say.' It was something which simply did not interest him.

Sarah worried as her savings dwindled. If it wasn't for her grandchildren, she would have gone mad thinking about it. The little girls twined their arms around her neck and put their fragrant faces next to her old, wrinkled one. Nomzamo had a baby boy. James had wanted to call him Ezekiel after his old teacher, Nomzamo's father, but Nomzamo said she wanted to look forward, not back. So they had called him Tambo. Such were the times they were living in that the name didn't cause any surprise among their friends and neighbours. Everyone was writing their rebellion on empty walls in the street, or even wearing T-shirts with slogans on them: One Education for Freedom ... The People Shall Govern ... Troops out of the Township ... Sarah didn't like to think that James might sympathise with such things - he'd been to prison once already and a second time would break her heart - but she knew better than to voice her misgivings, and soon the baby's name seemed an ordinary thing.

'Oliver ... Tambo!' she'd chant, pretending to toyi toyi like the school children, and the baby's sweet body would ripple with delight.

With three children to look after, there was more than enough work for her in the house, and slowly Sarah's old bustle returned. Although always at the back of her mind was the worry about when the pension would be paid out, and whether she would be able to manage on such little money. She didn't want James and Nomzamo to be out of pocket because of her. The money Nontu sent wasn't enough to cover more than minimal expenses for Nomhle and

226

Nozinzile. She knew Nontu was struggling to send even such a small amount, so it was no good asking for more.

Three months passed. In the beginning, she began every day fearing that William would appear suddenly at their front door. She expected him to order her to return at once to Glen Bervie. Furtively she looked out for him so that she wouldn't be taken unawares. At night she dreamed he stood over her as she lay sleeping, scolding her for not being at work. She dreamed he held a gun at her head and made her run all the way to the farm. She dreamed that Vera forced her to scrub the dining room floor twice over, saying she hadn't done it properly the first time. Indeed, when she looked, there were inexplicable muddy footprints all over where she had just cleaned. When she opened her eyes in the morning, it took a moment before her panic subsided, and she allowed herself the luxury of snuggling against Nozinzile's warm body. Slowly the dreams became less urgent. Slowly she began to feel at home in this house. She began to plan another kind of life.

Then, one day the white Cortina parked in the street outside. Heavens! He had really come after all this time! He was opening the new wooden gate, which James had recently put up. The next door dog began to snarl.

'Voetsak!' shouted William, but the dog, a large angry animal, mottled brown and black with a suspicion of a bull mastiff in its ancestry, only barked more fiercely and began to worry at the wire fence between the two houses. Hurriedly, Sarah pulled out the suitcase of clothes from under her bed and searched through the neatly folded layers for her white apron. There it was! She pushed the rest back like a bundle of washing. She was busy tying the apron when he knocked loudly on the door. A safety pin? Her fingers felt clumsy like a handful of sausages.

He was rattling the door handle. He wasn't a someone you could keep waiting. She opened the door.

'Good morning, Sarah!' Although he had to raise his voice to be heard, he was trying to make it sound breezy and without anger.

'Good morning, Baas William.' She held tightly onto the door frame. The dog was hysterical - it did not like the scent of white people. 'Thula!' she shouted at it, and it cringed, but kept up a quiet growling.

'We thought you were sick. We were worried and went to your house. Why didn't you tell us you were leaving?'

She stared at the ground and hardened her heart.

'You should have given proper notice,' he was beginning to scold like he used to. 'You know it's against the law to go off the way you did.'

What could she say? Didn't he remember how he had looked at her? How he had told her his mother's promises were none of his business? What would be his comment if she told him straight out that he had betrayed her - that they had all betrayed her?'

'Well? Don't just stand there. You must have some explanation.'

She couldn't keep up her silence, but she still stared down at his feet, imprinting the image of his polished brown boots and white woollen ankle socks under the stiff pleat of his khaki trousers. 'I'm old now, Baas,' she whispered.

'I've already told you we're willing to give you more time off. Miss Vera said I should say that particularly. She wants you to come back and she sent me to find you.' It seemed he was not allowed to return without her. She had some value then.

She rebelled at the very idea of working in that house again. She'd made her break - there was nothing at all that invited her nicely. Miss Millie and her old Missis were gone, together with their kindnesses and their promises.

'You're not supposed to come to town. It's illegal for you to stay here. You're a farm girl, you aren't allowed to live in the location.'

It couldn't be true that she wasn't allowed to stay with her family. 'I've put money into this house.' She gestured towards James's addition to the small dwelling. 'Mr Freeman knows I'm here. I did the building a long time ago.'

'What?' He didn't understand what she was talking about.

'When James came back to Fort Bedford, after ... When James came back, I built on a room for him here. It was Nozuko's house then. Miss Millie gave me the seventy rand I needed, and ten rand more. It wasn't borrowed, it was given. Mr Freeman knows it's my

228

money.'

'My sister had no right to do that without asking me. You were my girl ...' He spoke slowly, as if thinking about something else rather than the words. She knew he had said he would never forgive James nor let him come back to the farm, yet his own sister had built James a place to live. On top of it, she'd left James her car in her will. Sarah could almost see the ideas catch fire in William's head. Let him think what he liked. Although she feared him, she wasn't going to let him take away anything that was hers. She kept a sullen silence.

'I'm taking you to see the location manager. We're going to sort this thing out right now.'

She had to go with him. The dog threw itself against the fence as they passed. Pink and brown lips were drawn back to reveal strong sharp teeth that, given a few inches, could have sunk themselves into William's leg. William pretended not to see it. He unlocked the back door of the car.

'Get in.' She obeyed. Her will was strong, yet hidden. She smoothed her starched apron across her lap.

They were at the location office. He strode ahead of her, not even waiting to make sure she was following him. He pushed the policemen aside and walked straight into the inner office. Mr Freeman, looking shabby and tired, came forward with his hand outstretched. William ignored the hand.

'Look here, Freeman, this girl of mine is living illegally in the location. I thought it was your job to make sure things like this didn't go on.'

Mr Freeman's mouth, which had been smiling politely, set into a sad grimace. Instead of replying to William, he turned first to look at her. 'Molo, Sisi.'

'Molo, Baas Freeman,' she whispered, standing as close to the door as she could.

'What?' William turned for a moment, surprised at the interruption. 'Oh ... What do you have to say to that, hey, Freeman? Speak up.'

'Dr Crewe, I know this old girl well. I know her children. If she wants to live with them, I don't have any objections.'

'She's my girl. She lives on my farm. It's illegal for her to move to town.'

Mr Freeman relaxed a little. 'If I'm not mistaken, Doctor, your place is near that old black spot on this side of the river?'

'Yes?'

'The position is, Doctor, we had clear instructions that Bantu from that part, because it is situated within the three mile radius from town, if they have connections with Fort Bedford - work or family connections - may be considered eligible for housing in the location if such is available. She is living with her son. Besides that, the family have occupied that stand for a long time. You could say they have rights there.'

Mr Freeman sat down behind his desk, and started to write something on a piece of paper. His action seemed to dismiss William.

'But she's my girl.' William wasn't as sure of himself as before, but he still acted as if he could tell Mr Freeman what's what.

'Dr Crewe, she's an old girl. Isn't it better for you if she moves now and you get someone younger? Think of the future; she's going to be a liability to you. Then you'll be coming to me begging me to find a place for her - and where will I put her? If her own family will look after her, isn't that less trouble for both of us?'

William couldn't stand still. Tap, tap ... his heels were hitting the wooden floor. Mr Freeman still wasn't offering him a chair, but William looked far too angry to sit down. 'Mr Freeman, I'd appreciate it if you'd keep out of what isn't your business and didn't tell me how to run my affairs. I'll report you to the magistrate, who, by the way is an old friend of mine, for interfering between me and one of my employees ...'

'Dr Crewe, you won't be able to substantiate that complaint. I'm not telling her where to live. She can still work for you - I'm not stopping her.' Mr Freeman was beginning to be quite happy with himself. He tilted his chair back slightly, and looked slyly at William, almost like a child who knows he has got away with something naughty. William had made a mistake thinking he could order Baas Freeman about.

'All right, Freeman. Have it your own way, but I'm warning you, I

230

won't forget this in a hurry.' Sarah knew William never asked for anything twice. He was out of the door in three strides. 'Come,' he ordered as he passed her.

He got straight into the front seat and started the engine. His fingers drummed on the steering wheel as he waited for her to shut the car door. She had a sudden panic that he would drive her all the way to Glen Bervie, like in her dreams, but he stopped in front of the house in the township, keeping the engine running.

'Could you live here, but still come to work on the farm, like Mr Freeman says?' He didn't turn his head, but his voice pinned her down.

'I'm old now Baas William. I can't walk so far anymore.'

'If I pay for a taxi to bring you in the morning and fetch you home in the afternoon?'

He, who never compromised, had bent over to accommodate her. She couldn't deny him any longer. Besides, the wages would be a help, until the pension came through - and even afterwards, if the money wasn't enough. There were plenty of youngsters living nearby, who were at a loose end, who wouldn't mind a small job looking after the children for her during the day.

THIRTY-NINE

For five rand a week, James drove his mother to the Glen Bervie turn-off, and then fetched her again in the afternoon. When the white people had finished their midday meal, and the left-overs had been divided amongst the servants, when the dinner service was washed and put away, the stove burnt out and the kitchen swept, Sarah would sit down under the shade of the waterless gum tree which had once marked the boundary for the houses on the plots, and wait for her taxi.

Vera had expressed the wish that on no account should the taxi bring Sarah all the way to the farmhouse. Allowing a native taxi onto the farm, especially as a regular feature, would, she said, make the place look like a slum. Her guests would be surprised at such a vehicle. For this reason, neither William nor Vera recognised James as the taxi-driver who brought Sarah to work each morning, especially as, a few years back, he had exchanged Millie's old Chevrolet for a newer second-hand Chrysler.

Sarah realised that the move to town had been a turning point in her attitude towards Glen Bervie. When she trailed along the dusty lane that joined the farm to the main, tarred road, she wondered where she had found the strength to run to work all those years. As if being on time for these people was the most important thing in the world.

Emily, Freddie's widow, now came in only two days a week to do the washing. Sarah lingered with her over breakfast, watching the bees feast on the smoky flowers in the plumbago hedge, which hid the two of them from the sight of the house. 'I should get back to work,' Sarah sighed.

'Let the young ones do it now, you can afford to stay a little longer before she will notice.' Emily's hands gave off a strong smell of blue washing soap. She'd not complained when Freddie was alive, but now, with most of her life behind her, she grumbled all the time. 'I've never tasted anything except soap,' she said. 'Samp, porridge, meat, potatoes - ugh! All soap! My stomach must be as shiny as a new pot!' She laughed generously, opening her mouth in a wide O, showing four front teeth missing in a smooth gap. 'When I'm dead they must cut me open to look. I'll be a miracle, cleaner than any madam!' She clapped her slender hands together at the thought.

'Cleaner than her,' Sarah replied, her laughter bitter with hate. They both fell silent, thinking of Vera's soft white hands, her clipped English vowels. How she fussed if Sarah's brown fingers touched the inside of the vegetable dish, as if they carried some disease that only black people had. For most of her life Sarah had accepted that white people thought that way about her, but now the idea boiled inside her, making her want to put down the serving dishes and tell them to help themselves, and not make her wait on them at their meal-times if they couldn't respect her.

The two new maids pulled faces at Vera behind her back, and giggled together after she had scolded them. Tenjiwe boasted that she could clean a bedroom in less than ten minutes and they raced each other through the housework in order to have a longer time to sit gossiping under the pine tree, where they would be pretending to clean vegetables. Sarah did most of the cooking, unless Vera wanted to prepare something special. But Vera seemed tired too, and no longer entertained as often as in the old days. She'd sit for hours listening to the radio with her eyes closed - stories and plays mostly, or an occasional concert from Cape Town - but when the news came on, she'd switch it off angrily, and stare out of the window.

Old Mrs Crewe had always listened to the news before coming to the dining room for lunch - the pips were a sort of signal that Sarah should make everything ready. Now, as soon as the news came on, Vera would storm into the kitchen and order Sarah to dish up immediately. If William was still listening, Vera would ring the dinner bell imperiously to summon him. She avoided the sun, and her eyes would blaze in her white face.

Sarah watched as millions of small ants dug their way through cracks in the walls, and swarmed onto the window sills and across the pantry shelves. Occasionally she'd wipe them off, but there were so many, a few dead ones didn't make any difference. They were looking for jam or sugar or any fresh meat or butter, the food Vera kept locked away in cupboards or in the fridge. Millie used to discourage predators by setting the table legs in tins of lime, and by keeping a watchful eye out for the first signs of their invasion, but Sarah found herself welcoming them, as if she had called them up. She deliberately didn't draw Vera's attention to their moving columns. Vera herself didn't seem to notice, or if she did, she didn't know what to do to stop them.

Occasionally, when Sarah had a chance or reason to look in at the bedrooms, she noticed spider webs looping across the ceilings. The kitchen shelves were sticky with a film of grease. Sarah decided that if Vera wanted to tell the young 'girls' to clean up, that was fine, but it wasn't her job to scold them. She hadn't the energy to make it all shine as in the old days. In fact, it pleased her that, without her care, the house deteriorated.

She kept the dining room table a small bright island in the midst of this dingy house. Its mahogany surface gleamed with polish scented with rosewater. The silver butter dish and the knives and forks sparkled at the cut-glass water jug and salad bowl. William's cucumbers, tomatoes, beetroot and lettuces were heaped onto the table. His gem squashes, green beans and peas overflowed the vegetable dishes. The potatoes, as firm as beautiful white apples, were piled high with plenty of butter and parsley. She served the onions in a delicious thick sauce, which nestled round their shiny skins. She used all the tricks Millie had taught her to make the vegetables taste marvellous, but William and Vera sat at the table like two dried-up sticks. They ate almost nothing. The left-overs were heaped onto the large enamel bowls Sarah and Emily and the others carried home on their heads at the end of the day.

'Grandma, have you brought beetroot?' Nozinzile would ask. She loved all the salad things. Seeing the children's healthy faces shine with pleasure made Sarah feel less tired. When they'd finished eating, she'd allow them onto her lap, and they'd all three rest, until it was time to do the evening chores.

The farmhouse was old, like she was. Sometimes she fancied she was pulling it down around her! Except for the dining room table, which she kept just so, for Millie. Occasionally, when she gathered mint from the garden, she'd pick roses to fill the centre vase and mass them together like Millie used to do.

Vera would even remark on it. 'Oh, you've put flowers on the table, Sarah.' In that surprised voice of hers, which was a calculated insult.

Sarah said nothing, but inside her mind, she answered, 'I didn't do it for you. I'm putting flowers on a grave you can't even see.'

FORTY

'They're raising the rents by R1.80 a month.'

'Yehova!' Sarah was appalled at the idea of having to find the extra money.

The young man looked at her as if measuring her anger. He wore a pair of skinny blue jeans and a dark T-shirt. Smart, she thought, not lazy. The girl with him, who wore a faded blue and white cotton dress and sandals, was still a child, but perhaps nearly a woman.

'Gogo, you know me. I'm Sizwe Zwakala.'

'Of course - Sizwe! How are you?' Sarah could not get over how much he had grown from the youngster that used to accompany his mother so quietly to church.

'We are all well, Granny.'

'I remember when your mother was pregnant with you. You were such a big baby. We used to joke and say she must be carrying twins!' Laughingly, Sarah put out her hands to indicate Beauty Zwakala's size.

The girl giggled shyly.

'Granny, this is Nodumo Sigibi.' He put an arm round her shoulders to bring her forward.

'You should be ashamed that you are not both in school.'

'We will go to school later on.'

Sizwe explained to Sarah how everyone's rent was used to support the Bantu Local Authorities, which had been appointed to run the townships. 'They're making us finance their apartheid. The councillors are just government stooges - we didn't elect them. That's why we say everybody must stop paying rent.'

'But where will I go if they throw me out of my place?' Sarah looked involuntarily back through her open front door to where Nozinzile and Nomhle were playing quietly so as not to wake Thambo.

Sizwe's white tennis shoes came to attention. 'If everybody refuses, they won't be able to pick on one person.'

'They could still ... '

'Granny, you have to do as we say. It's been decided. We are the Comrades. We are not waiting any longer for democracy and we have grown hard. The government doesn't represent us. The councillors don't represent us. I don't want to threaten you, but we burned the beer hall. We burned the school. We can burn down houses too.'

That night James said the same thing: that they should join the rent strike. 'We've got power if we can stand together in this,' he explained. 'A tree can't grow if its roots are cut off. Apartheid puts its roots in Africa, in the African people, but it is a foreign tree and its fruit is eaten by the white colonists. We must kill the tree, not nourish it.'

She hadn't heard such talk from him for years. He'd been so quiet since coming out of prison, just building up his taxi business, loving Nomzamo and his son.

Nomzamo nodded. Her face was in repose and you would have thought she was agreeing to something quite ordinary. 'It is time to do this. You will see.'

Sarah saved the rent money, and gave fifty cents to Sizwe when he came to collect it every week for the Comrades. The rest she put in a tin, which she kept hidden under her clothes in case the council ordered her to pay up or leave. The council refused to collect the rubbish in an attempt to force the residents to pay their rent. James and two other volunteers hired Mzizi's pick-up and raced round early every Monday at a crazy speed to pick it all up and take it to the big dump on the top of the hill behind the township. The streets had never been so clean!

The government-appointed black councillors didn't like not getting the rent. They called a residents' meeting, but no one came. Then, one late afternoon, the new 'Mayor's' house went up in flames.

Because it was the smartest house in the 'location', white visitors to the town used, before the troubles, to be brought to gawp at it. The Fort Bedford businessmen would explain that this proved how well-off the natives were under apartheid.

Beauty Zwakala came to fetch Sarah when she got home from work. 'Quick,' she urged, 'or the house will be ashes before you get there.'

Somehow the curtains in one of the front rooms had caught alight. Yellow tongues were licking the roof timbers and the corrugated iron buckled and cracked as the fire pushed its way upwards and out into the air. Sarah used her hands to shield her eyes from the intense heat. 'The flames are so hot you would think the devil himself were in there!' she joked with Beauty.

The 'Mayor' was desperate to save his furniture. Because no one would give him a helping hand, he alone had carried out as much as he could before the fire had begun to rage too fiercely. His lounge suite stood forlornly in the street, but it was still close enough to the house to be in danger of being burnt by a falling spark. Every time a piece of the roof timber exploded onto the ground not far from where his things were piled up, the 'Mayor' jumped to stamp out the flame.

Then the police vans and the fire engine pulled up. It was an occasion for the crowd to gossip together asking when was the last time a fire engine had been called out for a house in the township. 'This must be a very important somebody,' a man's voice called, and they all laughed.

But the laughter died away as three Casspirs and a Buffel pushed their way through the people. The huge armoured vehicles threatened and dwarfed those who stood in the washed-out, muddy street. Soldiers with guns poured from the belly of the Buffel. They wore combat uniforms, which speckled against Sarah's eyes and shimmered in the air, which was watery from the heat of the fire. They had hard faces, and their smooth hair was hidden under army caps. Then more police vans screeched to a halt, so close they were spitting up stones and dirt against Sarah's body. Policemen were right inside the crowd, grabbing young people and forcing them into a

238

van. Beauty screamed that they'd taken Sizwe. She moved towards the van and Sarah went with her.

Beauty had Sizwe by the arm and was trying to pull him back. A shoulder of one of the men who was throwing children inside, got in the way and she lost her hold. 'Baas,' she screamed, 'Baas, please, he's my child ...'

'Fock off - blerrie meid - ' he jerked her away. 'Gaan huis toe!' he yelled in her face, striking her body a hard blow with his rifle so that she fell to her knees. Sarah rushed to help her up again.

The sergeant with a loud-hailer spoke what must have been a command to disperse immediately, but Sarah, who was trying to calm Beauty, did not hear the exact words. There was a pop on the ground a foot away, and white smoke billowed out from what looked like a beer can. She heard herself scream before the breath burnt her lungs, and then she too was running. There were gun-shots, and she saw a boy with his arm around another, who had fallen. She was too old to run fast. She had lost Beauty. She was choking. At last Beauty was with her again. Running and falling, crawling together along the road towards her house, she thought her body would break.

That day, forty-seven children were taken into custody. Parents of children who had disappeared gathered at the police station, but the sergeant said he could not say who had been detained. James was phoning Port Elizabeth to find a lawyer or a white politician who could speak to the police, because they would not talk to the parents.

There were so many gunshot wounds to treat in the clinic that Nomzamo did not come home at all on the first day. On the second and third, she was only home to sleep. Her face was grey with tiredness.

'We're trying to treat people in their homes now, because the police are watching the clinic. If anyone has a bullet wound, they are arrested,' she told the family. The estimated number of detained rose to seventy-eight.

Four days later, a policeman called at Beauty's house to inform her that she could fetch Sizwe's body. He told her that Sizwe had been taken to Port Elizabeth where, using his shirt, he had hanged himself suddenly when the policeman, who had been interrogating him, had gone down the passage to make Sizwe a mug of coffee. In death, his face was swollen from a broken jaw, and his eyes were buried in the dark bruises that were all around them. There was dried blood in his ears. There were wounds all over his body, and burn marks too.

The police made a statement at the inquest, which was held in Port Elizabeth. They were in such a hurry to get it over. They said they were sorry there had been no time to inform the family beforehand of the inquest. They blamed the unrest in the townships for their haste. James read the newspaper report to Sarah and Nomzamo. There had been a fight among the prisoners, it said, which accounted for the condition of the deceased's body. The matter was under investigation and the police were interrogating all those detained with Sizwe, but so far no one would admit to being involved in assaulting him. Black people were naturally violent towards each other, the report said, and it was not unusual to have riots amongst prisoners. The police had proof that the fire which had burnt down the 'Mayor's' house had been a deliberate act of arson. From their investigation, the police had evidence that Sizwe was implicated in this and he had probably hanged himself because he was too scared to face trial and imprisonment, or possibly the death sentence. His suicide was thus proof of his guilt as a terrorist, and as an undercover member of the ANC.

Sarah sent a message to Glen Bervie to say she was ill. She helped Beauty wash Sizwe's broken body, and stayed with her through the nights before the funeral. The house was crowded with the many people who came to pay their respects to Sizwe. Two more children died from bullet wounds sustained that day, and it was decided that all three youngsters would be buried together in a joint funeral service. Beauty hardly left Sizwe's side, so she had very little to do with the arrangements, which, it seemed, were being made more by the community from which he came, than by his mother and family. Mourners from towns all over the district would be attending, and the Bishop of Port Elizabeth himself would speak at the service.

Miraculously the police and army stayed away from the township on the day of the funeral. It seemed as if they'd had orders to give the people this one day of freedom so that they could bury their dead. Buffels and Casspirs blockaded the roads leading into the white town, but they refrained from patrolling the streets, which had been kept from sleep throughout the previous night by the screech and thud of buses arriving from places all over the Eastern Cape as well as other, far away cities like Johannesburg and Cape Town.

Early in the morning the football stadium, where the funeral ceremony was to be held, began to fill up. The young people had held a vigil there throughout the night. Sitting up with Beauty and other members of the family, Sarah had heard their singing; the voices amplified the family's more private sorrow.

Alala engalele
Amabhunu ekhaya
The boers can't sleep
Alala nezibhamu
Amabhunu ekhaya
They sleep with their guns

Adubula abantwana
They shoot at the children
Bantwana e Soweto
The children in Soweto

Adubula abantwana
They shoot at the children
Bantwana KwaLanga
The children of Langa

Adubula abantwana
They shoot at the children
Bantwana e Fort Bedford
The children of Fort Bedford.

By ten o'clock everyone was packed so closely together that latecomers had to be satisfied with standing room only. James had helped with the arrangements for the funeral, but although many of the planning discussions had taken place in her home, Sarah could never have imagined what she experienced that day. She sat with

Beauty near the three coffins which were draped in green and gold and black - the colours of the African National Congress. Where had the flags come from? When she whispered the question, Beauty merely shrugged. The ANC, she seemed to imply, was still there, even though it had been banned for more than twenty years.

Sarah watched as two athletic youngsters climbed onto the scaffolding above the unfinished stand opposite where she was sitting. They were finding a good vantage point from which they could watch the ceremony. Further along the scaffolding four young people were tying up a large banner - black letters on a white ground - TROOPS OUT OF THE TOWNSHIPS. Next to the banner, a flag flapped red and yellow and black in the slight morning breeze: UNITED DEMOCRATIC FRONT. At first Sarah had tried to count the people streaming into the stadium, but there were too many too close together to separate into numbers, and they were still arriving. Thousands. Tens of thousands. A hundred thousand. Sizwe has put Fort Bedford on the map of the history of our country, she thought. A sixteen-year-old boy!

Buses continued to arrive. When one stopped, you could see everyone standing up inside, and as the door concertinaed open, the youngsters jumped out, toyi-toyi-ing towards the stadium, their arms raised, their feet stamping the ground. Yet when they entered the great mass of people, they joined the silence of the crowd. The day's temperature was climbing, and the sun began to burn Sarah's neck. She opened her umbrella, making sure Beauty shared in its shade. Beauty stared straight ahead of her, seeming to notice nothing of what was happening around her. All her weeping seemed to have flattened out her features as if they had been washed away. Sarah did not want to imagine how it would be if it were her own son in that coffin. Although she herself had lost two before they had grown even a little bit, this death was different.

The Bishop opened with a prayer. Father O'Reilly read from the psalm: 'Thou preparest a table before me in the presence of mine enemies. Surely goodness and mercy will follow me all the days of my life and I shall dwell in the house of the Lord forever. He prayed that the Lord send peace and reconciliation amongst all the people in

242

the country.'

Sarah didn't know who had decided that James be a main speaker. The loudspeaker crackled and then his voice was everywhere. Magnified many times it echoed from each side of the stadium. It seemed as if he had been speaking to great crowds all his life.

'This government is making war on our children. Sizwe Zwakala, Matthew Xulu, Xolili Mbombela were not yet adults. They should have been at school - learning Mathematics, learning History and Science and Languages - but we all know what our schools have become under apartheid and how our children have had to take up the cudgels to fight not only for a better education system, but also for our freedom, the freedom of their parents from all the unjust and humiliating laws we have to live under. We must never forget that they have sacrificed their lives for us. Apartheid has robbed them of their futures ... '

Beauty was wailing in a thin monotonous cry. The whites of her eyes tilted upwards. Sarah pushed Beauty's head down between her legs to stop her from falling into a faint.

James was finishing his oration. 'We must not be afraid to stand together. Freedom must come in our lifetime. If not in our lifetime, then, like these Comrades, we too must be prepared to die for it. We are the people of South Africa. The people shall govern. The struggle is ours. The strength is ours. Amandla!' He punched the air. He was asking the crowd to give the response. Arms were raised like a forest of trees.

'Ngawethu!'

Sarah beckoned to one of the young men, who were acting as marshals for the crowd, to fetch water for Beauty. He returned with a plastic bottle full, which she splashed on Beauty's neck. She crushed her handkerchief and poured water on it, spilling some on her dress. Never mind, it would dry quickly in the hot sun.

'Put it to your forehead, Sisi. We'll be moving soon.'

There was a moment of laughter in the crowd, and some clapping. What was the next speaker saying? She whispered to Zwelethu, Beauty's brother, who was holding her on the other side.

'What did she say?'

'She says,' he smiled wryly, 'the government is a lot of cockroaches.'

'Oh ...' How many times had she not pictured William and Vera like that?

They were all standing for the Black People's National Anthem. She raised her arm and sang with them.

Nkosi sikelel' iAfrica
Lord bless Africa
Maliphakanyis uphondo lwayo
Exalted be its fame
Yiva nemithandazo yethu
Hear our prayers
Nkosi sikelela
Lord grant Thy blessing
Nkosi sikelela

Yisa moya
Come Spirit
Yisa moya oyingewele
Come Holy Spirit
Usisikele
And bless
Thina lusapho lwayo
Us, her children

The women's voices took the refrain higher. Sarah had never heard the anthem sung by so many voices before, as if all the nation sang together. She imagined the sounds coming together like a map of Africa, with its rivers and mountains and open spaces. The men's voices were like the ground, the women's flying above them, like the sky.

The great crowd began to move towards the gate of the stadium. The young ones were in front, running and singing. Nomi kubi siyaya - even in our troubles we continue marching forward. Such a sweet tune for these strong words. Sarah sang with them. She took Beauty's arm and helped her up. Zwelethu was on Beauty's other side. Sarah's feet kept the rhythm of the song. They joined the crowd, which

244

surged out of the gate and down the road - ten, twelve abreast, packed closely together in the narrow road. The bearers, Sizwe's comrades, who carried the coffins on their shoulders were singing too. Siyaya. The downward slope of the hill tilted the coffins forward as they ran.

'Make way please - '

She had to let go of Beauty's arm as the young men ran past her with the coffins. One, then another, and yet another. They wore khaki uniforms and black berets. The green, gold and black flags were still draped over the wood. The young men's hands gripped the silver handles and they carried each coffin high, like a salute. Sweat was pouring from their faces, which looked ecstatic, as if the words of the song were keeping them going. Sarah, who had not cried yet, now wept. Oh, these dead ones! Oh, these young people!

She wanted to stop, to give herself time to weep, but she also needed to be part of that great forward rush. The young men were not hurrying their friends to their graves, they were running towards their freedom, taking their dead comrades with them.

Beauty was crying that she could no longer keep up. They broke from the crowd to drink water from a street tap, where a group of women were already gathered. Sarah could see how the people filled up the road as it dipped towards the small stream that ran through the township and then up the hill on the other side. There were no cars. Father O'Reilly passed them, walking with two nuns from the convent. There were hundreds of faces she did not recognise, as though, for this one day, Fort Bedford had been changed into another place altogether.

The cemetery was a hilly two acres of red earth. There was a large pepper tree at the gate, and a high hedge of prickly cactus. Sarah tried not to step on the graves, but she was pushed from all sides. The loose soil tripped her up, and she almost fell. Hands stretched out to steady her. The crowd parted to make way for Beauty and herself, so that they could stand at the open graves, their earth sides cut sharp and deep. The coffins were already lowered.

Sarah looked round at the mass of people pressing in on her. Everywhere umbrellas opened against the hot sun. A black and floral canopy covered the multitude, which flowed round and away from the still point at its centre. So must the thousands of people have stood, when Jesus preached. The thought reminded her of Ernest, telling his parishioners about the time when Jesus walked amongst the poor people of the earth. Sarah wanted to tell this to Beauty, but Beauty was staring downwards at Sizwe's coffin, as if nothing could comfort her.

Then, as the people sang again, many helped to fill in the graves. Beauty crumpled to the ground. When the three mounds were smoothed over, the young men, their faces full of pity, carried her home.

FORTY-ONE

Sizwe's funeral started James on a new life. First he changed his name.

'I want to be called Mkhuseli, Ma, like you named me when I was born. Why should I have a white person's name? When we work for them, they are too lazy to learn our language, and they give us names that are easy for them to pronounce, so that they can call us when they need us without thinking that we may be busy with something of our own. They believe we were born just to serve them, and that we have no culture that is our own. How often have you heard them say that we are backward and stupid, yet we have to be twice as clever as they are - more even, because we have to learn both their languages as well as our own. Why, some of them only speak one white language! I'm sick of all that nonsense and the false white mask they want me to wear. I'm Mkhuseli Khumalo like I was born to be.'

'Right!' Sarah smiled, seeing how well he was looking with eyes that were bright and strong. Amandla ngawethu! The strength is ours! She was proud of the way he spoke, and because everyone looked up to him and relied on his wisdom. But she was troubled that he was so seldom at home and worried if he was delayed past the time he was expected to return. He travelled to meetings in Port Elizabeth or spoke at other funerals in Uitenhage and Cradock. So many people were dying in the struggle that the funerals were becoming political events. How can the government ban a funeral?

She became accustomed to seeing Mkhuseli's photograph in the newspaper. Mkhuseli Khumalo speaks at the mass burial of the five victims of police shooting during demonstrations in Kirkwood. He was at the microphone, tall and serious, the mourners crowded round him. There was a UDF banner behind his head. Then: Mkhuseli Khumalo, with other members of the unofficial location committee meet with the Fort Bedford Town Council and representatives of the business community to discuss the boycott of the town's grocery stores.

Mkhuseli told her how he had coughed to hide his smile when he saw that Mr Albertyn was one of the businessmen on the negotiating group. Tommy Albertyn had pretended not to know Mkhuseli when he was introduced and Mkhuseli had thought it prudent not to remind him. Perhaps with his new name Mr Albertyn hadn't recognised him. Mkhuseli had joked that night with Nomzamo that now he had proof that all black people looked alike to a white somebody, and Nomzamo had shrieked with laughter. 'Do you hear that Tambo? Your father is learning how to make fools of the white people!' And as she'd danced the child round the room, their shadows played together on the walls.

'No, you must listen,' Mkhuseli told Nomzamo, holding her quiet in his arms while he talked. 'We were in the Mayor's parlour, the holy of holies! Dr van Zyl chaired the meeting and we blacks sat down on the leather chairs around their wooden table which was so polished we could see our faces in it - with ashtrays ...water jugs ... glasses ... note-pads ... free pens ...'

'Be careful,' Nomzamo was serious, 'you could get used to such luxuries, you know.'

'I spoke for all of us,' Mkhuseli's voice changed to a deeper tone, 'I said they should come and see for themselves how we have to live. I told them, "You should come and inspect our roads. It's not safe to drive on them, they're so rutted and full of holes that you easily damage a petrol tank or get a puncture, and who pays for that?"' He moved back to his chair and sat down next to Sarah, while Nomzamo still stood jiggling Tambo on her hip, trying to get him to sleep. The two women were carried away with him now, into that place, hearing him speak on their behalf.

'I told them,' Mkhuseli continued, '"We need more taps so that we don't have to wait so long for water or have to carry it so far. Besides, it's a health hazard when the water spills onto the ground and lies in pools where the people and animals have to walk." I said, "Sickness doesn't know the rules of apartheid. What affects us will spread to the whites as well. Our people have decided that we cannot pay rent when nothing is done for us where we live. We want the rubbish taken away and the streets cleaned up properly, and they should be lit at night. We spend money in your shops, but nothing comes back to us. It all flows one way. This must change. The have-nots must have something too."'

Sarah wrote to Nozuko about what was happening in Fort Bedford: 'I know Mzizi is more expensive for sugar and beans, but we have to buy there now because the children make sure no one shops in Main Street. Now the white shops are threatening to stop deliveries of food into the location if we don't also buy from them. Mkhuseli says the white businesses are losing too much money and they are afraid they will go bankrupt! I am pleased he is so much in the forefront. I'm hoping that this way the police will not put him in prison for being a trouble-maker. I know the council need to talk to him about what they can do to stop the boycott. The people in the township consult him all the time. He is at a meeting every night! Now the council has promised they will spend money tarring some of the roads. Can you believe they're saying that they will put electricity into the houses next year!'

Then there was the death of the policeman. Everyone knew he boasted to his friends about killing Sizwe and threatened other prisoners, saying that they should watch out, or the same thing could happen to them. No one admitted to being present when the petrol-soaked tyre had been placed around his neck, and his body turned into a burning torch. Mkhuseli was in Cookhouse on that day, so the police had no reason to believe it was him, although a week later they came to the house to fetch him.

They kicked open the door and shone their strong torches into the sleeping rooms. 'Khumalo! Come! Dress yourself. We're taking you to the station.' They didn't have a warrant, but Mkhuseli had gone anyway. You don't argue at four in the morning, when you have no clothes on your body, and there are three small children, your wife, and your mother, all up and frightened by the noise and the number of policemen in the house. Sarah knew he went without an argument in order to protect them and she prayed silently and urgently that he would return to them unharmed. 'Please God,' she prayed, 'You know he is a good man who has done nothing wrong. Keep him safe from the evils of that place.'

'I'll not speak unless I have to,' Mkhuseli whispered to Nomzamo, 'Ask someone from the negotiating committee to try to get me out.'

In the end it was the Mayor himself who had gone to the police, saying how could they detain the very man who was essential in the attempt to stop the boycott in Fort Bedford? Were they crazy? Did they want to derail the whole negotiation process and bankrupt everybody? Especially as they knew, and everybody else knew too, that Mkhuseli Khumalo could prove he wasn't even in town when the necklacing had taken place. Besides which, he, Dr van Zyl, could assure them from personal experience that Khumalo wasn't the sort of man to do a thing like that anyway.

Of course Dr van Zyl claimed credit for Mkhuseli's release at the next meeting of the negotiating committee, relating with some pride, his own part in the episode, and slapping Mkhuseli on the back like an old friend 'Now us two are going to sort this other business out in the same spirit, man. You owe it to me,' he said.

Mkhuseli thanked him, as he had thanked him already when he went to the doctor's house, standing even at the back door like a 'good Bantu boy', and not even being invited inside the house. He assured the committee that he had no idea who was responsible for the necklacing, adding that he himself was a man who was against violence. Yet he spoke up and said that in this matter of the boycott, he and the other representatives were only spokespersons for their community, who felt that there were still certain grievances that had to be addressed before the boycott could be lifted.

One evening when Sarah was on her way home from the white town, where she had been visiting a friend who lived in, where she worked, she was stopped on the corner leading into the township by a group of youngsters. Nodumo came to her, her hands placed together in a gesture of respect. 'Good evening, Gogo. Will Gogo please allow me to look inside her bag?'

Sarah was tired, and it irritated her to be stopped in this way by someone so young. But then she noticed how the girl's face was shadowed with sleeplessness, and that her dress, though clean, was threadbare, and she told herself to calm down because the child had not spoken rudely to her. She opened her bag to show she carried nothing with her.

Remembering Sizwe, and how he had protected this child, she wondered who was looking after her now. 'Are you staying at home?' she asked.

'Gogo, no. My parents are angry with me, and my father told me to leave.'

'And you? What do you think? Should you not listen to them and go back to school?'

The girl stood very still, her eyes downcast, but her voice was clear. 'Sizwe said the streets are our school, and prison is our university.'

Sarah could see a tear trickle down Nodumo's dusty cheek. Her heart opened. 'Child, please eat at my house tonight.'

'Thank you, Gogo,' Nodumo whispered.

After it was dark, there was a timid knock at the door. When Nodumo entered, Sarah could see how overcome with awe the child was, when she caught sight of James and Nomzamo. Her eyes glittered in the candle-light as she greeted them.

'Come, child, I have saved you some food.'

Nodumo's tense body could not accept the food easily - she ate a few crumbs only and then put down the plate. She said nothing, but made no effort to leave and later that night Sarah made her comfortable in a corner of the room. In the morning she was gone, but from that day on, Nodumo came to the house almost every evening after nightfall, leaving again before anyone in the house was awake. It became a challenge to Sarah to see if she could get her to eat well, and gradually, as the weeks passed, she seemed to relax with Sarah and with the children. She'd tell them stories that she said her grandmother had told to her, although her grandmother had passed away when she was still not yet at school. Sarah could see that Nodumo idolised Mkhuseli and Nomzamo because of their position as leaders in the community, but she knew it was to her, Gogo, that Nodumo came each night and that she was hungry, not so much for food, but for love.

It's like another child has been born to me in my old age, thought Sarah, and she cherished this new love in her heart. She saved special scraps for the child, as she had done for Mkhuseli, when he was young and in trouble twenty years ago. Was it really so long? When she looked around her she saw also a quite different spirit in her community, which no longer waited humbly for the white man to relent towards them, but was instead a place of anger and resolve. The township held itself ready for the next terrible event - an early morning raid, another mass arrest, a house burnt down or another necklacing.

Mkhuseli sat up until late at night, talking with Nomzamo, or with other men and women, neighbours and strangers. Sarah would say she was going to bed, and would see the sleeping faces of her grandchildren and her new daughter, but she herself would lie awake at night until the visitors had all left.

'We have to organise,' Mkhuseli explained to Sarah, sensing from her wakefulness that she did not understand the process they were going through. 'We must have street committees, so that if they arrest one person, someone else can take over their work.'

And in spite of the novelty of it all, Sarah felt drawn into this new life in the township. Although she travelled to Glen Bervie every day except Sunday, she took trouble only over the cooking, knowing that she would be taking her portion of it home to her family. She hardly thought about William and Vera, who seemed to her to wait for their food like pigs at a trough. They were of no account to her, just skinny old pigs, and the food she cooked was much too nice for them.

FORTY-TWO

Having made the decision to sell Glen Bervie, William allowed Vera to make all the arrangements. He told himself she knew his mind, and when she showed him the flat that was for sale on top of the new Barclays Bank building, he agreed immediately that they should buy it. It had a large sitting room, two airy bedrooms, one of which, Vera said, he could have as a study, and a small roof garden. From the sitting room window he could see the mountain rise above the line of shops on the opposite side of the street. When he saw that downstairs the bank was as secure as Fort Knox, he began to take a liking to the place. He told Vera he couldn't wait to move in.

Then he seemed to lose all his energy.

'You're in a complete slump,' Vera reproved him.

'I know,' he laughed, puzzled. 'I'll rest a little, and then I'll give you a hand with the packing.' But he found that, in spite of himself, he felt more and more inclined to leave it all to her. Whatever she decided, he agreed. It was less trouble, and besides, his mind was so foggy, he didn't really care much either way.

Whereas, before, he had, during the day, repeatedly caught glimpses of his mother in one of her characteristic poses, sitting on the lawn, or in her armchair at the dining room window - tricks of memory or of the light, he had assured himself - now it seemed that every time he entered a room, he got the overpowering sensation that she had just left it. He suspected a flicker of her skirt, or the hint of her slow footsteps receding down the passage. He could almost hear her talking with his father, and sometimes there was the faintest echo

253

of Millie's laughter, which was more likely to be, he scolded himself, the buzzing of a fly against the window pane. He decided he was hallucinating. He worried he was getting some serious virus.

He felt an overpowering sense that he had been deserted. He had relied, he now admitted, on her approving smile. He missed - his heart clenched in a sudden ache as he acknowledged the loss - he missed seeing his mother. He could no longer talk to her, reason with her, grumble and complain. It was no good confiding in Vera. He had made sure she hadn't the slightest idea of his visitations over the past couple of years. She'd have pronounced him a loonie, and part of him suspected that she would have been right. Yet, he had always believed that these visions were somehow in his power. His own familiars, conjured up by himself alone as an extension of his own reality. He was sure that they were only visual manifestations of his innermost thoughts. It was therefore doubly distressing to find them disappearing in such an impertinent fashion.

He couldn't concentrate on anything. It was impossible, when they were to lose the whole - Glen Bervie itself - to choose which bits of furniture, or which books they should take with them, which they should sell. When Vera asked his advice, he closed his eyes to make her go away.

'Right.' She was brusque. 'Don't blame me, then, afterwards.'

He barely heard her. His mind was on a logic of its own. He went through the house, searching.

'What are you looking for? Tell me.' Vera was exasperated. He'd emptied an entire wardrobe onto the floor.

He didn't know. He turned over what he had found: an old raincoat; a pair of black court shoes; a leather handbag; two navy straw hats.

A hat? Was that it? He'd recognise it when he saw it, and he did. It was on the top shelf of the bathroom cupboard - a white panama decorated with a narrow navy ribbon and a severe bow. He put it on.

Vera had not followed his clumsy, headlong search, but she gasped when she saw him coming out of the bathroom.

'William - what are you doing with your mother's hat?'

He glared at her. He didn't want her bothering him right now. He

254

felt much more energetic suddenly. She should be pleased about that, instead of making a fuss. Brushing her aside, he stalked onto the veranda, picking up a grass chair with one hand, and the round garden table with the other. He was delighted that the fog seemed to have cleared. The day sparkled. The gravel crunched underfoot as he made his way to the tennis court.

He spent some time deciding where to place the table and chair. Outside or inside the court? Under the tree or in the sun? He moved the two bits of garden furniture as if they were pieces on a chess board. Knight to Queen's Pawn. Castle the Bishop. Cheerfully, he whistled that old hymn tune with his tongue against his teeth.

Check. He'd found the place at last: dead centre of the tennis court. He adjusted the table so that it did not wobble. He stuck the chair legs firmly into a bed of carrots. What next?

Headlong back into the house to fetch the sunshade. His body seemed as light as air. How satisfying that each moment fitted so perfectly into place, like a jigsaw puzzle. Two white egrets floated across the sky towards the cows, which were grazing in the meadow below the house. The earth had that hum he hadn't noticed since he was a child - an orchestration of bees, cicada, and the noise the plants make, still wet from the night, growing in the morning heat before they keel over for the afternoon.

Vera found him sitting in the grass chair with the old floral sunshade stuck behind him in the chair. He was still wearing his mother's hat.

'William!' She stood directly in front of him so that he could not avoid seeing her.

He lowered his head.

'William!'

He knew that she was there, but feared, for some reason - he did not know what - to answer her. He concentrated on a row of cauliflowers slightly to his left, in an evasive action.

'William - I won't have this ... this charade!'

She snatched the hat from his head and stamped on it, trampling it into the ground, then picked up its loose brim and the broken crown and threw them as far as she could. She knocked over the sunshade, closed it, and put her foot on it to snap it in two. He heard a noise as if a thousand tons of rock fell from a great height. Then a silence so profound he thought he must have gone completely deaf, but he heard her voice as if in an echo chamber.

'Come with me.' Meekly, his hand in hers, he let her lead him away. She made him lie down in the bedroom, where she closed the curtains to keep out the light. He allowed her to say in that voice that was single and alone, that he was suffering from sunstroke. He was glad to hide in this dim, colourless room, as if he were a sick animal in a cave.

Vera no longer complained that he wasn't helping her with the move. She installed him in the sitting room of the new flat as if he were another piece of furniture.

'We can sack Sarah now,' she announced, when everything was over.

'Yes.'

'I've found out that she's been drawing her old-age pension for the past two months without telling us.'

'Cheek.'

'We could report her.'

He had stopped listening to her as well, but she was already interpreting his silences.

'I don't think so either. She's not worth the bother.'

Vera was very happy in the flat. She managed all the cooking and shopping herself, and engaged a maid who came once a week to do the cleaning and ironing. At last they were safe, she said triumphantly, reiterating daily how relieved she was that in her own home she was no longer surrounded by all those black faces. She never stopped congratulating herself on the move.

He seldom went out. During the day he sat with the newspaper in his hands, or stared at the flickering television screen, which made sounds he took no trouble to interpret. What he didn't confide in Vera was the loss of his familiar ghosts. He no longer saw his mother at the garden table, nor did he sense her presence or imagine that she had just left the room. He wasn't even able to conjure up a picture of her face or form.

256

He reasoned that this was because he was no longer living in a setting in which she would look at home, but one evening, poring over an old photograph album, he realised that he was not able to recognise his mother's face. In a yellowing snapshot, three women in their eighties stood in a group: his mother and her two sisters. Which one was she? He closed the album quickly to avoid having to answer the question.

He no longer wrote in his book of reckoning. Vera was pleased. 'The move's done you good,' she announced one evening after dinner, as if the move had been a sort of 'cure'. They were watching a French costume drama dubbed with the voices of South African actors. She glanced appraisingly at him. 'You're much more relaxed now, and you've put on weight. You'll have to be careful not to get a paunch.'

He said nothing. There was, as usual, nothing to say.

'You've lost your obsessions. You're much easier to live with.' With a smile, she put out her hand, and he took it. He would have held on forever, but she was busy with a tapestry in red and silver for a dining room chair cover. She stabbed the needle into the canvas, and pulled the thread through.

FORTY-THREE

Mkhuseli spotted the roadblock ahead, halfway down the long, straight stretch into Cookhouse. There were two police vans pulled up on either side of the road, their lights intersecting across it. As he drew closer, he could make out figures, and a man with a powerful torch slowed him down.

There was a heavy, sick silence in the back of the car. Sisa Njuza had asked him to fetch his wife and children from a farm near Middleton, where they had been staying with her family. Sisa sat in front. Two teenage girls, a six-year-old boy and a baby were with his wife in the back seat, together with her mother, who was coming back with them to Fort Bedford to stay for a while. They didn't have permission for her to be in the township, but were hoping that, by hiring a taxi, it would all happen so quickly that no one would be the wiser.

'Your pass.' The white policeman shone his torch onto Mkhuseli's papers, then took them away. He returned after what seemed much too long a time. There was trouble - he didn't have the reference book any more.

'Out.'

Mkhuseli turned to Sisa and put up his hand as if to say, 'I'll try to deal with this. I'm sorry.' He glanced into the back of the car. The two girls stared at him, their vulnerability equal to the dangers they clearly imagined. Behind them the women had effaced themselves, camouflaging fear.

Mkhuseli climbed out slowly, giving his eyes time to accustom themselves to the sweep of the veldt under the night sky. He avoided looking into the headlamps and the torches. Now he could see another car, a pale sports car with a Port Elizabeth number plate. The man in the passenger seat was getting out and walking towards him. Of course! He recognised the set of those shoulders, that short thick neck and, as the man came closer, the sleek brown hair and small, mean moustache. Gouws wore his sports coat casually unbuttoned to give himself the relaxed pleasure of putting his hands into his pockets as if he were merely strolling around his garden after lunch.

'Well, well, if it isn't my old friend, James Khumalo.'

Best not to reply. Mkhuseli was six inches taller than Gouws. One punch would send Gouws in an arc right into nowhere.

As if sensing Mkhuseli's thought, Gouws stopped a good few feet away from him. 'I suppose I must say Mkhuseli Khumalo now, hey?' The tone implied that using his Xhosa name had been a subversive act.

What was coming?

'You're up to something Khumalo and it won't help you to play footsie-footsie with the Mayor either. Don't think we don't know everything you do. When they had you in prison las' time they were too soft with you. That was because I was in Pretoria. Next time you'll see a difference. Who are those other kaffirs with you?'

Gouws was backed by a group of five uniformed policemen as well as another plainclothes officer. There was no way Mkhuseli could get away. 'It's just a family who've been to see relatives on the farm. I'm taking them home.'

'Check their papers,' Gouws ordered with a sideways twist of his head towards the people inside the silent car. The two youngest policemen collected the pass-books. They started joking, asking how old the girls were.

'Look Hannes - that one's quite well developed,' one laughed and pointed towards the shrinking girl.

'They're only ten and twelve years' old, Baas,' Sisa objected, begging them to leave his children alone. 'They're too young for such talk.'

'Ag, that's what you all say - we know you better, hey? Hey girls?'
The policeman had blonde curly hair and a pink tongue, which licked
round his lips as he put out a chubby red hand to tweak the elder
girl's ear. She pulled her head away sharply. 'Naughty!' he laughed,
delighted.

'I like them to have spirit,' commented the one he'd called
Hannes, approvingly. 'You know it will be worth it, then.'

The three older policemen laughed indulgently, as if they were
watching a show-jumping competition. Why didn't they clap? They're
animals, Mkhuseli thought bitterly. His anger was fuelled by the
knowledge that Gouws's dislike of him was the reason why such a
powerless family was being tormented in this way. But Gouws wasn't
finished with him yet.

'You're too much in the newspapers, Khumalo. You understand
what I'm saying, hey? Don't act dom. I'm telling you, you better
watch your step because any time now they'll be toyi-toyi-ing on your
grave too.'

'Sir?' He put all the hatred he felt into that one syllable, although
he kept quite still so that the man couldn't accuse him of anything.
This was no time to be arrested.

There was something glinting in Gouws's hand. He bent down
and there was a sigh as the blade of the knife sliced into the front
tyre.

'Oh dear. I think you have a puncture, Khumalo.'

'Please can I have my dompas, Sir.' Mkhuseli spoke each word
heavily, as if they were rocks he was throwing.

Gouws had already jack-knifed the blade and slipped it back into
his pocket. He clicked his fingers and the blonde policeman ran over
to him.

'You better give this kaffir his papers back, man - he's in a hurry.'
Gouws's voice teased like dirty water running out of a blocked sink.
The policeman loved it. 'He's got a puncture. Looks like he could be
here all night and his white boeties won't know where to find him.'

The men laughed as if they couldn't control their delight. They
teach them everything, thought Mkhuseli. He could smell their lust,
and feared for his life as well as the lives of his passengers. He

prepared his mind to defend himself: he wouldn't let them have their way without a fight.

'Doesn't look as if there's room for a spare in that old tjorrie.' The blonde policeman was still making jokes. Don't react, Mkhuseli told himself. Let them have their fun if it keeps them from doing anything worse.

'I'll be waiting for you Khumalo. Just for you.' The words poisoned the night air. Mkhuseli could hear how much Gouws hated him. It was personal, much more than just doing his job - or perhaps they were the same thing. Perhaps the hatred and the job were so mixed together that you couldn't do the one without the other. 'This is just a warning, for now. You're getting too big for your boots.'

Without giving Mkhuseli time to reply, Gouws returned to his car and bent down to say something to the driver, who started the engine. They accelerated away with a zoom of the exhaust, skidding on the rough ground before they hit the tar.

The policemen were preparing to leave also. The whole thing was set up just for me, thought Mkhuseli. Who told them I'd be coming this way tonight? They seemed subdued now, perhaps feeling the loss of Gouws's demonic energy. One tossed the four pass-books in a bundle at Mkhuseli. They weren't going to bother about the old lady's visit to Fort Bedford.

Mkhuseli and Sisa were lifting the spare tyre out of the boot when the police vans drove off. As they passed close to the car, the blonde policeman lobbed a teargas canister neatly through the back window.

'Dis vir julle, blerrie kaffir hoere!' he yelled.

Mkhuseli and Sisa jumped to open the car doors. The white smoke was spreading at an alarming rate. Mkhuseli helped out Mrs Njuza and the baby, while Sisa bundled the children onto the ground, and pulled his mother-in-law free. Only then could Mkhuseli cover his face and grope for the canister, which he threw as far away as he could into the darkness. His eyes were burning, and his skin felt as if his cheeks were melting. How could they do this thing to an old woman, and to children?

The granny had collapsed, and Sisa was trying to help her sit up so that he could rub her back to get her breath back. Mrs Njuza was wiping her baby's eyes, and jiggling him up and down, while her own tears fell freely. She had such a sweet, gentle face! The three children were sobbing and coughing.

'I'm sorry, friend,' Mkhuseli shouted above the wailing and choking. He did not know whether his voice was hoarse from rage or from the gas. 'I'm sorry, Sisa. It's my fault. They were waiting for me.'

'Brother, no!' Sisa's tears glittered in the moonlight. His face was scored with pain. 'We were lucky they were pursuing you. It's a miracle our girls are all right still. It's already happened to the daughters of my friends. The army comes into the school, and takes them away from the class ... when they come home, they can't even walk! This tear-smoke ... how can our children respect us when we cannot protect them from the harm these men do?'

He bent again to murmur to his mother-in-law, and, reassured by her reply, stood up, but he was still weeping when he came over to give Mkhuseli a hand.

Mkhuseli was pumping up the jack. 'It's not far to go now before we are home,' he spoke clearly, trying to reassure this small family, and to let his voice reach the children who had all huddled together. The car windows were wide open to let in the fresh air. The veldt was quiet again, peaceful and dark. Five miles away, the street lights of Cookhouse were like eyes of small creatures, hares or meerkats, watching them.

FORTY-FOUR

The airline passengers queued for more than an hour at passport control. Will they deport me? worried Jo.

'What's the purpose of your visit?' The official looked bored.

'A holiday.'

He flipped through her British passport in a leisurely fashion, then stamped it, handing it back without a word. She had expected to be interrogated. Had the Special Branch completely forgotten her?

There was Marge among the small crowd waiting in the dreary marble hall of Johannesburg airport. Outside, the sunshine looked as if it would last forever. Marge was older, but still healthy-looking and girlish, with freckles and bleached hair. 'Welcome home!' she said, as she hugged Jo quickly. You could cut her accent with a knife.

Marge drove for an hour to a house in a suburb far away from the centre of the city of Johannesburg, where she was introduced to Mike, who was already tending the fire for the midday braai. Mike worked as a technician in the hospital, where Marge was a ward sister. They had been married for a few months. Mike put out an enormous hand - he was over six foot and fleshy - then changed his mind and took Jo into a giant embrace.

First Marge served tea and home-made biscuits, then they started cooking the lunch. Mike couldn't do enough for his new cousin. He opened a bottle of special estate wine, served up barbecued chicken, pork and lamb chops, as well as boerewors. Jo was dazzled by the sun on a cerise and scarlet fall of bougainvillaea, awed by the mound of meat she was supposed to consume, affected by the fine wine.

'Give me a few days to get used to this high living,' she laughed, refusing another helping of sausages and chops. 'I haven't eaten so much meat in years!' She glanced at her arms and legs. 'I feel like a white mouse that has got into the wrong cage by mistake. You've a marvellous tan, Marge.'

'Don't envy us, it's us who envy you!' Marge was generous even in that, Jo thought.

That evening, Marge blurted out, 'Jo, we want to leave - there's going to be a bloodbath here.'

Jo felt tired and ill. It had been a long day and she was beginning to feel the strain. Mike shifted his buttocks and pulled down his shorts, which seemed to be hurting him. His legs were like tree trunks. 'I'm thirty-nine, but they told me I must enlist in the army for three weeks every year,' he told her. 'I don't want to go, but they give me this form to sign. It says, "Are you in the regular army, or are you a volunteer?" I ask them, "What must I put?" "No," they tell me, "You are a volunteer." "But man," I say, "I don't want to BE in the army, I don't want to volunteer." But they tell me again, "No, you are a volunteer. Put your tick where it says volunteer."' He deflated his rib cage with a huge sigh.

'Marge, you said I was wrong to leave. You said this country was great.' The words had rankled. Jo felt bitterly deprived by all those years in the London cold.

'I was stupid. Now the Government wants to improve things, but the Blacks want to go too fast, and the Verkramptes don't want any change at all.'

'Who scares you the most?'

'Oh - the Conservatives. They're mad. Things have got to change here.'

'How do you think it should be?' Jo was treading warily. She felt she had come back to an entirely different country from the one she had left.

'Ag, I don't know. Fairer, I suppose. Everybody agrees about that now. We didn't know we were doing wrong - we were brought up to think that way, but now ...'

'They want to go too fast - ' Mike interjected, sitting forward.

264

'They should just give us a little time to adjust, not ask for everything at once.' He pulled his shorts down again. They must be cutting him in half, thought Jo and the idea distracted her from the anger she was beginning to feel. What right had they to ask for more time - hadn't they had enough time already?

'You see,' continued Marge, 'they've still got to come up to our standard of education. It can't happen overnight.'

'How much time are you thinking of?' Jo was guarded. She could feel herself spoiling for a fight.

'Maybe ...' Marge was pouring a bedtime cup of tea. 'Maybe two years?'

It was as if she were a child asking to stay up a little later before going to bed. This is a ridiculous conversation, thought Jo. Does she really think they can make it all right in two years? And will they even try? Without a word, she took the cup of tea Marge handed to her. Why should I make her feel comfortable about this? she thought.

'Sugar?'

'No, thanks.'

Mike stood up, but he still hovered over Jo. His bulk was beginning to suffocate her. 'Let me get you a brandy,' he suggested.

'Why not?' She'd drink anything, she was so tired. Jo gazed at them through blurred eyes. Never mind what they say, she thought, this is what family means - people making this kind of fuss over me.

'I've been to England,' Mike couldn't stop demanding her attention. 'I was there for two weeks on a tour. It's really pretty: Oxford; Cambridge; Salisbury; Coventry; Scotland; The Lake District ...' He listed the place names like an incantation. 'Can't you get me a job there?' he begged. 'I'll do anything. I could drive one of those long-distance lorries. I've got an HGV licence.'

'I'll try.' How could she promise? She herself had only managed to stay because she was already teaching before they'd tightened the immigration laws.

Outside this house stretched the whole expanse of the country she'd not seen for more than ten years. In London, news from South Africa, which she always followed, had become more urgent. There was something happening almost every day. The crowds toyi-toyi-ing at funerals, which were shown on British television, made her acknowledge feelings that, with difficulty, she had managed to do without.

She had told her friends in London that she needed to check if the revolution was imminent. She had barely admitted to herself how much she longed to return. Now she wryly observed that it was ironic that she and Marge should again, so to speak, be changing places. Probably, she summed it up to herself, it was as unlikely that she would come back as it was that Marge would be allowed to settle in the United Kingdom.

'What about Glen Bervie?' she asked, wondering how Marge could bear to leave it.

'They sold it.' Marge's face had the pinched and bitter look of an abandoned child.

'Oh no!'

Marge was busy packing cups onto the tray, so she didn't meet Jo's gaze. 'It got terribly run down. Dad asked me to stay there, but I couldn't - not the way they live and not with my mother. Anyway, Mike and I had already ... I used to dream of restoring it one day to what it used to be - remember?' Marge's hand slipped and she jumped as the cups slid onto the floor.

'Oh! The new carpet!'

Mike was quickly at her side, enfolding her as if she were a tiny doll, squeezing her against his huge chest, but she wriggled free and ran back from the kitchen with a cloth to wipe away the tea stains. Keeping busy seemed to restore her composure.

'When? When did they sell?' Jo still couldn't believe it.

'It was just after we were married. We'd moved into this place already.' Marge calculated. 'About six months ago.'

'Who bought it?'

'Do you remember Bobbie Scott, the solicitor in Main Street - the one with the brass plate, opposite the church?'

'The one where we used to ring the doorbell, and run away?'

'His son. He married a farmer's daughter from Golden Valley. Between them they've got pots of money.'

Golden Valley: the name conjured up the evening sun, its

266

horizontal golden rays lighting up the Karoo bushes on the mountain slopes; baskets of ripe apricots and peaches; dark glossy orange trees hung with tangerine and lemon yellow orbs, so much more beautiful than any Christmas tree. Jo's mind flooded with nostalgia. She heard Marge only peripherally.

'I hear they've spent a fortune on Glen Bervie - more even than what they paid for it.'

'You haven't been back?'

'No.'

'What about Uncle William and Aunt Vera?'

'They're living in a flat above Barclay's Bank. It's all locked up at night so Mother feels quite safe there.' Marge's voice was sarcastic and her face took on a bitter look. How she hates her mother, thought Jo.

'She's got all her antiques, including the grand piano, crammed into the sitting room. Dad never goes out. He doesn't even read. He's changed completely - he never argues any more.' Marge was crying. This time she didn't refuse Mike's arms. 'He never says ...' her face crumpled like a child's, '... anything.'

'I can't believe it! No more Crewes at Glen Bervie! We built the place!' Jo was indignant. It was an injustice. Although she didn't say it out loud, she accused William, of course. How dare he sell something that wasn't his to sell? But then he'd always been good at taking things away from people.

'He just sits there ... as if there's nothing inside him.' Marge's voice was muffled by Mike's chest.

'We'll talk more in the morning. Come Bokkie, let's go to bed.' Mike spoke gently, turning her away from Jo, who felt rebuked for being too direct. She'd gone away when the system had become unbearable for her. Now, the centre no longer held, and those, like Marge, who hadn't cared to meddle in politics, were the losers. How should she comfort her, when her own heart was still so full of anger - even at her own cousin?

And William? She couldn't bring herself to think of him. She sat, fully dressed, in the spare room darkness, her eyes streaming with tears. 'Oh Mother,' she mouthed.

FORTY-FIVE

Jo took a bottle of Glenfiddich whisky to give to Father O'Reilly. He wore running shoes and grey socks and bounced energetically around her, exclaiming how pleased he was to see her.

'Come in - come in!' It was wonderful to Jo that he could remember her after so many years. He settled her in a comfortable, brownish room. On the linoleum under a sideboard was a saucer of milk with an unappetising crust around its rim. Next to it, a maroon velour cushion was hairy with cat fur.

'So, you've come from England,' he beamed.

'Yes - I'm on holiday.'

'You're thinking of coming back here for good? I know of a small house -'

Jo laughed, embarrassed. 'No, Father.' The idea of settling down in Fort Bedford had never occurred to her. Although its effect on her was mysterious to her, she no longer imagined the possibility of her childhood dream house on the river. She turned the talk away from herself. 'Do you still go on holiday to Ireland, Father?'

'I'm flying over in November, if I can get a priest to take the services here.' He brought her a tumbler with a tot of whisky, nicely measured. I think this year will be my last time. I find more and more of my old friends under the ground when I go over these days. I'm calling on cemeteries, Jo! The life here has kept me much fitter than those who were with me in the seminary. No, Fort Bedford is my home. I'll die here.'

'You'll retire here?'

'Retire?' I'll drop dead in harness, Jo. You should come back, though - it's really a great place now. We're developing the town as a holiday centre - there's even a new wandelpad, a tourist path, up the mountain!'

Jo looked into her glass. 'You don't worry about the future?'

Father O'Reilly's voice was untroubled. 'Oh no! It's coming right at last - I really think so. People are changing. Do you know ... ' Launching into a long anecdote, he poured another whisky each and settled down comfortably. 'The Council has built a beautiful new library for the Coloured folk. Beautiful. And the African people can read there too if they want, but the Council decided that they won't take books home yet. It's a sensible rule, Jo,' his innocent eyes were unblinking, 'because they haven't got proper facilities for reading at home.'

There it starts again ... thought Jo, this idea that in a few years' time there will suddenly be a miracle and everything will come right without anyone doing anything that hurts, or even changing their minds. 'Oh, Father - ' But Father O'Reilly was warming to the main part of his story.

'Last Saturday was the opening of the library - all the races were represented there. Beautiful. This town's come a long way, Jo. Victor Swanepoel - you remember Victor Swanepoel?'

Jo nodded. All the white South Africans she was meeting seemed to remind her that she was in a foreign country, even when they didn't mean to, but she heard his good will.

Father O'Reilly's legs were too short to cross over comfortably, but were spread out squarely in front of him. He clasped small hands over grey cotton shorts, which matched his socks and bush jacket. 'Victor's chairman of Rotary - they put up most of the money for the library. They've been very generous, Jo. He made a speech and he told a good joke. It had a message, mind.

'When the town was founded, the Mayor of Fort Bedford called together an Englishman' - Father O'Reilly said the word in Afrikaans, Engelsman - 'an Afrikaner and a Coloured.

'"What do you want?" he asked the Engelsman.

'"I want all the businesses."

269

"'Right - they're yours," said the Mayor. "And what do you want?" he asked the Afrikaner.

"'I want all the land," replied the Afrikaner.

"'Right - it's yours," said the Mayor. "And what do you want?" he asked the Coloured.

"'Ag, no, I just came along with the baas.'"

It was one of those bitter jokes that white South Africans tell against themselves, as a way of exorcising their unease. Jo laughed, in spite of what was becoming her habitual rage.

'The point is - he was saying that things must change. He told them straight out! Victor Swanepoel said that! So, you see, I am really very optimistic.'

'Father, I want to visit Sarah. She used to work at Glen Bervie. Am I allowed into the township?'

'Don't go into the location,' Father O'Reilly looked alarmed. 'Don't go, Jo, please. It's not safe. Even the police won't go in on their own. Believe me. The other day they stoned Big Jan Botha's van. He was delivering meat to an old boy that used to work for him. You never know what can happen. I'm serious, Jo. It's not safe for a white person to go into the location.'

Sarah was the key to all Jo's feelings about Glen Bervie, and about William. Her visit to the country would be fruitless if she didn't see Sarah and talk to her. 'Can you get a message to Sarah?'

'I'll try. Write down her name and the address. The trouble is I've promised to take someone to East London.' He looked at his watch. 'Good heavens! I'm late already!' He jumped to his feet.

Jo hastily scribbled the information on a scrap of paper.

'You'll be careful now, promise me, Jo?'

'Yes - yes, I promise.' The gate squeaked as Jo closed it. Father O'Reilly didn't wait for her to unlock her car, but rushed back inside the house to get ready for his next appointment.

FORTY-SIX

The next morning there was no message either from Father O'Reilly or from Sarah. Jo parked her hired car opposite the Chinaman's general store, which was situated on a corner on the edge of the Black township. It was a run-down building with the name AH YUI flaking off in orange letters over the doorway, which faced the white side of town. Ouma, Jo remembered, had pronounced it AH WHY, saying, once, that it was the saddest name in the whole world.

A small crowd were passing the time on the raised stoep running along two walls of the shop. They stood, or sat, quite still. They could be, Jo thought, an allegorical tableau illustrating Poverty. Jo left the car, and walked over the street to stand next to an older woman, who was sitting on her own, close to the edge of the stoep.

'Excuse me, I wonder if you can help me. I am looking for Mrs Sarah Khumalo. Do you know her?'

The woman gave her a blank, hard stare from an exhausted, wrinkled face. Her reply, in Xhosa, seemed to indicate that she did not understand English, and if she did, she was still not prepared to help. Two young men, leaning against a lamp-post, sniggered, confirming Jo's impression that the reply had not been accommodating.

A woman, barefoot, with a baby tied securely onto her back with a ragged blanket, moved closer, as if curious to find out what this white woman wanted.

'Sarah Khumalo: I'm looking for her. She lives in J Street. 21, J Street. Do you know her?' Jo asked.

Although they did not seem to be paying attention, the group had acquired a wary stillness. After a minute, the young woman replied, 'She's very old.'

'That's her. Is her house far away?'

'I know her.'

'Can I go there?'

A tall woman now approached Jo. 'No,' she told her decisively, speaking in perfect English. 'You can't go by yourself into the township. The police must take you to the house. It's best you ask them.'

'Is the house a long way from here?'

'Far.'

It seemed hopeless. How could Jo ally herself with the police when she herself had seen television footage of policemen shooting children who were throwing stones. Yet, surely, Sarah would be too old to walk the long distance to the shop. In any case, how would Jo get a message to her to say she was waiting?

The woman with the baby seemed to make up her mind. Hitching the baby up a little, as if to make her more comfortable, she started off at a fast pace down the dirt road leading into the township. 'I'll tell her,' she muttered.

Surprised, Jo ran after her. 'Thank you. Let me give you a rand for your trouble.'

The money seemed to make a difference to the group.

'I'll fetch her.' One of the two men stood up, lively. Jo felt a shiver of fear.

'It's all right, now, I think.' But, worried, she turned back to the women. 'Will she be able to walk so far? Wouldn't it be better if I went to her house?'

'They'll bring her in a car,' announced the very old woman, indifferently, speaking perfect English after all. She looked critically at Jo's clothes. 'You are too smart.'

Jo raised her arms apologetically. Wanting, like all travellers returning home, to make an impression, she had dressed carefully. She was afraid she might meet William or Vera, and, knowing their power over her, she did not want them to be able to say she was not

272

a success abroad.

She waited quietly for a few moments, then, unable to bear the scrutiny of the people on the stoep, she asked, 'How long will it be?'

'It's not far.'

This time the answer came from the woman who had told her to go to the police. The information she was being given was slippery, changeable. It seemed unreliable, protective, wanting to reassure her. Jo turned back to the safety of her hired car and sat inside it, staring at the mountain, which loomed larger and darker green than in her memory of it. In the afternoon its huge shadow would swallow up the town. I'll go and look at my grandfather's statue, she thought suddenly.

'If Sarah comes, please ask her to wait for me. Tell her please not to go away. I'll be back in half an hour.'

Although the two-storied shops bore names which she remembered from childhood, Main Street seemed unfamiliar to Jo. There was a great deal of new, yellow brickwork, and a supermarket where the Palladium Bioscope and Cafe had once stood. Jo picked out the shop fronts that she recognised - Johnston's Drapery Store and Cohen's Jewellers still had an archaic air. The street was as wide as in a cowboy film. The Dutch Reformed Church, painted a dull grey, was squatter and less impressive than she had remembered it. Now that she had visited the churches and cathedrals of Europe, she recognised that this building had made a bleak attempt to imitate their grace. Karoo Gothic, she giggled to herself, as she pushed open the tall, wrought-iron gate.

The dapper marble figure - sculpted beard, winged collar, coat-tails and bible - was still on its plinth, but there was a heaviness in the thighs, a fleshiness, which made him appear pompous and slightly ridiculous. It made her doubt the heroic qualities with which she had invested him. Jo walked round him critically. She read the inscription thoroughly. She looked up at the dusty windows which punctuated the drab walls of the church. They were not at all like the eyes she had imagined staring at her when she was a child. They were just empty, dirty glass. It was all so much less interesting than she had remembered.

This time her arrival at the Chinaman's provoked a ripple of attention. Someone pointed at her. As Jo got out of the car, Sarah separated herself from the group, and came slowly across the road. She was an old woman in carpet slippers, wearing a neat turquoise-blue woollen dress and a rust-coloured knitted cap. She seemed to have shrunk from Jo's memory of her generous bulk, but Jo would have recognised her anywhere.

'Oh Sarah! Thank you for coming to meet me - I'm so very glad to see you!'

'Miss Jo.' Sarah pulled out of Jo's embrace as if disliking such familiarity. Perhaps, Jo thought, she also feels embarrassed by the critical silence of all these people watching us.

'I've bought some flowers. Please will you come with me to put them on my mother's grave?' Jo wanted to take Sarah somewhere they could at least talk in private.

At the cemetery, they walked together under tall ragged pines, which seemed to drain all the life from that gravelly place with its rows of granite headstones. Millie lay with her mother and father under a single, polished slab.

AND THEIR DAUGHTER

MILLICENT RORIG

AGED SIXTY YEARS

The grave plot was fenced with an eighteen-inch high railing. It was not tall enough to lean on, and there was nowhere to sit down. Because Sarah was limping, Jo took her arm. 'You must be tired, Sarah. Forgive me - I've made you walk too far.'

'Oh no, Miss Jo. Look - I'm very fine.' To Jo's distress Sarah broke into a shuffle dance, reminding Jo immediately, not of the toyi-toyi-ing of the angry youth, but of the stereotypes of happy slaves that she had seen in old American movies.

The dancing was like a mortal blow to her, resurrecting, as it did, moments when Sarah had danced thus for her when she was still only a child. 'Stop! Please stop!' Jo did not want to weep - did not know even who she was crying for, herself or Sarah. 'Sarah, please, you mustn't do that!' Solicitous for Sarah, Jo did not have time to wonder whether Sarah's gesture was completely spontaneous, or one of deepest irony, perhaps even of deepest hate.

Back inside the car, the two women sat upright, constricted by the paraphernalia of driving. Jo gripped the steering wheel as if she was about to start the engine, but she didn't want to let Sarah go yet. When she was a child, she had taken Sarah's kindness for granted. She had come to make retribution. She turned the upper part of her body uncomfortably towards her companion, who was so very familiar, and about whom she knew almost nothing.

'When did you stop working for William and Vera?'

Sarah calculated. 'Five - six months ago. Miss Vera said because I am getting the government pension, it is wrong for me to work for her anymore.'

'Weren't you tired of working?'

'Tired.' There was such expression in that one word. 'Ek was gedaan,' Sarah continued. The Afrikaans meant used up, an adjective normally describing a broken, useless thing. Sarah was saying that Jo's family had used her up and discarded her like a broken bicycle or a worn out piece of clothing.

'Is the pension enough to live on?'

'Miss Jo - I am suffering hunger. I don't have enough to buy the paraffin, the sugar - even bread.' Sarah opened the palm of her right hand, marking these essential items by bringing her thumb down onto a different finger with each word. She stared at her hands. 'I've Nontu's children to look after now, and Leah is living with me also.'

'I've brought you something.' Jo reached into her bag for the R100 she had put into an envelope, and gave it to Sarah.

'Miss Jo is just like your kind mother. Thank you. Now I will buy meat!' Sarah seemed pleased, but instead of putting the envelope away, she opened it and counted the notes. When she'd finished, she said nothing, folding the money away and tucking it into the neck of her dress. It was clear to Jo that she was disappointed.

'I didn't know Leah was with you. I should give her something too … ' Hastily, Jo added another twenty rand. She inwardly calculated the cost of her trip to Fort Bedford - the car, the petrol, the hotel, the money for Sarah. Her travelling allowance was dwindling.

Sarah took out the envelope again, and added Leah's money to it. 'She will be very pleased,' she remarked, without enthusiasm.

Jo tried in vain to find the warmth she needed in Sarah's voice. She had wanted this money to make a difference to Sarah's life, yet she was also distressed that her visit had taken on such a financial aspect, especially as she had clearly failed to bring enough. As a last resort she attempted to revive old memories. 'How long did you work at Glen Bervie?'

'I came there in 1933. I was still eighteen years' old then. I didn't have schooling. There was no education at that time. Before that I worked for old Mrs Albertyn.' Sarah stared at the town's tin roofs and painted walls, the homes of all prospective white employers.

'And Ernest?'

'We came together. We were already married then.'

'You worked at Glen Bervie for over fifty years!'

'Yes.' Sarah turned at last to face Jo. 'It's me who nursed old Mr Crewe when he was dying, and also old Mrs Crewe. I looked after Miss Millie, your mother. Then I worked a long time for Dr and Mrs Crewe.' She paused as if counting all those years. 'Old Mrs Crewe promised me that they would always look after me. Now when I suffer hunger, I feel sorrow.' The word did not correspond to the anger that Jo heard in Sarah's voice.

'I'm sorry.' Jo was ashamed for them all.

'Mr Freeman is saying I can buy my house now,' Sarah began to speak more urgently. It was clear that she felt she should take advantage of Jo's sudden appearance in her life. This new concession, which allowed black people to buy houses in the townships bordering on white towns had been made during Jo's visit to the country. Jo had read in the paper that councils were being ordered to sell off council houses in an attempt to make black people also vulnerable to what was being euphemistically referred to as the 'status quo', otherwise translated in parliament by one government minister as 'the mess we are now in'.

'How much do they want you to pay?'

276

'A thousand rand.'

It was the equivalent of three hundred pounds. It seemed impossible that anyone could buy a house for such a small sum, but Jo knew it was miles beyond what Sarah could afford. 'Are other people buying?' she asked.

'Yes - many in my street.' Sarah was absorbed, urgent. 'Please Miss Jo, you must send me the money from England. If I can have my own house, I will make it so nice.' Sarah's hands and fingers seemed to sketch gleaming paint-work, a lacy veranda, a garden. It was a dream that Jo could not resist.

'I will, I promise you.' Jo felt foolish. She had not seen herself as a benefactor. She had wanted her visit to explore the past, to swap stories about her childhood. She had wanted to ask intimate, political questions. Fort Bedford was in the news. It had been mentioned more than once in the British media. She felt sick from the questions she hadn't asked.

'You taught me Nkosi sikelel' iAfrica. Do you remember, Sarah?'

Sarah laughed politely, 'I remember.'

'You should have taught me to speak Xhosa. I feel foolish that I never learned it.'

'Yes, I should.' Jo could hear no particular enthusiasm in Sarah's voice.

This conversation will never warm up, thought Jo, so she started the car. Where the cemetery road joined the main road into town, was the town's single industrial site: a glue factory. As she paused at the intersection, there was a revolting stench of boiling bones.

'Ugh! I'd forgotten the terrible smell!' Jo held her nose in a joke gesture. 'I remember when the wind blew the wrong way, how it came into all the houses. We were glad to drive back to the farm to get away from it. Does it often blow over the township?'

'Often,' Sarah grimaced, but she laughed too.

Suddenly, at last, intimacy had been established. 'What do you think about what is happening now?' Jo felt able to ask.

'Miss Jo?'

'What do you think about what the children are doing ... the Comrades ... the school strikes, the rent strikes ... boycotts ...?'

Sarah was quiet for a moment before she spoke, wary. 'I don't know.'

'I think the children are very brave.' As usual Jo was giving an emotional response. 'I'll be glad if they win - it's a war.' She waved her hands above the steering wheel.

Sarah's answer was contained, and, to Jo, entirely consistent. 'Maybe we'll get more money then.'

'Is that what you want most - money?' Jo had come a long way to get to know Sarah, and she wasn't going to let her off lightly.

'We are the have-nots,' replied Sarah. 'We think it is time we get more. If we need to ask, we must ask.'

'And the youth? Do you support all their actions?'

'They are our children,' said Sarah, with a finality that drew her life around her like an invisible cloak so that not even Jo, who felt rebuked for being still the inquisitive one, could penetrate further.

FORTY-SEVEN

No, it wasn't like a homecoming, Jo was forced to admit. She knew where everything was, as a blind man might in a familiar room, but all the same, the landscape looked different, as if an outer layer had been peeled off, exposing a raw, bleak quality that she had missed before. Having deliberately avoided seeing William and Vera, she drove past Glen Bervie on her way out of town. Father O'Reilly had said she should call in. 'The new owners would be most pleased to show you around. Really. They've spent a fortune on it - it's a show place now.'

Wasn't it before? thought Jo. I believed it was paradise. On the drive out, the azure mountains unfolded along the road. The sky was a fiery blue, the sun beat down over red-brown earth, burning up all other colours.

The old graveyard had been flattened and tarred over to widen the road for the Glen Bervie turn-off. Opposite, where so many small houses had sheltered the lives of a whole community, was a large, double-storied modern residence, with a white tiled swimming pool set into a bright green front lawn. A hedge of cannas blazed huge crimson blooms against cinnamon leaves. The effect was garish. It's tasteless, thought Jo, shocked to see jets from a sprinkler turning in silver arcs. What a waste to be watering in the midday heat!

The Glen Bervie farm road was flanked on either side by taut, shiny, barbed wire. The place seemed to be completely overhauled and cleared of people. Jo stopped at the front gate. The old brass name-plate was still fixed into position, but the white-washed pillars had been extended and crowned with grandiose wooden beams of a dark, oiled wood. Beyond the cattle grid, Jo could see how the oak trees, that Ouma had planted, had grown so tall that their branches met across the drive to form a green tunnel. Masses of blue agapanthus were flowering luxuriantly in their shade. The effect made Glen Bervie look more like a Louisiana slave plantation than the farm she remembered.

Across several fields, where Sarah had lived, another large house was in the process of being built. Two men were putting on roofing tiles. She could hear the rhythmic tick of their hammers below the hum and high whine of the cicada. At least the cicada were still here!

She drove further down the lane towards the cow-sheds. Here the old wattle and daub farm buildings had been rebuilt into a business-like complex of dairy and milking sheds. Behind them, she glimpsed the white-painted wall of the main house and the old fig tree next to the rain-water tank. Jo caught her breath at the memory of her mother tying brown paper bags over the ripening fruit in order to protect them from greedy sunbirds.

Her eyes jumped at something. Between the house and the cow-sheds, the new owners had put up a replica of an old Cape Dutch arch with, at its curve, a bell, like a slave bell. To her horror, Jo recognised it as the bell that had been fixed to one of the gum trees on the path leading to Sarah's home. Had Ouma ever used it to summon people to work, or to indicate the end of the day's labour? Jo was almost, but not quite, sure she had never heard it ring. Had the new owners re-instated the custom, or did they regard it merely as a picturesque memento of the old farm?

She couldn't walk past that thing. She would drive to the river, climb the krantz, see if there was at least one memory she could revive, with which she could be comfortable. In spite of her growing unease, her old excitement welled up at the sight of the krantz's high blue-grey surface, lightened by an occasional seam of glittering quartz. A heron perched on one of the tall poplar trees, which Ouma had planted to give shade for two generations of children.

Jo parked the car under a familiar pepper tree. She picked off a sticky cluster of hard seeds to run through her fingers as she walked down to the river. Holding the spicy aromatic seeds to her nose, she wondered for the hundredth time that day how she had managed to live for so many years without these fragrances, this heat, this sky, these mountains.

The heat gave the lucerne fields a watery look and she could feel the sweat trickling down her forehead. In spite of the general hum that the plants and insects were making, there was still a silence around her, which seemed to have in it the faintest echo of voices raised in leisurely conversation, of the sound of axe on wood. But how fenced it all was! Leaning on the shiny, new, padlocked gate, Jo gazed at a river that was no longer the wilderness she remembered. Barbed wire fencing ran across the river, cutting off the places where she had played from where she now stood. A young bull with a thick muscled neck and pinkish nostrils was grazing in a brand-new enclosed meadow under the poplars, which was irrigated by a turning spray. I'm not facing him, Jo thought. I'll have to find another route. She clambered over the gate and dropped into a muddy patch of grass. A jet of water from the spray, sharp and blissfully cold, caught her face and shoulder as she ran towards the river.

There had been good rains, and, just below the krantz, the brown water flowed too vigorously to cross. As Jo looked for stepping-stones higher up, rather than face the bull, a memory like an old tooth-ache told her she would be walking into forbidden territory. Mamsamsaba! Had she also been banished from her home? In the distance she could see a herd of cows grazing on the mud-flats where the river broadened and its banks shelved more steeply. Two pale Labrador dogs separated themselves from a man, dressed like a country squire in tweed plus-fours, who stood with them. They loped down towards where she struggled to jump across on the occasional flat stones. Then she was on the opposite bank and heading towards the high ground of the krantz. There was another fence to climb, and yet another. The dogs had joined her and now slithered easily under the fence wires. At last, twisting between rocks and stubborn cactus, she found the old path along the edge of the rock face, and became aware, without alarm, that the man had followed the dogs without crossing the river, and was within hailing distance.

'Are you all right?' he called.

'Yes, thank you, but these aren't my dogs.'

'No - they're mine.'

He must be the new owner, she thought. She stopped and shaded her eyes to look at him properly. 'I used to live here. May I walk along the krantz?'

'Oh yes, fine.' Now he had found out who she was, he was generous, hospitable. 'Would you like to come up to the house?'

'No thank you - I'm sorry, I don't have the time.'

He whistled to the dogs, who returned immediately to him. He sent them to police me, thought Jo bitterly. Fortress Bervie. When she reached the highest point, where she had been accustomed to stand, she deliberately surveyed, not the landscape below her with its deserted, fenced-in look, where the shine on the new barbed and razor wire dazzled her eyes, but the imagined paradise of her childhood memory.

Come back, she called to it. Just this once. I've travelled across oceans to see you again. I've been to lots of other places, but none as dear to me as you are. Come back, so that I can hold you close for all the years I have left to live. I'm nothing without you, and you also need me to remember you - for who else has been as loyal to you as I have?

As if in answer to her call, she saw the red roof of Glen Bervie farmhouse nestling amongst many trees, she picked out the path to Sarah's house and a glimmer of its white walls, while next door to Sarah, the Fourie's old windmill raised its dandelion head. Yes, there was the cemetery, a triangular wedge of red-brown earth right up against the black, tarred main road, and there, shrouded in a haze of blue smoke from the many cooking fires, were the plots.

FORTY-EIGHT

When the cheque came from Jo, Sarah took it to the township office. It caused quite a stir. The policeman who received it from her, offered her a chair to sit on. Dignity flowed into her, and she sat straight up, not humbled by problems of money. Mr Freeman called for her and she went right inside his room and stood in front of his desk, watching his face as he looked at her money.

'Well, well.' He glanced down to read her name. 'Mrs Sarah Khumalo. They've paid the full amount, hey? You've worked for very kind people.'

'I've worked hard, Baas.'

She didn't feel grateful. At long last there was a little back for all those years and years of running after them. If she hadn't asked and asked, she would have had nothing at all. You had to behave like a dog with them: either cringing or biting. That was all they understood.

Over the past years, when she had feared that her bitterness would drive her mad, she had deliberately kept it at bay by calling up memories of Millie.

Sarah, Sarah, where are you?

Here I am Miss Millie!

Sarah, Sarah, have you seen my car keys?

By the telephone Miss Millie, I saw them this morning.

And then the smell of roses and beeswax polish would come too. Even now, the hot smell in the back seat of Mkhuseli's car would bring tears at the memory of drives into town with Millie.

She told herself that the money for her house had been sent by

Millie's daughter, not by William, who had sold Glen Bervie and given nothing to those who had lived and worked there all their lives. She didn't have to thank him for anything. He had not treated her like a person. William and Vera still owed her for a whole lifetime of meals and beds and clean floors. Her hatred of them was fresh, like the sharp smell of new dung.

When the legal papers for the house were given to her, Sarah worried about where she could keep them safe. Mkhuseli wanted her to let the bank look after them, but in the end Sarah folded them into the same old cocoa tin she used to keep the birth certificates of all her children, together with Ernest's death certificate. It was the same tin in which she'd saved money for Nontu's schooling and teacher training, for Nontobeko's nursing fees, for the rent. It was, she told Mkhuseli, her safest place, and she wasn't going to start trusting the bank at her age.

But first, she and Mkhuseli and Nomzamo spread the large pages on the kitchen table. Nomzamo raised the wick of the paraffin lamp to make the light brighter for Mkhuseli to read the words aloud. The printed parts were in English and Afrikaans, but the words typed in were in Afrikaans only. Her name was on it: Mevrouw Sarah Khumalo, and the address: J Straat 21, Orlando, Fort Bedford. This paper was the proof that she really was the owner of the house.

For 99 years, it said.

'Not forever? Yehova! They've cheated me again!'

'Ag, Ma, don't worry. Everything will be different in ninety-nine years - even sooner.' Mkhuseli was delighted that she had bought the house and he wanted her to be content. But she hadn't forgotten the bulldozer that had pushed over the walls of Grandfather Gxoyiya's home before he'd even had time to dress. All those people had had papers of ownership for their houses too, hadn't they? She could still picture that cloud of red dust, as if flames licked at the people's lives, shrivelling up everything they'd worked for. The white people, she knew, even as she carefully folded up her title deeds and snapped the lid shut on the tin, could take away anything you'd managed to squeeze out of them. They didn't even have to do it in secret. It wasn't a crime to them.

284

Are you asking me or telling me? William had said. You'll do as we say. It's not your place to tell us what we should or should not do.

In the past, she'd always gone to her sleeping dead with her deepest fears. She'd stood by Ernest's grave and asked him to help her. Her parents, she was sure, had given her the strength to save for Nontu's and Nontobeko's schooling. She was so proud that her children had done well! But now, when the graves of her ancestors had been levelled under the road, how could she find them? How could she be sure they rested quietly when the unceasing traffic thundered above their heads? She dreamed at night that her father blamed her for what had happened there. 'But Father, what could I have done to stop it?' she begged him, appealing to her other ghosts for support as they clustered round her. She'd be joining them soon, but she was afraid they would punish her even before then, that they would not intervene if new laws were passed to take her home away from her.

'Please stop worrying, Ma. Come - I'll paint the roof for you tomorrow. Just tell me what colour you want it to be.'

'Red. Blood red.' And she'd laughed until the tears came, and she was frightening Mkhuseli and Nomzamo with her gasping sobs. Mkhuseli put his arm on her shoulder until she forced herself to quieten down.

'I'm all right now, Son.' She turned away from them. She wasn't going to be the kind of mother who burdened her children with her worries.

The next day, Mkhuseli painted the roof in broad scarlet stripes which glistened like fresh blood when she went outside to see how he was getting on. He was nearly finished, and paused to drink the mug of coffee she had brought him, sitting on the top of the ladder, with his legs dangling free. It was hard for her to believe he was nearly forty. Although he had been grey for years - since his time in prison - he had no fat on his body and his face was still smooth, without wrinkles. He grinned at her, his heels dancing in time to the radio, which was belting out a strong, happy melody.

Sarah felt she had waited her whole life for this moment: her own house, her son taking time off from his own business to help her fix it up, her two grand-daughters playing hop-scotch in the dusty earth outside the front gate.

She didn't notice what kind of car it was. She turned with a jump when it came round the corner of the street with a squeal of tyres skidding on the loose stones. The rat-tat-tat of the gun was loud and sudden. She yelled, 'Nomhle! Nozinzile!' although the two girls had already turned to flee towards the shelter of her arms. Nozinzile fell on the path. As Sarah ran forward to help her, she could hear Nomhle behind her, shrieking at further horror. Looking back at the house as she picked up Nozinzile whose body flopped like a doll, she saw red paint splashed down the wall, the ladder fallen, and oh no, not Mkhuseli, not Mkhuseli dead, not Mkhuseli, not her Mkhuseli.

She gave Nozinzile to Leah, who had rushed out of the house, and she flew like a ghost to Mkhuseli, who lay with his one leg right under his body, and his left arm in such an odd, twisted position. A bloodstain was seeping across his shirt, and there was more blood in a pool under his extended leg. She could see a bullet wound above his right ear, and another in his neck. The bullets had ripped through his body - she couldn't count how many wounds there were, but the blood that poured out was bright and shiny. He opened his eyes for a moment, but she could see he was already far away from her. She held onto his shoulder, trying urgently to keep him from leaving her.

'Mkhuseli ... Mkhuseli ... Son ...' she whispered, over and over.

Nokupumla Memani had run over from her house. 'Fetch Nomzamo,' Sarah begged her. 'She's at the clinic.'

Leah had carried Nozinzile inside. Someone else had picked up Nomhle, who was screaming with a high, terrified sound. Sarah noticed all these things as she crouched down next to Mkhuseli. I'll never leave him, she thought grimly. I'll fight anyone who tries to take him from me. I'll starve to death here next to him. But when Nomzamo came, out of breath from running all the way from the clinic, her eyes enormous with fright, Sarah knew she couldn't allow herself such a luxury, when another grieved as much as she.

Nomzamo knelt on Mkhuseli's other side, but he was already gone. Nomzamo stroked his head, pushing back the hair from his bloody forehead, calling his name, but the face, which was Mkhuseli's

286

face, did not move, the eyes, which were Mkhuseli's eyes, did not respond. Nomzamo wept and pleaded with him trying to force his silence to speak to her, but she could not raise him.

Sarah remembered the rest in a blur. She felt Leah pulling her gently away from Mkhuseli. She remembered stumbling into the house, and seeing Nozinzile resting so lightly on the bed, like a bird who has fallen from the nest, before the darkness of her grief overwhelmed her.

FORTY-NINE

Out of the dark night came Nodumo's fresh young voice. 'Come, let me wash you, Gogo. No, you don't have to do anything, I will take your clothes and wash them too. I loved Mkhuseli also, Gogo. He was a father to me, when my own father said I was no good and my mother told me to leave the house until I was ready to go back to school. After Sizwe was killed, I had no one to love any more. Baba Mkhuseli encouraged me to continue in the struggle, and you, Gogo, you sheltered me and fed me and looked after me. After Sizwe, it was your family became my family and gave me hope. Please Gogo, let me wash your face. I'll comb your hair nicely. Please Gogo, just drink a little sweet coffee, eat a little pap. Please Gogo, Nontu is coming home today. You will want to greet her like a mother.'

Sarah opened her eyes slowly. She was still unable to move her limbs, but she could see. She saw that Miriam Matama was staying in the house, and that Nozuko and Raymond and the children were back from Umtata and that they had brought Nontobeko with them. When Nontu, slim, in a black dress, held her wordlessly, both their bodies shook with their sobbing, and it was as if all those present echoed their wailing because the sound of sadness seemed to engulf the house.

Nontu was accompanied by Nozinzile's father, but Sarah had no words of comfort to say, for him or anyone else. Neighbours brought pots of stew and pap, and remained sitting in the kitchen or overflowed into the garden. Nodumo helped everywhere. Nomhle insisted on being most of the time on Sarah's lap, and Sarah was grateful for the small warmth lying against her when the rest of her was so very cold. For a week no one went to bed, but sat upright, or leaned against pillows, not changing at night from the clothes they had worn during the day.

They waited for the autopsy so that they could bury their dead. Mkhuseli was killed by one or all of the 27 bullets fired from a machine gun of the type used by the South African Police. Nozinzile had taken only three bullets into her small body, but she had been closer to the car, and they had sliced through her, stopping her heart instantly. Both death certificates stated: Cause of death: shooting by persons unknown.

The new government emergency regulations forbad a public funeral service, but about 300 people attended the private service. Relatives and friends crowded into a marquee outside the house. Sarah noticed that Dr van Zyl and another white member of the liaison committee had taken the trouble to attend, but she did not speak to them, and they left before Mkhuseli made his final journey to the cemetery. Mkhuseli and Nozinzile were buried side by side.

There were more empty graves already dug and waiting. Whose turn will it be next? thought Sarah. She lifted her head and caught sight of Beauty Zwakala. I could not have imagined myself in her place so soon, thought Sarah. Now I too have lost my only son, and darling Nozinzile has gone even before she could live a life of her own. A stale wind blew across the raw, red earth: unlike the sweet wind that has passed over lucerne or green mealies, it smelled sour and barren. Sarah felt grateful at that moment that Nomhle, who was being looked after at home, would not be able to remember any of this bleak ceremony. She herself felt exhausted by sorrow, although her heart went out to Nontu, and to Nomzamo, who had got very thin, and stood so quietly, her eyes dry and empty.

When they turned from the filled graves, Sarah noticed the police for the first time. Three Buffel-loads full, a hundred men in grey-blue uniforms stood shoulder to shoulder, with at least ten alsatian dogs on short, tight leads. More police than were usually deployed in Fort Bedford, they must have brought in reinforcements from other towns. The dogs appeared to pull forward, straining to attack. Even as she opened her mouth to warn others, there was the pop of the first tear-smoke canister, and the white cloud rising from the ground like a spirit out of a bottle.

Do they not even have the decency to allow us to bury in peace the ones they themselves have killed? Sarah's bitterness filled the high blue sky. It spread like a giant plant over Main Street, reaching with unstoppable tendrils over all the white people's houses, darkening their plate glass windows, their lawns and garages and parked motorcars. Her bitterness exploded the mountain, raining an avalanche of rocks and earth and trees onto the town, crushing and burying it so that there was nothing left to remember the people who had lived there: all those white faces who told her she was no good and couldn't have anything, and who took her Mkhuseli and all her hope from her.

She was too old to run from the tear-smoke. Indeed, it seemed that she herself would choke to death. Her hands clawed at her stinging eyes, but then Nozuko put a handkerchief over her face, and Raymond took her arm and they half-supported her, half carried her towards the waiting car.

Soon the mourners had to return to their own homes, but Miriam Matama stayed on with Nomzamo for a few weeks longer. Nodumo still kept close to Sarah. Sarah did not know how she would have managed without Nodumo. She was so weak, even though now she had only Nontu to look after, because Miriam was pleased to be caring for Tambo so that she could get to know her grandson better.

Nodumo washed Sarah's clothes and made her room tidy. She combed Sarah's hair and dressed her. How is it that I am so weak? wondered Sarah. She was stiff in all her joints and slow, slower than she had ever been.

About three weeks after the funeral, Sarah was resting on a chair outside the front door, while Nontu played with a wire car, which her cousins had brought her from the Transkei. Nodumo, who was going out, stopped a moment and leaned her slight body casually against the front gate.

'We know who killed him,' Nodumo spoke quietly and so casually that anyone watching would have concluded that she was merely commenting on the small vegetable garden on which she fixed her eyes. Sarah's gaze was suddenly keen, and she drew in a sharp breath.

'The white man, Gouws, Special Branch, was driving. It was his car. The man with the machine gun was Ebenezer Mgasa.'

'The Devil himself! Mgasa - I know him! What would they pay him to make him do a thing like that?'

'We'll get him.' Nodumo's tone was light, without emphasis. She laughed. It wasn't much different from any young girl's laugh. 'Gogo, I must go now, but I shall be back tonight.'

'Be careful.'

'Don't worry, Gogo.'

Sarah didn't forget what had been said, but as the weeks passed, she began to think that Nodumo was just like everyone else, swearing revenge, but never doing anything. So when Nodumo told her that she would soon be leaving town, Sarah didn't remind her about their previous conversation. Its implied content was too serious to spend words on. Besides, she worried about her child.

'Where will you go?'

'It's better that you do not know.' Nodumo suddenly hugged her fiercely and put her young face against Sarah's old, lined skin. 'Oh, Gogo - you know I don't want to leave you, but the police are looking for me, and I can't even sleep here any more because it is too dangerous for you to shelter me. I promise, one day I will return and look after Gogo all the time. Please give me your blessing.'

'Child, you will always have that. Go well. Walk carefully.' For the first time in many weeks, Sarah shed tears of love and not of grief. They were a life-giving fountain. 'I am grateful that you stayed to comfort me.'

Alone, Sarah's strength increased daily, but with her renewed vigour came a corresponding increase in her need for justice. Surely this crime should not be swept away without anything being done? She dreamed about sharpening a knife herself, and waiting for Mgasa to come out of the police station, but she knew she would not have the nerve to kill. Then, one evening, when the sky was turning a deep gold, and the clouds were dyed navy and scarlet, Beauty banged on her front door.

'Hurry!' called Beauty. 'You must come with me.'

'But I must stay with - '

'No time for that.'

Still not knowing what she was being called to do, Sarah picked up Tambo, and rushed to leave him and Nomhle with the neighbours next door. There wasn't time to lock the house. Sarah limped as fast as she could to catch up with Beauty, who was already further along the road.

Beauty took her arm to steady her. 'Lean on me.'

'What ... what is it?'

But Beauty would not answer. The crowd of young teenagers standing together in the cul de sac behind the beer hall parted to let the two old women through. What were they being asked to witness? Something tall moved and writhed and burned like a flaming torch. A man?

'Who is it?' whispered Sarah. She couldn't take her eyes off the fiery man. As she watched, the figure sank to his knees, and then, like a tree softly falling, to the ground.

'Mgasa,' Beauty breathed the name. The crowd was already moving away, as if there was no longer anything of interest happening. Was it her imagination, or did Sarah see Nodumo slip into the darkness?

Someone had placed petrol-soaked tyres around Mgasa's neck and body, pinioning his arms to his sides, and had struck a match. If she had been present to hear his pleading, would she have been merciful? She conjured up a memory of Mkhuseli sitting so carefree next to the tin of shiny red paint. She heard the squeal of the tyres, and the rat-tat-tat of the gun. There was Mkhuseli's body bleeding into the earth.

How else could she find justice except with another death? Yet this death did not cleanse her of sorrow, indeed it seemed to have added a further burden to the horror of her situation. Now the body lay still and the flames seemed to have eaten their fill. It was dark, but for a moment she glimpsed a face with hair white, like ash, a grimace of teeth.

292

She pulled at Beauty's arm. 'Come, we have seen enough, I am needed at home.' They did not speak further, but as she walked back Sarah thought, if I could find Nodumo again, I would tell her that I have lived too long when I must watch such things happen. Yet she was proud too, knowing that this child of hers had the courage to extract justice from those who used the law as a stick to beat her with, never to protect or to defend those whom she loved.

ACKNOWLEDGEMENTS

When I began Sarah's Story, writer friends kindly gave invaluable advice. My heartfelt thanks to Marsh Rowe, Tina Talbot, Gcina Mhlope, Miriam Tlali, Monica Mnguni and Bernadette Mosala who helped me at this crucial time. Many thanks also to my daughter, Susan Tacq who typed the first draft; to Maggie Friedman, Lily and David Goldblatt, Sandra Braude, Safoora Sadek and Chris Cunliffe, who gave me shelter and encouragement, and to Mothobi Motloatse who persuaded me to submit the novel for the Bertram's Literature of Africa competition. Finally, my unbounded gratitude to my son, Jannie Oosthuizen, who has lifted Sarah's Story out of the computer and onto the book you now hold.

Lightning Source UK Ltd.
Milton Keynes UK
UKOW052112171012

200755UK00008B/42/P